JOV

We at Jove Books are thrilled by the enthusiastic critical acclaim that the Homespun Romances are receiving. We would like to thank you, the readers and fans of this wonderful series, for making it the success that it is. It is our pleasure to bring you the highest quality of romance writing in these breathtaking tales of love and family in the heartland of America.

And now, sit back and enjoy this delightful new Homespun Romance . . .

COUNTY FAIR
by Ginny Aiken

Titles by Ginny Aiken

**OUR TOWN: CANDY KISS
COUNTY FAIR**

County Fair

Ginny Aiken

JOVE BOOKS, NEW YORK

COUNTY FAIR

A Jove Book / published by arrangement with
the author

PRINTING HISTORY
Jove edition / February 1997

The Putnam Berkley World Wide Web site address is
http://www.berkley.com/berkley

ISBN: 0-515-12021-9

A JOVE BOOK®
Jove Books are published by The Berkley Publishing Group,
200 Madison Avenue, New York, New York 10016.
JOVE and the "J" design are trademarks
belonging to Jove Publications, Inc.

PRINTED IN THE UNITED STATES OF AMERICA

10 9 8 7 6 5 4 3 2 1

County Fair

1

"*BA-AA-AH. BA-AA-AAAHHH!*"

Whirling around at the suddenly strident call of her favorite ewe, Willow Stimson froze at the sight that met her eyes. An enormous rutting ram was accosting the dainty Missy, trying to mount her. And Otis Hillenbaugh, this year's head sheep judge, not five feet away!

Willow tugged on the leather harness she'd put on Missy before leading her out of their assigned stall in the Sheep Building. Missy obeyed, bounding past her. Unfortunately, so did the randy ram.

"Go away you . . . you lecher. Oh-oh-oh, flapdoodle!"

A ripple of masculine laughter caught her attention. Mortified, Willow blushed. Glancing back, still trying to lead Missy away from her would-be swain, she stole a peek at the entertained male she'd heard.

Tall and large as a mythical god, the man loosely held the libidinous ram's tether. Blue eyes sparkled beneath dark russet eyebrows, and a wide mouth separated a matching beard and mustache. Shoulders wider than any Willow had ever seen shook with mirth under a broad expanse of brown flannel. Weathered denim trousers, looking as if they'd been constructed to order, housed his lower half. The indulgent expression on the face of the hulk of male humanity at the nether end of the ram's lead was as appalling as his features were appealing.

Controlling her indignation, Willow turned away from the attractive man and concentrated on assisting her sheep. Wherever she led the ewe, the ram followed, chuckling giant in tow. Again facing the brute, she demanded, "Don't just stand there laughing. *Do* something!"

"An' what would that somethin' be?"

Missy's back legs slid in the mud, and Willow's arm wrenched as the small ewe attempted to escape the much larger, stronger ram. "You should at least control your animal before he does Missy irreparable harm."

Another glance his way revealed an up-tilted brow on a face marked with mischief. She turned back to Missy, narrowly avoiding a foul-smelling mess on the ground.

A fresh burst of chuckles followed her. "Should he get her in 'harmed' condition," the stranger said, "I'd let you keep the lambs next spring."

Willow's eyes widened. She planned to sell Missy for her wool. What would a bellyful do to her value? Especially if she got that way by that man's randy beast?

She wasn't willing to find out. Time to return to their stall. "Come along, Missy!"

Then Willow heard a most censorious *tsk-tsk*. She stole a look around and groaned. Matters looked mighty grim. Otis Hillenbaugh, the head judge, stood shaking his head, his lips pursed tighter than a spinster's reticule.

That was the man Willow had to impress with Missy's best qualities? With her ewe's suitability to win the Best of Show ribbon? Oh, dear. This was hardly the way to begin a successful Fair Week.

"Here, now, sir," she called out between panted breaths. Missy darted to the left. "You simply must"—Willow tugged toward the building—"retrieve your"—the ram lunged at Missy's hindquarters—"undisciplined creature. He's distressing my ewe."

As if to emphasize Willow's plea, Missy let out another *ba—aa—AAAHHH* of outrage, skidding to the right. Willow again fought to lead her animal back inside the Sheep Building.

The ram persisted, charging Missy, nipping at her flanks.

Waving farewell to Judge Hillenbaugh, the giant grinned maddeningly, then shrugged as if to say boys will be boys.

Missy tripped and fell in the mud. The ram fell on top of her. The ewe grew frantic.

Willow became infuriated.

The titan turned serious, pulling back on the ram's leather strap. "Come along now, Lugh. Leave the lassies be."

When the ram ignored him, he sighed. Approaching carefully, dodging the ram's horns, he slipped a massive arm behind the animal's forelegs, then used his weight to bring his sheep to the ground. "Go!"

Willow needed no further encouragement. She ran back to where she now knew they should have stayed. But she'd wanted to brush out Missy's fleece before it became a hopeless snarl, since judging started tomorrow morning. A few extra knots to work out of Missy's wool were preferable to that unseemly display before the head judge.

Once safe in the stall, Willow dropped onto a bale of hay, holding her ewe close. "Oh, Missy-girl," she crooned, keeping her voice low and soothing. Missy still shook, clearly frightened by Lugh's unwanted attention. If only the judge hadn't been standing so near. If only Missy weren't going into her first heat. If only that beastly man had kept his obnoxious animal under control.

If only winning didn't matter so much.

But it did.

Willow sighed and hummed softly, trying to comfort the animal while she cleaned the mud off Missy. Before the wool could form tighter tangles, her fingers unraveled the knots that had provoked the miserable series of events. With a special long-toothed comb she worked on the fleece that should bring her the money she so needed.

Once Missy's tremors eased and her wool was again fluffy and unknotted, Willow came to a decision. Because of the inauspicious start to their County Fair week, she would redouble her efforts and ensure that Missy won Best of Show in the ewe division. She couldn't afford to lose that prize. Her future, her very livelihood, depended on winning the title. Prize-winning animals always sold for more, as did the other members of the winner's flock.

After last year's flood of the Codorus Creek devastated her crop and damaged her barn and home, Willow hadn't had seed for planting this spring. All she had now was her flock and the yield of her kitchen garden. Since she'd mortgaged the farm to effect the most desperately needed repairs, she stood to lose her heritage. In childhood she'd lost Mama and Papa. Two years ago she lost Aunt Lucie, who'd raised her since she was orphaned. Just days after Aunt Lucie's death, Willow lost her dreams of love and a family of her own when her fiancé jilted her for a wealthier woman. Willow refused to lose the farm, too.

"You, Missy-girl, are going to win this show," she said, determination steeling her voice. "I can't let this turn out any other way."

Later that afternoon as Willow set up her spinning wheel in Missy's stall, she tried to forget the more embarrassing moments of the day. But each time she thought back on the ordeal, the giant's mischievous blue eyes and smug smile materialized in her memory. Too bad such an attractive, good-humored man was so reprehensible. Why, it showed complete ignorance of propriety the way he'd let his wild beast accost Missy!

"The audacity of the man!" she exclaimed, sitting by the wheel.

Startled by Willow's outburst, Missy wriggled in her nest of fresh hay, tilting her head.

"Yes, indeed," Willow elaborated. "A distinct lack of moral pulchritude." Who knew what other shortcomings that bold male hid behind his amiable façade.

"Well, Missy, he can keep his inadequacies to himself. We didn't come here looking for questionable males. We came to win."

"Speaking to yourself now, Willow?"

At the question, spoken by a familiar feminine voice, Willow rose and turned, a smile on her lips. "What a pleasure, Mrs. Meister! I didn't expect to see you today until I finished settling the animals for the night."

Splendid in a slate-gray wool flannel suit, Aunt Lucie's lifelong friend, Reba Meister, took measure of Willow's surroundings. "I know, dear, but I felt it a mite chancy for you to walk home all alone in the dark. I wanted to let you know Mr. Meister will come for you."

Mr. Meister would ensure her safety? He was considerably older than his robust wife, a sprightly leprechaun, brilliant of mind and gentle of manner.

Stifling a chuckle, Willow said, "There's no reason to bother the professor. I can walk the short distance to your house. It's more than enough that you've offered me your spare room for the entire week."

Mrs. Meister's face took on a sad cast. "It's the least I can do, dear. Lucie was my best friend, and we both always sought your well-being. After all these years, I can certainly offer you hospitality and keep you out of harm's way."

Willow hadn't the heart to argue further against the lovingly offered protection, ludicrous though it was. "Thank you. You're as gracious as ever."

Mrs. Meister smiled, proud of accomplishing her goal. Then she grew serious. "Milford Philpott is back in town."

Surprised, Willow frowned. "I wonder what he wants. After all, he was in an all-fired rush to dump me and run to Philadelphia with his heiress not two years ago."

"I've heard he came to buy stock for his father-in-law's stockyards. He's also been asking about farm properties for sale. They say he wants to raise sheep."

Willow thought over Mrs. Meister's news. "Strange. He couldn't wait to get away from the drudgery of farm work. He said he wanted the easy life his wife's rich family offered."

"Oh, I don't think he intends to farm himself. He's likely looking for investment property."

Willow shrugged, amazed at how little she felt for the man. She'd once thought herself in love with him. Apparently his betrayal had killed what feelings she'd had. "Could be. It's none of my business anymore."

Mrs. Meister narrowed her gray eyes. Willow withstood the scrutiny, knowing full well her friend was checking for further evidence of a broken heart. She smiled, since it seemed hers had completely healed.

With a nod, Mrs. Meister smiled back. "So, tell me, how have you been this summer? I regret not getting out your way, but between my rheumatism and Mr. Meister's professorial schedule, I don't know where the time flew off to."

Willow clasped her hands. "Oh, it was . . . hot, dry. The sheep are well, though."

Mrs. Meister again narrowed her gaze. "And the harvest? Were you able to hire enough hands?"

Willow couldn't meet those keen gray eyes. "There was no harvest."

"Oh?"

Pacing the confines of the stall, Willow waved dismissively, trying to make light of her situation. "I mean, yes, the kitchen garden did beautifully. It's the corn and soybeans that didn't do well."

A glance at her late aunt's best friend told Willow she hadn't fooled the woman for a moment. "Actually, they didn't do well because I'd have had to plant them for them to do anything at all. I . . . lost my store of seed in the flood. I had no money to buy more."

Persistent as ever, Mrs. Meister leaned over the stall gate and lowered her voice. "But I thought you'd gone to Mr. Stoltzfus at the bank. Didn't you . . . mortgage the farm?"

Willow laced her hands and faced her friend. "I did, but the money went for repairs to the barn so the sheep would be protected last winter. And the house . . . well, the front steps were washed away, and the foundation had to be repaired."

"Hmmm," Mrs. Meister murmured, worry wrinkling her brow. "Now you've brought the flock to show."

"Exactly. And I intend to win at least one Best of Show ribbon. Missy is an especially fine specimen of Border Leicester ewe."

"What will you do once she wins?"

Willow gulped. As if in understanding, Missy butted her hand gently. Willow rubbed the soft head. "Sell her," she responded, her voice nearly a whisper.

Reba Meister slapped her left hand with the kid gloves she held in her right. "That makes no sense, Willow. Aren't you weaving cloth this winter? And what about knitting? How will you come up with enough wool?"

Please God, my plans will succeed. "I'm keeping Maizie and Stella and Erastus for breeding. The youngest Fritzmeier boy is watching them for me at the farm. I'll shear all three."

Crossing her arms over her pouter-pigeon chest, Mrs. Meister refused to ease up on her queries. "Didn't the ladies of the Horticultural Society place orders for a respectable number of shawls and sweaters?"

Willow sighed in relief; this question she didn't need to dodge. "I have enough wool at home to cover those orders. Enough, in fact, to make a few extra pieces to sell on consignment at Mrs. Mowbray's Philadelphia Millinery."

The creases smoothed out on Mrs. Meister's brow. "Then you'll soon pay off that risky debt on the farm, won't you?"

Willow took a deep breath in an effort to calm the queasies that welled up in her middle. "That's precisely what I aim to do."

What she *would* do. Remembering the letter she'd received just this morning, Willow added, "And pay the taxes, too."

"You think you'll pay the mortgage by selling the flock? And the taxes with the money from your homespun and knitted pieces?" Mrs. Meister's skepticism made the unease in Willow's middle bunch up in a lump at her throat.

Her efforts to reassure Aunt Lucie's friend died a rapid death. She swallowed hard. "I *have* to."

Shaking her head, and with it the ostrich feather adorning her fine felt hat, Mrs. Meister again sought Willow's gaze. Willow turned away and busied herself needlessly carding the wool she planned to spin in the demonstrations she was to present during Fair Week. She wished Mrs. Meister wasn't quite so accomplished an inquisitor.

An elegant black boot tapped its toe against the wooden

walkway ranging down the center of the Sheep Building. "Willow, dear, why don't you just let Mr. Meister give you the money? I'm certain Lucie would have taken it—"

"She wouldn't, and you know it."

"She certainly would have, had she run the risk of losing the farm."

"Not even then," Willow murmured, wondering if she really had a chance to avoid disaster.

"Then let's talk about you," Mrs. Meister persisted. "You needn't sell off the animals you love. Please let us help."

Mrs. Meister's plea was tremendously tantalizing, especially since Willow knew a sincere desire to help inspired it, but something in Willow—she feared it was pride—kept her from consenting. "Maybe if the situation worsens . . ."

The smile that bloomed on Mrs. Meister's powder-soft pink cheeks told Willow her friend had taken her evasion as agreement. They'd have this argument again, it seemed. As Willow would adamantly refuse to take charity, so would Mrs. Meister insist on helping her closest friend's niece.

But Willow was determined to win.

As the western sky caught fire from the setting sun, Daniel Callaghan sought to bring his conversation with this year's head sheep judge to an end. "Very well, Otis, I'll see you for breakfast."

With a careless wave, Daniel left his late father's friend and business contact near the Midway entrance to the York County Fairgrounds' Sheep Building. 'Twas encouraging to have a friendly individual judging this year's sheep.

"Mm-hmm, Lugh, sure and we'll be winnin' a ribbon for you this year. An' maybe a few others, as well." Not that Daniel had any misguided notion of bribing himself to a win. He just felt it was in his best interest to maintain the good will of the man who would decide the future of his latest venture.

When Lugh paused to drink from a trough outside the Sheep Building, Daniel leaned against the wall of the structure. Sheep. He'd decided to raise sheep as well as dairy cows.

Although Callaghan's Dairy was having a year more successful than any before, Daniel was determined to increase that success through his own efforts. It wasn't enough to keep his da's farm running at peak condition.

Wincing at the pang of guilt he felt each time he thought of his father, Daniel set painful considerations aside for the time being. There'd be time a'plenty to ruminate on those thoughts during the fast-approaching winter. At present he had ribbons to win, animals to market. No time for worries and mixed-up feelings.

Brooking no nonsense from the animal, he tugged on the ram's tether. "Get along with you, Lugh!" At the sound of his name, the large sheep followed Daniel into the building.

With a quick look around, Daniel noticed various acquaintances readying their animals for an evening in the unfamiliar confines of a fairground stall. The whir of bustling activity welcomed him.

A voice called out from his left. "Daniel! Goot to see choo!"

Turning, Daniel nodded toward the Pennsylvania-German farmer. "Same here, Mr. Müller."

It did feel good to be back in York, among sights, sounds, and smells that took him back to his adolescence. Surprisingly good. Once, he'd thought of nothing more than escaping the town. Provincial, he'd thought it.

And he'd escaped. Only to have fate wrench him back.

"Ah, laddie," he said to his ram, "ne'er thought I'd be

content in York. 'Tis strange to find myself so. Come along, now, it's near time for supper, and 'tis hungry I am."

Daniel looked toward his assigned stalls near the back of the building, hoping to find Hans, his farmhand. In the long, dim expanse of the Sheep Building, he spied many black-hatted pale blond heads, but none of them belonged to his helper. Although still a distance away from his area, he could see that before disappearing, Hans had taken pains to ensure the comfort of the Callaghan sheep.

Mischief had Daniel grinning. "Lad likely found himself a charmin' German lassie to woo. Seems he'd have plenty to choose from."

Suddenly Lugh charged ahead, his piercing cry plunging the building into a shocked silence. "For God's sake, lad, what are you up to?" Daniel muttered, seeking to halt the beast, who would have none of it. The leather lead cut into the palm of his hand, but Daniel dared not relinquish his grasp. He dug in his heels.

Lugh lunged again.

Daniel stumbled, then fought to keep himself upright as the ram galloped down the walkway, his hooves clattering against the wooden planks. Without checking, he knew himself the object of everyone's curious attention. "Stupid damn sheep," he spat under his breath, his legs following Lugh's pace almost of their own volition. "Would you stop, you *diabhil*, you!"

Unexpectedly, the demon did stop. But then he reared up. And tried to vault a closed stall gate. Daniel skidded into Lugh's back. One of the ram's back hooves smashed down on his toes.

Pain shot through him, and he cursed the day he'd entertained the misbegotten notion of raising sheep. Then he heard a familiar voice over the ruckus Lugh had set up.

"Have you nothing better to do than pursue me and my

ewe, sir?" asked the pretty but prissy farm maid whose ewe Lugh had taken a shine to earlier. Too bad she seemed so ill-tempered. Damned waste of good looks.

When Daniel didn't reply to her waspish question, she pursed her lips and glared at him. "Or is your control over your beast so scant? Honestly, someone is likely to be injured, and it best not be me or any of my flock!"

Still struggling with Lugh, Daniel gritted his teeth. "Neighbors, are we now?" *Splendid.*

He tested his injured toes with his weight, all the while pulling back on Lugh's tether. When he spared the lass a glance, he saw her standing, fists on slim hips, anger in her honey-colored eyes. Attractive, yes. As was her ewe. And his ram was most attracted. "Come now, you damn fool beast!"

"Hmph!"

Another glance at the girl showed her lips tighter than a Scotsman, outlined in white. Damned if he didn't wonder what those lips would look like curved in a rosy smile!

Allowing a hint of a smile to curve his own lips, he said, "Can't say I blame the lad, miss. He's enchanted by your ewe—"

"Then take pains to *dis*enchant him. Immediately."

Stubborn, the lady was. But before Daniel could do anything further about it, Lugh bellowed and pawed at her wooden gate. It gave off a creaky protest.

Daniel lost his smile. Avoiding Lugh's lethal hooves, he sidled up to the amorous beast. "Here . . . now," he said between panted breaths, feinting first to the right, then to the left, seeking a hold on woolly legs, protecting his head. "Can't have you tearin' down the place—now, can I? Even if I grant you—she's a fair lassie—at that."

Daniel again hugged the ram behind his front legs and pulled back, hoping to throw him off balance. Again, it worked, but this time it took all of Daniel's strength to wrestle down the sheep. Lugh set up an aggrieved wailing, fought to regain a foothold, and struggled mightily in Daniel's arms.

"Damn beast is likely to be the end of me," he muttered.

"We can only hope," said the farm maid.

"'Course, and you would feel that way. You and your troublesome ewe."

"*My* troublesome ewe!"

"Aye, 'tis too enchantin' you are by half!"

"I beg your pardon, sir!"

By God, what was wrong with the girl? "Take your accursed ewe elsewhere!" He wouldn't last much longer, fighting with Lugh. "Can't you see I'm fair bustin' my—"

"Why should we move?" she asked, her cheeks coloring. "I'll have you know we've done nothing to create this appalling situation. It's all due to your undisciplined beast."

Dragging Lugh away with difficulty and effort, Daniel shot her a final glare. "Undisciplined, nothin'! A healthy male animal, he is, just like any other."

"Then, sir, go accost another pair of females. We have ribbons to win."

Not if he could help it. Lugh's was one category Daniel intended to win. With a final monumental heave, he got his ram across the walkway and into his assigned stall. Lugh then rushed the stall gate.

Determined, that ram was. Just as Daniel himself was. Ribbons to win, had she? "We'll see about that!"

2

$\mathcal{A}$FTER CLOSING THE stall gate behind him, Daniel watched his female nemesis stalk down the center walkway of the building. He read determination in each step. What was she up to now?

Moments later he found out. Hiram Becker, a fair official, didn't look happy as he approached Daniel behind the returning farm maid. At Lugh's stall gate she came to a halt and gestured toward Daniel and his ram. "There! As you can see, considering that beast's behavior, he's too close to my ewe's stall. It would be highly unethical if my animal were disrupted so much as to be disqualified from the competition."

"Afternoon, Daniel," murmured Hiram. "I see we have us a problem."

Daniel acknowledged both the greeting and the assessment of their circumstances with a tight nod. What was the snippy lass hoping to gain? Or did she think she had a solution to the foolish situation?

With another breezy wave the girl directed Hiram's attention to her own sheep. "As you can also see, sir, my ewe is quiet." Turning toward Lugh again, she tipped her nose higher in the air. "That . . . overheated, snorting monster is the problem. You should reassign him to a stall as far away from my Missy as possible."

Daniel's eyebrows leaped toward his hairline. Audacious bit, wasn't she? Further scrutiny of her firmly set, stern expression had Daniel wondering if she was married. Her looks would attract males, but her temperament seemed the sort that would pose a powerful deterrent for many a man.

Then again, she couldn't be more than a year or two past adolescence. Young for marriage, in his opinion, but who knew? The farming folk around York tended to marry early.

The silence between the three of them grew deeper, the sounds of the animals in the building underscoring their differences. A sheep *baahed* softly from one of the farthest stalls. Another one answered from nearby. Generalized snuffling came from everywhere else.

Hiram scratched his graying head. "Don't rightly know, miss. We have us a lot of sheep in this year's competitions. All them stalls are filled. Cain't see where I could move the ram to."

Daniel watched the pretty girl bite her lower lip. She tapped the toe of her serviceable shoe against the wooden floorboards. A frown brought her arched eyebrows close. "If you can't move the ram, you can't move us, either, can you?"

"'Fraid not."

A wisp of silky brown hair fell across the farm maid's cheek. With a move that seemed instinctive, she blew it away. Her concentration never wavered. "Neither one of us can be assigned another stall?"

Hiram's homely features took on an obstinate cast. "Jist said so, miss."

Silent for a moment, the girl glanced down the row of stalls Daniel assumed she'd been assigned. Then she checked those across from her animals, as if to verify that they, too, were occupied. She continued to chew her bottom lip, the thoughts buzzing through her mind nearly audible. Moments later she appeared to arrive at a decision.

"Since you seem opposed to cooperating," she said, "I guess it's up to me to solve the problem."

Daniel's jaw began to ache from clenching it. He swallowed a comment.

She didn't. "I'll take my two rams from the stall they're in now, and move my ewe there. It's not as good as a different stall assignment, but I'll do my best to make it work."

Hiram quirked his broad mouth into a wry grimace and bowed. "Why, thank you *ever* so much indeed, miss."

Daniel stifled his sudden urge to smile. As he'd suspected, the finicky lass had irritated the older man. Still, as Hiram tapped the brim of his hat and left, the girl squared her shoulders and, in a dignified manner, strode toward a stall where two fine rams were comfortably housed. In the girl's proud gesture Daniel found more to admire than censure. Interesting female, that one.

"Trouble, Mr. Cal—Daniel?" asked Hans from behind Daniel's back.

"Hmmm . . . maybe. Maybe not."

"What is it?"

"Seems Lugh's taken a shine to her prize ewe," Daniel said, jutting his bearded chin in the young woman's direction. "But her ladyship's not as taken with Lugh himself. To prevent another ruckus—"

"*Another* ruckus?"

"Another ruckus, yes. Lugh's tried to . . . romance the lovely ewe twice now, and her owner wants to keep them apart at all costs."

Hans chuckled in a very male way. Daniel took a good look at his farmhand and noticed the lad was more a young man than a boy. He also caught the gleam of interest in the younger man's eyes when Hans observed the departing girl again. Hmmm . . .

Tucking away that scrap of information, Daniel went on. "Well, an' she's decided she'll move her animals around. Put some distance between the star-crossed lovers, y'know."

With another chuckle Hans leaned over the stall gate and scratched the ram's head. "Too bad, boy. Lady's not interested . . . happens to me, too."

Daniel again considered the expression on Hans's face as his farmhand watched the ewe's owner. If the girl wasn't married . . . and if Hans had the gumption needed . . . and the girl took to Hans better than she had to Daniel . . .

Nineteen-year-old Hans was young enough to tangle with the miss. A thirty-two-year old man like Daniel preferred his women more . . . cooperative, compliant, even.

Then the sounds of a struggle filled the Sheep Building. Above the indignant *baahing* of aggrieved animals Daniel heard the troublesome farm maid trying to recapture her animals' attention. Hans returned to Daniel's side. "What is she doing?"

Daniel snorted. "Jugglin' sheep, far as I can tell."

"None too successfully, either."

A distinctly indulgent note rang in his assistant's voice. Daniel observed the commotion, again remarking how attractive the harried girl was. As attractive as she was young. He turned to Hans. "Why don't you go give her a hand with her flock?"

Hans's grin broadened. "She could use a hand."

"A strong one," Daniel said, hoping to bolster the boy's confidence.

With a swagger the blond youth went toward the girl and her sheep. Once at her side he grasped a ram by its halter and said something to the lovely owner. A wobbly smile curved her pretty rosy lips.

"*Damn* fine-looking, she is. Lucky lad," Daniel muttered as he entered Lugh's stall and brought his thoughts back to his own flock of sheep.

As Jethro, Willow's black ram, was about to slip from her grasp, a pair of dust-covered work boots appeared in her lowered range of vision.

"Takes more than one person to handle these two," said the owner of the boots in a youthful tenor voice.

Willow glanced up and returned the young man's smile as best she could. "Never has before. They just don't want to be disturbed." She shook her head. "And it's all that horrible man's fault. His, and his unruly ram's."

The young man's smile broadened, but he held firm to Jethro's halter. "Here," he said, reaching for the lead attached to Zebulon, Willow's other ram, "let me do this for you. Just show me where you want them."

Willow straightened from her unladylike crouch and swiped the back of her hand across her damp forehead. "Over there," she said, pointing to the stall across from the libidinous Lugh.

The young man's step faltered. "You want these two in with that ewe?"

"No, of course not. She has to be moved to where they were."

"I . . . see. By the way, my name's Hans. Hans Brenneman."

"Pleased to meet you, I'm sure. I'm Willow Stimson."

Hans flushed to the roots of his blond hair, and his Adam's apple bobbed. "Pretty name."

Willow smiled at him, hoping to put him at ease. He seemed a very nice person. And not bad-looking either. But, oh, he looked so young . . . and self-conscious. On the other hand, he was polite, unlike the randy ram's owner. Too bad the handsome redheaded colossus didn't display similar good manners.

Putting aside all thought of the disturbing man, Willow focused on her sheep and Hans. "This is very kind of you," she said. "Do you have animals entered in the competition?"

Hans grunted his response as he sought to keep both displeased rams heading in the right direction. The grunt came with a negative shake of his head.

Willow frowned, puzzled. "Then why are you in the Sheep Building? It's hardly the most interesting exhibit at the Fair."

As he strained to control Willow's two sheep, Hans's face grew redder than a moonshine-sodden drunk's. "My— employer—does."

"Oh! I see," she said, wondering who Hans worked for. "Here, let me hold that gate open for you."

With a relieved sigh Hans shoved the rams into Missy's stall. In seconds Willow had her ewe by the halter and in her new quarters, too. Hurrying back, she narrowly saved her spinning wheel from the rambunctious play of the male tenants in Missy's former domicile. Hans followed Willow's every move.

After placing the wheel in a hay-covered corner, Willow turned to thank her rescuer, but crashed into him, nose to nose.

Again Hans's face colored. "Oh, Miss Stimson! I'm very sorry. I—I didn't mean to startle you. Are you all right?"

The youth's concern was touching, especially in comparison to the boorish, improper actions of the owner of Missy's attacker. Too bad the older man hadn't taken the time to learn proper responses to mishaps. It hardly seemed right that the beast had smiled benignly when his ram accosted Missy. The least he could have done was to offer an apology.

But, no. Seemed he didn't have it in him to acknowledge his mistakes.

Scolding herself for letting her thoughts wander again toward such an unseemly subject, Willow reassured Hans that she was fine. "In fact, I'm better than fine. You see, I had to move my ewe from the clutches of that . . . that *debauched* beast across from her original stall."

Hans's lips twitched at the corners.

Willow frowned. "Now, don't tell me you think it's funny, too."

Shaking his head and backing out of Missy's new quarters, Hans caused a shock of wheat-colored hair to cover his high forehead. His grin widened. "No, Miss Stimson, not in the least."

Willow stepped out of the stall and closed the gate. His smile made it difficult for her to give his words much credence.

"Honest!" he continued, protesting too much. "Besides, we took care of the trouble, didn't we?"

Willow glanced toward Missy's original stall. The sudden motion of a familiar rust-toned head caught her attention. Strange, she thought. Seemed the Irishman had been looking in her direction, but had averted his gaze to avoid being caught staring. Very strange.

She wished she'd found a vacant stall in another part of the building, anywhere to avoid those vivid blue eyes. So, had she really taken care of her trouble?

"Yes," she said, then realized she'd spoken out loud. "I do believe we have," she hurried to say to Hans. "Anyway, you were telling me that your employer was also exhibiting sheep. Who do you work for?"

Hans shot a glance down the aisle way. "I work at Callaghan's Dairy, and Mr. Callaghan needs my help during Fair Week."

"Callaghan's Dairy," Willow said, then frowned, remembering a time a while back when the York area had buzzed with criticism of Daniel Callaghan's flight to Philadelphia. "Good place to work, I've heard."

"Very. Mr. Callaghan is evenhanded and honest and hardworking."

"That's good. At least he has *something* to redeem him," she said. "I still remember when he abandoned his family and their farm in favor of fame and fortune in Philadelphia. Do you think age and the passing of time have taught him what his father's broken heart couldn't?"

Hans glanced away, refusing to meet her gaze. "I don't know, Miss Stimson. I don't judge a man by what he did before I knew him."

Willow found herself reddening at the gentle rebuke. "At least he's done right by his niece."

Enthusiastic nodding further mussed Hans's hair. "He's trying hard with that Maribeth. But she's a tough one, you know."

"Always heard the Callaghans were strong-willed."

Hans chuckled. "I'll say. Mr. Callaghan's nothing if not determined. That determination never fails to bring him success."

Willow thought a moment on Hans's words. "He's showing sheep, you said."

"Yes. Sheep. He intends to win, too."

Willow reached for Missy's woolly head. "I don't know about that. I'm here and I intend to win."

Hans's eyes suddenly widened in dismay. "Uh-oh."

"An' too bad it 'tis," offered the familiar, brogue-spiced baritone from only inches behind Willow.

Dismay, horror, dread filled her jumpy middle. It couldn't be, could it? Her luck couldn't possibly be that bad, right?

She straightened and turned. A glance had her stomach

crashing down past her knees. "Uh-oh, indeed," she mumbled. Squaring her shoulders, she faced the cause of her predicament. "You're not about to tell me that you're Daniel Callaghan, are you?"

A bark of masculine laughter seemed to bounce off the high ceiling of the Sheep Building. It teased Willow's senses, disturbing her immensely. *What a laugh*, she thought.

"Never been a liar, lass."

"You are." At his sudden glower, she hastened to add, "Daniel Callaghan, that is. What luck." She gritted her teeth against the effect of the Irish giant's restored humor. She allowed her gaze to meet his.

Mr. Callaghan cocked a rusty-colored eyebrow. "Luck? Why, 'tis of the Irish, of course!"

Luck of the Irish, indeed. With her lousy luck, Willow feared the imposing man had heard her unflattering remarks about his past behavior. But aside from a touch of irony in his crooked smile, his expression was so controlled she couldn't tell exactly what he'd heard. The full auburn beard shielded whatever he felt about it.

She suspected she'd soon find out, though. Daniel Callaghan didn't seem the sort who'd take criticism lying down. No, he was more likely one who took it as an affront to his manly pride. Or as a challenge to be met.

Heaven help her if he was.

After the irritating Irishman and his employee had gone their way, Willow set up her spinning wheel, made herself a stool from a bale of hay, and set up the motion that over the years had become almost instinctive to her. Her foot on the treadle pumped gently as she fed the carded fleece to the wheel. The caress of the wool was soothing, and it helped settle her rattled nerves. Soon the whirring had Missy sleeping at Willow's feet.

What a way to start Fair Week. First she'd tangled unknowingly with the one entrant in the sheep categories who would most fiercely challenge her for the Best of Show ribbons. Then she'd been an unwitting part of a spectacle that shocked the head sheep judge. She'd followed those two mishaps by befriending her foe's associate, and a short while ago she had probably offended the daunting Daniel Callaghan.

True, Willow should never have criticized the man's adolescent behavior to his farmhand, even if she was entitled to her negative opinion of those who followed the lure of glamour offered by large cities. Mr. Callaghan had the right to choose a way of life she opposed.

Now, she was sure of only one thing. Daniel Callaghan was a formidable obstacle to her immediate and future goals.

Willow glanced at Missy, then with a smile relaxed. Regardless of Mr. Callaghan's imposing personality, and what was surely a fine flock, Missy remained a superb example of the best traits of Border Leicester sheep. Her wool was lush, with a good crimp, strong, and made a perfect yarn when spun. Those qualities would stand them well against the power of Daniel's personality.

Unable to resist, Willow glanced toward the Callaghan stalls. To her amazement, she caught Daniel staring back at her, an odd intensity in his blue gaze. Good heavens, what could the man be thinking?

While inwardly chiding himself, Daniel deliberately met Willow Stimson's golden-brown gaze. He'd pried the girl's name from a reluctant Hans, who for some reason had turned oddly reticent when Daniel had questioned him about his new acquaintance. What did the boy think? That Daniel was interested in a fresh-faced farm maid?

What a load of blarney! At thirty-two he was clearly too

old to be sniffing around a young girl. Not that he would want to do so in the first place.

"Here," said Hans, startling Daniel. "Lugh's apples."

"Wondered where you'd gone," he responded, reaching for the bushel basket of Lugh's favorite treat.

"Couldn't have our boy missing his apples. Besides, we want to make sure his feed stays the same. You still plan to breed him before selling him, don't you?"

"Of course. Fine ram such as Lugh will give us a crop of splendid lambs."

Hans removed his black hat and patted his forehead with his crumpled handkerchief. "Like I said, then. We want to make sure his feed stays the same so he'll be ready to service the ladies."

"You spoil him too much," Daniel countered, chuckling.

"He's a fine animal. A lot of character to him."

Mischief bubbled up inside Daniel. "Too much for your little friend and her pretty ewe!"

Hans flushed. "Miss Stimson isn't my 'little friend.' She's a very nice young lady."

"Ahh . . . So you like a lady with a hint of tartness to her."

Shuffling his feet, Hans edged away from Daniel. "I didn't notice any tartness."

"Get on with you, boy! You aren't blind or deaf by half. Every word she speaks comes out splashed with vinegar."

Suddenly Hans straightened, and with obvious determination he met Daniel's gaze. "Seems ungentlemanlike to discuss a young lady in such unflattering terms. If you'll excuse me, I'll go see about storing Lugh's apples."

His jaw gaping, Daniel watched Hans stride off. What had Daniel started when he sent young Mr. Brenneman to help a lassie in distress? He'd only meant for Hans to engage the outspoken Miss Stimson in a mild flirtation. Had the boy taken a real interest in her?

A strange sensation crossed Daniel's middle. He wasn't sure what exactly it was, but he did know it didn't feel too great. Could it be regret? Disappointment? Perhaps even envy?

But no. It couldn't be. Willow Stimson was too young for Daniel to entertain an interest in her. Much too young, he thought again.

A rogue portion of his mind, however, reminded him of Willow's fierce defense of her ewe. He remembered the intense glow in her golden-brown eyes.

Perhaps she was young in years, Daniel admitted, but Willow Stimson had depth. He found himself wondering what precisely lay behind her devotion to her animals and her readiness to protect what was hers.

Shaking himself to derail the disturbing train of thought, Daniel realized it was now nearly suppertime. A good meal would serve as a splendid distraction, as he was sure he'd find old friends aplenty intent on supper chased down with good conversation. Just the thing a sensible man needed to keep his mind from straying toward dangerous territory.

With firm steps Daniel strode toward the doorway at the Midway entrance of the Sheep Building. In the still-bright autumn evening light he failed to keep his gaze from seeking and finding Willow Stimson.

What he saw moved him far more than he could have imagined. Sitting in a corner of her ewe's stall, Willow rocked back and forth with the motion that made her wheel spin. Her graceful fingers played out the tufts of fleece she was turning into yarn. A smile softened her already sweet features. Since he last saw her earlier in the afternoon, she'd allowed the braided coronet she'd worn to uncoil, and now a fat, glossy plait of brown hair flowed over her shoulder. At her side, the ewe gazed up at her mistress, as if deep in silent womanly communication.

Again Daniel found himself thinking that there was probably more to Willow than he wanted to believe. Despite much beauty, a young, impudent lass was easy to ignore. A young woman with hidden depths, a beckoning spark of fire, and a quintessentially feminine air was a different matter altogether. A woman like that could easily cause a man to forget the span of years that separated them.

To his chagrin, he found himself lingering in the doorway, absorbing the beauty of Willow Stimson. He called himself a fool for allowing himself to indulge his appreciation of Miss Stimson's attributes.

Before he could escape, she looked up. Their gazes met. A moment went by.

Then another slice of silence slipped away. A peculiar energy filled Daniel, speeding his heartbeat, warming him.

This time he failed to find his more logical, sensible self. Still holding her gaze, he was forced to acknowledge that deep inside he felt the strongest urge to discover what treasures hid behind Willow's prickly front.

3

"*She's a purty* little thing, ain't she?" Hiram Becker asked Daniel as he plunked down his ceramic coffee mug on the long table by a food stand.

Daniel spooned up his last bite of mutton stew, chewed, and savored the picture of Willow Stimson that floated through his head. "Yes, she's a lovely lass."

"Cuts a right nice figger, too."

Daniel let out an appreciative sigh. "Firm an' supple an' graceful."

"Don't know 'bout all that, son, but she sure is a treasure."

Treasure. The very word that came to Daniel's mind every time he thought of the spark of spirit in Willow's brown eyes. "A gem indeed."

"More'n I can afford," added Hiram, wiping his lip on his crumpled napkin.

With regret, Daniel nodded. "Me, too."

"You . . . too?"

"Too damn old."

Hiram frowned. "The devil you talkin' 'bout, son? Brigid's two years old. You said so yoreself."

Daniel felt his stomach lurch and his face redden in sudden embarrassment. Holy Mother of God, he'd been thinking of Willow when Hiram had merely been compli-menting Daniel's best ewe!

Clearing his throat, he pushed away from the table and tossed his napkin down next to his empty bowl. "Ahem . . . er . . . you're right, of course, Hiram. Brigid's just exactly the perfect age. An' when she wins, I'll only be considerin' the best offers for her."

Running his hand through his wind-ruffled hair, Daniel then placed his brown felt hat on his head. "'Tis a pleasure suppin' with you," he said, "but I'd best get back to Hans before the lad starves."

Hiram nodded and gave Daniel one of his trademark toothless grins. "Fine boy Adam Brenneman raised, dontcha think?"

The memory of Hans's interest in Willow brought a sudden niggle to the farthest reaches of Daniel's attention, effectively erasing the answering smile he'd offered his companion. But Hiram did have a point. "Hans is the best worker I've ever had. Decent sort, too."

"Yup, not a skirt chaser, neither. Had to let Max Sweitzer go. Boy couldn't keep his mind on work fer thinking of the ladies. Turrible waste."

Daniel flushed again. Although he couldn't call Hans a skirt chaser by any stretch of the imagination, he'd seen the lad plenty distracted by the lovely shepherdess they'd both met earlier that day. And Daniel didn't like how he felt about Hans's response to Willow's attributes. But he couldn't com-plain, since in all fairness, he himself had wasted entirely too many thoughts on the girl. "As I said, Hiram, I'd best get back. 'Twouldn't be fair to keep Hans hungry any longer." With a shake of Hiram's bony hand, Daniel took his leave.

Stepping away from the dining area, Daniel turned toward the Sheep Building. The scent of mutton stew still danced on the air, making him wonder if Willow had eaten yet. She didn't seem to have anyone helping her with the animals, and she'd looked as if she was well settled with that ancient spinning wheel she'd been plying when he last saw her.

As he remembered the sheep-moving disaster of that afternoon, he became convinced that she was indeed alone. "There's likely no one who cares whether the lass eats or not."

Instead of thinking about Hans's appetite, as he should be, Daniel allowed his concern for Willow to lead him back to where a black-bonneted Mennonite matron ladled out generous portions of stew. "Could you please add some biscuits?" he asked. "An' something to cover the bowl, too. I'm taking the meal back to the Sheep Building."

A kind smile and a nod accompanied the lady's spare movements. Moments later Daniel carried a towel-covered dish in hand. *It's just the neighborly thing to do,* he silently answered his taunting conscience. *Really.*

Still, a doubting corner of his mind seemed to mock him. The sort of thoughts he'd been entertaining about the shepherdess weren't of the neighborly sort. The way his mind seemed fixed on the curve of her rosy lips went way beyond cordial acquaintance. In fact, it bordered on the fringes of obsession.

Why the hell had he bothered with a supper dish for her? Although Willow was little more than an adolescent, she was old enough to keep herself fed. Daniel gave the offending bowl of food a glare and called himself all kinds of fool.

If he were to take the stew to Hans, the lad would think Daniel had lost his mind. Part of the fun of Fair Week was the opportunity it gave the residents of the outlying areas to renew friendships with those who lived in town. Hans hadn't stopped blathering about all the cronies he planned to look up. Supper was the prime social hour, and a bowl of mutton and biscuits in a sheep stall was not what the boy had been anticipating.

"Fool," he called himself again, wondering how to dispose of the damning evidence. He looked for a garbage receptacle, but found none at hand. By now he'd reached the entrance to the Sheep Building, and he stifled a curse and went in.

The colors of dusk were scarcely discernible in the western sky, but the Sheep Building was already painted in shadows. Some exhibitors had lit lanterns, and their yellow light puddled in random patches down the gray length of the wooden walkway. The different shades of darkness blended in subtle designs. Unable to resist, Daniel glanced in Willow Stimson's direction.

He found her in the same spot where he'd left her. Still in her ewe's new stall, Willow continued to sway to the rhythm of her wheel. Wisps of glossy hair captured the golden lantern light, forming a halo around her face. The rustle of animals on hay sang of life inside the building, and as his footsteps brought him closer, it seemed to Daniel that even the animals' breathing had joined in spinning her soothing tune.

Involuntary steps brought him abreast of Missy's stall. He watched Willow make yarn of airy clouds of fleece, getting something out of nothing with only the pressure of her foot, the touch of her slender hands. She turned the practical endeavor into something special, almost magical.

When she paused and saw him, her cheeks warmed to an apricot tint, making her eyes seem darker and more mysterious. A smile softened the line of her lips, giving life to a response in Daniel. She affected him in a strange, powerful way.

He shook himself, aware that such fanciful thoughts led

only to trouble for a fool like him. After all, he'd approached Willow in the spirit of neighborly kindness.

"Here," he said, holding out the food. "Since it seems that you're alone at the Fair, and that you're still at work— enjoying it, too—I thought to bring you something to eat."

Willow's eyes narrowed. A wary crease lined her forehead. "You didn't have to do that."

Damn and blast her, she was still bent on scolding him. "Of course an' I didn't! But you seemed so set in blamin' my animals and me for your troubles earlier today that I thought 'twould help get things back to normal if I brought you a meal and—and allowed you to stay . . . where you seemed to want to be."

Partway through his speech, Daniel faltered. He'd realized that his reasoning was as lame as a broken-legged horse, and it likewise deserved to be put out of its misery. "'Tis just some stew, and I've no ulterior motive."

She continued to eye him with questions in her gaze, her lips now crimped in a skeptical pout.

"'Tis only food, woman!" he burst out, feeling ridiculous as he held out the plate of meat and vegetables. "Get on with it. Take the dish."

Willow stood, her back to Daniel, and did something to her spinning wheel. Then she turned and slowly approached him, expressionless.

The deliberate blankness on the feminine features again made Daniel remember those hidden depths he suspected Willow possessed. Even her distrust of him, which in fact was quite reasonable since they'd only met that day, spoke of wise deliberation, a measured consideration of her circumstances.

While all these thoughts stampeded through his mind, the damnable dish of stew grew heavier in Daniel's hand. Still the lady held on to her reservations. "By Mary and Joseph, lass, I didn't poison it, you know!"

His outburst made her lower her lashes, and the apricot glow bloomed again on her cheeks. "I'm sorry," she said. "I've been rude when you've only tried to be kind."

Daniel shifted his weight from his right foot to his left. An itch developed smack in the middle of his back. Despite his best efforts, righteous anger couldn't break through the guilt he suddenly felt. He hadn't *only* been trying to be kind to Willow; it was quite an enjoyable pleasure to feast his eyes on the comely young woman. Somewhere deep inside, Daniel admitted he hadn't wanted her to retain a negative impression of him. He'd been somewhat self-serving when he'd brought her his white flag of peace spread over the top of a humble bowl of stew.

He shrugged and switched the dish from his left to his right hand. "Yes, well, I don't normally try to offend," he mumbled, wondering when she'd take the damned food and let him get the hell away from her flummoxing presence.

Her smile tipped higher, and mischief burst to life in her brown eyes. "That's good to know. I could have sworn you'd determined to make my Fair Week nothing but a nightmare."

Daniel found himself smiling in return. Even though he shouldn't. Even though he knew he had to leave. And soon. "I'd much rather inspire dreams of a pleasant sort," he found his mouth voicing without a conscious order from his mind.

Her eyes widened. Her lips parted and formed a delightful *O*. She glanced away from him, letting her attention flee everywhere but to his face. Willow Stimson obviously had no experience with flirtation, and Daniel relished that knowledge. "Here," he said yet again, his voice cajoling. "Take the food. In the interest of peace, of course."

Willow took a step that placed her just on the other side

of the stall gate. A sweet, herbal scent teased Daniel's senses, despite the heavy musk of animal in the air and the fragrance wafting up from the stew. She even smelled pretty, curse her youthful soul! She was nothing but troublesome temptation.

Willow held out her hand. Daniel gave her the dish. Her nostrils twitched when she caught the odor of the stew. She frowned. With care she lifted the edge of the towel and studied the contents of the ceramic bowl. Hastily dropping the cloth back on the proffered food, she opened the gate and stepped out onto the walkway where Daniel stood, the dish held well away from her body.

With narrowed eyes, she studied him. "Mutton?"

What could possibly be vexing the finicky female now? "Of course, an' 'tis mutton. What's wrong with *that*?"

Unexpectedly she pushed the rim of the dish into Daniel's middle, and if he hadn't rushed to grasp it, the contents would have landed on his boots. His temper, always a healthy part of his nature, registered an instant surge. But before he could recover from the shock brought on by Willow's peculiar actions, she spoke.

"Then *you* eat it if you can. I *don't* eat the animals in my flock, or their relatives, for that matter. It's equal to cannibalism, and I have yet to stoop so low." With an upward tilt of her chin, she spun and started down the center of the Sheep Building, jabbering all the way. "I should have known the degenerate owner of that lewd ram would turn out to be a cannibal—"

"Cannibalism?" Daniel repeated, stunned. "*I'm* a degenerate cannibal? The woman's mad! Absolutely stark, raving mad. She's naught but a walkin', talkin' blarney stone!"

Shaking his head, Daniel glanced down at the unfortunate serving of food. Well, and 'twas good he'd had this confrontation with Miss Stimson. It had shown him precisely what a loony creature she was. Despite her undeniable allure, he was best rid of her.

Squelching a touch of disappointment, Daniel strode back to Lugh's stall, fighting against the persistent mental image of Willow's sashaying posterior as she'd stormed away. What a sad waste of splendid womanly attributes. . . . She was lovely, but as barmy as they came.

At Lugh's stall Hans leaped up as if impelled by a coiled spring. Without allowing the younger man a chance to speak, Daniel thrust out the stew and muttered, "I got supper for you."

Hans frowned. "Something wrong, Mr. Call—Daniel?"

Daniel cursed. "Not a bloody thing, boy-o. Not with me, that is."

"Has one of the animals taken sick?"

"Sick? Nay." But considering his latest skirmish with Willow, Daniel was forced to reconsider. "Aye! Sick in the head, she is."

Hans tried to smile, but the gesture died as he continued to study Daniel. "What do you mean?"

With a sigh of frustration Daniel dropped onto a bale of hay. "They're the most damnably maddenin' creatures, you know."

"Sheep?"

Daniel shook his head.

"Cows?"

A sharper shake bounced his hat off his head. "Women!" he exploded, then realizing it had sounded more like a curse than a noun, he chuckled wryly. "Sit, lad. I've not really gone mad, at least not yet."

Visibly relaxing, Hans took a seat on a bale across from Daniel's. "More trouble with Maribeth?"

"No." The trouble was more with the uncle than with the niece. An uncle who'd wasted too much time thinking about plump rosy lips, a shiny brown braid, and the sweetest swaying hips he'd ever admired. "I'll tell you, son, women are naught but trouble of the worst sort."

Hans took the towel off the stew and plucked a soggy biscuit from the congealing mess. With a shrug of obvious resignation, he took an exploratory nibble. The well-seasoned food must have still been edible, since he took another bite, this one larger than the first.

Daniel leaned over and patted his farmhand's shoulder. "I owe you a decent meal, lad. A steak, thick as you want it, potatoes, pie. Just pick the time and place, only make sure you do it this week while we're in town."

Chewing, Hans nodded enthusiastically. Without wasting time on speech, he dug another blob of stew out of the bowl and, with the appetite typical of male adolescence, fed himself.

Ah . . . to be that young again. But youth bore pitfalls all its own. Take Willow Stimson, for example. "I have to warn you, Hans, that pretty little Willow is naught but trouble in a temptin' package."

The spoon fell from Hans's suddenly still fingers, clattering against the bowl. His fair skin flushed an angry red, and his eyes narrowed with indignation. As the young man's jaws were still occupied, Daniel hastened to explain himself.

"If I'm to be honest, I must confess I didn't buy the stew for you. On my way out to supper, I noticed Miss Stimson still workin' in her ewe's stall. On my way back I felt 'twould be the neighborly thing to do if I brought her a dish of stew. After all, I didn't want to leave her with the notion that I'd sought to offend her earlier today."

Hans picked up his spoon, cut more stew, and resumed eating. More than ever, Daniel grew aware of his farmhand's youthful vitality in contrast to his own maturity, and how appropriate Hans was for a girl like Willow.

"Anyway," he continued, "I took the food to her and spoke of makin' amends. Next thing I knew, she inspected the food and took offense at being offered mutton. Then she started spoutin' blarney about cannibalism and lewdness and degenerate ram owners. Finally she stomped off. Now, I ask you, is that the way to respond to kindness?"

A broad smile split Hans's fair Teutonic face. The boy's relief was almost palpable. "She didn't respond that way to mine."

A slow ache invaded Daniel's temples. He really hadn't needed Hans to make any more out of this, and he was especially irritated by the reminder of Willow's obvious appreciation of the younger man's efforts on her behalf and the foul response she'd had to Daniel's.

He didn't like it one bit.

"Hello there, Daniel Callaghan!"

A girlish voice tore Daniel from his bothersome thoughts. Turning toward the speaker, he smiled in recognition and stood, holding out his hand in greeting. "Why, if 'tisn't Katherine Meckler herself! An' what a lovely sight you are, m'dear."

A slow smile spread over the delicate blond features of Daniel's former flame. "You're a sight yourself, Danny. It's been a long time, hasn't it?"

At the old nickname Daniel chuckled. "Ten, twelve years, at least," he said, studying the changes wrought on Katherine by those very years. They'd been kind to her, since she looked even better than she had back then. His own smile broadened.

Shaking a graceful, gloved finger before his face, Katherine *tsk-tsk*ed. "You shouldn't be so quick to remind a lady of the passage of time."

"An' why not, m'dear? Especially when it looks so fine on you. You're lovely to behold."

Katherine Meckler was indeed a rare beauty. She wore her silver and gold hair swept up, leaving her exquisite face bare, showing off the flawless line of her cheekbones and the pure blue of her eyes. Pink lips smiled just enough to allow a peek at pearly teeth, and a rounded chin finished the oval of her face. Her features were what most would call classically perfect, and she knew how to display them to their best advantage. The burnt-sugar silk of her stylish suit made much of the lady's petite but well curved figure.

Katherine came closer, her eyes sparkling a sky blue. "And you're still a silver-tongued charmer! How are things at the dairy now that you've been back a while?"

"You knew I was back?"

What Daniel could have sworn was a wink teased him.

She went on. "Everyone's known of your return. Even if we haven't been personally honored with your presence."

Although her smile never wavered, Daniel felt the reprimand. "It's been . . . difficult since my father passed on. Then when Maggie an' Will were gone, Maribeth an' I had to come to grips with our loss."

Katherine removed a butter-cream colored glove and placed her delicate hand on Daniel's forearm. "You've needed comforting, haven't you, darling?"

Had he really heard what he thought he heard in Katherine's soft voice? And her a married lady! Daniel discreetly disengaged his arm from her grasp. Married women were not a'tall to his taste.

"No," he said, "'twasn't comforting I needed. What I needed was a great deal of time to learn to cope with my grief. Nothing takes away the pain of loss. One merely learns to live with the despair an' the void death leaves behind."

A hint of sadness and a faint smile appeared on Katherine's even features. "Oh, Daniel! You're as poetic as ever."

Uncomfortable with the description, Daniel frowned. Poetic? What nonsense! That weak description wasn't one a businessman wanted broadcast in the middle of a livestock exhibit. Besides, what had ever given Katherine the idea that he might be interested in resuming their long-dead romance? Especially this many years after she'd married Dr. Richard Meckler.

Then a crystal tear rolled down her cheek. "What is it, Katherine?" Daniel asked.

Another droplet followed the first, and a tight little shake of her head set a lush plume on her butter-cream felt hat to shivering. "You're not just poetic . . . you're absolutely right." A muffled sob followed. "I, too, have suffered loss. My dearest Richard went to his reward last winter."

Richard Meckler had died? "'Tis sorry I am, though I never heard a word of it, busy with the farm as I've been. What happened? Why, Richard was younger than I am."

Another louder sob broke forth. "Oh, Daniel, it was frightful! He was caring for a patient who came down with a violent fever. For days he stayed out at the fellow's farm, fighting for the man's life." Katherine's fingers popped open the clasp on her dainty leather bag and withdrew the most useless scrap of frippery Daniel had ever seen. With the bit of lace smaller than his palm she daubed her damp cheek. "He caught the same fever, and—"

"Here," he said, cutting off her tale. Feminine tears were something he'd never learned to handle. Passing her his generous-sized linen handkerchief, he added, "That thing there is useless."

A dazzling smile dawned on Katherine's lips. "Dependable as ever, Danny. You certainly know how to care for a woman in need."

Not if you ask Willow Stimson, he nearly blurted out, but caught himself before making an unpardonable blunder. "Just what any man would do."

Katherine shook her head, averting her face and studying her reflection in a minuscule looking glass she'd extracted from her diminutive purse. Then she waved the lace rag at Daniel in a pretty gesture of dismissal. "Not at all," she argued, then faced him, her face as pale and lovely as ever. "You'd be amazed at the number of brutes a lady is forced to endure."

An' you'd be the first on Willow Stimson's list, Danny-boy, his blasted conscience taunted.

"Ah . . . er . . . well, Katherine, perhaps 'tis your lovely delicacy that makes us men seem rougher than we mean to be." He extended his hands, which next to hers looked like smoked hams, solid and work-reddened as they were.

Katherine graced him with another pretty smile. "Don't be so modest, dear Daniel. Your company is always a pleasure." Then, with a birdlike gesture, she cocked her head. "In fact, why don't you let me know when you'd like to have dinner and see a production at the Strand Theater? It would be a delightful way to get reacquainted."

This time Daniel entertained no doubt that Katherine's invitation bore more than just the offer of a meal and a show. The beautiful widow Meckler was offering Daniel a rare prize indeed. But something about her frontal attack smacked of . . . just that, attack. A battle to be waged and won. Daniel wasn't sure he wanted to go to war just for the pleasure of a woman's company. Much less did he wish to be the field where she stabbed her flag of victory. Although he'd been without a woman for a while now, he wasn't anywhere near that desperate.

He took a step back. "I don't know, Katherine, we're

awfully busy right now, and after the Fair I can't say when I'll be back in town."

Her smile tightened at the edges. "It doesn't matter when, darling. Just keep in mind that I'm looking forward to becoming great friends again."

That was a strategic retreat if he'd ever seen one. "As soon as I find time to spend with friends . . . we'll see. After all, I'm Maribeth's only relative, and the wee lassie needs me."

Momentarily silent, Katherine folded her lace hanky and returned it to her bag. Then she nodded briskly, as if coming to an important decision. "I've heard your niece has become difficult. Have you considered the disciplined influence of a boarding school? I know of an outstanding Quaker establishment in Connecticut. Really, darling, you shouldn't deny yourself a life because of the child's tantrums."

Daniel clenched his jaw. He sought forbearance, but found little to call forth. "I don't think so, Katherine. We're Catholic, and should we need one, convents abound. For the present, I'll be keepin' Maribeth at home."

A tiny stiffening in her shoulders made it clear that Katherine had caught the gist of Daniel's message. He hoped she took his recommendation to stay out of his personal problems as seriously as he meant it. His niece was his business, and no one else's.

Twin pink circles marred the smoothness of Katherine's cheeks as, with jerky motions, she tugged her fashionably long gloves back on. "Just remember, Daniel, my offer remains open. Anytime you're in town and available, send me a message. I'll be happy to renew our—"

"*Friendship*, yes."

A nod set the arched feather on Katherine's hat to bouncing again. "Of course. Friendship." She leaned over the gate, grasped Daniel's shirtsleeve, and pulled him toward her. She rose as high as her tiptoes allowed and reached for Daniel's distant face.

Halving the span, he placed his lips against hers, then pulled quickly back. He didn't want to give Katherine any more ideas than she already had.

"*Do* remember my invitation," she repeated, then left.

Daniel took a couple of steps toward the back of the stall. With a heartfelt groan, he dropped onto his hay bale. 'Twas only then that he realized that his farmhand had witnessed the mortifying incident.

Hans wore a dumbfounded expression. His eyes were beamed on Katherine's straight back as she neared the entrance of the Sheep Building, and his sappy smile gave him the look of a moonstruck pup. It was clear the boy had never seen anyone who rivaled the stunning widow.

Daniel waved his hand in front of Hans's glazed eyes. The young man blinked, then shook himself. "She's something, isn't she?"

Nodding, Daniel leaned against another hay bale piled high behind him. "Yes, the lady is something else, an' up to something, too. But I'm afraid what she's up to is too rich for me."

Hans jerked his head around. "You mean—you're not going to take her up on her invitation?"

The disbelief on Hans's face told Daniel that the thought of turning down such an offer was unfathomable. He tried to explain. "I'm not ready to become her latest conquest, lad. No man should let himself be fooled by such direct flattery. Once he does, a forceful lady like Katherine has him totally under her control."

"B—but . . . Oh, hell, I just don't understand you, Daniel. First you tease Miss Stimson mercilessly, making certain she believes you're some randy old goat, and then you refuse to take advantage of the widow's offer. Is it . . . that you don't *like* ladies?"

"Now hold it right there, boy-o! I resent what you're hintin' at. Of course, an' I like the ladies. I like them just as much as the next man." How dare that upstart question Daniel's preferences? The boy couldn't have gotten that absurd idea from his actions. Then again, it didn't matter where the boy came up with the daft notion. Daniel had to set the matter straight.

"'Tis just as I was tellin' you before Katherine stopped by. Women are dangerous, Hans. An' you'd best be learnin' this while you're young."

"How can you call that vision of loveliness dangerous? And Miss Stimson—she's not dangerous at all! You're the one who riled her up."

"Ah, but, Hans, notice please, 'tis on the two of them that your mind remains. Have you once thought of checkin' on the sheep? An' how about the Callaghan cows in the Dairy Building? When was the last time you spared them a thought?"

Although Hans tried to hide his response by leaning deeper into the shadows, Daniel had no trouble spotting dismay on his face.

The younger man remained silent, clearly trying to remember. "Why . . . it was . . . Oh, yes! It was right before you brought the stew. I'd been wondering if I should leave and look in on the cows, since you were taking so long to eat. I wondered if I'd be better off settling them for the night instead of waiting for you. Then you showed up all steamed at Miss Stimson. I hadn't been thinking of her before that."

Daniel remembered the embarrassing end to his evening meal with Hiram. In all honesty, he'd been the one with the woman on his mind.

Catching a stray lock of mustache with a thumb and index finger, Daniel tugged, thinking of some way to change the subject, but his mind refused to cooperate. His thoughts refused to yield the memory of Willow.

He considered the events of the day. Had he really been that unpleasant toward Willow? Was he at fault? Or had something else been at work there? Then he realized it hadn't been something else a'tall.

"That's it!" he exclaimed. "Course, an' I didn't cause Willow's problems earlier today. 'Twas all her ewe's fault! The creature proved irresistible to Lugh. Poor lad was only respondin' as his Maker made him. As I said, Hans, females are crafty and dangerous. They make a man question his actions, his very intentions."

Hans shot Daniel a doubt-filled glance. He didn't look convinced.

Daniel persisted. "What happened today was caused by feminine wile. The next time I see that cheeky shepherdess I'll make her admit that her ewe tempted my ram. Just as Eve led Adam to perdition."

4

$\mathcal{M}$ORNING CAME TOO quickly for Daniel in his hotel room the next day. Try as he might, he failed to block from his sleepy eyes the stream of sunshine flooding in. With a quick glance he checked the time on the ornate clock atop the gleaming mahogany armoire by the sunny window. No matter how he looked at it, it was time to rise.

After performing his ablutions, Daniel found himself ready by seven o'clock. He still had time for breakfast, if he didn't linger over a second cup of coffee.

After a substantial meal of eggs, sausages, spiced apple slices, and abundant coffee, he felt fortified for the day ahead.

Today promised to be an important part of his first Fair Week as owner of Callaghan's Dairy. The preliminary judging was set to start by eight sharp. Despite choosing the streetcar over a cab, Daniel made sure he arrived at the fairgrounds with time to spare.

As he drank in the sights, sounds, and scents on the Midway, Daniel observed how little had changed from the York County Fairs he'd attended as a child. Oh, the buildings were a bit worse for the wear, but the brassy autumn sunshine warmed him as it always had, Pennsylvania German dialect sang along with English slang, and the spice of cooking pork sausages, roasting beef, steaming sauerkraut, and frying pastries bore the same perfume he remembered from years ago. The smells of the York County Fair were so vivid and his memories so sharp that he could almost taste the unique essence.

Near the Exhibition Arena he grew painfully aware of the devastating difference a scant year can make. A year ago in early spring Daniel had been at his office in Philadelphia almost round the clock, vying for a lucrative new contract to import Irish woolens. He won the business, but by season's end, he'd lost what he'd had left of what truly mattered in life. What hurt most was the careless disregard with which he'd turned his back on it years ago.

Although he scarcely remembered the time before leaving Ireland—he'd been so young—he did remember his childish disdain for the dairy farm that meant so much to Darby Callaghan. Daniel's father had worked endlessly to wrest a living from the rich Pennsylvania soil. Very early on, Daniel decided that his da's style of life wasn't for him. He'd never forgotten the excitement of the ship, the bustle of the crowd at the pier, the raucous call of sailors and stevedores, much less the wealth of goods that had come on the ship that brought the Callaghans to the New World.

When he was old enough to face Darby nose to nose, he'd informed his da that he was off to seek his fortune in Philadelphia. Although Daniel knew he was breaking his father's heart by turning his back on what the elder Callaghan had fought so hard for, Darby never argued with his only son over his choice.

But Daniel disappointed his father all the same. The day his son walked away from the dairy farm Darby built stick by board, inch by field, calf by cow, the relationship between father and son suffered what Daniel accepted as an irreparable blow.

Soon after Daniel's move to Philadelphia, his younger sister married the youngest son of a Lancaster County farmer. The newlyweds pestered Darby until he allowed them to take over the dairy. Shortly thereafter, knowing his farm was in capable family hands, Darby yielded his grip on earthly soil.

Mother lasted scant months after her Darby was gone. More years flew by. Then, at the end of spring last year, the flooded Codorus Creek took the last of Daniel and Maribeth's family when his sister and her husband drowned. The bridge they'd been crossing was ripped away by the roiling water.

Since then, he and Maribeth had tried to carry on, but Daniel felt unequal to the task of instant fatherhood. All he knew was that he *couldn't* fail the child. Not as he'd once failed his father.

"By damn, an' I'll be doin' right by Maribeth!" he muttered at the edge of the Exhibition Arena. With a look at the folk around the showing blocks, Daniel spotted Hans. As he strode toward his farmhand, he made himself a promise. From that moment on, the only female Daniel would allow into his thoughts was his orphaned niece, Maribeth.

"There'll be no more thinkin' of maddenin' shepherdesses for you, Daniel Callaghan."

Herding sheep had its rewarding moments, but preparing them for display at a fair wasn't one of them. Especially when one was as tense and anxious as Willow found herself this morning. It was to be expected, however, since today would decide her future.

When she had groomed Jethro and Zebulon, her two young rams, Willow returned to Missy's side. She again checked the ewe's fleece for ragged tufts, a pair of shears at the ready. Since she'd seen to Missy before tending to the rams, this was no more than a show of busyness, but it kept her hands occupied.

All she succeeded in doing was to make Missy skitter away. No self-respecting sheep was fond of shears.

"Oh, this just won't do, Willow Stimson!" she scolded herself. "You can't stay so nervous or you'll guarantee all your animals a poor showing. They don't deserve that. It's not their fault that you're in dire financial straits."

"Speaking to yourself *again*, dear?" asked Reba Meister from the wooden walkway, concern in her voice.

Willow turned, taking a calming breath. "I'm so glad to see you, Mrs. Meister. Maybe you can distract me enough that I won't get any more flustered."

"Dear child, if you'd only let Mr. Meister give you the money—"

"Please don't. Not today."

"As you wish," Mrs. Meister said, worry lining her brow. "But after the fair we're going to have us a very serious discussion."

"I hope that conversation won't be necessary after the fair."

"For your sake, dear, I hope so, too." Mrs. Meister took off her trim brown gloves, then opened the stall gate and gestured Willow to join her. "What's this I hear about an altercation with a certain Irishman?"

Willow wrinkled her features in distaste. "I can't believe someone ran to tell you tales."

"Small world, smaller town. You know how it is."

As she blew a loose strand of hair from her forehead, Willow allowed herself to remember the more wretched moments of the day before. "I'm afraid it's true. Daniel Callaghan and I got off to an unpleasant start. But I had nothing to do with it. In fact, it was all his fault."

Reba Meister arched a silver brow. "I've always thought

that quarrels happen when two can't find common ground."

"Honestly! I did nothing to the beastly man."

With a soft *tsk-tsk* Mrs. Meister shook her head. "Now, Willow, you know perfectly well he's reputed to be the most charming of men. How can you call him beastly?"

"You should have seen him as I did! Oh, it was awful," she added with a shudder, remembering the head sheep judge's expression. "I was working out knots in Missy's fleece near the Exhibition Arena when Mr. Hillenbaugh appeared, accompanied by two men and a ram. I had no idea who the other men were—not that knowing would have made any difference to me. Since first impressions are so important, I waited for an opportunity to greet the head judge properly. I continued working on Missy's wool, and the next thing I knew the poor ewe was *baa*-ing for her life! Mr. Charming Callaghan's brute of a ram was . . . he was all over Missy, trying to . . ." Willow checked for eavesdroppers. "*Accost* her."

"Accost her?"

She wrung her hands. Even though she'd grown up on a farm, the intricacies of animal reproduction remained an improper subject for ladylike discussion. "You know, climbing on her . . ." Willow lowered her voice to a whisper. "To *mount* her."

"But . . . isn't this about the time of year when ewes come into heat?"

Willow cast another peek around them. "Yes. But—"

"Isn't it normal for a ram to be attracted to a ewe in heat?"

"Sure, but—"

"Then why are you accusing Daniel of improper behavior? Seems to me his ram acted quite reasonably. The man had nothing to do with it."

Willow gaped. How could Mrs. Meister dismiss yesterday's mortifying fiasco so matter-of-factly? "He could've tried to control his beast! He didn't have to laugh at Missy's offended sensitivities and her rejection of his randy animal. In fact, he acted as if he was proud of that awful Lew."

"Lew?" asked Mrs. Meister, obviously stifling a chuckle.

Willow's frustration deepened. "Yes, that's the ram's name."

Mrs. Meister's laughter burst forth. "Oh, this is hilarious! Or, you would agree with me if you stopped taking it so seriously. Can't you see the humor?"

"No, not at all."

"Mr. Meister will be so disappointed. Can't you see how appropriate the ram's name is?"

"Lewis?" Willow shook her head. "What's so appropriate about a ram named Lew?"

"I also see that your scheme to save the farm with wool consumes you. The fleece seems to have blinded your common sense and smothered your thinking as well."

Willow tightened her lips. This sounded like a lecture, the sort given to a child who had misbehaved. As far as she was concerned, *she* hadn't earned the reprimand. She knew who had.

Before Willow could respond, Mrs. Meister continued. "How can you forget the time you've spent burrowing through Mr. Meister's books on Celtic myths and legends? Have you forgotten every tale, every scrap of whimsy the two of you culled from those books?"

"You mean he named his ram after Lugh? The Celtic sun god? The god of . . . fertility?"

Mrs. Meister chuckled once more. "More than likely it was Maeve Callaghan who named the sheep. She loved those stories more than even my dear husband does. Makes perfect sense to name a vital, virile ram after a god of fertility."

"Oh, I can't believe tiny Mrs. Callaghan was the one who

chose the name. It had to have been that vulgar man. You should have seen him cheer his animal. Why, if I hadn't pulled Missy away, that ram would have succeeded in breeding her, with Daniel Callaghan egging the beast on! He even offered me the lambs that could result from that appalling union. Utterly shameless. And to think he gave his animal such an obscene name."

"Doesn't look like I can persuade you, does it?" Mrs. Meister grew serious. "If I told Lucie once, I told her a thousand times. She made a grave mistake by keeping you sheltered from the earthier aspects of animal husbandry. Yesterday's incident shouldn't bother you so much. Just get used to it." Then Mrs. Meister winked, surprising Willow. "You'll have to discover Daniel Callaghan's charms on your own."

"What charms?"

"Why, dear girl . . . the man is gloriously handsome. With all that waving auburn hair, those blue eyes, that mustache and beard, and of course, that manly build. A woman would have to be blind, deaf, and stupid not to notice such a man."

"Handsome is as handsome does," Willow retorted, even though she sounded petty to her own ears. "I won't deny he looks quite splendid, but there's more to folks than just their looks."

"Of course, dear, but it seems you've forgotten that fact."

"Not after my experience with a handsome, shallow man. One who traded a meaningful life here in the country for riches in Philadelphia, just as Daniel Callaghan did, if you'll remember."

Reba Meister lightly slapped Willow's hand in reproof. "You can't compare Daniel to that weasel you almost married. Besides, Philadelphia had nothing to do with

Milford leaving you. Greed did. I tried to warn you. Lucie did, too."

"Yes, you did, but both of you hated Milford from the time he was a child. I couldn't see how you two would have better insight into his character than I did, biased against him as you both were."

"Why do you think we disapproved of him? Because we did see beyond his pretty face and manners. There was no substance to the fool. You're best off jilted, you know."

In a thoughtful voice Willow said, "It didn't feel that way then." She'd never forget the anguish of abandonment coming on the heels of Aunt Lucie's passing. "The least he could have done was wait until Aunt Lucie was cold in the grave before running off with that stockyard owner's daughter."

"Nonsense! The least he could have done was to leave town years ago without scheming to get his hands on the Stimson farm. York doesn't need rats like Milford Philpott, and neither do you."

"Well, he's gone now, and I'm here, and I have more important things to think about than foolish men."

"Absolutely. You're already twenty years old. High time you started thinking of good, solid men and courting."

Not again! Reba Meister was anything but a quitter. She'd been pestering Willow about her lack of prospects for months now. "Are you saying I should leave everything to a husband and become a proper missus?"

"I think it's time for you to look around and find someone to share your burdens and appreciate you for the prize you are. You're a lovely young woman with much to offer the right man."

She'd agree. For the moment. And in the interest of temporarily closing the discussion. "Fine, I'll do that once Missy wins Best of Show."

Mrs. Meister sighed. "It's time, dear. Let's get the animals to the show blocks."

Willow opened the stall gate and led Missy out. Mrs. Meister took the ewe's leather lead and, despite her elegant suit, competently led the animal toward the arena. That freed Willow to handle her two other ewes. She'd have to find the Fritzmeier twins, the boys she'd hired to help show her sheep, then send one of them after her two rams. She needed one of them to help her show the females.

As they made their way through the crowd that had begun to gather around the Exhibition Arena, Willow experienced tremendous relief. She was glad she had something concrete to do. Especially since it would divert Mrs. Meister's attention from what Willow knew was her favorite subject.

Mr. and Mrs. Meister, unlikely specimens though they seemed, had married when Reba was quite young, passionately in love with each other. That love had never dimmed, despite their failure to have the children both had wanted. As the recipient of their tenderness and support, Willow had benefited much from their attention. She knew she would never have weathered Aunt Lucie's death and Milford's betrayal without their love. She didn't like to argue with the Meisters, but she wasn't about to budge on her opinion of Daniel Callaghan.

"Now, if he doesn't sway Otis Hillenbaugh's vote, we can have us a fine Fair Week," she muttered to Missy, who was following closely.

"For heaven's sake, Willow," objected Mrs. Meister. "A Callaghan wouldn't stoop to bribery."

Hmph! She'd seen the two men together enough times now to raise her suspicions. "Well, maybe not an outright bribe, but they were quite familiar, chatting and smiling and patting each other's back."

Throwing her free hand up in the air, Mrs. Meister cried,

"I give up! This fair thing has made you lose your mind. Otis Hillenbaugh and Darby Callaghan were as close as brothers, and Daniel and his sister Maggie called the Hillenbaughs Uncle Otis and Aunt Heidi since they were sprouts. Of course they're close, as close to family as one can get. I'll just have to wait until this week is over to reason with you."

She *had* gone too far that time, Willow thought. "I didn't know. I guess they would be close under those circumstances. But I still fear that their family ties will favor Mr. Callaghan's flock."

"Think as you wish, Willow, but don't let anyone hear you say that. There's no one fairer or more scrupulous than Otis Hillenbaugh. Except perhaps Daniel Callaghan, himself."

"Hmmm . . . that remains to be seen."

Silence descended on the crowd as soon as the judging began. It was a tense silence, the nervous energy of the contestants and onlookers nearly a living thing. Although the humans knew to keep quiet, their animals didn't share that sort of discretion. Each time a sheep was prodded, pushed, or closely examined, its *baa* of protest seemed louder and more strident than it otherwise would have.

Her bottom lip caught between her teeth, Willow watched Mr. Hillenbaugh and his colleagues approach, her nerves tautening with every step they took. Their verdict was too important to her. It mattered too much.

Those exhibitors whose animals had been judged were free to take their entries back to their respective stalls. Results would be announced later and ribbons awarded accordingly. Willow watched those who left the circle with envy. She wished she was already done and on her way back to the relative comfort of the Sheep Building.

When Mr. Hillenbaugh approached Daniel Callaghan, Willow studied the ewes the Irishman had entered in the competition. One in particular was as close to perfection as Willow had ever seen a sheep come. Like his ram, Daniel's ewe was a stylish creature, a naturally dark Border Leicester sheep, with long, lustrous wool, and of an admirable size. The animal's wool would be especially attractive when spun into yarn. Missy had a worthy adversary indeed.

After meeting the lusty Lugh, Willow had known in the back of her mind that Daniel Callaghan would present stiff competition. She just hadn't wanted to admit it.

When the judges left the Callaghan ewes, Willow saw Hans speak momentarily to Daniel, then lead the judged sheep away. Although she couldn't see the animal whose tether Daniel took from Hans, it looked as if he had a contestant entered in an upcoming category.

Then there was no time for Willow to wonder about Daniel's fair showing. The judges were in front of her, studying Missy's form, her wool, the soundness of her teeth. They checked her hooves. They inspected her ears. They looked at her eyes and her skin and her belly, too. They took notes in small books.

Just as Willow felt that she could no longer bear the strain of exhibition, she heard one of her other ewes give a strident *baa*. She didn't dare turn to see what was happening, and since she'd already paid the Fritzmeier twins, she knew the animals were well watched. She followed Missy's all-important judging. But soon Daisy joined Rosebud's chorus of discontent, and although she tried, Willow couldn't see them through a group of bystanders who blocked her view. She wished the judging was over; she just wanted to take her sheep and collapse on her sweet-smelling bale of hay.

A rustle of movement close by suggested that the onlookers had gone on to other exhibits. She glanced toward the boys and her ewes, but instead saw Daniel Callaghan intent on the judging of her best ewe.

When two of the judges brought their heads together and conferred, apprehension began to jell in Willow's middle. The nerves, the anticipation, the fear of losing . . . she'd never experienced anything so intense in her life. Missy bore Willow's future on her elegant, woolly shoulders.

Suddenly the expectant silence in the Exhibition Arena was rent by the cry of an agitated ram. Missy trembled. Willow recognized the animal's voice. The culprit was none other than Mr. Callaghan's randy ram.

Missy began to fidget. Willow turned and spied the libidinous Lugh fighting his owner in an effort to reach the object of his desire. No wonder Daisy and Rosebud had cried out! As any healthy ewe would, they scented the aroused ram and worried about the monster's attack.

He was headed straight for Missy.

Someone tittered to Willow's right. A young man across the arena whistled his admiration. Murmuring spread. Soon everyone was discussing the antics of the Callaghan ram and the lovely white ewe he fancied.

Willow prayed for the earth to open up below her.

No such miracle happened.

The laughing grew louder.

Missy joined her voice with those of Daisy and Rosebud.

Mortified, Willow spun around and demanded Daniel's intervention. "This is no longer tolerable, Mr. Callaghan. You are now causing a general disturbance, not to mention undermining my ewe's chances to win. You simply *must* do something about that . . . that satyr."

The tittering became outright laughter as Daniel shrugged, grinned, and tugged again on Lugh's lead. Ineffectively, of course.

"Good day, Miss Stimson," the Irish bawd called out.

"Not likely!" she shot back, looking to the judges for dismissal. Taking pity on Willow and Missy, since the ewe continued to tug on her lead seeking escape, Mr. Hillenbaugh smiled anemically and waved them along.

As she fled the humiliating scene, Willow looked for Mrs. Meister. She spotted her friend and proceeded that way. Once she reached the older woman's side, she shot a venomous glare at Daniel Callaghan, who was again in the throes of mirth at her expense. "Now do you see what I meant?"

Mrs. Meister's lips twitched suspiciously; a merry glint lit up her eyes. She nodded, then lost her battle to control her laughter. "Oh, my!" she exclaimed between peals. "That's a fine ram Daniel has there."

Shocked, Willow took another look at the offending animal. "How could you think that? Can't you see how scared Missy is? How jumpy she became during her judging? Don't you see how badly that will affect her scores?"

"Dear child, I see a lot more than you do right now. I see healthy animals responding to their most basic instincts. It's up to Lugh to pursue and to Missy to make the pursuit exciting."

"You can't possibly find Missy guilty of this catastrophe."

"No, dear. She's not guilty of anything, and neither is Lugh. They're behaving normally. As are you and Daniel."

"If I'm behaving properly, how can he possibly be, too?"

"Because you've paired up for the most exciting dance of your lives."

5

"*BECAUSE YOU'VE PAIRED up for the most exciting dance of your lives.*"

Hours after Mrs. Meister had left the fairgrounds, her words continued to plague Willow. How could something so laughable be true? There was nothing Willow found interesting, much less exciting, about that overgrown, debauched Irishman. Why, he lacked the basics of common decency, never mind having desirable attributes.

She would, however, concede that if one were the sort who put emphasis on a man's looks—which she wasn't—then one had to admit that Daniel Callaghan was a fine example of male beauty. His eyes burned with cobalt fire. His hair bristled with vigor. His smile, hidden by that luxuriant growth of rust-colored whiskers, burst forth with disarming regularity, lightening an already open face. And if one studied his physical build . . . well, even Willow would agree that few men possessed the physical perfection Daniel displayed. In fact, he looked strong enough to fight and win any battle, protect his own from any foe, and bolster even the most weary of partners.

If only in that respect, Willow longed for a man like Daniel.

But *her* mate would have to present evidence of moral

rectitude and propriety. She needed someone who not only fought and won, but also did so honorably, someone who could comfort when she needed it, someone who had something special to bring to their union.

As of yet, Daniel Callaghan had failed to demonstrate anything beyond his questionable character and magnificent build.

Besides, Willow had better things to do than waste hours wondering why Mrs. Meister considered Daniel such an outstanding catch. Especially for a woman like Willow, who bore so much responsibility.

Not only was she fighting to salvage her livelihood, but also to preserve her heritage. Her father, Richard Stimson, whom she scarcely remembered, inherited the family farm when he was quite young. He married soon thereafter and insisted that his sister Lucie remain with the newlyweds until she, too, married. Willow then made a prompt arrival into the family. Since Lucie Stimson never found a man to her exacting standards, when Richard and his young wife died of cholera, she inherited the farm and Willow's care. By dint of constant attention, she continued to coax a rich harvest from the fields, while all along indulging her love for her small flock of sheep and the joys of working with the animals' wool.

When Aunt Lucie died two years ago, Willow was devastated. Then, when Milford abandoned her just days before their wedding, Willow felt as if her life had ended. She'd lost her parents and her beloved aunt, her fiancé had never really wanted her, and in the end he threw her over for a rich city miss. . . . What did she have left to live for?

The response came quickly, by way of her surrogate parents, the Meisters. Reba Meister placed the newborn Missy in Willow's empty lap and showed the younger woman the trust the animal placed in her. The sheep needed attention; they couldn't fend for themselves, as they were accustomed to human custody. Aunt Lucie's, in this case.

Aunt Lucie had shared a special closeness with her sheep, and Willow learned early on that she, too, could communicate with the animal residents of the farm. In her time of need, that bond lifted her depression, replacing it with the joy that comes from love shared. She loved her sheep. They were curious individuals, each one endowed with unique traits and a distinct personality. They in turn provided Willow with a reason to go on.

Then came the flood. Her fields, always so fertile thanks to the richness of Pennsylvania's soil and the abundant moisture from the Codorus Creek, were ravaged by the water's fury. The floodwaters surged onto the farmyard and whirled around the house, stealing Willow's front steps and weakening the foundation of her home. The barn collapsed.

Willow was forced to mortgage the farm. She wouldn't otherwise have been able to repair the house and rebuild the barn for the sheep.

The mortgage money, however, hadn't stretched to buy seed for planting this spring. The only thing Willow had left was the yield of her small kitchen garden, the wool she'd saved from previous shearings, and the potential income from the sale of her flock.

Nothing else really mattered now. She had to find the funds to pay the mortgage, as well as the taxes. She couldn't waste time admiring a cocky Irish bawd's good looks, especially since he seemed to be the biggest obstacle to her goals. His animals would be difficult to beat.

Even though Willow didn't have a four-year-old ram competing against the lusty Lugh, she did have her hopes pinned on Missy. After seeing Daniel's ewe, she knew she had reason to worry. Her two-year-old rams, entered in the Young Ram category, also faced stiff competition from other Callaghan entrants, but nothing so monumental as going up against the dark Lugh and Daniel's matching ewe.

Missy had been acting strangely ever since the judging that morning. The ewe hadn't displayed her usual perkiness, choosing instead to lie at Willow's feet while she plied her spinning wheel. She'd also slept more than she normally did. Willow was beginning to worry.

"Hello, there, Miss Stimson."

Looking up, she smiled at Daniel's young farmhand. "How are you this evening, Hans?"

"Doing fairly. Looks like Lugh will win Best of Show, and his lady, Brigid, is a strong contestant in . . . her . . . Oh, how rude of me! You're hoping to win that category, too."

Willow smiled tightly and waved away the young man's concern. "It's an open competition, Hans. Anyone can aim for the ribbon. It's what the fair is all about. Finding the best animal of its kind."

He sighed in relief. "I'm glad you don't hold that against me. I'd hate to offend you on account of my job."

"Don't give it another thought. I have plenty of worries, so I don't fret over what's out of my control."

"Worries, Miss Stimson?"

"Please call me Willow," she said, standing and approaching her visitor. "It seems that my ewe isn't feeling well. I'm wondering if she could have caught cold during yesterday's rain."

A frown scored Hans's forehead. "You mind if I take a look at her?"

"No, it's probably to her benefit. I could use another opinion."

Willow opened the gate and ushered Hans in. His serious expression justified her decision to let him examine Missy. Maybe she was too anxious about the outcome of the judging and was imagining problems where there were none. A stranger would keep a cooler head.

"Can't say for sure there's anything wrong with her," Hans finally answered, rising from where he'd crouched to study Missy. "She's breathing kind of fast, and it looks like she's using her stomach instead of her lungs but . . . it could be too soon to tell. You should keep an eye on her. Has she been eating regular?"

Willow tried to remember. "I—I don't know. With all the fuss of the Fair, and the special grooming, and the judging . . . I haven't paid much notice to her appetite." She leaned over the feeding trough and to her dismay found quite a bit of grain in the bottom. "Looks as if she's off her feed. And I always measure her portion. She does best if I give her regular amounts at regular times."

"Well, all sheep do better that way. Now that you've noticed, you can watch her and see how she does." Hans dropped down to Missy's side again and tipped her face upward. Docile and well-mannered as always, Missy cooperated, allowing him to study her eyes and nostrils. He rubbed his thumb over her nose, and Willow knew he was checking for fever and nasal discharge.

That would be frightening indeed. A cold was nothing small to sheep. It could lead to pneumonia, and that, more often than not, to death. Willow shuddered at the thought.

"Her nostrils aren't wet," Hans said, "nor is she real hot. But if she's not frisky and she's not eating, then you need to watch her."

Willow nodded, her bottom lip caught between her teeth, her fear-chilled fingers laced tightly. "That's what I thought, and I did check her nose a couple of times. Thank you so much. I appreciate your concern."

Hans blushed. "Anything I can do for you, Miss Stimson, just ask."

"Anything the lass asks, eh? I'd worry if I were you, lad!"

Willow jerked her head around at the unexpected interruption. Daniel Callaghan, big as a sunset-haloed mountain, stood at the walkway side of the stall gate, a strange light blazing in his blue eyes. His whiskers hid from Willow's scrutiny whatever he felt or thought.

That irritated her more than his words. "Hans has nothing to worry about," she said in a starchy tone. "I'm not in the habit of asking for illegal or immoral assistance."

Hans rushed to her side. "Mr. Callaghan! You're not hinting—"

"Ah, get along with you, lad! I wasn't insinuatin' a thing. I was just commenting that you seem mighty taken with the lovely lady."

Willow tightened her lips. "*I* think you're being horridly rude, barging into a personal conversation as you just did."

An eyebrow danced up Daniel's forehead. "Personal . . . and private?"

Hans nudged Willow deeper into the stall and, squaring his shoulders, confronted Daniel. "I resent the way you're speaking to the lady. When Miss Stimson told me that her ewe wasn't eating and was less active than usual, I offered my help. She wanted another opinion."

The reddish eyebrow plunged back into place. "Any sign of fever?"

Willow shook her head, trying to control her anger. She had to avoid letting this man unnerve her each time he appeared. Otherwise, the rest of her Fair Week was sure to be even more calamitous than it had been so far.

Without asking her permission, Daniel opened the gate and entered the now crowded stall. Noticing the crush, he bobbed his head toward his pens and said to Hans, "Go back to our area, boy-o. I'll take a look at the ewe, then meet you there in a minute or so."

For a moment Willow feared an argument between the two men was inevitable. Hans's eyebrows drew menacingly close. His cheeks sported ridges of tightened muscle. His lips grew white-edged with restraint.

Daniel waved, urging Hans on. "You've nothin' to fear. I won't hurt the lamb or her mistress one bit."

With a sharp nod, Hans did as asked, but his strides down the walkway sounded sharp and clipped to Willow's ears.

"You really shouldn't have done that," she started, then realized Daniel was oblivious to her presence. Crouched next to Missy, he softly scratched the ewe's head, his other hand busy seeking the cause of the sheep's problem. He stared into Missy's black eyes, then rubbed her nose a few times. He shook his head and stood, shrugging.

"Can't say I find anythin' wrong, lass, but she's breathin' shallow. I'd keep an eye on 'er, especially with all the cold rain we've had. I'd hate to see her go down. She's a fine one, indeed."

Willow swallowed hard. What she had to say next was sure to prove difficult, one of the most humbling utterances she'd ever voice. "Th-thank you, Mr. Callaghan. I appreciate your opinion, as well."

The whiskers tipped in a lopsided smile. "Ah, lass, call me Daniel. I'm old, but not that old yet!"

Willow smiled at his small vanity. "How ancient are you, Daniel?"

A broad smile betrayed his mock frown. "Watch your mouth, lassie! Just because you're little more than a girl doesn't mean I'm ancient. I'm thirty-two and countin'. How about you?"

Willow chuckled. "Ancient indeed. I'm twenty myself."

An eyebrow rose. He seemed surprised. "By all the Saints, I won't stand here and be insulted! Especially since you're older than you look. I'll go back where I'm appreciated." Chuckling under his breath, he saluted Willow with two fingers to the rim of his brown hat, then let himself out of the stall. "Let us know if there's anythin' we can do for your sheep."

Willow found herself again smiling at the man she'd sworn was the worst that the male gender had to offer. "Thank you, I will."

"Happy dreams, lass!"

"Thanks . . ."

Who would have known? Daniel Callaghan wasn't a monster after all.

Deep in the silence of the night, the anguished cry of a child pierced the veil of Willow's dreams. Startled, she looked around, wondering if she had just dreamed the sound. The Sheep Building wore the dark mantle of midnight and echoed with the peaceable song of slumber.

Many a sheep's lament resembled the weeping of children, so Willow rose from her bed of quilts and hay and looked in on the members of her flock. The two rams slept, heedless to the sound. Daisy and Rosebud, lying close together, were awake and alert. The cry probably awoke them. Willow no longer thought she'd dreamed it. When she checked on Missy, she found her as the ewe had spent most of the evening, resting in the hay. She, too, was awake.

The Sheep Building remained dark, the murmur of healthy animals breathing the only sound in its depths. Not many farmers stayed in the stalls with their animals. Most visited family or friends in town to ensure themselves a good night's sleep. After Hans and Daniel both advised her to keep an eye on Missy, Willow knew she wouldn't have slept had she gone home with Mrs. Meister. As lovely and comfortable as the Meisters' guest room was, she would hardly have napped for worrying about Missy.

She'd sent the Meisters a message by way of the Fritzmeier twins, explaining her situation. She knew the older couple would understand her concern, although she suspected they'd hold strong reservations about her decision. Still, she was an adult, with adult responsibilities. She couldn't charge the twin adolescents with the burden of seeing Missy through a possible illness.

To offset the feeling of helplessness, Willow had repeatedly inspected the stall to make sure everything was as it should be. The pen was clean and dry; the hay on the ground sweet and fresh. The Sheep Building, with its open-arched sides, allowed fresh air to circulate freely, and as always, she supplied Missy with abundant cold water and feed. For additional insurance, she'd covered Missy with an old quilt, as the night had turned cooler than expected. For now that was all she could do.

A final glance around her assigned area revealed no change from when she'd hunkered down to sleep. The cry that roused her couldn't have been serious, as the animal appeared to have gone back to sleep.

Willow rolled herself back up in her other quilt, glad she'd brought two of her larger ones. Not only had Aunt Lucie been a successful farmer, she'd also woven magnificent blankets and shawls, and her intricate quilts had always won ribbons at the fair. Better than their beauty, however, was the warmth they offered. Aunt Lucie always used wool instead of cotton to fill her quilts.

As Willow allowed herself to relax, her eyes grew heavy. Through the curtain of golden slumber that settled over her, Willow perceived the hint of lantern light. She briefly thought that someone must have come to check on his animals, but let the notion drift away as sleep overtook her. She welcomed the darkness and the rest. Especially since it brought a whisper of music, soft, mellow notes that danced with her dreams.

"Because you've paired up for the most exciting dance of your lives."

Mrs. Meister's words took hazy shape, melding into the form of a dancing couple. The man was tall, strong, bearded. The woman, graceful and slender. She smiled up into her partner's eyes. The music swelled around them, coaxing them to glide, to spin, to whirl to the sweet notes of an invisible violin.

Turn after turn made the woman's cloud of skirts ripple, each spin lifting the fabric just enough to allow the dancers to become one with the music, to weave together in a mystical union too poignant for words.

The music played, its notes growing richer, louder. The dancers kept up with the song, joy shimmering in their radiant expressions. The violin filled the night with magic and brought longing to Willow's heart.

She awoke on a sob. The dream had been . . . more than a dream. It had felt so real that Willow wept, for she'd tried to reach it, to touch the dancers and share their emotions, but they'd eluded her. She now knew it had only been a dream.

A questionable one at that. She could have sworn the man was Daniel Callaghan and the woman herself. Although she'd learned earlier that evening that he had at least an ounce of goodness to him, he was still miles away from Willow's ideal man.

She blinked, seeking to clear the odd feelings that had filled her during the glorious dream. She could scarcely accept that the image of Daniel dancing with her had such power to move her. That she still felt a sense of excitement in her heart, a yearning, a wish to dance to the music that still played in her mind.

She knew she no longer slept, but strangely enough the music played on, and in the far end of the Sheep Building a lantern gave off its golden glow. What was going on? It was the dead of night. She'd thought herself the only human in the structure, and she'd yet to meet a fiddling sheep.

With the comfort of her quilt hugged tight around her, Willow stood. She looked toward the light.

Was she still dreaming? Could what her eyes saw be real?

She stared, captivated by the unexpected sight of Daniel, a delicate violin held up to his shoulder, anchored by his bearded chin. His right hand held a bow, leading it in a masterful dance over the strings.

Daniel's eyes were closed, and his shoulders swayed as he lived the music he made. A wealth of emotion rose from the violin, affecting Willow in a way she'd never known before. She took a step toward the man and his instrument. Then another. But she stopped herself, suspecting that she was witnessing something few people ever did.

As large and hard as Daniel Callaghan appeared, there seemed to be another side to him. One he kept hidden, a private part of the man. Willow felt the pull to approach that man, a desire to touch the essence of the violinist who brought tears to her eyes by simply skipping a bow over a string.

A lump of emotion caught in her throat.

Tears slid down her cheeks.

Daniel played on.

The music changed; another piece warmed the night, taking the nip of autumn from the air, replacing it with a warmth that Willow wanted to keep forevermore.

Angels, she thought. Angels played like this. Up to the heavens they sent their songs, offering God their most magnificent sounds. Daniel's music joined that of heavenly hosts.

Willow had never known such spiritual perception, such instinctive recognition of her Maker. But that night, in a humble sheep pen, she listened to Daniel's God-given talent, and wept for joy. The majesty of creation surrounded her; life, vibrant and potent, lifted her spirits, and she rejoiced in being alive.

Her skin tingled. Currents of energy swirled through her. As she listened to the praise Daniel offered, she noticed a child at his side, mesmerized as Willow herself was. Tenderness softened the man's expression; love was surely present, as well. The child's eyes were open, wide with wonder, a smile upon her lips.

Still, Willow wept. Not with pain or sadness, but with reverence for Daniel's gift. What sort of man could seem so earthy, yet hide within him a treasure so rare? What man could spend his life carving a living from the soil, yet produce a sound so sublime?

The answer was touchingly clear. Daniel. And that brought another question to Willow's mind.

Could Mrs. Meister be right? Had Willow and Daniel paired up for the most exciting dance of their lives?

6

*L*ATE IN THE night Daniel wrought a sweet lament from his violin. What should he do about his situation?

No answer came.

While his eyelids burned with the pain of loss, his niece, Maribeth, gazed up at him, trust in her sky-blue eyes. Those eyes of hers . . . they haunted him. They came to him in his worst nightmares, beseeching his help to raise a motherless child.

After his sister's death, he'd gladly assumed the care of Maggie's child, a little girl who looked just like her mother had at twelve. It was clear Maribeth needed Daniel, but he didn't know precisely what it was she needed from him.

As far as he could tell, she needed a father, but hers was dead, and Daniel didn't know how to become the father Maribeth needed. All he knew was to bargain in business, and perhaps raise cows and sheep—nothing that would help him bring up a niece.

He couldn't fail her. He was all she had left.

Fear filled his heart, then poured from his violin, creating a sound not unlike the weeping of angels. As always, Daniel found the outlet for his rawest emotions in the strings of the old violin. Although often engulfed by the ferment of feelings, he'd never been able to share those emotions with anyone. Except his mother.

Maeve had been a creature of excitement, of feelings, of impulse and wonder and love. Daniel had always confided in her, confessed his fears, voiced his goals, shared his joys. Now Maeve Callaghan was gone. It seemed she'd been gone for a lifetime. He still missed her and the fancy-filled shelter her stories had offered during the storms of his youth.

It hurt that Maribeth didn't have Maeve. The child should have a grandmother to offer her comfort. She needed the sweet scent of lilies and the soothing warmth of Maeve's embrace. Maribeth needed the stories her grandmother wove of Irish faeries and legends and myths, of a world of mystery and magic she could escape to when the hurt pierced too deep.

Just as Daniel needed his fey mother's comfort these days.

He wished he could cry instead of having to be strong, but a glance at Maribeth revealed the tremulous blooming of a smile to brighten her pixie-like face. That smile prefaced the disappearance of her tears, and a victory over the apparitions that woke her with frightening regularity.

As he played, Daniel gave thanks for the gift his mother had left him. She'd taught him to play the violin, and although he never felt he could touch the magic she'd crafted out of silver scraps of sound, he knew his music, sincere as it was, found a home in Maribeth's aching heart.

Each time the dreams came to haunt her, she'd race to Daniel's room, weeping, calling out for the parents who'd died. Daniel shared the pain of the child left behind, and together they'd cling, tight childish arms wrapped around his bulk, his arms shielding her from any further despair. Then, when the sobs dried to droplets in her eyes, Maribeth would beg for a song from Uncle Danny, and, needing an outlet for his own regrets and losses, he gladly took up the instrument of their peace.

He wished he had someone to help him find his way through the maze of parenthood. He wished, for the first time in his life, that he'd done as Darby and Maeve had wanted him to do. He should have married young, stayed on the farm, shared with his family the love he felt for them. Instead, he'd run away in a burst of selfish independence.

He'd wanted what he wanted, when he wanted it, how he wanted it. No one else merited consideration, or so he'd thought. By the time he grasped the extent of what he'd turned his back on, shame deterred him from doing what his conscience and heart begged him to do. Crippled with guilt, he never saw his father again, never felt the man's rugged embrace, never said he was sorry or heard "I love you, son" in that richly toned, Gaelic-spiced voice again.

Then, before he could tie things up in Philadelphia, since his plan was to return to York, Maeve followed her Darby into eternity, and once again Daniel failed to say half the things he'd wanted to before she was gone.

Since the dairy thrived under his sister and brother-in-law's care, and his remorse made the farm a reminder of his failures, Daniel returned to Philadelphia from Maeve's funeral more driven to succeed than before. It wasn't until that damned creek stole Maggie's and Will's lives, and he took one look at his grief-ravaged niece, that he resolved to stay in York for good.

But he had no idea how to go about reclaiming this sort of life. He'd plowed right in to the intricacies of farming, learned all there was to learn about feed, breeding, finances— the elements needed for success on a dairy farm. Aside from the heartbreaking midnight serenades, he'd mostly left Maribeth in his Mennonite housekeeper's care.

The woman had raised nine children. She should have

been the perfect candidate to help Maribeth heal and go on, but for some reason something seemed to have been lost in the effort of mothering her own. Maribeth had closed herself in, and except in the aftermath of the nightmares, she resembled a shadow of a child.

Then she'd turned twelve, and Daniel was forced to set aside his compulsion to build on Darby's success. He'd spent the last month chasing Maribeth home from wherever she'd chosen to run away that time.

Tonight she went too far. She'd left the farm earlier in the evening and walked the miles in to York. She showed up at the Sheep Building as the sky turned dark, demanding a corner of a stall to sleep in, because as she said, the sheep never left her behind. It was Uncle Danny who'd taken them from the farm and brought them to York. He'd left her behind, but she refused to stay with the housekeeper at the farm; she refused to sleep again without Uncle Danny's violin for when the nightmares hit.

How he wished for a wife right now. Someone who understood the complexities of impending womanhood. Maribeth was poised at that awkward threshold better known as adolescence, and since Daniel didn't know what it took to become a woman, he couldn't seem to strike any chords his niece could respond to.

Except his music.

He'd play for Maribeth for the rest of his life if it came to that. But, oh, how he wished he had a woman at his side to share the cares of parenthood, to reach a lonely little girl's bewildered heart, and to help her reach her destiny. To help her grow into the lovely woman Maribeth showed promise of becoming someday.

Daniel slipped into another melody; his longing soared on winged prayers of sound. He confessed his loneliness, his need for a partner by his side. He needed a woman strong enough to face the coming days with courage and love. One with a heart large enough to embrace a man and his niece, but there didn't seem to be too many plucky, loving ladies around. To his dismay.

After that piece, he segued into a favorite tune from childhood, the folk song his mother had played for him when she'd wanted him to sleep. "Danny Boy," she'd called it, and its notes never failed to bring back to Daniel the memory of Maeve's love. He would always thank the Heavens for the gift his mother left Maribeth, for without knowing, she'd endowed her clumsy son with the means to comfort the child.

He played as Maribeth's blue eyes closed, and the tension in her slender shoulders eased.

Closing his own eyes, he continued to play, and a vague feminine form began to materialize in his mind. His dream woman, he thought when he spied the hair pulled up into a simple knot, the slender waist, the graceful fall of skirts. She was the ideal he longed to touch. He knew she'd welcome him, reaching for him even as he reached for her.

Lustrous brown hair wisped around her face, making sweeter the soft contours of her features. Then he saw her eyes, deep, dark pools of emotion, brimming with life and love. He needed her, that partner for life, that mate of his dreams.

Damned if she didn't look like that sassy shepherdess, Willow Stimson! Nobody could accuse him of poor taste in females. Although she certainly was pretty, she was too prickly for his taste. Too bad, as she had enough pluck for a dozen damsels, and didn't dither with her words.

He chuckled. The man who ended up with that lass would never know boredom, and if her lively wit was anything to go by, a spicy intimacy was sure to satisfy the most demanding of males. Willow Stimson . . .

He'd never know what made him glance her way, besides his failure to banish her from his thoughts. She was persistent in her presence, coming back, time and again, to invite his attention to stray her way.

And so he saw her.

He blinked. Then again. Could that be her, wrapped in a whirl of white, as if a cloud embraced her lovely form? All he could see was her face, rising like a vision above the snowy froth.

His fingers missed a string, causing him to skip a note for the first time that night. Daniel closed his eyes. He concentrated on his music, and tried to cast the otherworldly image of Willow from his mind.

It worked, for when he opened them again, she was gone. No sign of white shone from the shadows in the building, and no face peered at him with fascination in a pair of large brown eyes.

He'd dreamed her. But, why?

Even at twenty Willow was a wee bit young. A lass her age wouldn't have the depth, the strength, the maternal maturity he needed his woman to possess. It wouldn't do for him to continue fantasizing about Willow Stimson. It was a waste of time.

Despite her allure, and the passion in her actions, her youth rendered her ill-suited for his needs. Willow could never be Daniel's dream come true.

Early the next morning Willow inspected Missy, then went to freshen up and find some breakfast. A just-fried dough-nut, a glass of fresh milk, and a red-ripe apple filled the bill.

As she munched her food, she remembered her dream and remarked how odd it was that the only dream she'd had that night was that suggestive vision where she'd danced with Daniel. Her subsequent sleep had been restful, and she'd risen with the sun to tend to her flock. Still, through all her early-morning actions, her mind had refused to surrender the image of Daniel Callaghan seducing songs from a violin.

The man was dangerous, far more so than his brawny build and easy smile had led her to believe. His attractive exterior and quick wit deterred Willow, reminding her of Milford Philpott's treachery, but the soulful violinist, the loving uncle, the caring farmer who'd taken the time to examine her sheep appealed to her on another level. She had to take care around Daniel, or she could find herself in trouble. It wouldn't do for her to become infatuated with the man.

Clapping sugar off her hands, Willow stood. "The doughnut was wonderful, Mrs. Schott!" she called, waving goodbye to the pastry maker. "And your apples are sweeter than ever this year. I'll want a bushel, so if you'd like some squash for the fruit—"

"*Ja, ja*, Villow," responded the plump matron, her rosy cheeks glowing beneath her starched white bonnet. "Squash is gut. *Danke*."

With a nod and a wave, Willow turned toward the Midway.

"Villow!" Mrs. Schott cried out. "Don't choor umbrella fergess. Ve haf much, much rain!"

Dismayed by her distraction, Willow returned, gathered her umbrella, and as she stepped onto the Midway, opened the contraption to protect herself from yet another downpour. It seemed as if all the weather knew to do anymore was rain. Cold, gray-skied rain. She was fast growing tired of the showers, the mud, and the damp. Besides, if the weather didn't change soon, Missy could have a hard time of it if she did come down with a cold.

Now that she had turned her mind back to matters of importance, Willow felt the need to return to the Sheep

Building to take another good look at Missy. What would she do if the ewe became ill?

"Don't go borrowing trouble," she chided herself under her breath. "Concentrate on the fair and win some ribbons."

Outside the entrance to the Sheep Building stray bits of hay bonded with the dirt and the water to form a dusky, slurping, sucking paste. There was nowhere to go to avoid the mess, so Willow plunged ahead.

Just as she stepped into the shelter of the building, her umbrella hit something and bounced back at her. Its eight-rib paragon frame flipped inside out and broke. A deep-voiced "Ooomph!" told Willow she'd hit someone rather than something.

"I'm so terribly sorry! I—"

"Sure an' you'd best watch where—"

Both grew silent.

Willow peeked around the umbrella, unwilling to believe her persistent misfortune. Why did she have to bump into Daniel Callaghan of all people?

Daniel's face appeared from behind his own umbrella, moving slowly, as if not ready to credit his ears. Willow glared at her now useless umbrella.

"Flapdoodle! Sorry," she added, then averting her gaze, entered the building. But the fates had been against her all day, and it seemed they weren't about to change course. As she stepped around Daniel, Willow's bootheel caught on the ooze on the ground, which glommed on thickly and showed no intention of letting the footwear escape. She lost her balance, slipped, and fell.

Daniel's arms flew around her. His umbrella plopped into the slop. His arm sent her own broken gadget muckward, by way of his leg. "Ouch!" he yelped. "Damned nuisance, that thing is. An' you, lassie, don't you think it might prove prudent to watch where you're goin'?"

"Me?" she cried, then wiggled to separate herself from the irritating man, but only managed to lose her footing again. She caught his arms on her way down. "What do you mean I need to watch where I'm going? I was using my umbrella because I was walking in the rain. You were in a roofed building. You should have made certain no one was in your . . . way when you . . . opened . . ."

The words died on Willow's tongue. The strangest warmth seeped from his arms into her fingers, traveling up her arms and to her head. She felt light-headed. A tremor shook her.

Willow found herself so close to Daniel that she detected a fresh, just-washed scent coming from him. It had a rich undertone, a spice she couldn't identify, but it suited the large man so well she wondered if it wasn't the natural fragrance of his skin that so appealed to her.

From her vantage point near Daniel's breastbone, Willow spied a tuft of mahogany hair at the open neck of his crisp white shirt. He didn't wear a tie today, and a spark of curiosity tempted her to reach up and touch that wisp of hair.

She barely managed to keep herself from doing just that. Screwing up her courage, she tipped her head back and sought Daniel's face. What she found there stunned her. An expression that surely matched the befuddled one she knew she wore widened his eyes, ruddied his cheeks, and sent the pulse in his temple to a visible beat.

His eyes sought hers.

A wild rushing sounded in Willow's head. Her breathing grew shallow, quick. Her skin felt flushed; her middle tightened. Then Daniel trembled. Her eyes opened wider still. His face approached, coming closer every second. Willow's breath caught. She waited . . . poised . . . ready—

"There you are, Daniel," called Hans from inside the

building. Willow could have sworn his words were akin to a pail of ice. She pulled away from Daniel, unsteady on her feet.

Without waiting for Daniel's response, Hans went on. "Where did you rush off—" Interrupting himself, he nodded at Willow. "Well, hello there, Miss Stimson."

Daniel's hands, which had steadied her, dropped from where they'd clasped her arms, and she felt her knees begin to crumble again. She mustered up her gumption and stood tall. "H-hello, Hans."

His eyes narrowed at the reedy sound of her voice. "Are you all right?"

Daniel ran his hand through his hair, then tugged at his mustache. "Er . . . ahem! You see, Hans, Miss Stimson—"

Oh, how awkward this all seemed! "Call me Willow, please. Both of you."

Both men nodded, but each eyed the other with suspicion.

Hans kept his eyes on Daniel, but again asked Willow, "Are you all right? Your voice sounds strange."

Willow tried to eke out some words, but failing, ran damp palms down the sides of her skirt.

In an affable gesture Daniel laid an arm across Hans's shoulders. "Aye, an' I believe Willow's quite fine, aren't you?" he asked, his gaze delving deep into hers.

Who knew what he sought? She didn't, yet she felt as if he reached the very essence of her, the depths of her heart. She managed to nod in response.

Daniel continued. "Er . . . you see, boy-o—"

"Hans, if you please."

Daniel's cheeks burned red above his beard. He took his arm back. "Hans, then. I . . . er . . . wasn't watchin' my step, an' I ran into Willow, who was strugglin' with the rain an' her umbrella, which broke in the end."

Three pairs of eyes followed Daniel's down-sweeping

hand. The two umbrellas wallowed in brown goo like pigs in a pen.

She had to say something and then get away. After taking a quick breath, she thought she might succeed. "So you see, Hans," she blurted out in a bright, brittle voice, "I'm quite all right. I slipped, and Daniel caught me before I joined that useless pile of wire and cloth. But I really must run along. I have to see to Missy."

"An' how is the wee Missy farin' this wet mornin'?"

Without meeting Daniel's gaze, Willow stepped into the Sheep Building, then turned to smile at Hans, who was by far the less dangerous of the two males. "When I woke up, she seemed no different than last night, but I've been gone a while and should get back to her. I also have a spinning demonstration scheduled for this morning, and I wouldn't want to be late for that. Have a lovely day!"

At a rapid clip Willow made her way back to Missy's stall. She needed time to sit, quiet her rattled nerves, sort out her reactions to Daniel.

How mortifying. A second day had now started with a mishap involving Daniel Callaghan. As Willow thought about the moments just passed, she found the memories of a midnight serenade fading, leaving in their place an image of the brawny farmer who so thoroughly vexed her.

She let herself into Missy's pen. The ewe seemed to be in the same spot where Willow had left her nearly an hour ago. With a murmur she knelt beside the animal and touched her black nose. It was warm, not hot, and dry. That was good, but Missy seemed uninterested in rising, and she'd scarcely touched her food.

Willow's concern deepened.

"There you are, dear child."

Willow donned a smile. "Mrs. Meister! I'm ever so glad to see you."

A silver eyebrow arched up at her effusive greeting. "Has anything of interest happened since I left last evening?"

Willow shook her head. "It's just that I'm worried about Missy, and it's good to see a familiar face."

"Then you'll be doubly glad, since Mr. Meister is on his way."

"Really? He left his books to come to the fair?"

Mrs. Meister chuckled. "It wasn't easy to talk him into coming, but when I told him you'd be spinning today and weaving later in the week, he decided to take the time and watch you work. He's fascinated by the way you turn wool into pieces of art."

True to her friend's words, the slender Steven Meister approached Missy's stall, and Willow's smile broadened. "I'm so happy to see you, Professor! And honored. It's not often you leave your library."

"Ah, dear girl, I wouldn't miss your demonstration for the world!"

Reaching over the stall gate, Willow wrapped her arms around the elderly leprechaun. "I'm about to go to the exhibition area. Why don't the two of you go and find a good place to watch?"

Mr. Meister nodded, then turned to his wife. "Mrs. Meister, you go ahead and secure us a spot. I'll help the child with her wool and the wheel."

"Excellent, dearest." With a bob of her felt-and-lace-hatted head, Mrs. Meister left.

As soon as her footsteps faded, Mr. Meister's face grew serious. "Now, Willow dear, Mrs. Meister tells me that you're still in financial straits and have refused her every attempt to offer our help. I understand pride, child, but pride makes a mighty poor companion."

She nodded, then shrugged. "I do understand. It's just . . .

I don't know, just something I have to do myself. The farm's all I have left of them."

"I understand. It's your mother and father and aunt rolled in one, is it not?"

Willow nodded, fighting the lump in her throat.

"What worries me most," Mr. Meister continued, "is that you've tied your future to the wool from your sheep. I don't feel that's wise."

She swallowed hard and answered in a strained voice. "I know it's not particularly smart, but the wool and the sheep are all I have left."

"And you're still opposed to selling the animals for their meat."

"As always."

A sigh lifted the old man's concave chest. "Might I remind you of one of my favorite legends?"

"Sure." As if she could keep him from doing so! It wasn't in Steven Meister's nature to fail to use his vast knowledge to hammer a point home.

"Remember the words of the Celtic god Angus when he warned Diarmait, who had stolen Grainne from her betrothed Finn MacCumhail. Angus told Diarmait not to hide in a tree with only one trunk, or to rest in a cave with only one entrance, or to land on an island with only one means of approach."

"I do remember," she replied. "And I know how Finn defeated Diarmait by tricking him into stepping on a boar bristle with the heel of his foot—his only weak spot—and inflicting his mortal wound. It's a wonderful story, and if I could I would follow Angus's advice. I placed my hopes on the wool because it's all I have, and, yes, my weak spot is the sheep. I also know that you want to help because you care, but this is something I must do on my own."

Mr. Meister's features sagged with a hint of sadness. "I

understand what you're saying, even though you've set yourself up for a painful fall."

Willow felt the queasy rumble of fear in her middle. "Then it's a fall I must take, although I hope it won't come to that. Here," she added, handing him a sack of carded wool, "it's time for my demonstration. And just so you know, I don't intend to lose that Best of Show ribbon."

"Then what?"

"I'll sell the sheep."

"Who will buy them from you?"

"Not a butcher or a processor of meat!"

"Do you think you'll have the choice to make?"

I'd better. "Of course."

7

$\mathscr{A}$LTHOUGH SHE'D BEEN somewhat apprehensive about attending her first meeting of the York County Agricultural Society, by the time the members present were seated, Willow lost every qualm she'd held. Yes, she seemed to be the only woman in the room, but with the lively barrage of debate going on, she doubted anyone would take notice of her presence.

The main topic of interest was whether or not to purchase seventy-three acres owned by Samuel Smyser in West Manchester Township for the purpose of relocating the fairgrounds. Many supported the move. Just as many seemed to oppose it. Although everyone, including Willow, was used to the fair being held at its present location in the southeastern section of town, she had to admit that the much larger acreage would be beneficial in view of the ever-increasing number of visitors to the York Fair.

For the longest time it appeared the various members of the society would never come to an agreement, but eventually someone proposed a vote, and the count was taken. A majority supported the purchase, and the decision was made. The York County Fair would have a new home next year.

Since she'd sat toward the back of the room, Willow was

able to slip out once the voting had been tallied. She set off toward the Sheep Building. The evening was cool, as it often was in the fall. Even though it finally stopped raining earlier in the day, the crisp spice of autumn showers perfumed the air. Willow was glad to see the change in the weather. Missy's breathing remained shallow, and her heart beat faster than normal the last time Willow checked the ewe's condition. Rain would only aggravate the problem if it proved to be a cold she'd caught, as Willow now believed.

Heavy feet trod behind her, and although she knew she was probably safe in the fairgrounds, Willow picked up her pace nonetheless. The footsteps sped up as well, and she cast a glance behind her.

"Lovely evenin' to you, Willow Stimson," Daniel said.

Did she have a previously unknown trait that allowed this man to find her everywhere she went? It was becoming difficult for Willow to purge Daniel's presence from her every thought about the Fair.

"A good evening to you, too, Mr. Callaghan."

"No, lass, it's Daniel, remember?"

Heat rushed to Willow's cheeks. Yes, she remembered, she remembered every disturbing moment, every vexing, irritating, enervating second she'd spent in Daniel Callaghan's presence, and their unexpected closeness earlier in the day stood out from among their other encounters. A ripple of excitement flashed through her, and she found it hard to draw her next breath. "Ye-yes, I remember. Daniel it is."

"An' would you be goin' back to your sheep?"

"Of course. I'm afraid Missy has indeed come down with a cold."

"'Tis a pity, then. Will you be callin' a vet'rinary?"

Willow sighed at the thought of the added expense. "If it comes to that."

Daniel shook his head and smiled wryly. "Fool that I am, I'm only troublin' you more. An' I remember you sayin' you had plenty to worry about." At her nod he took her elbow to lead her around another of the countless mud puddles in the dirt walkway. "Tell me this, lass. Have you managed a moment to enjoy the fair?"

Once Willow grew used to the warmth of Daniel's clasp on her arm, she returned his wry smile. "I'm afraid I've been too busy to do more than rush out for a bite to eat every now and then."

"Have you no one to help you?"

"I'm the last Stimson left."

Daniel's reddish eyebrows crept up toward the tousled hank of matching hair that fell onto his forehead. "Didn't I see the Fritzmeier boys showin' your ewes? Haven't you hired their help?"

Oh, dear. What an uncomfortable subject he'd picked. Again. "I can't afford hired help on a regular basis. I only paid the twins to show the ewes because I couldn't handle all three animals at one time."

"I see," he answered, and Willow suspected that he did indeed see the gravity of her plight. Then he swept his free hand through the air, directing her attention to the attractions up ahead. "Have you taken a stroll down the Midway?"

Willow looked with longing toward the lights that lined the center of the fairgrounds. Only a deaf man could have missed the blast of the calliope music, and only a dedicated grumbler would have condemned the merrymaking going on. "Not yet."

"Well, then, lass, hold tight to my arm an' follow my lead!"

Willow gasped as Daniel picked up his pace, and she was forced to do as he suggested. She held on to his solid arm as if she'd never let it go.

Moments later she found herself in the very heart of the excitement that characterized the York County Fair. In the lavender air of dusk, the Midway lights sparked excitement in her. Passersby sang along with the calliope, everywhere the scent of local foods teased her senses, and the night resonated with vitality. York County was indeed celebrating life.

As they continued on their way, sideshow hawkers called out enticing descriptions of what they had to offer.

"Come see the bearded lady!" cried one.

"No, no, no," responded another from across the way. "Don't waste your time there, ladies and gentlemen. Come see the nee-eu-west wonder! We have an authentic, gen-neu-wine three-headed bull calf!"

Directly before them, a nattily dressed man with impressive handlebar whiskers winked at Daniel. "I offer you the most stellar collection of dancing ladies straight from Paree, France!"

Willow stole a peek at her companion to gauge his response to the bait the man offered. She found Daniel gazing at her, a smile spreading to his eyes. "Ah, lad! Too bad for you, but I've on my arm the loveliest lady here tonight. I won't be needin' your bevy of beauties a'tall."

Although she laughed along with the sideshow promoter, a thrill of pride rippled through Willow at Daniel's flattering words. She'd seen the honest admiration in his gaze. Perhaps that appealing, hidden man was about to make another appearance.

All of a sudden her knees rivaled blue ribbon grape jelly.

"'Tis a mite thirsty I am, lass," Daniel said. "Would you be carin' for a glass of lemonade?"

As she gazed at his handsome face, all Willow could do was smile and nod. Yes, perhaps a tart lemonade would wash away the dangerous excitement she'd begun to feel.

Daniel purchased the refreshing drink, then led Willow to a bench at the edge of the Midway. She sat down, glad for the support, as her knees were still wobbly from Daniel's appreciative glance. She accepted the glass he offered, and took a large, cooling sip.

"You know, lass, I'd almost forgotten what these fairs were like."

"That's right. You were gone a long time."

"Too long, and most heartlessly, so you said."

A glass provided poor protection from his knowing gaze. "You heard."

"Aye, so I did."

Flustered, Willow set the lemonade at her side on the bench. "I owe you an apology. It was wrong for me to criticize you to your employee."

"But 'twould have been fine to do so to someone else?"

Willow's ears burned with the upward surge of a blush. "Now you're playing with words, trying to trap me into saying something you can poke fun at. I'd best be going my way." She stood. "Good night Mr.—"

"Daniel," he said, cutting her off as he caught her hand in his. "You may be right about the teasin', but in the interest of a pleasant evenin', can't we set the bickerin' aside? 'Tis enough we're pitted to compete for ribbons. I'd rather not fence with words, too."

As the rough texture of Daniel's fingers enfolded hers, Willow was stunned anew by the sensations his touch set off. She nodded, then sat again, tugging on her hand. He released it slowly, surprise in his gaze. It seemed that he, too, enjoyed the contact, unnerving though it was.

Willow folded her hands in her lap, trying to disguise the tremor that shook them. This simply wouldn't do. She had to take control of the moment, divert the conversation, whatever it took to make her remember how rough and rude Daniel often appeared.

"Tell me, what was the appeal of Philadelphia?"

He groaned. "I thought we'd agreed not to bait each other again, lass."

"I wasn't baiting you. I really want to know." She'd been ditched by a fiancé for the good life to be found in that great city, and this man had walked away from all she'd ever dreamed of having. She really wanted to know what it was about Philadelphia that tempted men to behave like fools.

Watching Daniel, Willow saw him close his eyes and lean his head back. How difficult could it be to answer that question? The word *money*, simple as it was, would do the trick.

Then he sighed. "I guess you could say it was to follow a dream. You see, lass, when my family came from Ireland, I saw the ship, the freedom of the sailors, the easy friendship between the stevedores at the docks, an' the cargo the ship had brought. I decided right then that I wanted to be a part of that. I knew I could make good."

Hmmm, Willow had yet to hear the word she expected, and Daniel sounded sincere. Could there be more to this leave-the-country-for-the-city passion she'd now seen affect two men?

With a wry chuckle Daniel laid his arm across the bench's back, coming even closer to Willow. "It wasn't easy to leave. I loved my family, but I had this hunger inside, and the dairy just didn't satisfy. I wanted the excitement I'd seen, the action of the port. I felt that in Philadelphia I'd be findin' the opportunity to succeed, to achieve what I aimed at an' my drive carried me to. I had a mighty craving for the challenge of the quest."

"Did you ever appease it?"

"Aye, that I did. But before I knew it, both my parents

were gone. I saw no reason to be comin' back to York. My sister an' her husband had the dairy in fine form."

A faraway look took hold of Daniel's strong features. "I worked hard an' succeeded in business, but I've had to battle my share of demons, too."

Willow sat, mesmerized by the story that flowed out in Daniel's musical brogue. Yes, she thought, this was the midnight violinist, the caring man she'd caught glimpses of before.

"When the Codorus flood took Maggie and Will, I came back. Before leavin' Philadelphia, I knew that part of my life was done. The first time I saw wee Maribeth lookin' like a lost lamb, an' all those tears she couldn't keep from spillin', I knew I'd never go back. So I've concentrated on the dairy an' buildin' the flock of sheep."

"What do you want with the sheep?"

Daniel closed his eyes for a moment. "When I returned, I vowed to build on my father's success. I realized there's a growin' market for mutton at the hotels and restaurants in York. So I started lookin' for a sheep farm, but since none were for sale, I just bought a starter flock."

Willow winced at the thought of slaughtering Lugh and Brigid for the sake of overfed patrons in York's eateries. Then Daniel's words about wanting a sheep farm sank in. At least he seemed to have decided against that. Willow's sheep farm was on shaky financial footing, but only until Missy won that Best of Show ribbon.

Suddenly Daniel slapped his solid thigh, blinking. Willow knew he'd said more than she'd expected, probably more than he'd expected, too. But she was glad. This man she could talk to.

Even if he ate sheep.

Then Daniel's lopsided smile kicked up the corners of his

mustache. "Enough of this, lass! I started out tryin' to cheer you up a mite."

Willow shook her head. "Goodness, don't feel bad about me! You lost your family in a short time. I'm sorry for your loss, and especially for my criticism. It wasn't my place to judge—"

Daniel's finger pressed on Willow's lips, silencing her. Her eyes widened. Her lips tingled. Butterflies rose and fell and swirled in her head. What was it about this man's touch that could so totally dismantle her guard?

"Hush, *a sto'ri'n*. I shouldn't've rambled on like that. My woes are all my own. I know better than to spill it out at the first pretty lass I see." He stood, nearly knocking over the forgotten lemonade.

Willow picked up the glass and drank deeply. She needed to do something, anything to avoid the power of those blue eyes. Those eyes looking so fixedly into her own.

He smiled and took the glass from her nerveless fingers. "May I?"

His eyes still on hers, he took the cup and drank from where she had just moments before. The intimacy of his action stunned her. Her mouth still felt the thrill of his touch, and she remembered the moment in the morning's rain. There was nothing she could think or say or do, but to wish that moment were here again. Now. That he felt the same impulse he had earlier today. She wished he'd kiss her, more than she'd ever wished to be kissed before. Even during her engagement to Milford.

Without any warning, Daniel stopped drinking lemonade, frowned, and turned away from Willow. He cleared his throat, then said in a gruff voice, "Give me a minute to return this glass. I'll be right back."

His frown and harsh tone hit her like the cold rain this morning, pelting her with reality. What on earth had she been thinking to wish this man would kiss her? Just because he had the Irish gift of blarney didn't change the fact that he was the same insufferable beast who'd encouraged his rutting ram to attack Missy. With a talent for words like Daniel Callaghan displayed, it was no wonder he was so adept at flirtatious games. And Willow, an unsophisticated, country bumpkin shepherdess, was hardly a match for him.

Even if he seemed to have a few good qualities sprinkled in among the bad. She just had to remember those mortifying, horrifying moments that proved Daniel's lack of propriety, no matter how his eyes bewitched her, or his story moved her.

But those good traits had given her unforgettable moments. To her dismay.

"You *will* win that Best of Show ribbon," she whispered, firming her resolve. "You will not let his handsome face distract you. And you will *never*, under any circumstances whatsoever, wish again for his kiss."

A deflated sensation momentarily struck her, but she straightened her spine and murmured, "No more wishes about kissing. No, sir, not for Willow Stimson, owner of the Best of Show ewe."

Large and warm as ever, Daniel's hand clasped her arm, startling her. "You were sayin', lass?"

Oh, Lord, what if he'd heard these comments, too? It was well past time to go. "Just that I need to get back to my ewe."

He nodded and guided her in the right direction. She could have sworn she saw disappointment in his eyes, but then again, with all that manly beard so thoroughly shielding his expression, she had no further evidence to give credit to that possibility.

The silence between them grew. The noise of the Midway seemed to fade and move away. Tension tightened. Willow picked up her pace. She thought about Missy, Aunt Lucie, the farm. She remembered the mortgage on her property, the taxes she had to pay. But no matter what she thought of, she couldn't ignore the fact that where Daniel's fingers held her arm little pinpoints of excitement teased her, testing her resolve. This wouldn't do.

"Where is Hans this evening?" she asked, knowing talk of his farmhand would divert her thoughts from the magic of Daniel's touch.

He frowned. "Any reason you'd be wantin' to know?"

"Oh, nothing special. It just seems that every time I see you, Hans is there beside you."

Daniel shot a narrow-eyed look her way. Those blue eyes . . .

"He had some friends he'd been wantin' to see, so I guess he's still with them."

Willow stole another look at her companion. Then those long fingers holding her arm tightened. What on earth was Daniel's problem? Any more pressure, and he'd bruise her elbow! She discreetly tried to retrieve her arm.

He had other ideas. His fingers remained tight, but his thumb rubbed the flesh it held, in a seemingly soothing fashion. By now Willow was so acutely aware of Daniel— his presence, his touch—that the tiny motion set off ever-spreading, highly disconcerting sparkles of feeling in her arm.

She stumbled, then murmured an apology.

"Are you all right, lass?"

"Of course!" Willow cringed at the shrill squeak that betrayed her nervousness.

Silence again draped a pall between them. They continued dodging mud holes as they approached their destination. Willow knew they were passing interesting stalls and displays, but she was unable to drag her attention from the man at her side.

"Funnel cakes!" he suddenly exclaimed.

Willow's nostrils twitched. "Yes, smells like funnel cakes. That's probably something you missed while in Philadelphia."

"I'll say! Come on, I've been fairly dyin' to have one." Daniel's laughter chased the awkwardness away.

Relieved, Willow laughed, too. She picked up her pace to avoid being dragged to the food by her arm. The closer they got to the stand, the more the delicious aroma of fried sweet batter lured them on.

At the appropriate stand Daniel bought one of the large, golden pinwheels. When the woman who'd cooked the treat asked, "Sugar?" he answered an unequivocal, "Of course!"

Then he turned to Willow. "Would you like one, too?"

Not hungry, Willow shook her head, smiling.

"You'll be missing it, then."

She chuckled. "I never left York. I've had them often enough."

He shook his head, his eyes wide. "No such thing as often enough, a *sto'ri'n*. Not when it comes to funnel cakes."

Willow fought down the surge of pleasure at his Gaelic endearment. She'd heard the earlier one, but hadn't wanted to make much of a word she was sure he tossed out with effusive ease. Knowing its meaning made the term seem more personal than perhaps Daniel had meant. More the fool you are, she chided herself, and worked at ignoring her response to him. "Enjoy the cake."

Breaking off a large portion, Daniel took a bite, rolled his eyes in ecstasy, and munched contentedly.

Willow couldn't stem a chuckle.

"Sure, an' you won't have one?"

"I'm sure. Besides, it's more fun to watch you behave like a boy."

He swallowed, then swiped his mustache to remove a dusting of sugar. "Ah, yes! An' you're likely to say that men are naught but overgrown boys."

"I don't need to. You did it for me!"

Daniel let out another of those rollicking laughs of his, full of vitality and male humor. His eyes sparkled. More sugar dusted his beard. "Come on. 'Tis plenty I have here to share. Have a piece." His eyes begged. His smile beckoned. Willow now knew how Eve had felt in the presence of the snake.

Her determination capitulated. She held out her hand, but, shaking his head, Daniel broke a bite-sized portion from the pinwheel, then held the sweet up to Willow's lips. Surprised, she paused a moment, then opened her mouth. Daniel slipped in the piece of pastry, and as she closed her lips, she caught his finger between them.

Heat exploded on her lips as the flavor of the cake burst in her mouth. She stood frozen, unable to move. Daniel slid his finger from her clasp, lightly dragging it across her bottom lip.

More heat.

More sparkles.

More swirling sensations that stole Willow's ability to think, even breathe. Good Lord, if this was what Daniel did to her by simply touching his finger to her mouth, then it had certainly been wise to decide she didn't want to experience his kiss. Heaven only knew what a kiss would do!

With unsteady steps she backed away from the dangerous temptation that was Daniel and found herself inside the arched entrance to the Sheep Building. Shadows welcomed her, offering her discreet cover to compose herself.

"Thank—" She broke off when her voice failed her. She tried again, although her breath was still caught inside her,

her heart still pounded, and her lips still tingled. "Thank you, Daniel."

Then she looked up, intending to say good night, but the farewell remained stuck in her good intentions. Daniel's eyes were again fixed on her, flashing cobalt fire, reminding her of the missed moment earlier that day. Something told her Daniel was not about to let this one go the same way.

A heartbeat later he was at her side, so close that his fresh, warm scent enveloped Willow in her cocoon of shadow, and she knew she'd been lying to herself. She wanted his kiss.

His lips grazed hers. A dart of response, swift and shimmering, flew from her lips to her head and stole what ability to think she had left. She could only feel the pressure of his lips against hers, the heat of his body against hers, the tickle of his beard against her skin. Especially the dizzying caress of his lips.

Moments later Daniel lifted his head, a puzzled look on his face. Willow understood that look; it mirrored what she felt, the stunning discovery of what it truly meant to be kissed. In the distance she heard music. Her legs wobbled. She trembled. Then Daniel's large hands cupped her face and held her for another kiss.

Fireworks! She saw stars behind her eyelids, felt honeyed warmth flow from her lips to her head, her heart, her middle. Her thumping heart sped with the heat that encompassed her, and Willow felt a soft, strange murmur build inside her and burst in her throat.

Daniel shuddered. They were so close that Willow felt the movement. So close that she felt his breath soughing by her cheek. So close that private parts that rarely made their presence known grew sensitive, only serving to heighten the effect of the feelings Daniel had unleashed in her.

Now she knew what his kiss was like. It was the Fourth of July and more. A celebration, a jubilation, an exultation.

Then abruptly it stopped. He stepped back, his eyes blinking. He rubbed his lips and his mustache with his thumb. Immediately Willow identified the prickle of that fringe upon her skin. She still felt it, probably would for a while. It was something she would never forget, the soft-rough thrill of Daniel's mustache against her mouth.

"Ah . . . I better be leavin', lass."

She nodded.

"Sweet sleep."

She nodded again.

"I'll likely see you in the mornin'."

"Mm-hmm."

Then he turned and took off down the Midway, his steps as close to a trot as a walk could get.

Willow watched his departing bulk, surprised by his sudden awkwardness. He'd seemed so suave, so flirtatious. But moments ago the same sort of distraction she felt seemed to have stolen what expertise he'd ever had.

Could that kiss have affected him as much as it had her? She hoped so. She'd hate to think she was whirling alone in this fascinating dance.

8

*H*OURS CREPT PAST Daniel that night. He tossed. He turned. He rose and paced. He tried to read. Nothing worked. Willow was permanently etched in the pewter-gray landscape of his thoughts. Willow laughing, angry, stunned by his kiss.

He couldn't blame her for her obvious shock. He hadn't dared examine his own response to that incredible, impossible moment they'd shared in the shadows of a fair exhibit building. How could something that inspired such magical feelings happen in so mundane a place? How could he have lost all prudence as a result of the innocent touch of Willow's lips? How could her spicy, herbal scent have reached him and transported him nigh unto heaven, making him forget all reason?

He didn't know, but he now knew that Willow Stimson was an intoxicating blend of angel and woman, a shepherdess with a touch of sorceress hidden deep. And it seemed she'd cast a spell on him.

Which, of course, was ludicrous. He was a grown man, a full thirty-two years of age. He'd known women, all sorts of different ones. But none had stood so distinctly apart from the others, none had affected him too deeply. Now there was

Willow, and although he believed she was just another woman, something in his heart taunted him with the fact that her lips had left him feeling like a youth in the throes of first love.

'Twas a scary thought indeed.

As was the realization that he no longer thought of her as a girl.

But he had to remember her youth, her scant twenty years. A young man was precisely what Miss Stimson needed, what she probably dreamed of. Not a thirty-two-year-old bachelor with a mountain of regrets and the burden of raising a difficult child.

Hans. Willow needed Hans, and Hans had certainly been attracted to her. Since that was the case, Daniel would have to make sure that Hans stayed in frequent touch with her for the remainder of Fair Week. After all, a lass who looked a scant seventeen or so was ideal for a youth of nineteen. She didn't need a jaded man like Daniel.

Exactly what did Daniel need?

Well, he'd have to give that further consideration, and he would do so as soon as he ejected Miss Willow Stimson from his thoughts.

A wicked little demon on his shoulder chuckled, but Daniel refused to listen. He took up his violin and slipped right in to a poignant Irish folksong, then another, and another after that.

As always, the music consumed him. It transported him to a world where magic flourished, where dreams were the order of the day. When he played, Daniel took flights of fancy through his mother's legends of Celtic gods, of faeries, little people, leprechauns. Tonight he felt nearly desperate to remember a tale of courage, of successful battle, of sound defeat for an opposing foe. But the only myths that came to him were those of wonder and spells and love attained. Those yarns his mother had particularly held dear, that he'd loved to listen to, but that had also irritated him, as they'd seemed to transport her into a world of make-believe where he couldn't reach her.

He played until his hands, arms, and shoulders ached. Until he admitted that no matter what he did, the memory of Willow in his arms, her sweet lips against his, her lovely form in his embrace, was impossible to dislodge. He remembered how she trembled, how she sighed, how her lips molded to his as if she'd been created just for him.

Damn it all, she was too young, too caught in the same youthful fervor that had led him to follow the images planted in his mind by his mother's stories. With her fantastical tales, Maeve had encouraged Daniel to dream of valiant quests and heroic adventures. He'd reached adulthood hungering for the challenges posed by those myths, those accounts that eventually lured him away from his family, that made him wound those he loved as he followed his quest. Daniel could see Willow's idealism, and he recognized her passionate commitment to a goal. He'd trod that path before and knew better than to come too close to someone headed that way.

So he lay down and tried to sleep.

The clock on the hotel room's fireplace mantel continued to mark the agonizingly slow seconds of the night. Daniel forced himself to stay still, deliberately keeping his mind blank. Eventually, deep in the abyss of darkness, slumber stole upon him, blessing him with oblivion.

Then . . .

Music swelled, bearing Daniel higher and higher on its notes. Around him clouds eddied in billows of gossamer mist. Heavenly music flowed past him, and he felt the soft caress of the ephemeral haze. The swirling mass rose and fell, slowly thickening, then taking form. That was when he saw her, the enchantress in the cloud.

Cloaked in white, her face appeared above the haze. Long streamers of silky brown hair rippled behind her. The distance between them served to blur her features, all but a pair of dark eyes. Mysteries hid there, veiled answers whose search demanded rapt devotion. Something deep inside him echoed with the need to plunge into the treasure trove within. Full rosy lips smiled secretively, making him yearn for just a taste of their sweetness.

Again the swells of white thickened, allowing him only glimpses of the enchantress. Impatient, he reached out for her, but all he touched was the airy whiteness as it climbed heavenward. When it descended in lily-white petals, they revealed her neck, her shoulders, her enticing shape.

Clad in the sheerest of cloth, the enchantress stood still, a knowing smile on her lips. She knew what she was doing to him; she knew the depth of Daniel's longing. The silk clung softly, revealing curves and valleys, swells and dales. He reached for her again, and failed to touch anything but air. The breeze flowed by. Her skirt began to undulate, its length shimmering around her, drawing down more mist from heaven to conceal her hair, her arms, her face.

His longing grew to need, to a hunger for something he couldn't identify. Yes, he wanted to touch her, but he knew touching would never be enough. He ached to join her, to enfold her in his arms, to make certain she would never leave his side again. She stayed just beyond his reach.

The clouds then rose, hiding inch by inch the enchantress's form, until he saw her no more. Daniel felt sadness and knew fear, the fear of never finding her again.

A cry escaped him, but it did no good. She was gone; she

*couldn't hear. The pristine vision turned to fog. Gray puffs
roiled before him, spinning wildly out of control. His heart
pounded. His breath caught in his throat. What lay beyond
the shroud of storm cloud up ahead?*

*After moments of anxiety, the slate faded to silver, then
back to white. Fluffy balls formed before Daniel, bouncing,
rolling, running in circles, finally turning into sheep.*

*When they noticed Daniel, they ran away, all but one. She
was gentle and pretty and content to stay where she was,
just beyond Daniel's reach. Then the texture of the scene
changed. A jarring ball of black wool bounded toward the
white ewe, setting her to flee. Relentless, the ram followed,
intent on satisfying his urgent need. He wouldn't give up the
chase—*

"No!" Daniel cried, and sat up. His throat was raw from
his cry, and he wondered if the hotel would send someone
to inquire about that yell. To make matters worse, he was
aroused, painfully so, his loins begging for release.

Hell of a way to spend a night. First, thoughts of Willow
kept him from sleeping. Then, when he finally managed to
nod off, she returned to haunt his dreams. What dreams
those had been, full of nonsensical fantasy, the likes of
which he hadn't experienced since his mother's last retelling
of the tales of Arthur and Guinevere and Merlin. The very
myths he'd tried to trade for those of battle while he'd
played his violin.

"D'anam do diabhal!"

Hell, even consigning the lass's effect on him to the devil
did him no good. He was afire, burning with need. He now
felt monumental sympathy for Lugh. Poor beast. Missy
probably looked as good to him as Willow did to Daniel,
and both those females spelled nothing but trouble.

Besides, Daniel was man enough to know what the
foolish dream meant. He'd been too long consumed with

grief, guilt, and the need to succeed on the farm. He'd worried about the dairy and Maribeth, ignoring his intimate needs. He needed a woman. One who would satisfy his physical urge. One who'd make him forget the ridiculous desire he felt for a young country lass.

"By God, and maybe Katherine was on to somethin'." He rose, stretched, and stepped before a mirror atop the chest of drawers. A good long look showed him a man with the flush of sensual need on his cheeks and the black of a sleepless night under his eyes. Hell of a mess, he was.

Perhaps he should take Katherine up on her various offers. She could satisfy a man's physical needs, and she'd be a fine companion as well. Dinner, a show, followed by a night to remember . . . yes, that would take care of his immediate problem. As a bonus, perhaps he'd find in Katherine the woman he needed. Maybe she was right, and Maribeth needed the strictness of a convent school. The sisters would take no nonsense from the child.

Ignoring the distaste he felt at the thought of sending his niece away, not to mention the certainty that his sister would not have approved, Daniel decided that a bath and breakfast were what he needed first.

As he flung a thick cotton towel over one shoulder, he entered the private bathroom attached to his suite. He knew one thing for certain. He would keep a discreet distance between Willow and himself. In turn, he would pay more attention to his own needs. He wouldn't continue to deny himself, for that had only served to leave him vulnerable to an inappropriate attraction. He would simply not be tempted by any more unsuitable females. He would contact Katherine and give that affair a chance to progress; he'd investigate the possibility of a future with the elegant, sophisticated widow.

After he bathed and dressed, he went to the hotel dining room for another hearty breakfast. That was something else Daniel had missed in Philadelphia. The generous portions of fresh foods that were so much a part of life in the country. York County was rich in agriculture, and everyone celebrated that bounty thrice daily during meals.

As he was leaving the main salon of the hotel, guilt suddenly made his step falter. Maribeth! He'd forgotten the child! Damn that pretty shepherdess and the dreams she spawned.

Turning on his heel, Daniel took the stairs two steps at a time. After Maribeth appeared at the fair the night before, Hans had fetched the housekeeper, and Daniel had set the woman up in the hotel to share a room with Maribeth. Although he knew how the child felt about being left with Mrs. Hulbert, he had no alternative. He had business matters to attend to, and couldn't very well do so with his niece at his heels.

Short of breath, he arrived at Maribeth's door and knocked. He got no answer, so he knocked again, harder this time. Impatiently he knocked a third time, calling, "Maribeth, 'tis Uncle Danny. Open up, lass."

The door to the room on the right of Maribeth's opened, and a burly, white-haired man stuck his head out into the hall. His brow was runneled with a frown, and the glare he shot Daniel would have downed a lesser man. "Sorry," Daniel offered, wondering how to wake his niece and his housekeeper without being ejected from the hotel.

Then he tried the doorknob. To his amazement, the brass ball turned, and the door yawned in. He stepped into the still-dark room, hoping he didn't offend Mrs. Hulbert's sensibilities by barging in on her so early in the day.

He needn't have worried. She wasn't there. Neither was

Maribeth. And it was only eight o'clock in the morning! Where could they possibly have gone?

If Maribeth had cajoled Mrs. Hulbert into taking her to the Peter Wiest's Sons Mercantile on West Market Street, wouldn't they have stopped by his own room and let him know? Or if they'd decided on an early morning walk . . .

They hadn't been in the dining room. He would have seen them. It was obvious he wouldn't find his answers in the empty room; there was nothing for him there.

Tamping down his unease, he approached the green-suited, lemon-sour man behind the desk in the hotel lobby. "Excuse me," he said. "I'd be lookin' for my niece and her companion. Perhaps you've seen a young girl and an older lady leavin' today?"

The man studied Daniel down his beaked nose, his thin lips pressed tight. An eyebrow arched, and beady black eyes behind the spectacles blinked. "A young girl left about an hour ago, and an older woman left shortly thereafter, but they weren't together."

Damn! "Did they leave a message for me?"

"And who would you be, sir?"

"For heaven's sake—I'm Daniel Callaghan. Did they say anything before they left?"

The odd bird frowned, looking more like a parrot by the moment. "The older lady left a message. Let me see if it's for you."

Who the hell else would Dorothea Hulbert be leavin' a message for? Daniel tapped his nails against the countertop. He didn't like this one bit.

"Here," squawked the parrot, extending a piece of hotel stationery.

Daniel grabbed the paper, but as he read, dismay and fear began to boil in his middle.

Mr. Callaghan:

I have tried to care for your niece nearly a year now. I find the effort to be more than my old nerves can bear. Maribeth disappeared again this morning while I saw to personal needs. I'm going home to my son's family. His children don't run away.

Dorothea Hulbert

Where had Maribeth gone this time?

"Hans, m'lad! Have you seen Maribeth?"

At Daniel's call, Hans straightened from where he'd been grooming Brigid and sent a puzzled look his way. "What do you mean, have I seen Maribeth? She was at the hotel with you and Mrs. Hulbert. At least, that's what I thought."

"Yes, well, boy-o—"

"Hans, if you please."

Daniel waved dismissively, then ran a hand through his tousled hair. "Very well, *Hans,* I thought her at the hotel, as well. But when I went to see her this morning, the room 'twas vacant, and both had gone. Mrs. Hulbert left a letter. She's goin' back to her son because Maribeth ran away again."

Worry lined Hans's brow. "I haven't seen her. And this is where she came the other night."

"Aye. That's why I came straight here. I was hopin' she'd be here with the sheep. And you."

Embarrassment on his face, Hans said, "Yes, she's made it plenty clear she . . . likes me. But this time she didn't come looking for me."

"I know, I know. I guess I'll be havin' to call the police again if we can't find our wee lass. But I'd hate to be doin' that, then havin' her show up where we should have found her."

"I'll keep an eye out for her. When I finish with the animals, I can go look for her in other exhibit areas if you want."

Daniel nodded. "I'll take this side of the Midway, you can take the other. If you find her, come back here, and for God's sake don't let go of her!"

With a nod Hans returned to his work. "That should make her happy."

Daniel laughed, knowing how embarrassed Hans was by Maribeth's blatant hero worship. If it meant they could keep her where they could watch her, then the boy would simply have to put up with it. Maribeth couldn't continue to pull these frightening stunts.

A child alone. He shook with fear at the thought of what could happen to Maribeth. His gut clenched, and beads of perspiration popped on his forehead. This was another aspect of parenthood he didn't know how to handle, the constant worry over the lass's well-being.

As Daniel went toward the opening of the Sheep Building, he caught sight of a group of women clustered around Missy's stall. He hoped the dainty ewe's condition hadn't worsened during the night, and although he knew the urgency of finding his missing niece, nothing said he couldn't start his search in the Sheep Building. After all, Maribeth was nearly as fanatical about sheep as Willow seemed to be. She could be as close as the next stall.

Surprised by the silence of the women, he approached, trying to catch a glimpse of whatever it was that had them so engrossed. Although he towered over the gaggle of them, and despite stretching his neck to see if Missy seemed worse, he had to elbow his way to the gate.

Then he heard a familiar giggle. In the next heartbeat he saw the cause of the commotion. And he saw red. "Maribeth!" he roared. "What are you doin' here, young lady? An' without leavin' me word of where you'd be!"

The women at his either side backed off, most of them heading toward the Midway entrance of the building. One or two stayed, rampant curiosity fixing them in place.

"Mr. Callaghan!" Willow returned. "How dare you speak to the child in such a tone of voice? It's no wonder she's avoiding you this morning."

"An' what else would you be knowin' about my niece, Willow Stimson?"

"Very little. Just that she loves sheep and is learning to spin."

A good look at his niece showed Daniel that indeed the girl was at Willow's wheel, valiantly trying to imitate the older lass's artistry. "Saints preserve us, so she wants to learn to spin. An' does that make her vanishin' act just fine?"

Willow's eyes seemed to darken, her lips pursing in disapproval of his sarcasm. "I didn't say that," she answered. "I simply objected to the way you addressed her. Is that how you'd like her to address you in return?"

"Now you're an authority on children as well as sheep?"

"I didn't say that, either. You, on the other hand, seem to claim to know all there is to learn about both. Then you encourage your sheep to perform unmentionable acts in public, and you rant and rave at a child. Surely you must know you're insufferable!"

For some reason Willow's insult cut deeper than Daniel would have expected. Especially in view of what had transpired the night before. "Insufferable? Why, lass, last night you didn't think so when I—"

"That's hardly the subject to bring up in the presence of an impressionable child, don't you think?" Although she spit responses at him quickly and confidently, a peach tint darkened the curve of her high cheekbones, and her eyes failed to meet his. 'Twas an improvement, knowing she was discomfited by his allusion to their kiss.

"Fine," he said, storing the kiss for later discussion. "We can pursue the subject of my runaway niece."

"Runaway?"

"'Tis precisely so, Willow Stimson. The wee lassie ran away from my housekeeper earlier this mornin'. She left no word of where we could find her. An' if you look closely you'll notice she's a child, one who could end up in danger by wanderin' the Fair alone."

Willow's chin dropped a notch. "She's safe on the fairgrounds. Aunt Lucie always let me have the run of the fair, as long as I let her know where I'd be every so often." A pair of tiny vertical lines appeared between her eyebrows. "If I'd known she didn't have your permission, I would never have invited her into Missy's stall."

Her tone of voice was so serious, and the look on her face so earnest, that Daniel felt his anger at Willow melt away. "Ah, lass, forgive me. I lost my blasted temper because I'd been fearin' trouble. Ever since her birthday last month, we can't seem to keep track of the child."

"Can't keep track of her?" Again Willow's chin went skyward. "What on earth does that mean?"

Daniel snorted impatiently. "What do you think it means? Maribeth has made it her life's work to vanish as often an' as routinely as the sun rises an' sets."

Narrowed brown eyes made Daniel feel squirmy. They seemed to see too much.

"Hmmm," Willow murmured. "The girl vanishes. Every

day. And you left her behind this morning? Why, any child left to his or her own means will set off immediately in search of mischief. What did you expect when you left her . . . and where *did* you leave the poor—"

"Poor! Think a bit on her poor uncle, lass. I didn't leave the child alone. She was supposed to be sleepin' in her own Hotel Penn room. The room she was sharin' with my *housekeeper*. Somehow, she slipped away. I have never left Maribeth to her own means, as you put it."

Then Daniel felt a tug on his shirtsleeve. It was Maribeth.

"You know, Uncle Danny, I'm right here. You could be asking me your questions instead of Willow."

"Aye, Maribeth, I'm aware of where you've been hidin', an' we're goin' to be havin' us a very interestin' discussion on your disappearance this mornin'. Once you come out from behind Willow's self-righteous skirts." Daniel ignored Willow's sharp intake of breath.

Maribeth's features turned stony. "I just wanted to be with you. And the sheep."

"And Hans?"

At that his niece's blue eyes turned stormy. Her jaw clenched. Her shoulders stiffened. "Ooohhh! I hate you, Uncle Danny! You're the most horrid man. I'm not going back to nasty old Mrs. Hulbert!"

"Well, an' you'll be happy to know you won't be doin' that, after all. She's gone. She up an' quit after you ran off this mornin'. How do you like that? Are you ready to eat my cookin'?"

Maribeth's face went from a sly grin, to a pucker, as if she'd suddenly bitten a green persimmon. "Yuck! If there's anything worse than Mrs. Hulbert, it's your cooking."

"Well, then, an' what shall we do now?"

The girl's anger seeped away, making her look younger

than twelve. "I . . . I don't know. I didn't think she'd leave."

"Well, lassie, I think it's about time for you to be doin' some thinkin'. I'd like you to go back to our stalls. Hans is tendin' to Brigid an' Lugh. You can help him until I get there."

Mulishness squared the child's jaw. "Why can't I stay with Willow?"

Startled by Maribeth's question, Daniel glanced at Willow, who pounced on the opportunity, asking, "Why *can't* she stay with me? I'll watch her."

Daniel didn't want to answer what really came into his mind, so he turned back to Maribeth. "What would you be doin' with Miss Stimson's animals that you wouldn't be doin' with ours? With Hans, to boot."

Again storm clouds blew over Maribeth's features. "You just don't understand! You're . . . you're just a . . . a stupid *man*."

Daniel had never had his gender so virulently maligned. "An' that's somethin' I won't be changin', Maribeth." He ran a hand through his hair, feeling like pulling a hefty handful out. The problems with Maribeth were driving him mad. Utterly insane. "I thought you *liked* Hans. Don't you want to help him today?"

With a sullen "Oh, fine," Maribeth yanked open the stall gate and stomped off, leaving Daniel with his mouth hanging open.

"You know, Mr. Callaghan—"

"How many times need I tell you my name is Daniel?"

Willow shrugged. "Allow me to start again, then, Daniel. Maribeth seems to need a woman's company. I'd wager she spends an enormous amount of time with you and Hans out at the dairy. She might see her time at the fair as an opportunity to pursue feminine interests. I'd be more than happy to keep your niece with me as long as I'm not giving a demonstration or showing my animals. She's interested in spinning. I'd love to teach her."

Completely at a loss, Daniel gave her opinion some quick consideration. "I'm not sure it's a woman's company she's needin'. If that were the case, then she wouldn't have run away from our housekeeper. She was a woman after all."

"Where has she been running off to?"

Persistent little thing, the shepherdess was. "Oh, to the schoolhouse, Peter Wiest's Sons Mercantile, Mrs. Mowbray's Philadelphia Millinery. Then, night before last, she came here."

"You mean she's been leaving your farm and coming all the way into town on her own?" Willow arched an eyebrow. "She has a lot of courage. And a lot of anger, I suspect."

Daniel exhaled forcefully as the pain of loss stung him again. "Aye. The anger I understand. I feel it, too. Her parents' loss hit both of us badly. But I can't bring them back for her, an' I can't let her run wild."

Willow's brown eyes took a slow voyage over his face, and Daniel felt that scrutiny as if it were a tactile exploration. Suddenly the memory of their kiss rushed to his thoughts. He recalled the softness of her lips, the warmth of her breath, the satin smoothness of her skin, the perfect fit of her body against his.

". . . asked to be with anyone before today?"

Daniel shook his head, trying to clear the sensual haze that had enveloped him. He'd missed most of what Willow had said. He scrambled to remember. "You're asking if she has wanted to be with anyone in particular before today?"

Willow nodded, eyeing him with questions in her gaze. She didn't speak.

He continued. "Up to now, all she's been wantin' is to be with me in the dairy or with the sheep. Especially with the sheep. An' she often follows Hans, so much that the lad's embarrassed by her infatuation."

An accusatory gleam burned in her bewitching brown eyes. "Oh, yes. I can see why she thinks you're horrid. I can't believe you teased her about her feelings for Hans. She doesn't know how to deal with them, and now, after your comments, she's sure to feel even worse. I'm convinced she wants, and needs, the company of a woman. I'm offering to be that woman for the duration of the fair. She seems to like me, I certainly was taken with her, and I even come equipped with sheep of my own."

"I'm not sure I believe you're right."

"Give me the opportunity to prove it."

"Maribeth's not an experiment, you know."

"I never thought of her as one."

"I'd rather keep her with us."

"With two men? One of whom she thinks herself in love with, and the other, the one who just made fun of her feelings?"

"Well, if you put it that way . . ."

"How else should I put it?"

"Ah . . . er . . . ummm. Fine! Teach her to spin. Just don't be lettin' her out of your sight."

"I'll do my best, Mr. Call—Daniel."

"Seein' how you care for your sheep, I guess your best will do for one difficult lassie."

Willow tipped her chin back up in the air. "I would happily go to battle for one of my sheep. Be assured I'll also go to battle for Maribeth, should the need arise."

Daniel shook his head. "Fine, fine. I'll send her to you right away."

Barmy. Willow Stimson was positively barmy. And he was sending his niece to her. How had things gotten so far out of control? His life had shown all signs of settling until Willow waltzed her ewe in front of Lugh. Now, he'd be doing well if he remembered his own name.

Hers was impossible to forget.

9

$\mathcal{W}$ILLOW WATCHED HIS solid bulk walk away, shaken by this latest encounter with Daniel Callaghan.

"My, my, my!" Reba Meister said, catching Willow unawares. "I'm glad I came early this morning. That was an interesting exchange."

Willow groaned inwardly. She'd been so busy coping with Daniel's perturbing presence and Maribeth's problem that she hadn't noticed they were being observed. With a quick glance she realized that Mrs. Meister wasn't the only one who'd enjoyed the sight of Daniel Callaghan and Willow Stimson arguing at the York County Fair.

Oooohh! That man. "I'm glad we entertained you," she said sharply, then winced. It wasn't Mrs. Meister's fault that even the mention of Daniel's name proved unsettling. "I'm sorry. It's just that bickering with Mr. Callaghan—"

"I heard you call him Daniel."

"Yes . . . yes, you did," Willow said, her cheeks warming. "He insists I call him by his given name, although I'd prefer to do otherwise."

Willow felt Mrs. Meister study her. Such close scrutiny left her itchy and twitchy and uncomfortable indeed. "I do!" she insisted. "Honestly. I've had nothing but trouble each time he's appeared, and beside his unseemly behavior, he displays the worst possible manner around his niece."

Curiosity shone in Mrs. Meister's eyes. "Do tell! I've heard the girl is a constant source of trouble."

"She's not trouble," Willow said, still irritated. "Not deliberately. From what I saw today, I'd say she's lonely. Her mother's gone, and she wants a woman's company. Someone who sees her as a person, not just another chore. She's tired of the housekeeper, tired of chasing Mr. Callaghan around the farm, and tired of mooning after his farm-hand."

"Seems you know a lot about the child without knowing her."

"Oh, but I do know her. That's what caused the argument. You see, Maribeth slipped past the Callaghan housekeeper this morning. She came to the fairgrounds, and my spinning wheel piqued her interest. I invited her to join me, then asked if she wanted to learn to spin. When she said yes, I began to show her. Before we knew it, we'd gathered spectators. Then *he* showed up."

"You drew an audience when teaching Maribeth?" Mrs. Meister asked. "Larger than at the exhibition arena?"

Willow nodded. "I think they became interested when they saw a child try. I counted more observers than at yesterday's demonstration."

Mrs. Meister removed her white gloves and stored them in her handbag. She remained silent, but Willow could almost see wheels in her friend's mind churning the information. She herself had recognized the benefit of helping Daniel with Maribeth while advancing her own cause.

"You know, Willow, you're fighting an uphill battle."

Mrs. Meister's words surprised Willow. She'd expected a scolding about her self-serving decision. With a shrug she returned to the spinning wheel, and with only a glance, beckoned Missy to her side. The ewe slipped her head under Willow's awaiting hand, allowing her to rub the animal's neck. "I know, but it's one I must fight. Most spinning wheels and weaving looms were abandoned some time ago, but they're wonderful parts of homemaking, ones that let a woman feel she's more than a drudge."

An indulgent smile tipped Mrs. Meister's lips. "True, you make spinning and weaving look more like an art form than the time-consuming jobs they are. Still," she went on to add, skepticism in her voice, "I think most women are satisfied to come to Wiest's Mercantile and buy the fabric they need."

"Some said the very same thing," Willow replied, "but others did note that spinning couldn't be too difficult if even a child could learn."

A nod made the white rose on Mrs. Meister's navy hat bob. "I know what you're planning to do."

"Well, of course!" Willow leaped to defend her position. "I can teach the child a dying art, just like Aunt Lucie taught me. Since Maribeth needs a woman's touch and I need a pupil to demonstrate that spinning and weaving are well worth the time, why shouldn't I take advantage of the situation?"

"Have you mentioned it to Daniel?"

She refused to meet the older woman's knowing eyes. "Nooo . . . but I will. As soon as I find the opportunity."

Mrs. Meister made a doubt-filled noise. "I'd make sure he doesn't object to his niece being used to promote your personal interests."

"I don't plan to *use* Maribeth. I just want to make the most of a bonus."

"And you think teaching the child to spin will coax women to try?"

With a shrug, Willow began working the treadle, and the wool flowed from her fingertips once again. She was glad to have something to occupy her hands; she didn't want Mrs. Meister to catch her fidgeting, as she felt the urge to do. "It can't hurt," she said. "Besides, I've seen old school friends on the grounds. I'll invite one or another to come watch. When they see how satisfying the work is, they might be inspired. Who knows? Maybe some will start flocks and raise the animals for wool instead of their meat."

Mrs. Meister didn't look convinced. "You're as stubborn as Lucie was. Do you realize you're the last spinner in York County?"

"At the moment . . . but we could soon see a growing desire for home-grown, home-spun wool, yarn, and cloth." Warming to her subject, Willow stood and picked up a brown-paper parcel. Untying the length of twine that kept it closed, she unfurled a cream-colored shawl she'd woven for the fair. "Just wait till I display this and some of my knitting. A new market for wool-producing sheep could spring up in no time."

"I'm afraid you're letting your love for your flock distort your vision of reality."

Willow caught her bottom lip between her teeth. Yes, there was that possibility. "I have to do something. Otherwise, I'll be forced to sell the flock for mutton, and I can't see doing that."

As Willow shuddered, compassion and love bloomed in Mrs. Meister's expression. "You know, dear, should it become too difficult, Mr. Meister and I are here, waiting for the opportunity to help—"

"I know," Willow said, with a tight nod. "I just can't sit and watch it all die, much less the sheep. It seems so . . . brutal to raise them just to kill them. And for what? To feed ourselves? There's plenty of other ways to keep our bellies filled."

"Yes, there's always chicken, beef, pork, and turkeys, too. Heaven help us if you decide to champion those! You'll cause an uprising. York County is an agricultural area, Willow. Most folks raise animals for food."

"I know. Don't remind me. I . . . feel guilty each time I eat a chicken leg or a slice of ham."

Mrs. Meister sighed in resignation. "What am I to do with you?"

As she slapped a cheerful smile on her lips, Willow forced herself to hope for the best. "Just be there for me, as always."

Mrs. Meister reached over the stall gate and caught Willow's hand. "As if anything could change the way I feel about you, child. You know quite well you're the daughter I never had."

Willow's eyes prickled. "You and Mr. Meister are like family to me."

"And Lucie was . . ." Mrs. Meister's voice thickened with emotion. "Lucie was Lucie. Stubborn as they come and too indulgent when it came to your own headstrong tendencies." She waved dismissively. "Oh, such nonsense! What a pair we are, leaking like old roofs in a rainstorm. Besides, I want to know what you *really* think of Daniel Callaghan."

Groaning, Willow sought words to describe the man. It was a pity she couldn't voice the less acceptable but more accurate terms she privately used to describe Daniel. "Oh . . . he's irritating, rude, ill-mannered, boorish, vain, full of himself, and—"

"Horrid!" cried Maribeth, opening the stall gate. "Uncle Danny's horrid, mean and nasty."

Mrs. Meister's eyebrows rose. "That bad, dear?"

A sharp nod made red-gold plaits slap against the girl's back. "Just exactly so." Curiosity drew her eyebrows together. "I'm Maribeth Miller. Who're you?"

Taking a step back, Mrs. Meister studied Maribeth. "I'm

Mrs. Meister, a friend of Willow's. Tell me, why is your Uncle Danny so evil?"

The plaits flew from side to side in denial. "I didn't say he was evil. He's just mean. And nasty. And a terrible tease."

The older woman laughed. "That just comes from being a man."

Maribeth's blue eyes widened. "You mean they're all that bad?"

Mrs. Meister made a show of thinking. "Hmmm . . . I'm afraid so. Tell me, what are you doing here with Willow?"

Maribeth sidled toward the spinning wheel, casting longing glances its way. With a cautious finger she caressed the work-worn wood. "She said she'd teach me to spin."

"And you'd rather do that than go back to the farm?" Mrs. Meister asked, although Willow had told her the answer beforehand. What was her friend up to?

Maribeth grimaced. "Who wants to stay all alone in that big old house? Especially now that old Mrs. Hulbert's gone."

"So you feel alone in the house."

The plaits bounced in assent.

"And you came to the fair because your uncle Danny was here."

Another nod.

"But you'd rather be with Willow than with him."

"Well, sure!" the girl exclaimed. "He's too busy with the sheep and the cows and those old farmers, Granda's friends. They used to come and . . . and visit my . . . my da be—before . . ."

Willow pulled the grieving child into her arms. "It's all right, Maribeth. Cry it all out with me. I don't have a mother or a father, either, and I lived with my aunt Lucie while I grew up. I know how you feel."

The sobs came out in earnest. The slender shoulders under Willow's arms shook uncontrollably and tears soaked the shoulder of her rose-cotton shirtwaist. Memories of times she'd cried at the injustice of orphanhood brought stinging tears to her own eyes.

"Willow," whispered Mrs. Meister.

When she looked up, the love in her friend's gaze soothed her own wounds, as it had for many years. "She's found the right place for her," the older woman said. "I'll see you later this afternoon."

Willow nodded, rubbing Maribeth's heaving back. The sobs went on for quite some time. Then hiccups shook the girl. Finally Willow heard mumbled words, but couldn't make them out.

She set Maribeth just a few inches away, then studied the tear-stained face before her. "Feel better now?"

Maribeth lifted one shoulder. "Some."

"There's still something else wrong, isn't there?"

A nod.

"I hope you trust me enough to tell me. I won't tell a soul."

Maribeth stared at her clasped fingers. "At least your aunt Lucie was a girl—I mean a lady. Uncle Danny's just a man."

So take *that*, Mr. So-Certain-You-Know-Everything Callaghan! Satisfied she'd correctly read the girl's needs, Willow smiled. "You know the lady who was just here?"

At Maribeth's nod Willow went on. "She was my aunt Lucie's best friend. When my parents died, Aunt Lucie got me and the farm, and she was by herself, like I am, too. Her best friend, Mrs. Meister, wanted to have children, but she never did. So they helped each other. Mrs. Meister took care of me many, many times when my aunt was busy with the farm, and Aunt Lucie trusted her friend to take good care of me because Mrs. Meister loved me as if I'd been her own."

Yearning softened Maribeth's features. "You were lucky."

"Oh, yes, dear. I was very blessed to have both Mrs. Meister and Aunt Lucie." But what could Willow say to the child who only had Daniel Callaghan to count on? Good Lord, what sort of blind corner had she talked herself into? "Ah . . . er . . . let me tell you what we can do. I'll be your Mrs. Meister, and you be my little girl."

A shrewd gleam brightened the blue eyes. "You can't have children?"

"Oh, my, no, not exactly. I mean . . . I don't know." What sort of verbal quagmire had Willow opened up with her well-meaning comparisons? Good heavens, the child could and probably had talked circles right around her unsuspecting uncle. Willow doubted that Daniel had noticed what a quick mind Maribeth had. She would make absolutely certain he knew before the end of Fair Week. Maribeth deserved no less. "You see, like my aunt Lucie, I'm a farmer. And I'm not married. That's why I don't have children."

"Oh, then you're *too busy* for me, too."

"I never said any such thing!" Willow cried, nearly out of breath from chasing Maribeth's thought processes. "What I meant was that I'd like to be a friend to you as Mrs. Meister has been to me."

Maribeth's blue eyes narrowed, much the way her uncle's did. When she studied Willow so piercingly, the resemblance between man and child was astounding. Like Daniel's gaze, Maribeth's made Willow feel as if she were being judged, her measure being taken. She was more disconcerted now, however, since it was a child who did the measuring.

Then Maribeth shrugged. "Will you teach me to spin?"

Sighing in relief at the apparent favorable verdict, Willow led her charge to the spinning wheel. Slapping a hay bale nearby, she said, "Let's get on with it, then. Take a seat."

Maribeth did as asked, then waited while Willow took a puff of wool from a large cotton sack. Her eyes gleamed and she smiled in anticipation. Willow wished for more Maribeths to carry on the old art.

"This wool is already carded," she said. "We can start spinning right away. If you want, I can show you the carders and how to use them."

"I want to learn it all!"

"Then you shall. Look here," she said, showing the girl a tuft of wool. "This is called a sliver or a rolag. It's combed wool that's ready for spinning."

Willow spread the end of the rolag in a fan shape across her palm. Taking up the end of yarn left on the bobbin, she went on. "This is called the leader. It's a short piece you leave attached to the spindle when you're done spinning a quantity of yarn. You use it to start spinning your next batch of wool."

Carefully Willow sat by Maribeth on the hay. "To start spinning, I have to join the combed wool and the leader. To do this, I twist them a bit to the left, then hold the spot where I joined them between my left thumb and forefinger. With my right hand, I give the wheel a clockwise turn and start treadling."

Maribeth stared at Willow's hands, clearly fascinated by the process of turning a puff of fibers into strong, supple yarn. Willow felt the child's excitement and remembered how she'd felt as a girl learning to spin at Aunt Lucie's side. Tranquillity descended upon her, and despite the lively interest in her expression and the sparkle in her eyes, Maribeth also seemed affected by the innate peace of spinning.

Some time later Daniel interrupted. "Ladies, I'm off to see to the cows."

Flustered, Willow stood. "That's nice, I guess."

Daniel chuckled. "If you say so, lass. I mean that I'm leavin', an' if Maribeth is needin' me, she can find me in the Dairy Building."

"I'm fine, Uncle Danny," Maribeth piped up. "You go with your cows."

"Just don't be pesterin' Miss Stimson."

Willow sniffed. "The child wouldn't know how to pester. Besides, she has a wonderfully quick mind, and dexterous fingers to match. She's already spinning on her own."

"She pesters us plenty out at the farm, but if she's fine bein' here, then it's your decision when to send her to Hans at our stall, or to me at the Dairy Building."

Another comment Maribeth should have been spared. Willow added it to the rest of her ammunition for the now inevitable conversation she would have with the girl's uncle. "I'll do just that."

With a tap to the brim of his brown hat, Daniel turned and headed toward the doorway of the Sheep Building. As he approached the opening, Willow saw him greet an exquisitely garbed lady decked out in parasol, gloves, and peacock-plumed hat. When he bent at the waist, took the woman's hand, then brought it to his lips, Willow felt a strange twinge dart right through her heart. Only last night those lips had been pressed to hers, as close as they could possibly get. Now the lusty brute was smacking them on that woman's fancy white gloves.

Willow glanced at her own hands and had to wince. Hers weren't of the delicate, lily-white variety. She worked too much and too hard with them. Sturdy and strong, they served her well on the farm, but in dainty kid gloves? No, they'd probably look ridiculous, large and awkward.

Then she considered the hat the woman wore. Willow sighed. It was indeed a lovely creation, but as tall as Willow was, she'd never dare sport a head covering so large, never mind that tall, iridescent peacock plume on top. That is, she wouldn't unless she was sure she'd be in the company of someone as tall as Daniel, since she'd tower over most people.

In the company of someone . . .

Hah! What a silly notion for her to entertain. She was Willow, always in the company of sheep, who didn't care what she stuck on her head as long as she fed them.

For the first time she could remember, Willow longed to wear something frivolous, feminine, and to have a man to wear it for. After all, it seemed even Daniel brought out his rarely used manners in the presence of a lady like the one in the plum silk suit.

Intent on the tableau up ahead, she heard Daniel say something about tonight. Then the woman laughed, gazing up into his eyes, adoration on her features. Shameless, Willow strained to see if she could make out what they were saying.

"Then we're set," said the woman in a breathy, almost childlike voice. "I'll expect you at seven this evening, and after supper we'll catch the show at the Strand Theater."

Daniel nodded. "I can hardly wait."

A satisfied smile tilted the woman's mouth. "I'll be waiting," she said, then rose on her tiptoes to kiss his lips.

That intimate touch sliced right to Willow's pride. To think she'd actually liked that kiss last night! Why, it was laughable to consider it half as wonderful as she'd first thought. After all, Daniel handed out kisses as if they were penny candy, a cheap treat.

A likely treat, indeed. Those were worn-out, used-up, third- or fourth-hand lips he had. And she wasn't particularly interested in seeing firsthand where else he'd been smacking them. It sufficed to know he didn't value his caresses.

How foolish to believe that a kiss could create its own brand of magic. The tingling she'd thought she felt had probably been nothing more than a bout of indigestion, and the heat she'd thought came from his touch no more than a fever from the intestinal disorder.

"Indeed! He's nothing more than dyspepsia on legs."

"Can people actually *be* dyspepsia, Willow? I thought it was a sickness that afflicted people."

Oh, dear! She'd forgotten Daniel's precocious niece was at her side. At least the child seemed not to know who Willow had referred to with her unflattering comment. "Some beastly folk are true afflictions, I'm afraid."

The fickle, skirt-chasing, lusting, cheap-kissing, infuriating sort.

At half past seven that evening Daniel knocked on Maribeth's hotel room door.

Willow ushered him in. Although he'd known to expect her, her presence sparked a response in him. His heartbeat kicked up its pace, his breathing shortened. Heat swirled within him, and damned if he didn't feel something like indigestion flutter around his middle.

He cleared his throat. "Well, lassies, I'm off for the evenin'. I don't expect to return till late, but I trust you'll both be comfortable."

Willow's eyes glittered with a brittle flash, making Daniel think of animosity. Why was this woman constantly angry at him? And why did her anger bother him so much? Damn her pretty, appealing face . . . and her shape . . . and her energy . . . damned if 'twasn't time to leave!

He gave civility one last chance. "I appreciate your

willingness to stay with Maribeth. I'd no one else to turn to."

Willow remained silent, and Maribeth, staring avidly at her new friend, clamped her mouth shut in imitation. Neither seemed willing to speak. Fine! All the more reason to hasten to Katherine—where he *was* wanted.

Through clenched jaws, he growled, "Have a pleasant evenin'. I expect no trouble tonight."

Willow lifted a shoulder but gave his poorly veiled warning no audible response. Her eyes shot dark darts of displeasure his way.

Daniel turned on his heel, then slammed the door behind him. If that was the way she wanted it, then that was the way Daniel would play it. In fact, in a few short hours, he'd be well fed, entertained, and his most bothersome symptom would have been ably dealt with by the lovely Katherine. He didn't need Willow Stimson; he didn't need her smiles, her touch, her lips . . . her anger, her moods, her damned aggravating silence. He just needed her to keep his niece put while he pursued his night to remember.

He hadn't wanted to leave Maribeth with Willow. He didn't want to be indebted to the lass. But since Hans had informed him of his plans for tonight as early as yesterday afternoon, Daniel hadn't wanted to impose upon his farm-hand. Besides, he didn't think it wise to leave an adolescent girl alone in a hotel room with the object of her romantic notions. Still, he'd fought the idea of Willow for a long time. Then, when he'd faced the inevitable and approached her with his request, she'd acceded with a silent nod.

Willow. Silent.

For a woman so normally full of complaints, her silence was truly disturbing. Something had to be troubling her, and Daniel could swear it had something to do with him. Could it be last night's kiss?

No. Surely she hadn't made a big deal of the simple smooch.

The demon on his shoulder laughed wickedly, reminding him precisely how *un*-simple that kiss had been.

Daniel shoved the imp and the thought aside. Maribeth. She was all that should occupy his thoughts. And he really should set the worry aside for tonight. Maribeth liked Willow, and Willow had agreed to stay with the girl. He'd solved his problem.

A niggle of unease, however, refused to be squelched. What if Willow began to work on Maribeth? What if she persuaded his niece to adopt her more outlandish notions? What if she had the child believing 'twas a crime to eat mutton? What if Maribeth, like Willow, took up sleeping with sick sheep?

Maribeth was fanciful enough as it was, and he didn't think it healthy for her to grow up in a world of fantasy and superstition.

'Twas just as well he was on his way to Katherine. He needed to direct his interest elsewhere. He had to find a more appropriate woman to influence Maribeth. Katherine would do.

As he left the hotel's lobby, he ran to the waiting carriage, ducking his head to avoid the worst of the rain. "'Tis awful weather we're havin'," he said to the doorman.

The man closed the carriage door behind Daniel. "Seems the same most Fair Weeks."

"True," Daniel said, remembering fairs from his youth.

The driver started the horses, and the rig rolled down Beaver Street. Although he was about to see to his personal needs, Daniel found himself strangely lacking anticipation. Had he lost his physical urge?

No, 'twasn't it. He remembered his condition first thing this morning. Well, then, and 'twas the problem Katherine?

Possibly, since he also remembered how he'd felt about her waging war for his affections.

Still, he knew no other women in York, and he liked Katherine well enough.

Although he didn't like feeling this way, since he'd never been the callous sort, he refused to think too long on his lukewarm anticipation.

He would pursue a relationship with a woman, so long as it wasn't with the young shepherdess. A woman who would capture his interest; one who could wrest his thoughts, his dreams, even his traitorous eyes, away from the disturbing, highly unsuitable Willow Stimson.

But . . . did such a woman exist?

10

THE WEATHER DIDN'T turn vicious until Daniel scooped up his last spoonful of crab bisque. Although dinner with Katherine had turned out to be the epicurean delight he'd expected, nothing could have prevented his dropping the spoon on the pristine white lace tablecloth.

Apologizing, he tried to dry the coral-hued cream with his napkin. All he managed to do was stain the square of damask the same shade of soup.

Then another thunderclap detonated. Daniel jumped, worry bursting in him at the horrific sound. Since the deaths of his sister and her husband, he'd been unable to function normally during a thunderstorm. His vivid imagination kept replaying the events that led to their deaths.

In his mind he saw the Codorus Creek, usually a gentle waterway, seething, roiling over its sides, roaring downstream, ravaging everything in its path. He saw the fated bridge. He saw the carriage. He heard the cries his sister and brother-in-law must have uttered.

His grief ripped open the wound in his heart once again.

If the storm could do this to him, an adult, he knew what nature's fury was likely doing to his poor niece's mind.

He tried. He really tried to pay attention to Katherine's chatter.

". . . and tonight's presentation promises to be one of her more spectacular performances. Did you have an opportunity to see her while you lived in Philadelphia?"

Daniel forced his wandering mind back to the conversation. A performance? What the devil did Katherine want to know? "Ah . . . no, can't say I had much time to catch shows. I worked long hours."

"Then I'm doubly glad you decided to accept my invitation. It's past time you allowed yourself some pleasures."

Damn! There she went again, insinuating and pushing harder every time. If he didn't know they'd be dining on a prime rib roast, he would've sworn the elegant widow was planning to have him as her main course. He didn't like feeling like a dressed, skinned, and roasted rabbit.

"I do take time away from work," he said. "I have Maribeth."

Katherine *tsk-tsked.* "Daniel, darling, that's just what I mean. You're denying yourself a full life by taking on every bit of the child's rearing. That's why I wrote down the address and the name of the headmistress at the Quaker school I mentioned the other day."

Rising, Katherine put beauty to shame. The red satin gown she wore had minimal adornment. It needed none, since her spectacular figure provided all the embellishment a gown could ever want. As she walked toward a massive walnut sideboard, Daniel watched the play of fiery fabric over delectable feminine curves.

Well, at least he was noticing what he was being offered. The storm hadn't yet rendered him blind. Nor had it made him stupid. "Katherine, I won't be needin' the address for that school. I told you that if I sent Maribeth to school, t'would be to a Catholic convent school."

Katherine turned around, a folded piece of lavender paper in her hand. As she approached, the molten flame of fabric rippled with each step, blazing in the light from the elaborate candelabra at each end of the dinner table. For a moment, Daniel fought for air. Then he remembered they'd be going to the Strand Theater. Katherine was going to wear that . . . that red thing in public?

"Katherine, dear, are you plannin' to wear that . . . ravishin' gown to the theater tonight?"

"Isn't it wonderful? It's the latest fashion, and I love it!"

Daniel didn't dare voice his concern as she twirled for his benefit. He frowned as he took notice of the gown's neckline. He had no wish to be seen in public with a woman wearing less than an excuse for a bodice. The scarlet cloth of Katherine's dress was cut so low, Daniel feared that in a moment of excitement she could end up displaying more than she'd bargained for to more viewers than she'd planned on.

With a swing of rounded hips, she reached her chair and poured herself into it, sweeping the disgraceful dress's train around to curl about her feet.

Another bolt of blue-hot lightning crashed nearby, the vivid color visible even through the drawn draperies on the dining room windows.

Daniel leaped up, his heart galloping. Maribeth!

The poor child was alone with Willow. Would Willow know how to cope with a hysterical girl? Would she be able to ease his niece's fears? He cursed himself for having failed to warn her about Maribeth's problems with storms. He'd known there was a good chance for a storm tonight. He went to the window and drew the draperies aside.

No, he hadn't been thinking about Maribeth tonight. He'd been thinking of his loins, and look where that train of thought had brought him! Straight into the lair of a blatant seductress whose garb could incite a riot.

". . . *Daniel!*" Katherine cried, tugging on his coat

sleeve. "Are you all right? Why, you jumped a mile high!"

He ran a shaking hand through his hair, noting how unaffected the widow was by the power of the storm. "'Tis naught, Katherine. The thunder caught me by surprise, an' I'm worried about Maribeth. Since her parents died in one she's had trouble with storms."

"Oh, pooh! Maribeth isn't a baby anymore. She'll just have to adjust." The Widow Meckler gave Daniel a teasing look. "Don't tell me that a man as strong as you"—she ran a hand over his lapel—"is bothered by storms?"

The taunt in her voice sent icy prickles running down his spine. The caress did something strange to his insides, something unpleasant, and he felt an overpowering urge to run.

But he'd accepted the invitation to dinner and a theatrical performance. It would be the height of rudeness to run out on Katherine that way. Then the Widow Meckler turned, the red satin emphasizing full, round breasts. She clasped her arms around the crook of his right elbow.

"Come back to the table, then," she said. "Cookie can bring the roast now."

Putting several inches between him and Katherine, Daniel returned to the table, but as he went to sit, fire once again rent the sky, shaking the house with the impact of the bolt of energy against the earth, the roar of thunder momentarily deafening him.

With jerky motions, he freed himself from Katherine's clutches. Manners be damned! His niece, fearful of storms like the one that had taken her parents, was in the hotel room with a lass who might not know what to do in a case like Maribeth's. He consigned Katherine and the sin she called a gown to their home in Hell.

"I must be goin', Katherine. My grievin' niece needs me more than you do. Thank you very much for the soup."

Katherine bolted up, her action tightening the fit of her gown. "B-but you *can't* leave. Cookie has dinner . . . and we have seats for this evening's show . . . and . . . and you *said* tonight was for me!"

Katherine's little-girl voice ill suited a woman whose gown left naught of her charms to a man's imagination, and her pettiness made Daniel pity the poor sod who'd married her. He wouldn't be surprised but that life with Katherine had weakened the good doctor's heart!

"No, thank you, Katherine. I'll be havin' none of what you're offerin'."

He threw down his napkin, then headed toward the front door. The indignant widow followed him, sputtering objections as she went, the train of her ridiculous red rag hissing along behind her.

"Ah, Katherine," Daniel said, reaching for the black dress hat he'd hung on a hall tree, "allow me to give you a word of advice. No man alive wants to share what's his with every other male. 'Tis best to be discreet." He gestured to her nearly bared bosom. "Fashion notwithstandin'."

"Y-you ingrate, you! You're rude . . . a boor . . . a beast!"

"Aye," he said, donning his hat. "'Tis a beast I am, but a beast with pride, unwillin' to be shamed."

He threw open the door and ran through the torrents pouring down the overhanging roof of the house. What a disaster tonight had turned out to be! Katherine had changed. She'd never been the retiring sort, but this . . . she was actually frightening. Blatant and embarrassing, too. He wondered how many other men would escape her clutches.

Climbing into the carriage he'd engaged for the night,

Daniel asked the driver to return quickly to the hotel. He collapsed on the seat, giving himself a chance to catch his breath. The rain pelted the vehicle, playing a harsh drumbeat that reverberated in the small enclosure. Lightning still lit the sky in intermittent displays of rage.

He'd had a close escape, indeed.

He'd never known another woman quite like the Widow Meckler, for which he was truly thankful, and it wasn't personal prudery that had made him respond so negatively. It was just . . .

Take Willow Stimson, for example. Her simple shirtwaists and skirts fit her perfectly, and her lovely, slender form was enhanced by what she wore. Still, he'd never seen her with her chest half uncovered, and he'd swear no other man had, either. It wasn't a matter of Katherine having been previously married, either. Daniel just felt that what became his should remain his.

Ah, yes. The man who managed to get past Willow Stimson's prickly exterior was sure to find delights aplenty. And if she ever wore an elegant evening gown, he was sure she'd not forget to cover what needed to be covered.

By damn, he was doing it again! He was thinking about Willow when he should have been worrying about Maribeth. He was doing it despite his growing concern for his niece's reaction to the storm.

This—this obsession with women had to stop, even though the path he'd taken to do so had been the wrong one for him. It was obvious tonight had been a monumental failure. Tomorrow morning he was likely to wake up twice as hot and unsatisfied as he had today.

The carriage pulled to a stop, and Daniel descended. He quickly paid the driver, then ran inside to escape the rain. With a nod, he sent the doorman a brief "Good evenin'," and took the curving stairs two steps at a time.

Another peal of thunder crashed outside. Daniel ran for Maribeth's room and pounded on the door. "Open up! 'Tis Uncle Danny."

Dead silence slapped his ears. Damn it all! Not again. "Open up, lassies, I don't find this humorous a'tall."

Nothing.

He tried the door, but this time it remained locked. Outraged, and with a final pummeling, he called, "Maribeth! If you're playin' some foolish game, you will be punished."

The door to the adjacent room opened, and the same displeased gent stuck his head out. "Having trouble keeping track of your wife? I'd suggest not threatening her or scaring the stuffing out of her with your yelling."

After mumbling an unnecessary explanation to the uninterested fellow, Daniel took the stairs down to the lobby. Again, fear for Maribeth filled him. He had to find his niece.

At the desk the now orange-suited parrot was again keeping guard. "Evenin', sir," Daniel started, trying to control the fear in his gut. "Have you seen my niece tonight?"

A jaundiced look came his way. "You've misplaced the child again?"

Daniel clenched his jaws. "Just tell me if you've seen her."

The beak pointed skyward, while the head shook tightly. "No, can't say I have. But I just came back from supper . . ."

Daniel didn't wait for the man to finish his explanation. He ran outside and looked from side to side. All he saw were angry clouds boiling in the darkening sky, sheets of water overflowing their bounds. Where in God's name could the two of them be?

He hoped Willow was with Maribeth. He'd thought her trustworthy, but by the looks of it, he'd put his trust in unworthy hands. As long as Maribeth was fine, he wouldn't be too hard on Willow. Still, she should have known better than to leave the hotel with his niece. Assuming they'd left the hotel.

Something told him to go east toward the fairgrounds. He didn't like the idea, didn't like thinking they'd gone that far in a storm, but he knew it was at least a reasonable possibility.

Then he identified that other pesky feeling that had been bothering him since he'd found the empty room. Not only had Willow proven untrustworthy, but she was still as distracting as ever. He couldn't shake the idea that something had gone wrong. Half of him wanted to blame her for irresponsible behavior; his other half assured him she wouldn't have been guilty of such a thing. He was worried about her.

Worst of all, despite his internal arguing, Willow was simply becoming more deeply entrenched in his thoughts. Would he ever be rid of the woman?

Did he even want to be rid of her?

Hell, he didn't want to ask himself that question, and it certainly didn't matter at the moment. Glancing at the western sky, he saw no sign of breaking clouds. The storm looked as if it had a ways to go yet.

Despite the rain, Daniel dashed out onto East Philadelphia Street. Loping toward the southeastern corner of town, he ignored the dirty water splattering his ankles and shins. He lowered his head, and fought the buffeting wind gusts. Nothing much mattered right now. Only Maribeth and . . . Willow.

There! He'd admitted it. He had strong feelings for the lass, the most upsetting one currently being fear for her safety. Hers and Maribeth's.

He arrived at the York Fairgrounds, and after a minimal explanation to the guard at the gate, he was allowed to enter. As he headed toward the Sheep Building, another jagged spear of lightning illuminated the frenzied sky just ahead of him. His nostrils rebelled when they caught the sulfurous scent of fire searing earth.

His fear heightened. Was Maribeth out in the storm? His gut twisted, and he failed to stanch the image that filled his mind. He saw Maribeth and Willow on a bridge, watching the river rising. Finally he saw the water rear up, swallow the bridge, stealing the two slight forms in its ravenous madness.

"No!" he cried at the sky. Where was God now? Where had he been when Daniel's sister and her husband had drowned?

He prayed for divine assistance, but expected none in response.

"Maribeth, Maribeth, Maribeth." He repeated his niece's name like a litany. His heart responded, "Willow, Willow, Willow."

The storm was upon him. That last flash had come less than half a mile from the fairgrounds. It had been close enough to feel the energy of the fire, the stench of scorching earth. He had to be careful; if he were hit he'd do Maribeth and Willow no good. But he still had to hurry, had to find them, before they were hurt.

Before they were taken from him, as all his other loved ones had been.

Lightning struck again. He heard it whistle through the air. He heard it strike the ground. He smelled the sulfur; he smelled his fear. The boom of thunder deafened him.

He had no choice. He had to find cover. He had to wait until the worst of the storm went past York. He prayed Maribeth and Willow were safe. He prayed that his fear turned out to be for naught. He prayed he'd find them as soon as the thunder and lightning abated.

As he dodged between closed stands on the Midway, he

kept looking for protection. They were padlocked, offering no cover, but the Dairy Building was only yards away, and the Sheep Building just past that. If he could make it to a stand before the next heavenly attack occurred. . . .

With the drenching the paths were getting, Daniel was forced to slosh his way between mud lagoons. The last thing he needed was to stumble, or hurt an ankle, and the mess underground was slimy and slick enough to do just that.

Suddenly he found himself abreast an open, vacant stand. He had no idea what it had housed earlier, but it looked like paradise right now. A burst of speed carried him to the shed, and he gratefully took shelter in its scant space.

Panting, he leaned against the back wall, then covered his ears when the next thunderclap hit. The ground beneath his feet shook, and Daniel couldn't control his own shaking. Fear made him hot. He knew the moisture on him wasn't all due to the rain. "Maribeth," he moaned. "Willow!"

No one answered. Nothing could be heard but the continued battering of the rain. The roof of the shed was made from tin, and the attacking water pounded a hellish refrain directly over Daniel's head. When would this damnable storm be over? He could have sworn days had already rushed by. And yet, when he took out his pocket watch and looked at its face by the light of another spear of lightning, he realized only an hour had passed since he'd decided Katherine was not the woman for him.

But in an hour much could happen. Especially to a child and the young woman charged with—

Suddenly a body hurtled into Daniel, knocking the breath out of him, making him stumble. "Ooof!"

He quickly recovered and wrapped his arms around the intruder. The fetid odor of manure, the slimy feel of mud, the prickle of straw, and the all-pervasive wetness of his rain-soaked assailant transferred onto him. And him in evening dress, no less.

The wet, darkened form fought him, its arms flailing and feet kicking, even as he sought to steady himself from the blows. But his strength served him well. He held on until another bolt of lightning crossed the sky, lending him light inside the shed. Shock paralyzed him momentarily. Under the thick glop of mud, manure, and straw, he found none other than—

"Willow! What in the name of all that's holy are you doin' out in this rain? And where in blazes did you leave my niece!"

Rage, red-hot and uncontrollable. Dismay, bitter and disappointing. A sudden weakening of the muscles he still needed to keep tough and functional. All these sensations punched him at the same time, joining his still vivid fear.

But Willow didn't answer. In fact it seemed as if she had no intention of honoring his demands with a response. She was instead consumed with scooping fistfuls of mud from her face, her head, her arms, her clothes, much of it landing on his once-elegant suit.

"What the hell have you been doin', lass? Wallowin' with pigs?"

"Oh, you beastly brute!" she muttered, obviously clenching her jaws. "I fell. Water and mud were everywhere, deep enough to cover my shins. I tripped on a rock and landed in the worst puddle. How dare you mock me?"

All the while she'd been spitting words at Daniel, her hands had scraped off more glop, and her taut body had wrestled against his restraints. He set her back a few inches and took a look at her. In the shadowy confines of the shed, he saw only a squirming lump of darkness.

But he heard her. And everything he heard cast aspersions

on his forebears, his manners, his moral fiber, and even his gender.

Another lightning bolt lit the inside of the shed, and Daniel had to fight down the nervous, relieved laugh that tried to rush from him. She was a sight! Gobs of straw-bedecked muck slithered from her head, down her cheeks, to her blouse, and on to her equally ooze-encrusted skirt. She was filthy, but she was safe.

"An' where did you dump my niece, Miss Stimson? As I remember, I asked you to stay with her tonight. What have you done with her?"

"Why, you presumptuous fool! Are you insinuating I did something hurtful to that beautiful little girl?"

Daniel remained silent. He wanted an answer, not another question. But inside him, hearing Willow's hot defense of her as yet unexplained actions, the knot of his fear loosened a bit. He didn't let it unravel all the way, though. Willow had some clarifying to do.

"You are a pig, you know?" Willow took steps away from Daniel, but he followed her retreat. He wasn't about to lose her again when it had taken every ounce of his courage to come out in the storm to look for her.

"No, you're not a pig—"

"Heaven be praised!"

"Worse! Pigs are decent animals. You're a fool of a man. A far worse being than the lowliest beast. *You* were the one who left this evening. You were the one too interested in a light skirt to watch your own, orphaned niece. I was the one who held her when the storm worsened, and *I'm* the one who was summoned to see to a sick sheep!"

"Where the hell is Maribeth?"

"She's safe, dry, and possibly having the best time of her life."

"What are you talking about? We're in the middle of a

killing storm, my niece has been paralyzed in thunder and lightning since the Codorus Creek killed her parents, you've done God knows what with her, and you have the arrogance to question my actions? To tell me she's havin' the time of her life? You're barmy, absolutely stark, ravin' mad, woman!" He slapped away a persistent drip from the hair that fell on his forehead, then pulled out his sodden handkerchief to remove some of the mud Willow had smeared on his evening clothes. "Where is Maribeth?"

"She's at Professor Steven Meister's home, being entertained by the two kindest, most loving people on earth."

"Meister? The York Collegiate Institute professor?"

"Yes." Aside from uttering her sharp response, Willow seemed oblivious to Daniel's presence; she was so busy wasting time and effort trying to clean herself. Anyone could see it was a lost cause.

"Here," he said, offering his soggy handkerchief. "You need this more than I do."

By the light of another thunderbolt, Daniel saw her grudgingly accept the piece of cloth. She buried her face in the fabric.

"Willow, lass, could we backtrack a bit? I need a better explanation. Why are you here at the grounds? Why did you take Maribeth to Steven Meister's home? What happened?"

"Mgerth ciefh neiozdh heihnf," she said into his handkerchief.

Daniel grasped her hands and gently drew them away from her face. "There. That's better. Start explainin' again."

"It's simple. The Fritzmeier boys were keeping an eye on Missy while *I* watched *your* niece." Daniel ignored Willow's stressed word. She went on. "Shortly after you left, Matthew came for me. Missy was running a temperature, and her eyes were glassy. Her nose was running, and her coughing wouldn't let up. She hadn't been that sick before I left."

"And . . .?"

With the back of her wrist, she shoved slop-caked hair off her forehead. Daniel shuddered in disgust.

"I had to do something. The Meisters have been like family to me since I was a child, and I knew they'd treat Maribeth like a princess. I called a carriage, took her to their home, made sure she was fine about staying there—which she was and happy, too—then came back to the fairgrounds."

Daniel's anger soughed out in a sibilant sigh. Maribeth was fine. So was Willow. "Then what were you doin' runnin' out in the rain?"

He could have sworn she stamped her foot, but since it was again pitch dark in the shed, he couldn't be certain.

"I sent Lucas for the veterinarian and kept Matthew with me," she said. "But Lucas isn't back, and I began to worry."

Although he was glad Maribeth was at least safe, dry, and out of the storm, Daniel wasn't pleased with matters as they stood. He understood the need to care for sick animals, but 'twas his niece he'd left in Willow's care. Despite his attraction to Willow, this latest episode detracted considerably from her appeal. She'd left Maribeth in a stranger's house so that she could rush to an animal's side.

This, her odd refusal to eat mutton, and the powerful connection between her and her sheep served to persuade him that Willow was truly an inappropriate companion for his niece.

Taking a bolstering breath, Daniel sought words with which to inform Willow of his feelings. "I'm glad my niece is safe, even though I can't agree with your actions. My niece is a child. You neglected your duty toward that child to run to an animal's bedside. It shows poor judgment on your part. I won't be leaving Maribeth with you again. You can consider the spinning lessons finished."

To the west, the clouds had begun breaking up, and a sliver of a moon crept out from between two midnight-blue billows. The light allowed Daniel to see Willow stand taller, her bearing turn regal.

In a dignified voice she said, "After the Codorus flooded my farm last year, I can't afford to lose even one sheep. My fields were ruined, and I have no money left to buy seed or replace the ewe. My farm and my future depend on my selling my flock. I must get the highest price possible for them, and Missy, as my best wool-producer, is the heart of my plan. I regret your decision, since I truly care for Maribeth."

She turned around, gathered her dirty skirt, and exited the shed. At that very moment another shaft of lightning pierced the sky to the east, startling Willow. She slipped.

On her way down, Daniel went to catch her, but his chivalry backfired, and he lost his footing. Together they landed in the mud.

11

FALLING HADN'T BEEN difficult. Wallowing in the mud, on top of a squirming female, was. Daniel tried to brace himself against the ground, but each time he went to take his weight off Willow, the muck slithered between his fingers, and his palms found no purchase. To make matters worse, Willow's limbs were again waving madly, and her mouth was running at the very same speed.

"I can't breathe, you mountain of mule! Get off me before I start screaming. . . . I will, you know. They'll come running to see what you're doing to me—"

His hand muffled her prattle, but in seconds her sharp teeth latched on to the fleshy pad beneath his thumb. "'Tis a ravin' lunatic you are! Let go my hand. I *am* trying to get off, but I'm as stuck in the mud as you. Besides, yellin' won't help. There's no one to hear you."

When the moon came out from behind a cloud, Daniel got a good look at Willow. Despite the mud, the straw, and her undeniable anger, something in her grimy features touched him, perhaps her intensity, her determination. Her eyes were as mysterious as ever, bombarding him with darts of fury. Her lips, full and rosy, caught his eye despite the abuse cannonading from them. Her firm chin, cocked in defiance as usual, never wobbled despite her predicament.

As he studied Willow's vivacious features, Daniel became aware of his wet garments. The layer of mud that inevitably seeped between them drenched what items of clothing had remained dry despite the onslaught of the rain. He noticed the warmth of her body seeping into his.

Tall and slender, Willow's figure lacked nothing, as Daniel realized while lying atop her. The curve of firm breasts, the length of sleek thighs, the flatness of her belly, the roundness of hips. All fit perfectly against the sharper planes and angles of his body, the two of them melding like pieces of a child's puzzle.

But there was nothing childish about his body's response. A sense of rightness grew in him. This woman was made for him, for his body, or so his heart said. No matter what he thought of her peculiarities, no matter her youth. Daniel had to admit that her delectable body appealed to him, in powerful, instinctive ways. He felt the pull of need draw him closer to her all the time, and he knew the need to kiss her once more.

Aside from his sensual response to Willow, Daniel began to see that his constant preoccupation with her went far beyond the physical. He'd been worried about her. He'd feared for her safety during the worst of the storm. And he cared about her sick ewe. He was beginning to see the reason for her determination, her trigger-ready temper. He realized that her fierce defense of her ewe, her every action, was motivated by fear, the fear of losing what she considered hers. Daniel had lost much; he understood.

And that scared him. Everything about Willow scared him.

As they lay in the mud, a strange ripple of fear winnowed through Willow. It wasn't fear of Daniel as such; she doubted he'd ever hurt her intentionally. It was more a fear of the unknown, fear of the feelings she acknowledged were brought to life in her by Daniel, by his presence.

She fought to escape his all-consuming appeal, but they were too close, and he was so large, so powerful, no amount of fighting did her any good. And, Lord, he was there! Right up against her. Closer than anyone else had ever been.

She could see every individual eyelash, damp and spiked. She could see a tiny scar above his left eyebrow, and she wondered what had caused the wound. She saw the thick fringe of mustache, the cushion of beard, and between them she saw masculine lips, slightly parted, the lower fuller than the top. And they were close. Willow remembered their kiss, the warmth she'd felt, the delicious currents that had surged through her, making her believe in magic. The magic of a single, perfect kiss.

Suddenly she lost the urge to fight. She felt the strength of the muscular body pressed intimately against hers, a chest laced with bands of sinew, long strong legs, their power latent but ready. Against her breasts, his heart pounded, a steady rhythm that seemed to pick up speed with every second that eased by. Nestled in the cradle of her lower body, that most masculine part of Daniel taught Willow the difference between women and men.

The tension between them was nearly palpable. It practically roared with a thunder all its own. She knew she wanted his kiss. She knew she didn't, too. That confusion in her mind, however, didn't mirror the wishes of her heart. Willow feared that despite his ornery disposition, his bawdy tendencies, his ineptness with his niece, Daniel was taking over the deepest corners of her heart, her emotions, and yes, perhaps even her love.

Frightening. It was indeed frightening to feel the attraction toward a man she knew she shouldn't care for. But now, in his arms and at his mercy, his lips drew nearer and scattered all her reservations, leaving her vulnerable to his touch, his presence, his kiss. . . .

Without warning, he pulled back, the look on his face mirroring shock, perhaps the same surprise she felt at the sensations he brought to life in her. With a determined grunt, he planted his fists on either side of her head, and reared up, his knees taking his weight off her body. Then he slid sideways, separating them.

"Here," he said, offering his hand, his voice gruff. Willow took the offered assistance and sat next to him. She then scrambled up, horrified by the layers of filth that clung to her. She tugged her skirt from her legs. It came away with a slurping sound.

Feeling awkward, she mumbled, "I have to get back to Missy."

Daniel's "Mm-hmmm" followed her, sounding equally disturbed.

Before she'd gone five steps, he called her name. She pivoted, nearly falling in the mud once more.

"Careful, lass." His voice again sounded rough. He cleared his throat. With obvious reluctance, he asked, "You're sure the woman's dependable?"

"Mrs. Meister?"

"'Course, an' who else would I be worryin' about?"

"You are so thickheaded! Of course she's dependable. I would never have left Maribeth with anyone who wasn't."

He made a noise in his throat like a grunt. "An' you're headin' back to your sheep?"

"Where else would I go, Daniel?"

He shrugged, then ran his fingers through his hair. Obvious distaste appeared on his features as he brought down a hand full of muck. He shook his hand, trying to rid himself of the mess. "Disgustin'," he muttered. "Well, lass, if you're goin' to doctor the ewe, an' you're sure Maribeth will be fine where she is . . . p'rhaps you'd be likin' some help. Seein' as the vet'rinary isn't here yet."

Willow's eyebrows shot up in surprise. She'd hardly expected him to offer assistance. She wasn't sure she should accept it, either. After all, they ended up arguing each time they met face-to-face. But Missy was doing poorly, and Willow was scared for her sheep. At this moment she would have taken help from Mephistopheles himself.

"As long as you stop baiting me, Mr. Callaghan, I could use some help."

"Baitin' you! Why, you're the one who's always prickly and angry—"

"Thank you for the offer, but you can see why I must refuse."

"Blast it all to hell, lass! Let's go see to the damn ewe."

Willow followed Daniel down the walkway of the Sheep Building, but instead of continuing toward Missy's stall, he stopped at one of his own.

"Here," he said, handing her what looked like a bundle of rags. Upon closer examination, she realized it was a blue cotton shirt and a pair of denim trousers. "They're not the height of fashion, nor will they fit you to perfection, but at least you'll be dry."

Willow looked up at him, surprised by his generous actions. "Dry sounds heavenly, Daniel. Thank you. I have a problem, though. Where shall I change?"

He looked up and down the rows of stalls, then peered through the open sides. "Looks like you'll have to improvise. I don't see where you can go. It's still rainin'. If you went elsewhere you would get wet when you returned."

Willow thought for a moment. "I know! I have some quilts I've been using for a temporary bed in Missy's stall. If you have some twine, or a length of rope, we could tie it to the building's pillars and drape the quilts over the rope."

Daniel nodded. "Clever, lass. Let's see what I have."

Moments later, armed with a substantial amount of brown twine, Daniel and Willow hurried to Missy's stall. When they arrived, both were dismayed by the ewe's condition. She coughed, then coughed again, the harsh sound rattling in her chest. Her breathing was shallow, almost a quick panting. Willow knew Missy was suffering.

Matthew Fritzmeier stood and came to Willow's side. "I'm sorry. She's vorse getting by the minute." In his distinctive, Pennsylvania German accent, he added, "I know not if she vill—"

"No. Don't say it," Willow cut in, fear shrilling her voice. "Go on, I'll stay with her the rest of the night. You can still catch some rest at your uncle's house."

"*Danke*," he said, then dropped his plain black hat on his flaxen hair. "I'll early come tomorrow. Unt Lucas, too. I know not vhere he ist."

"Thank you, Matthew. I wouldn't worry about Lucas. The veterinarian might not have been home. If I know your brother, he won't budge from the doctor's front stoop until he has the man in hand. They'll come as soon as the doctor can."

"Goot night."

Willow dropped the borrowed garments on her bale of hay, dismayed that she'd transferred a couple of splotches of sticky brown mud onto the denim trousers. Still, the trousers were a far sight better than the mess she had on. Rubbing Missy's head, and noting the animal's effort to respond, she felt a pang of sadness. Missy simply couldn't die. Willow would do whatever it took to prevent it.

"Could you help me with the rope, Daniel?"

"Give her some water. I'll be worryin' about the rope."

Willow sighed in relief. It was a luxury to know she could

depend on someone else, even if it was for something as minor as tying a rope to a post. For so long she'd had to handle everything herself. From her display of utensils at the front of the stall, she took a glass bottle intended to feed orphaned lambs and filled it with clean, cool water. She then tried to coax a few swigs into Missy.

It took heroic effort. By the time Daniel had tied two ropes to two sets of parallel posts, one at the front and one at the back of the stall, Missy had only taken half the small bottle. It was better than nothing, Willow told herself, not willing to lose hope.

"Do you want me to leave so you can change?"

"No!" The vehemence of her response surprised her. She needed company to make it through this night, but she didn't want to give Mr. Full-of-Himself Callaghan a bigger head. "I mean, you don't have to leave, just take care of Missy while I duck between the quilts."

With that, and refusing to wonder if he'd do the decent thing and not steal a glance while she changed, Willow threw the two blankets, one over each of the two lengths of rope, then taking the clothes, she proceeded to strip.

After removing the sticky, ruined garments from her body, Willow used the upper, less muddy part of her petticoat to scrape off as much as she could of the filth on her arms and legs. Her hair was a lost cause. It would have to wait until she could spend time in the Meisters' elegant bathroom.

She put on the blue shirt. It fit perfectly, except for the long sleeves. She rolled up the cuffs. Although the denim trousers were a bit snug around her hips and buttocks, the button-front closed. The sensation of fabric encasing each leg was highly unusual, but Willow recognized the ease of movement they afforded her. She wondered why women had never adopted the trouser concept. It seemed practical, especially for farm wives.

As she stepped out from behind her makeshift tent she caught the thunderstruck look on Daniel's face and stopped. "What?"

"Ah . . . er . . . Ahem! Nothin', lass, absolutely nothin'."

Willow emitted a rude snort, knowing something had stunned the giant sitting by her ewe. She suspected it was the scandalous fit of her borrowed garments. "They're Hans's, no?"

"Ah . . . well . . . yes. Mine would never fit you."

"True."

But he still looked odd; his eyes continued to stare.

"Do you mind not gawping at me? It was your idea to lend me these in the first place. It's not my fault if I look indecent."

"Oh, no!" he hastened to say. "Nothin' indecent about you, lass. Er . . . it's just that . . . I guess I'm not used to seein' a lady in men's clothes."

Willow could have sworn Daniel flushed, and she was charmed by the awkwardness he'd just confessed to. So he wasn't as jaded as he first appeared. "There's nothing to do about it now. I have to take care of Missy. So if my costume offends you, you're free to leave. I can handle things from here."

Although she'd given him an easy form of retreat, Willow fervently hoped Daniel wouldn't leave. As nervous as he made her, and as often as he drove her mad with rage, she didn't want to face the prospect of Missy's death alone. She needed someone at her side.

Daniel shook his great russet head.

Willow sighed in relief. "Aren't you going to change clothes?"

"I'd have to return to the hotel, an' I don't want to leave

you alone. I don't know how much we can do for her, but I'm willin' to try to save her."

Willow flashed him a smile. He responded likewise.

Silence descended, and they took turns feeding Missy water. After about an hour footsteps alerted them to the veterinarian's arrival. Willow sent Lucas Fritzmeier on his way, then returned to Daniel's side as farmer and doctor examined the ewe.

After listening to Missy's breathing with his ear pressed against her side, the doctor shook his head. "Can't say it looks good for her. She's mighty sick."

A trembling shook Willow's body. *Missy couldn't die!* "Isn't there anything we can do?"

Dr. Wirtz shrugged, then stood. "Sure. There are things you can try, but I can't assure you they'll work. Pneumonia is serious in sheep. Most would leave the animal to die or shoot it. That's how serious it is."

Willow shook her head. "Absolutely not. I'd like to know precisely what I can do to help her. She's still alive, and as my aunt Lucie always said, where there's life, there's hope."

"Ah, Lucie Stimson," the doctor said. "She was something, wasn't she?"

"The sort of something who wouldn't let her sheep die."

Dr. Wirtz laughed. "You're right, Miss Willow, you're very right." The veterinarian rummaged in his black leather satchel. "Here's what I can do. Every six hours give her three grains of quinine in half an ounce of whiskey. Then, every four hours, give her two grains of saltpeter and two drops of aconite. Make sure to wait one hour after you've given her the first mixture before beginning the second remedy."

Willow caught her bottom lip between her teeth. She watched as Dr. Wirtz measured out the medicines. "What will they do for her?"

"Do for her?" asked the doctor. "The quinine will lower her fever, and it can kill bacteria, too. The aconite, while it lowers fever, will calm her down and help her clear her lungs. The whiskey?" He shrugged. "Maybe it keeps the sheep happy?"

Willow dredged up a weak smile and took the containers of medicine. Then she realized she was missing something. "Where on earth will I find whiskey at this hour?"

A warm chuckle reminded Willow of Daniel's presence. "Don't worry, lass. Haven't met the Irishman yet who doesn't keep a medicinal dose close by. I'll get what I have in Lugh's stall."

As Daniel walked away, Dr. Wirtz gathered his belongings and snapped his satchel shut. "I'll return early in the morning, Miss Willow. I can see how she's doing then. For your sake, I hope she pulls through."

But you don't expect her to, do you? "I'll see you then, Dr. Wirtz. And thank you for coming out so late."

"It's my job, Miss Willow. I know I'm needed at odd times. A body gets used to it. G'night!"

Willow sat on the hay bale and listened to the doctor's departing steps. It was clear he'd already given up on Missy. He'd simply made a kind gesture by giving her the remedies. She wondered if Daniel had likewise counted Missy dead.

"Here you are, lass. Let's see how we get this in her."

Without looking up, Willow said, "You don't have to stay any longer. I can take care of her now that I have medicine."

"Willow," he said, his voice soft and gentle. "Look at me, lass."

When she didn't, a large finger tipped her chin up, and Willow was forced to meet his brilliant gaze. "I already told you I didn't want to leave you alone. This won't be easy, you know. I want to help."

Such tenderness, such kindness . . . Willow's eyes over-flowed, and Daniel's finger caught a tear on her cheek. "Thank you," she whispered. "It's been a long time since someone—since I had someone to help me."

"I know, *a sto'ri'n,* but you're not alone now. Here's the whiskey. Let's take care of your ewe."

They took turns persuading Missy to take the remedies, despite her distaste. And they talked. In soft murmurs Daniel told Willow about growing up at the dairy farm and how he'd dreamed of going to sea. Once on a ship, however, he discovered he didn't have good sea legs, and he decided his one trip had served him fine. He told her of importing Irish woolens, laces, whiskey, and of helping others come to America, as his parents had done years ago.

In turn, Willow told Daniel about Aunt Lucie, her constant energy, her lack of artifice, her gruff love. She told him about the Meisters, how she'd felt the first time she saw their lovely home. She told him how those two dears determined that she would lack nothing, not in opportunities to learn, or other more basic needs.

"Then why won't they help you now?"

Willow chuckled. "You have it all wrong. They constantly try to get me to accept their help. It's me who refuses. I need to do this myself."

"Oh, I know that feelin' well, and it can cause a lot of grief. Be careful you're not bein' obstinate instead of steady on your course."

She nodded tightly. "That's what they tell me, too. But I have to do this one last thing. The farm is all I have left of my parents, Aunt Lucie, the family I came from."

They fell silent again, still watching the ewe. Finally, before even the first hint of dawn appeared, Missy's fever broke. Relief made Willow shaky, and exhaustion took its toll. "You can go now, Daniel. I'm just going to spread my quilt on the hay and catch a nap."

"Determined to be rid of me, aren't you? Here, an' I thought we were gettin' on well!"

Willow caught the thread of humor in his voice. "See? Teaches you not to take anything for granted."

"Around you?" A laugh boomed from his lips, and Willow joined in. "Trust me, lass, no man could grow complacent around you. You're . . . you're—"

"Fine! I understand. I'm beyond compare."

"Aye, that you are. An' I'm not leavin' you here alone. Now, let me get those quilts, and we can put them to good use."

They sat with their backs against the bale of hay, each wrapped in a quilt. When they were finally comfortable, and the hay beneath them ceased crackling, Willow whispered, "Thank you, Daniel. This is the nicest thing anyone's done for me in a long time."

"You know, lass, if you'd only stop sendin' me away—"

"It's your choice to stay. I haven't imposed."

"That's just what I mean! Put away your quills more often. I'd bet you'd have all the help you need."

"Quills, you say?"

"Mm-hmmm."

"Porcupine. Hmmm . . . I'll have to give that some thought."

From far away Willow heard a child's chatter. An adult responded. A sheep *baa-ed*. Seeing how stiff her muscles were, she decided to open her eyes before moving, but even her eyelids rebelled.

". . . and all that *stuff!* How awful."

Stuff? Awful? Just who was there?

Finally she pried one eyelid open, just enough to let in a

sliver of light. It took a few moments to lever the other one open, but eventually she succeeded. When she was finally able to focus, what she saw dismayed her.

It was morning, as bright and sunny as only Pennsylvania autumns could be. And she wasn't alone. Wrapped around her was Daniel's massive arm, and she'd burrowed right into his broad, firm chest. Worse yet, on the other side of the stall gate stood Mrs. Meister and Maribeth Miller, both enjoying her plight.

How mortifying! "Have you been here long?" she ventured.

Maribeth giggled.

Mrs. Meister smiled. "Oh, long enough, dear. I see you did stay all night with Missy."

"Mm-hmmm. Dr. Wirtz came and gave me medicine for her. Her fever broke just a couple of hours ago. She's not over it yet, but she should live."

As Willow tried to lift Daniel's arm from around her middle, he began to object. In an aggrieved tone she whispered, "Oh, hush! Just get up. It's late. People are walking around already. Go, go!"

"Go?" he asked in a deep burr. "What do you mean, lass? I'm here to help you."

"That's what I mean. Go! You've done more than you know."

"'Morning, Uncle Danny," a child singsonged.

"Maribeth?" he asked, sitting up suddenly, running a hand over his caked hair. "Where—what's happened? Where is Maribeth?"

"Right here, Uncle Danny."

With a monumental heave Willow threw Daniel's arm off her body and leaped up. The quilt dropped from around her, and she suddenly felt naked instead of clad in Hans's clothes.

"Oh, dear!" Mrs. Meister exclaimed, then waved at Willow's clothing. "You are in a state, aren't you? And what *is* that on your hair?"

"Yes, I am in a state, and you really don't want to know what all is in my hair. *I* don't want to know. As soon as the Fritzmeier boys get here, I'll need to use your bathroom."

"It's always ready for you," the older woman answered, mischief sparkling in her eyes. "Good morning, Daniel Callaghan. I'm Reba Meister. We've never met, but your mother and I were friends. I'll never forget the lovely evenings when we visited. Your mother was the best storyteller, and had it not been for that, I think your father would have worked round the clock. Here's your niece, safe and sound. I thought you'd be worried."

Slowly, with lumbering movements, Daniel stood, absorbing the comments about his parents, but found himself too groggy to fully comprehend what Mrs. Meister had said. In an effort to wake up, he rubbed his face with his hands. A look of revulsion twisted his features when he felt the crust of dirt come off on his fingers.

"'Mornin', madam," he muttered, his voice still a deep rumble. "And what did you say your name is?"

"I'm Reba Meister, dear. I took your niece in last night."

Suddenly his lax posture vanished, his shoulders clicked erect, his head lifted, and he saw Maribeth. "Fancy seein' you here, little lady."

Willow took offense at his tone. "Now, Daniel . . ."

Maribeth didn't seem to notice. "Oh, Uncle Danny, you should see Mrs. Reba's house! She has things from all over the world. She makes the best hot cocoa, and she read me the most wonderful stories! Can I go back with her? I really don't want to stay with you and the cows today."

The shock on Daniel's face made Willow laugh. "I told you so."

"Don't you know you're never supposed to say that, lass?"

"When one's right . . ." She let her words trail off, her smile wide.

"Well, Uncle Danny? Can I?"

"I don't know, Maribeth—"

"Before you say no, son," Mrs. Meister broke in, "consider how busy you'll be today, and I know Willow has more demonstrations scheduled for this morning. I'd be delighted to keep Maribeth with me. We were having a marvelous time."

Daniel shook his head, a crooked smile making a tuft of his mud-stiff mustache tilt up. "I'm outnumbered, it seems." Turning to Willow, he added, "Go on. I'll stay with Missy until the lads get here. I'm sure you want to clean up."

"But you're still wearing those awful clothes."

He glanced at his ruined formal garb, then chuckled. "Awful they are, indeed. But go on, I'll stay."

Just then three youths approached Missy's stall. The Fritzmeier twins and Hans Brenneman came to an abrupt halt. Three faces registered shock.

"What . . . ?"

"What . . . ?"

"What . . . ?"

"You don't want to know!" answered Willow and Daniel in unison.

Laughing nervously, Willow turned to Daniel. "You can go clean up, too. The boys are here. I'm not wasting another minute talking when I could be washing. Ready, Mrs. Meister? Maribeth?"

As the three females walked away, four male faces registered admiration. Finally one of the twins let out a short whistle.

Daniel frowned. He now regretted giving Willow Hans's

clothes. It didn't set well with him that the boys were getting an excellent view of Willow's round posterior—even though he himself was relishing the view.

"Hey!" cried Hans. "Those are MY clothes."

"And they never looked half as good on you, lad, as they do on her!"

12

$\mathcal{H}$OURS LATER DANIEL could still see behind his closed eyelids Willow's rear gently swaying as she left the Sheep Building. She'd been followed by more than one scandalized look, many appreciative ones, and even some full of envy.

His constant preoccupation with the delectable porcupine was beginning to rankle, though. Daniel was sitting with Heywood Adler, the manager of the Hotel Penn, and François, their new French chef, and although they were discussing the fate of Daniel's flock, he damn well couldn't keep his mind on selling mutton.

". . . and can we count on Easter lambs, too?"

Daniel blinked, realizing he'd been asked yet another question he hadn't listened to. "Ah . . . Easter, you say? Aye, we'll have lambs then. How many would you be needin'?"

Heywood turned to his chef. "François?"

With a shrug the chef turned to Daniel. "*Je ne sais pas*. I vill haf to zee how many peeples comes to zee restaurant regularly."

Daniel stood, ready to bring the dull meeting to an end. "Fine, fine! You can decide how many you need, let us know, an' Callaghan Dairy will supply all the lambs you want."

Heywood also stood, taking his cue from Daniel's abrupt behavior. "Then we have an agreement for four ewes now, and once François determines how many lambs we'll need in the spring, we can count on you for those as well."

"Precisely." As an afterthought, Daniel added, "I intend to buy new stock for our flock. I'm expectin' lambs aplenty in the spring."

Heywood lifted an eyebrow. "Expanding? Are you cutting back on the dairy?"

"Of course not! Callaghan's is first a dairy, then a sheep operation. I'm just increasin' the flock. I've noticed how often the hotels in town serve mutton. I don't mind addin' those profits to the healthy dairy ones."

"Hmmm. Must be doing well indeed," commented the hotel manager.

"Can't complain," responded Daniel. "My father was very successful, an' my brother-in-law built on that success. Now that I'm here, I intend to follow in their footsteps."

"Ah, yes. My condolences. It was quite the tragedy."

Daniel swallowed hard, wondering if the shard of pain would ever stop piercing his heart. "Aye, a loss."

Obviously uncomfortable with the turn the conversation had taken, Heywood stuck his hand out at Daniel. "Yes, yes. Now, at the close of the fair we can meet at your stalls to collect the ewes, right?"

"Precisely," answered Daniel, glad to return to the simpler subject of business. "I'll have them ready for you."

"I'll see you then."

"Aye, then."

Pivoting, Daniel headed for the East Philadelphia Street entrance to the Hotel Penn. A sense of elation lifted the gloom he'd felt at the mention of his recent loss. It looked as though his gamble would pay off. The Hotel Penn was eager for his mutton, and he still had appointments with representatives from two more hotels. He'd have to buy more sheep, and the fair offered him the perfect opportunity. Secure in the knowledge that his entrants would take the Best of Show ribbons in their categories, Daniel planned to buy animals from those other farms whose sheep placed behind his winners. He'd be assured of excellent stock that way. He wouldn't let his da down this time. He'd add to the success of Darby's beloved farm, just as the elder Callaghan would have done.

Feeling lighter than he had since his father's death, Daniel started walking toward the fairgrounds. He'd take care of Darby's dream. He'd carry it to the heights Darby had always envisioned. And he'd take care of Maribeth as if she were his own. Not only did he love the child because she was his sister's, but because Maribeth, despite her current difficulties, was a bright, lovable child.

All Daniel wanted was to become the father she needed.

He realized that Willow had the knowledge and ability to deal with his niece. But despite his personal interest in the lovely shepherdess, he wondered if he should allow the two of them to grow any closer. Yes, Willow was hardworking, kind, and had formed an amazingly close bond with his niece from the moment the two met, but Daniel still held reservations about Willow's excessive idealism. She reminded him too much of his wonderful but fey mother, the woman who'd encouraged Daniel's weaker tendencies, that fanciful part of him that grew up determined to pursue adventure, to follow his quest.

Although Maribeth was a female, Daniel knew he had to prepare the girl to be strong. He didn't think Willow's idealism was any more strengthening than Maeve Callaghan's Celtic tales and myths had been. He didn't know how far to let the relationship between his niece and Willow go.

Hell, he didn't even know how far to let his attraction to Willow go.

Last night had been a topsy-turvy swirl of emotions, Willow thought as she toweled off her hair. She'd started the evening disgusted with Daniel's interest in a renowned coquette, then grew dismayed. She'd hoped the kiss they'd shared had meant as much to him as it had to her. His casual change of interest suggested otherwise.

A knock came at her door. "Willow, dear, may I come in?"

She took a bracing breath. "Of course."

Reba Meister entered, bearing a fragrant tray. Since Willow hadn't had an opportunity to eat, Mrs. Meister had bustled to the kitchen to rustle up a meal when they arrived home, and had shooed Willow to the bathroom.

"Mrs. Martin had plenty of ham, biscuits, and fried potatoes. She even made you a fresh pot of coffee. There's more than you'll likely want, so go ahead, dear. Enjoy your meal."

For a moment Willow thought she'd get off easily. Then Mrs. Meister sat on the blue satin-covered bed. "Now, Willow, child, you must know I'm dying of curiosity. How did you end up in Daniel Callaghan's arms? Not that I blame you—he's perfect to snuggle up with."

Willow rolled her eyes. There went Mrs. Meister again, dreaming up romances out of whole cloth. "Actually, it was unexpected and unintentional."

Mrs. Meister's eyebrows shot up. "Oh?"

Willow turned away from her scrutiny. "Stop with your 'Ohs'! Nothing you'd find interesting happened. When he realized how sick Missy was, Daniel stayed to help me. After her fever broke, I told him he could go, but he refused to leave me all alone. We sat, and seeing how tired we both were we . . . dozed off, I guess. That's it."

"Hmmm . . . " Mrs. Meister murmured, clearly unconvinced. "Then how did you end up in boy's clothes? And asleep on Daniel's impressive chest?"

Willow feigned great interest in her hairbrush. "The clothes are Hans's. I need to wash and return them."

"Fine. Mrs. Martin will get them ready for you. Now, dear, I'd really like to know how you came to be sleeping in such a public spot with the well-known Mr. Callaghan. You must admit it's sure to give plenty of grist to the gossip mill."

"Mrs. Meister, the York gossip mill doesn't need grist! It runs freely at all times." Apparently Willow wasn't going to get off easily. She'd have to explain to her friend what she herself didn't understand. Why *had* she woken up in Daniel's embrace? And how did she get there?

"As to sleeping in Daniel's arms . . . I don't how that came about. We sat side by side, and the next thing I heard was Maribeth's giggle waking me up. I was just as stunned as you to find myself so . . . improperly draped over that man."

And loving it, her conscience added.

"Oh, it was indiscreet," Mrs. Meister responded with a broad smile. "But I wouldn't worry too much. From what I can see, that dance of yours is proceeding just as I expected."

At her friend's romantic notion, Willow took a moment to consider the kiss she and Daniel had shared. She remembered the electric moments in the mud. And she remembered the sharp thrill that coursed through her when Daniel refused to dislodge his possessive arm from her middle earlier that morning.

Could Mrs. Meister be right? Were she and Daniel dancing to the tune of romance?

After hurrying back to the fairgrounds, Willow was encouraged to see Missy drinking from the bottle she'd used the night before. Matthew Fritzmeier waved her on, telling her he'd stay with the ewe while Willow did her spinning exhibition.

Although the turnout this morning was healthier than the time before, Willow had to admit it was hardly encouraging. She didn't know how else to spark interest in working with wool and the animals who provided the fleece. It was frustrating indeed.

When done, she returned her spinning wheel to Missy's stall and found Lucas Fritzmeier attending to her flock. She caught her lower lip between her teeth, concerned with the amount of time the boys were putting in with her animals. She knew she couldn't afford to pay them fairly for all the work they were doing.

"Lucas, you really don't need to stay with my animals anymore. I—I can't pay you and your brother, even though you deserve not only fair pay, but also a bonus for all the special effort you put out."

Lucas stood and played with the rim of his plain black hat. "It fine ist, Villow. Ve vant to help choo. Ve don't pay need."

"That's very kind of you, but I can't let you work for no pay."

The plain black hat made another circle in the youth's hands. "*Das ist* fine. Ve chust vant to help choo. Please don't vorry choorself."

"But you can find paying work with any farmer here. Everyone knows how hard you both work and how well, too. I can't accept that much in exchange for nothing—"

"There you are, lass! Have you had dinner yet?"

Willow spun around, surprised by Daniel's silent approach. "N-no. I just finished my demonstrations and returned to find Lucas taking care of my animals. I was thanking him for his help, but I don't need it anymore. I'll take care of my flock—"

"Has the lad done anythin' wrong?"

"Of course not! He and Matthew are wonderful with the animals."

"Well, then, what is your problem?"

Willow lowered her head. She really didn't want to discuss her personal finances, but Daniel left her no alternative. "It's just that they do so much, and I don't have the money to pay them."

"Have they asked you to pay them?"

"No, that's just it. They say they want no pay. It just wouldn't be right not to pay them."

"Villow," Lucas said, "ve don't need choo to pay. Ve chust vant to help. Honest. *Vater unt Mutter* vouldn't let us choor money take. They said ve vere to help. Like neighbors."

"Seems to me," Daniel said in a drawled brogue, "we're seein' that wee porcupine's quills again. Listen to the lad, Willow. His family wants to help. In a neighborly way. You aren't as alone as you think. There are plenty who care. Don't be throwin' away what's best in life. Friendships, *people* matter. Go on, tell the lad what you need done. Besides, I'd like to escort you to dinner."

When Daniel called her a porcupine, Willow stiffened up, but when he called friendships the best life offered, emotion clogged her throat. His invitation to a noon meal threw her nerves into a tizzy.

She wanted to spend the time in his company. There *was* a different side to Daniel than the boorish male he often seemed. She liked that man just fine, but she feared that with increased closeness, her unruly response to him would only worsen, and she really had no business getting involved with a man. She had no time for flirtations or even courting. She had a farm to save, animals to raise. Besides, he also wanted to win Best of Show for his ewe.

Still, she wanted to go. Against her better judgment, she nodded. "Just do as you were doing, Lucas. They need clean hay in the pens, and I always freshen their water around noontime." Facing Daniel, she said, "If you're not busy, then dinner is a welcome break."

As he held his arm out for her, Willow again felt that thrill he always set off deep inside her. Was she dreaming this? Was she *really* strolling down the Midway with the most attractive man in town?

Then she realized that if it was a dream, she wasn't interested in waking. At least not yet.

Although it was early in the day, the carousel was running, and the three-fourths beat of the calliope's waltz spun through the air. Just beyond the merry-go-round a group of food stands clustered together. Willow took a deep breath, and caught the scent of pork and sauerkraut, roasting chickens, beef in tangy tomato sauce, cinnamon, vanilla, and the sweetness of baked goods. The fragrance of mutton also wafted by.

As they approached, a man called Daniel's name.

Willow turned. "It's Hiram Becker. He wants you to join him."

Facing the older farmer, Daniel shook his head. "I think, lass, we'd best avoid that stand. They're servin' leg o'mutton today."

Willow grimaced. "Thank you. I really don't enjoy eating animals. It probably comes from spending so much time with them."

"Oh, I don't know. I grew up on the farm an' I have no trouble eatin' beef, chicken, pork."

With a shrug, she said, "Maybe it's just me, then."

Daniel chuckled. "P'rhaps we should find out what porcupines eat."

Willow sent him a quelling look. "I'm not sure I like that comparison you seem so fond of making."

"'Tis most appropriate. Every time you're nervous or worried or embarrassed, the quills pop out."

She ignored his comment. "There! Vegetable soup. Just what I want."

"Then that's what you shall have."

They sat at a small table close to the stand where Daniel bought two bowls of soup and fresh-baked rolls. Willow, who'd been too rattled to eat much of Mrs. Meister's lovely breakfast, was ravenous and ate with relish. Daniel, as befitting a man so large, consumed various bowls of the savory mixture. Soon they were done, and although Willow had truly enjoyed the time with Daniel, she knew she had to get back to Missy.

Daniel didn't argue this time. "Let's go, then," he said, offering his arm again.

Returning down the Midway, the music of the carousel seemed livelier than ever, the horses smartly rising and falling, the many riders laughing. Willow tried to spy the brass ring above the horses, but she was too far from the ride to see something so small.

"What are you doin', lass?"

"Oh, nothing. I was just looking for the brass ring. It brings good luck, you know."

"Don't know about luck, but good eyes and a long arm will catch it."

"Are you saying that a person smaller than you couldn't get the ring?"

"Not exactly. 'Tis just that certain conditions must be present."

"Oh, flapdoodle! The ring goes to the one who'll receive good luck."

"Want to test that statement?"

"Yes! Let's see if luck or favorable conditions prevail."

When the ride came to a standstill, those who'd enjoyed the spin descended, and a line of eager customers lined up before a man collecting a fare. Willow studied the steeds and chose a midnight-black horse who wore a silver-studded saddle. Without waiting for Daniel's assistance, she scrambled up and waited for the ride to start again.

Daniel chose the caramel-colored horse next to Willow.

"Have you brought Maribeth to ride the carousel?" Willow asked.

He seemed surprised by her question, then a sheepish expression crossed his face. "Hadn't given it a thought, but you're right, I should bring her. She'd love the ride."

Satisfied with the results of her small nudge in the right direction, Willow was now convinced that Daniel wasn't neglecting his niece. He seemed more inexperienced than anything else, and if she could help him notice Maribeth's needs, perhaps the child wouldn't continue to run away.

Suddenly the ride began. Willow's horse went up, then down. Regardless, her gaze was glued to the bars overhead. Nothing.

The music blared, and riders laughed. Others chattered. Some, like Daniel, smiled benignly, entertained in their own way. Willow focused on her mission. She was going to find that brass ring if it was up there to be found!

A shimmer of exhilaration bubbled up her spine, and

Willow laughed just from the joy of the moment. Seconds later Daniel joined her mirth. Their laughter soared with the calliope music, and as Willow's horse went up yet again in its round of the carousel, she spied the brass ring.

Scarcely controlling her excitement, Willow aimed, stood in her horse's stirrups, stretched . . . and snagged the ring!

When the merry-go-round came to a stop, she bounced off and ran to the Midway. "Did you see?"

"I saw."

"Now do you believe it was pure luck?"

"Hmmm . . . I don't know. You were on the horse closest to the ring—it rose just when you needed it to, an' you're tall for a lass. I'm convinced you had all the favorable conditions on your side."

"Oh, flapdoodle! It was luck. Pure, blind luck, and it means good things will come my way."

Daniel frowned. "That could very well be, but I doubt it has anythin' to do with that trinket."

"And I think it's luck. My luck is changing. Oh, I just knew Missy would win Best of Show! Now she can't lose."

"I wouldn't count your chickens yet, lass. Brigid has a good chance."

"But Missy's going to win."

"Willow," Daniel said patiently, "Missy is ill. How can you still expect her to win?"

"She wasn't sick for the judging."

"She is now, and the judges are all over the buildings during the week."

Willow didn't like the turn the conversation had taken. She'd needed the boost catching the ring had given her. She wasn't ready to let Daniel dampen her spirits, not when she was close to achieving one of her fondest goals. "Can we agree to disagree?"

"Looks like we'll have to."

"May the best ewe win," she added, not wanting to sound churlish.

Daniel nodded, then fell silent.

Willow followed suit, but she couldn't help wondering what so thoroughly occupied his thoughts. Was he still silently arguing in Brigid's favor?

As they continued their stroll down the Midway, Daniel lost most of his good humor. Willow's nearly frenzied faith in good fortune didn't sit well with him. Superstition bothered him. It had for a very long time.

Maeve had held myriad odd beliefs she'd sworn to, and she'd always quoted tales and legends from old Erin to support her irrational notions. Daniel couldn't give credence to ancient stories or superstitions. The future was the future, and anything could happen. Signs and omens, chivalric quests, and magical kingdoms offered naught to a person. One had to be strong, face the future with reality in mind, not with ancient stories that elderly folk half forgot. It didn't matter how appealing they were to a child, or to a person who, like Maeve, was more than a bit fey. Fantasy tempted one to do irresponsible things.

Willow's faith in a circle of brass, coupled with her odd refusal to eat meat, sounded a warning to Daniel. It rang a signal for caution. Maribeth was an orphan. She needed practical tools to face the future. Daniel doubted Willow's peculiar ways would be of service to the child.

With that in mind, Daniel had to keep his head about him. He couldn't allow a powerful attraction to blind him to reality. The last time he let idealism take the reins of his life, he'd broken his father's heart, wounded his mother, and disappointed his sister. Nothing could change the past, but nothing said he had to repeat his mistakes, and Daniel feared that getting too close to Willow, exciting a prospect though it was, would prove to be a mistake. Willow was too much like his mother, fascinating but impractical, living in a world far removed from the one he inhabited.

He couldn't risk Maribeth adopting Willow's fey tendencies. He couldn't fail his orphaned niece.

13

$\mathcal{H}$IS RESOLVE FIRMLY in place, Daniel continued down the Midway, only too aware of the woman at his side. No matter how irrational his interest in Willow was, it didn't seem he could ignore his feelings, much less her presence.

It wasn't just for Maribeth's sake that he should pull away from Willow as soon as possible. He was altogether too susceptible to her. He didn't want to fall back into a pattern of actions similar to the one that had caused his family so much pain. He couldn't allow her idealism to court his into making another appearance in his life. The results could be disastrous.

He had to stay away from the lovely but fey Willow Stimson.

Unable to resist, he cast a sideways glance at her. A distant look was in her brown eyes, a faint smile curved her rosy lips. Her silky brown hair was pulled up into a swirling knot, leaving the clean lines of her features in relief.

She was lovely. Not in the nearly impossible perfection of Katherine Meckler's classic beauty, but with a spark of spirit, a vibrancy all her own. And if her mouth was a bit wide, it simply added to its generous appeal. Her chin, too square for feminine perfection, reflected her resolve and her pride.

To tell the truth, the fact that at times she resisted his advances made her all the more desirable than the overly aggressive Widow Meckler. Daniel felt an urge to defeat Willow's suspicion of him, to turn her negative impressions into positive acceptance.

Even if she was the wrong woman for him.

As they approached the Sheep Building, Oliver Winfield greeted Daniel. With a smile, he responded, "Top o' the day to you, Oliver."

Nodding to Willow, the middle-aged farmer then asked, "Will you be bringing your lovely lady to our barn dance this evening?"

"Oh, sweet Mary and Joseph, to be sure an' I'd forgotten all about it." For a moment, Daniel regretted the pressure his friend had put on him to invite Willow to the dance. But only for a moment. "You heard the gentleman, lass. Will you be comin' with me to his party?"

"You don't need to invite me just because he put you on the spot—"

"Put away the quills, Willow. I'm askin' because I'd like you to come with me. No other reason."

With a chagrined expression on his kind, broad face, Mr. Winfield cleared his throat and began to sidle away. "It seems I put my foot in it. If you'll excuse me, my missus is waiting for me to go eat. I'll see you later this evening, Daniel."

Daniel nodded, his gaze still on Willow. "Lass? Will you keep me in suspense?"

Willow studied Daniel's face. She wasn't happy about the sudden turn of events. She'd spent the whole walk down the Midway silently arguing against her interest in Daniel Callaghan. Now, because of a friend's slip of the tongue, Daniel had invited her to a barn dance. She didn't think accepting was the right thing to do.

On the one hand, she'd never been to a barn dance, and she felt intimidated by the prospect. On the other hand, she'd never been invited by a gentleman to any sort of social event, as Milford had always been happy to visit at the Stimson farm. Although Daniel's classification as a gentleman was highly subjective, he had invited her to come as his partner. It was a heady moment.

She spared a glance his way and blushed when she saw a gold watch in his hand, his eyes focused on her. "Well?"

The mischievous twinkle in Daniel's blue eyes told her he knew he was irritating her. On the other hand, his grin told her it was all in fun. And the answer to his question was all about fun. She'd never had the opportunity to participate in much play. She'd always been busy studying with Professor Meister, or working on the farm with Aunt Lucie. She didn't regret the time she'd spent in those endeavors, but she did feel less than equipped to handle an evening in the company of Mr. Wicked-Pleasures Callaghan.

Despite her indecision, something inside her made her answer, "Yes."

Daniel laughed, seemingly in relief. How surprising. Willow hadn't thought he would feel anxious while awaiting her response. Goodness, was he as confused about her as she was about him?

As he went to slip his watch back in his pocket, he fumbled the timepiece and had to make three attempts before finally returning it to its rightful place. He was nervous. Incredible. A successful, citified, former Philadelphia businessman was worried about *her* response to his invitation?

Oh, Lordy. What had she let herself in for? "I'd best go," she said, hating the breathless quality in her voice.

"Of course," he said, but took a step closer to her.

Willow backed up. "Where shall I meet you?"

"Meet me?"

"Yes, for the barn dance. That is, if you really want me to go."

Daniel's blue eyes rolled. "I asked you, didn't I?"

"Under duress."

"*This* is duress, lass!" Another step put his open shirt collar scant inches from Willow's eyes. That tuft of auburn chest hair caught her attention again, and a rush of warmth flooded her.

"Ah . . . er . . . but you didn't say where I should meet you."

"You'll be at the Meister home, right?" At her nod he continued. "Then I'll come by in a cab to fetch you."

Willow's eyes opened wide. "Oh, you needn't go to so much trouble. I'm sure I can meet you—"

Daniel's finger pressed against Willow's lips. "Hush," he said. "I said I'd take you, and if you don't mind, lass, that's just what I'll do."

But Willow scarcely heard Daniel's words. All she registered was the presence of his warm, slightly rough finger on her lips, gently rubbing, increasing that burst of inner warmth he always inspired. Her eyelids grew heavy. Her breathing grew shallow. Anticipation grew greater. Was he going to kiss her?

Did she really want him to?

Of course she did! Willow was no fool. Daniel's kisses, as dangerous as they were, were forbidden pleasures. Something she knew she shouldn't have, but she couldn't resist the wonder and magic in them. She had no intention of avoiding the impending caress.

Under the pressure of that finger, Willow parted her lips. She watched him approach. Slowly, carefully, just as he'd done before. He seemed to be giving her the opportunity to back away. She smiled around his finger, and her eyelids descended some more.

Daniel's warm breath fanned her cheek. His lips parted. He was only a heartbeat away.

"There you are, Daniel!" called Hans from inside the arched entrance to the Sheep Building.

Daniel jerked his finger away from her mouth as if he'd been singed. Equally startled, Willow took a step back and found herself flush up against the building's outer wall. Her every nerve ending quivered, and she didn't know whether in embarrassment at being caught in another indiscreet situation with Daniel Callaghan, or if her heart, her mind, even her body screamed in frustration at the loss of Daniel's closeness, at the loss of a kiss.

When she felt herself composed enough to face the young man, she pasted a smile on her now-stiff lips. "Hello, Hans . . ."

She allowed her greeting to trail off when she read the disappointment and perhaps even hurt pride in his expression. Hans hadn't liked finding her virtually in Daniel's arms. Coming on the heels of the embarrassing morning episode, she could see where he wouldn't be pleased. She'd sensed his attraction to her from the moment they'd met.

Unfortunately, although she liked Hans, he didn't turn her into mush the way his employer did. And, Lordy, did Daniel ever have the touch! It was best if she beat a hasty retreat, otherwise who knew what further mortifying predicament the cocky Irishman would lead her into.

Regretting Hans's disappointment, but with a healthy dose of annoyance at the entire male gender, Willow took a few steps into the building. "What time should I expect you, Daniel?"

The skin above his beard ruddied. "Seven," he bit off.

"Oh?" she asked, not liking his tone of voice.

"Oh, yes," he responded, again rolling his eyes. "Seven. Don't make a fuss about it, an' you'd better be leavin' your quills behind, too!"

With a "Hmmph," Willow turned and stomped away from the two men.

Daniel watched her go, knowing Hans was doing the same. He was embarrassed by being caught again with the pretty shepherdess, but he was also glad that Hans's expression reflected his understanding of how matters stood. He'd been a fool to push Hans in Willow's direction. Especially since he'd wanted to pursue her himself.

He'd admit it. He'd been jealous of every smile, every word Willow had sent his farmhand's way. If it took a public display of interest now to discourage the youth, then that was all for the best. Even though he'd earlier decided to avoid further involvement with Willow. Even if she was a bit younger than he. Even if she was fey, idealistic, impractical, superstitious . . .

It seemed Daniel Callaghan was fated to pursue Willow Stimson.

He turned to Hans, clearing his throat. "Sorry, lad. I know I nudged you toward her, but I can't seem to stay away from her. She's the most infuriatin', aggravatin', flummoxin' female I've ever met."

Hans stared at Daniel for a long moment. Then he shrugged, a wry smile tilting the corners of his mouth. "Isn't she wonderful?"

Daniel barked out a laugh. He shook his head in helpless surrender. "Aye, that she is, indeed. Willow Stimson is the most wonderful condition that could afflict a man."

Hours later Willow found herself staring into the mirror in the Meisters' guest bedroom. Her hair, done by Reba Meister herself, was piled in a softly swirling knot. But it wasn't pulled tight, not at all. Its softness surrounded her face, and when the individual strands caught the light from the gas lamp on the wall, they turned a golden brown, haloing her features.

She shook her head. "Are you sure it will stay up?"

Mrs. Meister clucked and pulled Willow's hands away from her masterpiece. "Of course, child. Now stand still so I can finish fastening all these buttons down the back of your dress."

Stand still, she'd said. Hah! How could a body stand still when a battalion of buzzards had taken refuge in her middle? Willow was so nervous, so twitchy, she couldn't imagine surviving the evening. She was sure she'd go down in history as the only woman to die from exposure to a man!

Mrs. Meister had no sympathy for her plight. In fact, Willow couldn't remember when her friend had ever seemed happier. The woman's matchmaking bent was dangerous; it served to make Willow all the more aware of the powerful connection between her and Daniel. An odd connection, true, but most assuredly present whenever they were together.

Like during the almost-kiss earlier that afternoon.

"I wish I were going, too," muttered Maribeth from Willow's bed.

"Great!" exclaimed Willow. "*You* go in my place."

Maribeth's eyes twinkled in excitement, reminding Willow of another pair of devilish blue eyes. "Can I really? Really, really?"

"Oh, hush!" chided Mrs. Meister. "Of course you can't, Maribeth. This is an evening for your uncle Danny and Willow to enjoy themselves. They both work hard, and it's time they took a break. Your chance will come, dearest. In only a few years, too."

Maribeth's bottom lip pushed out.

Willow's winged scavengers made another sweep through her middle.

Mrs. Meister tugged on the white taffeta bow at the back of Willow's waist. "This is the perfect dress for you. We were very fortunate that Mrs. Heil had it in her dress shop. You can't always count on finding something ideal at the last moment."

Willow took another peek in the mirror. Mrs. Meister was right. The green-and-white dress did look perfect on her. The fitted, gingham bodice hugged her torso, its neckline forming an eyelet-framed, discreet *V*. Bouffant sleeves were banded in white taffeta at the elbow, and her waist was enhanced by the white bow. The skirt, cut in a gently flaring line, was also of the green-and-white fabric, and whispered deliciously with Willow's slightest move. The dress was simple enough for her taste—and for a barn dance—but it was definitely a party dress. She'd never felt more feminine than she did at that moment.

"Can I have the dress for my party, Willow?" asked Maribeth.

Willow chuckled. "If you still want it. I think, though, it'll be out of style after a few years."

Then Maribeth grew quiet. Willow studied the girl's suddenly serious expression in the mirror. "What's wrong, Maribeth?"

To Willow's surprise, the child lowered her gaze to her twisting fingers. "Will a boy ever want to take me to a barn dance?"

Willow understood Maribeth's question far better than anyone else would. She approached the bed and carefully sat, protecting the pretty skirt of her new dress. "Look at me, Maribeth."

When the child did, Willow continued. "I was twelve once, too, you know. I didn't have a mother, either. I only had my aunt Lucie, who knew nothing of parties or dresses or boys. But I had a friend, a very special friend who always knew too much about dresses, parties, and men."

She shot a glare in Mrs. Meister's direction and caught her friend exiting the room, an impish grin brightening her solid features.

"Was that Mrs. Meister?" asked Maribeth.

"Of course. I remember asking her a question very similar to the one you just asked me."

"What did she tell you?"

"She read me a story about a princess and the man she married."

"A princess?"

"Um-hmm, a princess just like you."

"Me!"

"You. How about if we go to the library? That's where Mrs. Meister read that story."

The girl scrambled off the bed and trotted downstairs, more animated than Willow had seen her yet. She'd snagged Maribeth's attention.

As she entered the library, Willow thought back to that wintry afternoon many years ago. She'd sat on the brown velvet settee with Mrs. Meister, a fire crackling in the hearth, Professor Meister perusing one of his endless tomes of history, myth, or literature. Mrs. Meister, who had been reading the latest issue of her favorite *Peterson's Ladies' National Magazine,* set the publication aside when Willow voiced her question.

"This is the story Mrs. Meister read to me. . . .

" 'There once was a king of Erin who had a daughter, precious just like you. The day came for her to find a husband, but the king knew not who would suit. So he made an announcement and was surprised when the son of a king of the East appeared at his castle, asking for the girl's hand in marriage.

"'Now the king of Erin was wise, and wanted only the finest man for his child. He told the prince, "You must first prove yourself worthy of my daughter. In a castle near a Loch to our north, a giant lives. He came by that palace through murder and deceit. Before you can marry my daughter, you must bring me the giant's tongue as proof of your victory over him.

"'The prince was surprised, but as he knew the king of Erin's daughter was fair indeed, he took off on his quest. When he'd only been gone but a pair of hours, hunger overtook him, and he paused by an oak at the side of the road. He'd packed some cheese and bread in a sack he carried, and had his fill.

"'After eating, he grew sleepy and lay down at the foot of the oak. In his sleep, a wee man in a suit of velvet approached him and asked him why he was there.

"'When the prince told the wee man of his quest, he smiled. "You must beware of the giant, me lad. He is evil indeed. But he has one weak spot. There's a brown stain on his breast, and if you shoot him there, he shall die. Then you can safely claim the tongue the King has asked for.

"'The prince awoke after thanking the wee man. He'd never had such an odd dream, and he wondered if his visitor's advice would prove helpful.

"'Looking up at the sky, he realized how late it was. He hurried along the road and soon came upon a glittering castle of the whitest stone.

"'A hideous roaring came from inside, and moments later the giant appeared on the drawbridge. The prince tried to approach without notice, but the giant had already scented him. As his foe approached, the prince saw inside the beast's shirt a spot of brown skin, and he knew the wee man hadn't lied. Taking aim, he shot a lance at the giant and watched it hit its target.

"'With a final roar the giant was dead. Moments later the prince cut out the tongue and was back on the road to the castle of the king of Erin. There, he laid the tongue before the king, then noticed a wee man standing behind the King's throne. It was the man from his dream.

"'The wee man whispered to the king, and the king spoke to the prince. "You have done well, lad. Now you shall receive your reward.

"'The wee man came forward, walked around the cutoff tongue, and magic took place. When the wee man retreated behind the King's throne, the tongue became a cask full of golden coins.

"'The next day the prince and the princess were married, and with the riches of their reward, they ruled happily after the king no longer lived.'"

Willow reached over and slipped a coppery curl behind Maribeth's ear. "And so, Maribeth, when the time is right, the finest prince in all the land will come, conquer what giant torments you, and win the right to be your loving spouse."

Maribeth's blue eyes burned with excitement. "Really? Oh, Willow do you *really* think that will happen for me?"

"Absolute—"

"Ahem!" Daniel's cough cut off Willow's answer.

She jumped, startled. Then, seeking to compose herself, she stood, surreptitiously wiped her suddenly damp palms on her skirt, and faced Daniel. A very odd expression seemed to darken his eyes to a navy blue. But he said not a word.

Willow approached Maribeth's uncle, not knowing what to say. "Good evening. I'm sorry, have I kept you waiting long?"

"Long enough," he said in such a low voice that Willow wasn't sure he'd actually responded so rudely. But she didn't put it past the maddening Irishman.

"Well, I'm ready now," she said, gathering her purse and her wrap. Tilting her chin upward, she left the cozy room with a brief "Goodbye" for Maribeth and a tight smile for politeness' sake.

Daniel grunted.

Willow had no idea what was bothering Daniel Callaghan this time, but he'd invited her to a barn dance, she'd prepared herself to attend a barn dance, and by golly! he was taking her to a barn dance.

Mr. Quieter-Than-a-Crypt Callaghan held the Meisters' front door open as Willow stepped out onto the porch. He helped her down the stairs, then ushered her into the black carriage waiting by the front gate. They both sat down, and Daniel gave the driver his cue.

Still, he'd said not another word.

She was fast growing tired of his rude behavior. Hadn't she told him he didn't have to take her to the blasted dance? Hadn't she had the decency to offer him a way out of having to perform an undesired chore? And he was *still* behaving like a petulant child?

Aaargh! Men. Just exactly what went through those confusing, befuddling brains?

Daniel gnashed his teeth. He was doing his level best to keep his temper under control, but it was hard, harder than he'd ever imagined anything would be. Willow had been filling Maribeth's head with the very same tales peopled with kings, princes, wee folk, giants, heroes, and magic that his mother had loved so well. The same sort of tales Maeve had often told him, right before she brought out the old violin. Those same tales that had inspired him to set off to seek his fortune, prepared to vanquish whatever giant got in his way.

Foolish nonsense it had all been. Dangerous nonsense, at that. The only giants Daniel had fought were people's intolerance and disdain. As an Irishman, he'd found himself unwelcome in many places in Philadelphia. He'd had to fight twice as hard to attain half as much as other men. And for what?

To abandon the family farm, to fail his father, hurt his mother, disappoint his sister, and himself as well. He'd made much money, but the money would never replace what he'd lost in favor of pursuing his ridiculous quest.

Willow had been prattling in the same vein as his mother. By all the Saints, she even knew the same Irish folk tales Maeve had so often told! Who had filled her head with that nonsense in the first place? And how had he come to be attracted to such an inappropriate woman? He'd known she was odd from their very first encounter. After all, what farm-grown maid would be so damnblasted skittish about a ram's normal response to a ewe in heat?

Stealing a glance at Willow, Daniel saw her looking more beautiful than ever. A shaft of silvery moonglow entered the carriage window, gilding her with its pure light. Her hair looked lighter, softer than usual, her eyes dark and mysterious. Her lips were tilted in a womanly smile, one that hid secrets he longed to learn.

He'd asked her to the barn dance. He'd come to pick her up. The fact that he'd found her proving his worst suspicions right had no bearing on his need to at least attempt politeness for the rest of the night.

Then the scoundrel on his shoulder laughed again. *Politeness, indeed,* he seemed to say. Daniel was forced into honest confession. He wouldn't need to feign polite behavior. He had all intention of enjoying this evening to its fullest. Tomorrow the ribbons would be handed out, the fair would come to an end. Tomorrow he would bid good-bye to Willow Stimson.

But tonight . . . ah, yes, tonight. He still had tonight.

14

$\mathcal{W}$ILLOW SWORE IT took them ten years or more to get from the Meisters' home to Mr. Winfield's farm. It actually took a half hour or so, but riding in a closed carriage with a tooth-gnashing, ill-humored colossus was not a pleasant experience. Certainly not one that went by in a flash.

The moment the carriage pulled to a stop in front of the large stone farmhouse, Willow threw open the door and scrambled out. She wanted not one more second in the presence of a man in a monumental grouch. This was to be her first barn dance, and she meant to enjoy herself. Even if she had to be equally rude as Mr. Green-Persimmon Callaghan himself. Even if she had to find another partner for the dancing. Even if she had to walk home when it was all over.

Smoothing her skirt as she went, Willow made her way around the house, past a neatly tended kitchen garden and beyond a chicken coop. The enormous red-painted barn rose skyward like a rustic castle before a field of shorn and dying corn stalks. Its wide open doors smiled a welcome to new arrivals. From inside Willow heard the squeaks of someone tuning a fiddle, the trill of a musician testing his harmonica. Above all, voices chattered, laughter filled the evening air, and the sweet scent of hay lured her closer to those gathered within.

She faltered when she stepped inside, not knowing where to go amid the bustling, milling group gathered there. Taking a deep breath, she scanned the cavernous area illuminated with myriad kerosene lanterns, seeking at least one familiar face. A couple of Aunt Lucie's friends were busy setting out what looked like a banquet. Pies of all sorts ranged down a long table, tin cups were stacked high at its far end, and a barrel of what she suspected was spiced cider brought up the rear behind the food. While she debated going in, a woman teetered past her, straining under the weight of a massive kettle filled with something savory and hot. Her face was damp from the steam, red from her efforts. Two bearded men in denim trousers and checkered flannel shirts rushed to her rescue, and she nearly collapsed in relief.

Willow shot another glance around. She smiled in relief when she spotted Tessa Hampton, a former classmate she'd always liked. Dressed in a red calico dress, the young woman stood with five others, the six forming a colorful bouquet. Squaring her shoulders, Willow took a step toward renewing old friendships, but a massive paw caught her elbow, and she was held right where she stood.

"Exactly what do you want now, Mr. Callaghan?"

"I brought you here, I did, an' I intend to dance with you. An' you needn't be treatin' me to any more of your hoity-toity independence or sass."

"Me! You're the one whose behavior is deplorable. Not one blasted word have you said to me since you muttered something in the Meisters' library. And I don't want to be treated to another dose of whatever it was you said back there, since I've noticed that when you mutter, it's a warning to take cover."

How dare he? Not even a "Good evening" had he offered, and yet he dared accuse her of inappropriate behavior. The gall of the man! She narrowed her gaze and met his blue eyes. They were dark, as dark as they always grew right before he let go one of his less acceptable comments. Willow rushed to forestall another of his pronouncements.

"I don't relish the thought of spending the rest of my evening humoring your foul mood. I was invited to a party and I intend to enjoy it. It's not as if I have such opportunities too frequently. You will *not* succeed in ruining my night!"

With that she yanked her arm from his grasp, irritated that he'd kept her by his side all that time. She stalked toward Tessa, not once checking to gauge his reaction to her words.

"Willow!" the pretty brunette called out when Willow approached the group. "It's been so long since I last saw you! What a pleasant surprise. Do you know everyone here?"

With sincere verve the young woman made Willow feel more comfortable than she ever remembered feeling among strangers. Once the introductions were over, and Tessa resumed the telling of an anecdote, Willow stole a peek at Daniel and was stunned to catch him staring at her, a crooked grin on his lips, admiration in his eyes.

So there! Satisfied with his response, and with an upward tilt of her chin, she returned to the general conversation and found herself able to join in. A mellow feeling winnowed through her, comforting and cheering her as it went.

At least it did until she remembered a brogue-spiced baritone saying something about putting her quills away and not refusing others' offers of friendship. That wickedly attractive, boorish brute couldn't have been right about that, could he? She wasn't putting people off with her determination to be self-reliant . . . was she?

She stole another glance at Daniel. He hadn't moved and

was studying her, an unreadable expression partly veiled by his rusty whiskers. Was she putting him off, too?

Her gaze tangled with his, a rush of tingles filling her middle. Why? Why did that man affect her so? Why *him* of all possible men? And, flapdoodle! Why did he keep on staring at her as if she were the greatest puzzle on earth? As if she were the most intriguing of mysteries? As if she held the answers to all the questions in his eyes?

Or was she superimposing her own muddled feelings onto his irritated expression?

Before she could waste any more time on her impossible musings, Oliver Winfield called for silence from a corner of the barn. "Ladies and gentlemen, I'd like to welcome you to Winfield Farm tonight. As you can see, Charlie Davis and Bernie Woolsey have brought their fiddle and harmonica, and we're about to start the dancing. I've been tapped to do the calling, so gents find your ladies, if you please."

Willow watched the threesome in the corner and saw Charlie Davis take a generous swig from a brown and cream crockery jug at his side. Heavens, there was even moonshine at this party. She'd heard all about the evils of imbibing spirits, but it seemed she was going to have an opportunity to witness those effects. What a night this promised to be!

Moments later the two musicians leaped up and began plying their instruments. The tapping of many toes immediately joined the sounds, and soon the men crossed the great expanse of the barn to approach the lady each would twirl in the steps of a Virginia Reel. Groups formed, and soon the rustle of dancing feet was heard, keeping the beat of the lively music. Willow's foot tapped in accompaniment.

"Shall we?" asked that familiar, Irish-flavored voice.

Willow turned and narrowed her gaze. "Why are you

asking me to dance if you didn't even care to speak to me earlier?"

Daniel exhaled forcibly, then ran a hand through his unruly dark red hair. "I'll never understand women! First you're complainin' about what I said, then you start in fussin' about what I didn't say. Damnblast it, woman! All I want is to dance with you tonight."

So there they stood, squared off in yet another apparent impasse. But Willow wanted to join the dancers weaving through the formations Oliver Winfield kept calling. And with Daniel standing before her, she doubted any other man would approach her. She didn't think she could get rid of him too easily, either. There was a determined set to his bearded jaw, and his blue eyes seemed to pierce directly to her heart.

She did want to dance with him, with Daniel Callaghan, despite his churlishness, his irritating tendencies, his occasional rudeness, his perennial mischief.

"Very well," she finally said, and grasped his hand. The usual shot of energy flew up to her shoulder, up and down her spine, making her head spin with the lush sensation of Daniel's touch. "Be warned, however," she murmured, hesitant, "I don't know what to do."

Patting her hand, he then folded it in both of his. The sensation was heady indeed. "Not to worry, lass. Oliver's callin' is easy to follow, and I'll be nudgin' you in the right direction, I will."

"Yes, but what about all the other people out there? How will I know who to follow? Whose hand to take next?"

"Everyone helps everyone else. You'll see."

So off they went. At first Willow felt a bolt of panic each time Oliver made a new call. Then, trusting in Daniel's words, she followed his lead and that of the other dancers in their square. Soon she found herself recognizing the individual formations and finally began to enjoy herself in earnest. She was glad she'd come, even if Daniel had been less than the ideal escort.

As they wended their way through numerous songs, Willow found herself anticipating the moment Daniel would return to her, allowing her to clasp his strong warm hand. She met his cobalt gaze when his fingers clasped hers, when he swung her on his arm. He held her gaze as he danced away, then swept back to her as he completed the dance circle.

A bubble of excitement, happiness, and joy blossomed in Willow's middle. It grew, then burst into a cascade of laughter. Just for the pleasure of it. For the enchantment of a magical night. For the thrill of being with Daniel Callaghan at her first dance.

After a raucous rendering of "Turkey in the Straw," Oliver called a refreshment break for himself and his two musicians. Willow found Daniel instantly at her side. "Oh! I didn't realize you'd ended up this close."

"Well, an' I did," he answered, the sparkle in his eyes growing darker, more intimate.

A feathery flutter teased her heart. This was the man she liked so well. The one who'd ridden a carousel with her. The man who'd spoken of chasing dreams. The one whose kisses burned themselves into the deepest reaches of her heart. The man she feared she was falling in love with.

"Cider?" he asked.

She made an assenting noise, but it wasn't even a murmur. Her voice remained stuck in her throat, the feelings inside her too strong to allow her to speak. Oh, Lordy. She was *really* in trouble now. In love with Daniel Callaghan . . . oh, my.

She scarcely noticed his departure from her side, much less his return with a tin cup full of cider scented with cinnamon and cloves. He lifted the cup to his lips and took an appreciative drink. "Splendid!" he exclaimed and held the cup out to her.

But he didn't let go of the blasted thing. He tapped her lips with the rim and waited for her to part them. Mischief made the corner of his mustache dance, but only until he came so close to her that she felt the heat of his large body, heard the sound of his breathing, saw the pulse at his temple beat faster. Then that deep blue stare lost its playfulness, turning serious, intense, deliberate.

He lowered his eyelids, and she knew he watched her sip from their cup. A flush colored his cheekbones, and Willow wondered if he, too, was remembering the kiss they'd shared . . . perhaps the one they'd missed sharing. She took another sip, aware that he'd quenched his thirst with that cider, as she was quenching hers. Did he crave another kiss, hunger for another caress?

Would he satisfy her longings? Would he fill her need for that other caress?

When she stopped sipping, he replaced the edge of the cup with his thumb, rubbing her sensitive bottom lip. "Willow," he murmured.

She didn't offer a reply; she had none to give. She'd been reduced to a mass of sensations, emotions, of yearning. All she knew was she wanted his touch to continue, to last forever, to reach her heart as he was touching her mouth.

A sudden wild whoop broke the spell around them, and Willow blinked owlishly in her Daniel-induced haze. What was going on?

Daniel stepped protectively to her side, grasping her elbow. His instinctive gesture thrilled her. He'd thought to protect her at the sound of something strange. The masculine nature of his action thrilled her newly discovered femininity, and she smiled up at him. His mustache twitched in response.

Another bellow drew her gaze to the corner of the barn where Oliver and the musicians had gathered again, Charlie Davis hugging his crock of 'shine. Bernie Woolsey, harmonica bouncing against his belly, reached around the wire-thin body of the fiddler, and with his paunchy strength wrested the coveted crock away. He took his turn imbibing the wicked spirits, but Charlie wasn't willing to share.

Quick as a whip, he grasped the loop near the neck of the jar and pulled, making Bernie spill the liquid fire down his shirt. "Aw, Charlie! Look whatcha made me do. I waishted a perfeckly good gulletful a'shine. Don' be so sh—shellfish wit yer drink."

"I ain't shellfish, ya dolt. Them's—*hic*—queer bugs what grow in th'ocean. Me, I ain't messin' with no big—*hic*—hole a'water. Uh-uh. I'm shtayin' on dry lan' wid my 'shine." Tipping up his jug, he proceeded to swill the stuff down.

Willow's eyes widened in amazement. "How can he just drink and drink and drink? Isn't it supposed to burn?"

Daniel chuckled. "Good 'shine should blister paint, lass. Charlie hasn't a thing to worry about, though. By now, he's burned everything that could be burned."

"But won't he get silly? Won't he fall down drunk?"

"An' you don't think he's silly enough already?"

Daniel's dancing eyes told Willow he was again teasing her. "Of course he's silly, but how will he play? Or is the dance over now that Charlie is . . . incapacitated?"

This time Daniel's rich laughter boomed out. Willow found herself joining him. "Ah, lass. Charlie's not nearly close to bein' incapacitated. He'll play for hours yet."

"Good!"

A russet eyebrow rose. "Liked the dancin', then?"

Willow's cheeks warmed. "Of course."

Daniel's voice dropped to an intimate level. "Maybe they'll grace us with a waltz."

The warmth in her cheeks flared into flames. "I don't know how."

"Have I yet led you astray, lass?"

Willow's eyes popped open wide, so startled was she by Daniel's suggestive question. When she dared look at him, she saw to her surprise that he'd embarrassed himself.

He cleared his throat. "I didn't mean that how it sounded."

"You should know I'm not easily led, Daniel."

"As Mary, Joseph, and all the Saints can attest," he muttered.

Willow tipped her chin up in the air. "If you start muttering again, I'm going back to Tessa and the others."

A warm paw captured her hand. "I'd like to see you try, lass."

Daniel's thumb drew circles on the palm of her hand, stealing her very breath. A tremor shook Willow, and she instantly knew he'd felt it in her fingers. Curse the beast, he knew exactly what he was doing to her! He knew she could no more walk away than she could run to Charlie Davis and join him for a drink.

She looked up at Daniel. Their gazes caught and held.

As if by their express request, Charlie then drew his bow over the strings of his fiddle and the sweet silver notes of a waltz stole sighs from the ladies, painted smiles on the lips of the men.

Daniel hooked the handle of the empty tin cup on a nail that stuck out from the rough wooden wall behind Willow. He led her by the hand toward the other couples already dancing. When they reached the center of the barn, he continued to hold her hand, then slipped his other arm around her back. "Just follow me," he whispered into her ear, the kiss of his breath warm and sweet in the sensitive shell.

At that moment Willow realized how much her feelings for the Irishman had grown. She recognized at that very moment that she would gladly have followed him to the ends of the earth and back.

She leaned into his clasp and boldly met his gaze. They took up the gliding three-fourths sweep of the music, and Willow saw her reflection in brilliant blue irises. She couldn't look away; he didn't, either. Still they danced, their steps matched, their bodies moving as if one. They turned, they spun, they twirled, all the time held together by the vibrant communion of their eyes.

Then Willow remembered her dream. The one where she'd danced with Daniel. They'd been fated to dance, to recognize the pull between them, to admit to the powerful attraction that transcended logic, sanity, common sense.

Feelings had no logic.

Love wasn't sane.

When the pace of the music again changed, and Oliver went back to calling, Willow and Daniel slowly parted and joined a square. Something had happened during that dance, though. Both seemed to know it. Willow knew she'd never be the same woman she'd been before those magical moments of realization in Daniel's arms.

She wove through the paces of the dance, her mind busy considering what she now knew of her feelings for Daniel. So this was love. This volatile surge of emotion, the heightened sensitivity in the presence of another, the longing, the frustration, the heat and desire and . . .

How did *he* feel about *her*? And how would she know?

She knew he'd liked kissing her. She knew he liked touching her lips. He seemed to have liked waltzing with her, and he seemed to love irritating her to distraction. But did that approach the intensity of love? Did he long to be with her, regardless how inappropriate she was, how far-fetched the notion of love between them was?

She found no answers. Certainly not while they danced this far apart. Would Charlie again do them the favor of striking up another lushly romantic waltz?

Willow cast a glance at Charlie and was surprised to see him swaying unsteadily despite the fact that his feet weren't moving. His thin body sagged, then bobbed up like a jack-in-the-box each time he righted himself. It seemed Charlie's 'shine was hitting him with a vengeance.

Screetch! cried the bow as Charlie lost control of his instrument. The dancers came to a standstill. As they watched, a strange expression of surprise, disbelief, and loopy inebriation bloomed on Charlie's lined face. He began to fold down, accordionlike, as his body gave in to the effects of the spirits he'd so imprudently imbibed.

"Whoo-eee!" he cried, just before his head *thunked* against the floor.

"Oh, my goodness!"

"Charlie Davis, how disgraceful can you get?"

"Did you see that?"

"Is the dance over, then?"

Questions flew from every member of Willow and Daniel's square, Willow's disappointed one bringing everyone to silent contemplation.

Oliver Winfield bent over Charlie, flapping a hat before the fiddler's cherry-red bulbous nose, all the while exhorting his lead musician to remember his duty to the dancers.

But he registered no results. Charlie was down. Out cold.

"Silly old coot," complained their host. "Sorry, folks, it don't seem there's anything we can do but let the fool sleep it off." Scratching his head, Oliver scanned the disappointed faces of his guests. "There's still plenty food, though. Help yourselves."

"Can't you fiddle?" cried a young man standing near Daniel.

Oliver laughed. "I'd sound like a pair of cats at each other's throats."

Then Willow's gaze flew to Daniel, who was busy inspecting his shoe. Or maybe it was the crushed hay on the barn floor he was studying. Or who knew what he was staring at. Who cared? Willow knew precisely *why* he kept his head down.

He didn't want anyone to suspect that he played the violin.

But she knew. Willow would never forget how his music had touched her heart, her soul. She would always remember the spare gestures of his large hands as he seduced magic from his violin. Did she dare . . . ?

Her heart beat like a drum. She could easily have led an orchestra, as her pulse pounded so hard. She didn't know whether she should speak up or not. Daniel would probably treat her to his surly silence afterward, but at that moment she realized she was going to do it nonetheless.

"Mr. Winfield," she called through the hush, "would you mind if someone else took up the fiddle? That way the dancing could go on."

"Why, no, missy. I don't mind at all. If there's someone here who can play, that is."

Daniel's gaze bore into her, but Willow didn't flinch under the onslaught of those angry, warning blue eyes. Straightening her shoulders, she tipped her chin toward the corner of the barn where the musicians reigned, silently urging Daniel to volunteer.

When he shook his head, she shrugged in response, then

took steps toward their host. "There's someone here who fiddles like a master."

"Who?"

"Who is it?"

"I dunno. D'you know who?"

The chorus of curious questions rang around Willow, but she turned to stare at Daniel. Furious, he again shook his head. Again she ignored his refusal and approached him warily.

"It's Daniel," she announced. "Daniel Callaghan is a splendid musician."

"*Splendid,*" muttered the musician at her side. "Have you never learned the meanin' of the word *no*?"

"Sometimes it's best to forget it exists. This is one of those times."

"What if I don't want to play?" he shot back, fury burning in his eyes.

"You can disappoint everyone and explain why you hide such a marvelous gift. I don't understand the secrecy. You've a magnificent talent that should be shared."

"Dammit, woman, I knew you were trouble from the moment we met."

"Only for the best reasons, you must admit."

"I'll do no such thing!"

"Of course you will, after you play some songs and realize how silly your refusal is."

"How do you know 'tis silly? You don't know how I feel."

"Maybe you should tell me, then. On the way back to the Meisters' after the dance."

"Sweet Mother Mary, you're as obstinate as a mule—"

Suddenly Daniel grew silent. His cheeks turned a bright red, his forehead matching them.

An odd feeling sprang to life at the base of Willow's neck.

An army of ants seemed to march over her skin as she suddenly became aware of the ear-splitting silence. Stealing peeks around the room, she realized they'd become the center of attention. All their neighbors strained to catch the gist of the argument, their eager faces alight with curiosity.

Then Oliver Winfield cleared his throat, breaking the uncomfortable silence. "Daniel, is it true what your young lady says? Would you take up the fiddle for a while?"

From the corner of her eyes, Willow watched Daniel nibble on the end of his mustache, then run both hands through his dance-tousled hair. "I guess I could," he said as if each word were ripped from inside him. "But I'll warn you, I've never done this before. I've only played for myself and Maribeth."

"And me," Willow whispered. "Don't forget I heard you play."

"Don't see how I'll ever be able to, lass." His muttered comment came back toward her as he picked his way up to where Bernie was now tippling the crock of 'shine uncontested.

Standing next to the paunchy harmonica player, Daniel took up the fiddle and bow, nestled them on his shoulder, and tentatively put one to the other. A pure, golden note swelled from his hands, vibrating in the still-silent space of the barn.

Then his blue eyes sought Willow, and she felt his scrutiny in the deepest recesses of her soul. He captured her gaze, and only when he seemed certain of holding her attention did the bewildering Irishman begin to play.

A waltz. That blasted brute was playing the very same waltz Charlie had earlier played, his eyes boring into hers. Nothing could have made her break the visual contact between them, it felt so strong, so vibrant, so alive.

When that piece came to an end, Daniel launched into a

lively Irish jig. Appreciative listeners broke into clapping, many willing to improvise steps to the sprightly tune. Still, his eyes held Willow's, and their touch seemed more intimate even than when his thumb had rubbed her palm, her lips.

So he went on, playing brilliantly, providing the music the revelers demanded. Finally, after one last run through "Turkey in the Straw," since Oliver was losing his voice from so much calling, Daniel paused before starting another piece. Staring at Willow, he gave her an enigmatic smile before bringing the bow back down to the violin strings.

In that seconds-long pause, everyone in the barn followed the path of his gaze. Eyes widened when they noticed how he held Willow in thrall. Whispers sprouted, and Willow registered them only at the edge of her thoughts. Her mind, her heart, her soul could only consider the essence of Daniel Callaghan at that exhilarating moment.

Then the soft, wistful notes of an Irish folk song filled the silent void. It was one of the songs he'd played for Maribeth, the piece that had brought tears of wonder to Willow's eyes. It was the tune she'd heard Mr. Meister at times call "The Londonderry Air," and at others he'd dubbed it "Danny Boy."

Willow knew that for the rest of her life that song would bring back to her the moments of magic she'd known thanks to the gifted Irishman, the very Danny Boy who'd grown into a tantalizing, mesmerizing man.

The man she loved.

15

As THE FINAL notes of "Danny Boy" escaped into the night, Willow remained where she'd been standing, mesmerized by the beauty of Daniel's gift. To think those sturdy, farming hands could take an instrument and wring from it sounds worthy of angels. To think those hands had held Missy's head, coaxed her to drink, and helped keep her from certain death. To think only moments before taking up the violin, those hands had held hers.

She smiled at him, a private smile that carried the depth of her admiration and, she was sure, betrayed the magnitude of her feelings for him. But she didn't care. At that moment she would have confessed her love. What kept her from doing so was the very public nature of the gathering, the number of others who were also intent on admiring a certain, talented Irishman.

He smiled back, a smile with so much tenderness, her heart ached. A smile so laden with promise, that her pulse sped up. A smile with just the right dose of spice for her to experience again that forbidden tingle Daniel inspired at private moments—as during a kiss, a caress of her hands, her lips.

As she watched, Daniel set down the violin on a bale of hay at his side. Then he turned, winked mischievously, and took a step toward her. That was when the spell he'd cast over the barn broke. Murmurs caught fire, and soon the sound of many conversations created a pleasant din.

The newly mobilized guests, however, pinned Daniel where he stood. A crowd formed around him, and from what Willow could tell, the individuals tried to outdo each other praising his musical genius. She settled back to await his return.

But as the minutes crawled by, Willow noticed a change taking place in the group around her escort. Whereas initially the throng had contained a fair number of men, as time went on, they walked away, going for more pie or cider or just to gather their companions and head home. The thinning cluster now comprised only women. Tall ones, short ones, slender ones, well-upholstered ones, too. As she watched, Willow became aware that the women weren't merely praising Daniel for the wonderful music he'd provided. They were vying for his attention.

Willow considered her situation. Daniel had been tricked—albeit innocently—by Oliver into inviting her to the barn dance. Even when he'd picked her up at the Meisters' home, he hadn't displayed any measurable enthusiasm for her company. Now, when he was able to choose a favorite from the assortment of ladies before him, he was stuck having to take her home.

The last thing Willow wanted was to become a chore to the handsome Irishman. Despite those seemingly intimate, flirtatious moments of the past few hours, Willow couldn't see where he would want to return to the side of the woman he'd been burdened with earlier that day.

As Willow watched, a dainty, curly haired blonde laughed at something Daniel said, then clasped his arm in both her hands, the gesture patently possessive. Daniel smiled back.

He never made a move to separate himself, he didn't even glance toward Willow.

Willow remembered the elegant widow who'd claimed Daniel's attention the night of the storm. The girl with Daniel looked like a younger version of that practiced coquette.

The smile Daniel gave the blonde made up Willow's mind. As she'd suspected all along, he was too far out of her reach. She should never have allowed him near enough to capture her interest, much less her heart. After all, he was a man who'd pursued the gloss of Philadelphia, the sophistication of that great city. The pretty girl at his side looked more the type Daniel would seek than Willow ever would. Or could.

Willow was a farmer. She'd always be one, and she would never aspire to the level of polish Daniel seemed to look for in his companions. He seemed drawn to a veneer of glamour, a certain shallow sparkle that covered up an internal void. He obviously lacked the depth of character she wanted in a man. It was best if she tore herself away from his influence, went back to the life she knew had meaning for her.

Besides, he ate sheep.

Silently she ducked out of the barn and began the long trek back to town. York seemed an eternity away in the nippy autumn night. Willow didn't care. The cold would likely slap some sense into her, would serve to remind her how badly Milford and his love for the money, the glamour of Philadelphia, had hurt her. She should never have allowed Daniel's appeal to seduce her. She should have remembered his years away from York.

As gifted as he was, as much as he loved Maribeth, as hardworking a farmer as he was, Willow should have remembered the successful Philadelphia businessman who hid behind the York Countian's facade.

Daniel Callaghan would never be the man for her. No matter how much she loved him.

Hot, tired, and thirsty, Daniel tolerated the congratulatory group that gathered round him when he put Charlie Davis's violin back down. With a touch of concern, he glanced at the snoring old coot and noticed the smile on the man's thin lips. Most likely Oliver would let Charlie sleep off the effects of the 'shine in this corner of the barn.

When he glanced at Willow, however, his entire mood changed. Damnblast the woman! She'd disappeared. Grinding his teeth, he managed to say, "If you'll excuse me, there's someone I need to find."

As easily as a dog sheds its winter coat in spring, Daniel left behind his disappointed public. At the moment the only thing on his mind was Willow. "An' I'll be damned if I don't find that maddenin', irritatin', bewitchin', aggravatin' shepherdess of mine," he muttered.

He was finally willing to admit how he felt about the exasperating Willow Stimson. She *was* his, by all that's holy! He knew damn well how she felt. Those delightfully expressive eyes of hers had revealed her newly discovered desire. She wanted him. As much as he wanted her.

But God only knew where in hell she'd taken off to and why.

After asking if either Oliver or his missus had seen Willow, Daniel requested and obtained the use of one of the Winfield farm horses. With a short farewell, he set out after his lady. If she'd decided to walk back to the Meisters', he'd catch up to her on the road.

Unwilling to yield to the fear that was growing in his heart, Daniel rode toward town. What if she hadn't just up and left? What if something had happened to her? Not that Daniel suspected any of the guests at the barn dance of harboring malevolent intentions, but a stranger on the road was a different matter altogether. Some crazy could have seen her, caught her, done any of many hideous—

"No."

He wouldn't let fear cloud his mind. The only thought he could entertain was his need to find Willow. Oh, yes, and demand to know why she'd abandoned him to the gaggle of giggling geese that had cornered him. The least she could have done was rescue him from those silly chits.

He'd wanted her to come and demonstrate her feelings for him. She was such an independent sort that Daniel feared she didn't need him for anything. But he needed her. Not just to help him with Maribeth, although Willow had already proved herself far more adept with the child than he was. He needed her to keep him alert, excited, on his toes at all times. He needed to spar with her, to dance with her, to laugh with her. He needed to hold her, to kiss her, to love her.

He loved Willow Stimson. "I love Willow Stimson," he repeated, this time out loud to the darkened, deserted road. Only the stars twinkled in response.

If he hadn't fallen in love with her before then, he'd certainly done so when she'd snagged that brass ring, no matter how irrational her superstitions about the metal circle were. No matter how worried he was about the influence her more fey qualities could have on Maribeth. No matter how much Willow reminded Daniel of his fascinating, fanciful, eccentric mother, who'd always kept her head in the clouds instead of on the family farm. The mother who had taught him to dream silly dreams, when they both should have been helping his sorely overworked da.

Then he remembered what Mrs. Meister said when they

met. She believed Maeve's stories had provided a respite for Darby from his work. She also seemed to feel that unless his mother captured his father's attention with her tales, his father would have labored round the clock. Could that possibly be true? Had Maeve provided valuable help in her own singular way to Darby? Daniel had never thought of it that way.

Even if she had, that didn't change the effect of her stories in Daniel's life. But knowing didn't seem to make much difference. Just as he had adored his mother, who could never have known that her stories had fueled her son's fantasies to leave the farm someday, hungry for high-sea adventures and dragon slaying of all sorts, he found himself feeling forbidden emotions for another unique, whimsical woman.

There was absolutely no logic to it. He just loved Willow.

What had finally toppled him over the edge into love was the neverending vibrancy of the woman, the enthusiasm with which she pursued her goals. She hadn't yet learned to let common sense or reality temper her excitement, as Daniel had.

Or at least, as he'd *thought* he had. His feelings for Willow certainly threw doubt on his supposedly wise judgment, his diligently pursued logic, his highly esteemed reason. Although that should have scared him witless, if not served to dampen his ardor, Daniel knew he was going to throw caution to the wind. He was going to explore his feelings for Willow and hers for him. He'd worry about the problems later, once he knew how deeply involved they were likely to become.

Now, where the hell was she?

Pulling up before the Meisters' elegant home, Daniel sought to calm his racing heart. He'd seen no sign of her on the road to York. He only hoped she'd somehow learned to fly and beat the Winfields' horse into town.

"Why, Daniel!" exclaimed Mrs. Meister as she opened the front door. "What are you doing here?"

"Where is she?" he asked, following the robed-and-slippered woman inside.

"She's upstairs in bed. Where else would she be?"

"An' how did she do that? I only just got here, an' I rode a horse!"

Bewilderment crinkled Mrs. Meister's broad forehead. "Daniel Callaghan! Have you been drinking? You're making absolutely no sense."

"You're right, dear lady. I've lost what common sense I ever had. 'Tis all because of *her*."

"How can you say that? She's just the sweetest thing!"

"Sweet as a dill pickle, you mean!"

"That child is certainly *not* a sour pickle. You'd best watch what you say about her in my presence."

Daniel frowned. Something was wrong here. Could this woman actually not know how tart-tongued Willow could get? Was Mrs. Meister blinded by her obvious love for the maddening shepherdess? God knew it was possible. He himself was willing to overlook her many faults. He just wanted to know why she'd left him behind in the barn. "Then the best thing is to call her down."

"I'll do no such thing," announced Mrs. Meister, tightening the knot at the waist of her navy blue robe. "Children need their sleep."

"Ch—children?"

"Of course, Daniel, she's not likely to be tractable if she's tired all the time. Have you kept her to a regular schedule? If she hasn't been sleeping well, and with all the grief she's carrying she can't be expected to think things through. It's no wonder she's run away from you!"

"Regular schedule . . . ? Mrs. Meister, madam, are you speakin' about Willow, or my niece, Maribeth?"

"Why, Maribeth, of course! What made you think I was referring to Willow?"

"Because 'tis Willow I came for."

"But she's with *you*!"

"No, she *was* with me. Then she . . . disappeared. She's the most aggravatin', infuriatin', flummoxin' creature on God's green earth!"

"She's not here." Worry carved parallel furrows between Mrs. Meister's silver eyebrows. "Where could she have gone—"

"The fairgrounds!" both cried in unison.

"'Course, an' I should have thought of it. She's likely gone to her sick ewe!"

"Dr. Wirtz took Missy home with him this afternoon. He was amazed by her rally and wanted to watch her for the next few days. Willow wouldn't have gone to his place. I think, son, you'll find her at her spinning wheel."

Then Mrs. Meister's eyes narrowed. She scoured Daniel's face with her piercing gray gaze. He squirmed under her scrutiny.

"You didn't *do* anything . . . offensive to her, did you?"

"Hell, an' of course I didn't!" he cried in outrage. "I danced with her, I gave her cider, I played my heart out for her on Charlie Davis's fiddle. What more could she ask for?"

"The words, Daniel. The ones you've been keeping to yourself." With a gentle shove and an understanding smile, Mrs. Meister showed Daniel out. "Go find her. Talk to her. I'm sure she's ready to listen."

"Can't go bein' too sure about that. Not with Willow, one can't," he muttered as he stepped out onto the porch. "Good night, Mrs. Meister. 'Tis sorry I am for wakin' you. I certainly hope you're right about Willow."

Her "Me, too" followed him down to where he'd left the horse. With an easy swing, he mounted and turned the animal around toward the fairgrounds.

It took some talking to persuade the night watchman that he was an exhibitor and had the right to check on his animals, even this late at night. Through the long moments of arguing his point, all Daniel could think of was how long Willow had been alone. Without protection. He prayed she was unharmed. Since many of his adult prayers had gone unanswered, however, he held little faith this one would have different results.

Finally the stocky policeman allowed Daniel to tie the horse near the gate and proceed to the Sheep Building.

The moment he stepped inside the arched entranceway, he spotted the smoky glow of a kerosene lantern above Missy's stall. Willow was there. Her beautifully coifed hair had escaped its bounds during her flight and cascaded around her shoulders, reflecting the golden glow of the lantern.

Mrs. Meister had been right. The swaying motion of Willow's shoulders suggested that she was working, and since Daniel remembered seeing the old spinning wheel in a corner of the stall, he was certain she was making yarn.

He remembered the first time he'd seen her so employed, spinning yarn from ethereal puffs of fleece. He'd been surprised. Spinning was an old craft, and Daniel hadn't seen a spinning wheel in years. Most modern women bought ready-made goods. Few seemed wont to expend the hours needed to make sturdy thread, much less to knit or weave it into cloth.

But Willow did. And the fiddler in Daniel understood. Moments later he gathered up Maeve's old violin and,

settling it under his chin, approached Willow. Drawing the
bow across the strings, he sent their pure notes to the woman
in the light, speaking to her with his fiddle's voice. Rich and
evocative, the music twined around them, drawing him
closer to her side.

Then she lifted her head, eyes wide with surprise. Daniel
spied the tears on her cheeks.

His hand faltered as he drew the bow back over his violin.
Had she been hurt after all? Had someone accosted her? He
continued playing, knowing the balmlike qualities of his
music would help soothe whatever hurt she'd sustained.
And he continued walking.

The closer he came, the more he saw. She looked none
the worse for the wear, except for her tumbled hair and
tear-stained cheeks. But something had upset her; that was
clearly the case. Daniel would find out exactly what had
caused her pain. But first he had to dry those tears and bring
a smile to her berry-sweet lips as she continued to ply the
old spinning wheel.

When the piece came to an end, he began to play the
lovely waltz they'd danced to earlier that night. Something
powerful flashed between them. Daniel played on.

Partway through the waltz, he noticed that the tears no
longer fell, and he knew how to bring that dreamy soft smile
back to her lips. As soon as he finished playing the waltz, he
opened the gate to Missy's stall, smiled, and launched into
"Danny Boy."

As the lush, sentimental notes rose from his hands, Daniel
came close enough to hear the sound of the spinning wheel.
Its murmur blended with the violin's song, filling the air
with sweetness and magic. As the song soared, Willow's
hands went still. She clasped them loosely in her lap, her
attention on him. Daniel felt the touch of her gaze as if it had
been her very hand on his flesh. A tremor shook him, and he

found himself staring at her lips. Waiting was hell, torture. But he knew that to claim a kiss he had to give her time to compose herself, to desire his touch as much as he wanted hers.

As Daniel played, Willow felt her love for him fly skyward with his music, every second making her more aware of her feelings for him. Why was he here? Why had he followed her? Could it be he *hadn't* felt obligated, wanting instead to be with her as much as she wanted to be with him?

Slowly she allowed herself a smile in response to his. Where hers was a tentative curve, his was broad, his eyes shining with a sensual glow. Willow remembered their kiss. Heat filled her again, just as his caress had done. She longed for another of Daniel's kisses.

She was fast becoming familiar with "The Londonderry Air." As he came to the end of the song, she stood. He'd come this far after her, so it was only fair for her to meet him halfway.

He stepped closer, and she responded, coming closer still. With a clarity that rang through the cool night air, he played the last notes of the piece, then laid the violin and its bow on the bale of hay where she'd sat only moments ago. "Willow . . ."

Emotion pooled in her throat, and she found herself unable to answer. She simply nodded and smiled again. His hand came out and slipped a thick lock of hair behind her ear. The feel of his warm finger on her earlobe made her tremble, wanting more, much more than just that fleeting touch. She wanted him to hold her in his arms, to kiss her as he had that other night, to prove to her that the memories she held were real, that his kiss had brought to life all this wanting, this passion inside her.

As if he'd heard her silent wishes, his palms cupped her

jawline, and his thumbs rubbed her lips. Willow's eyes closed, and her lips parted. She felt the tickle of his beard, the warmth of his breath, the whisper-soft brush of his mouth against hers. His kiss was as magical as she'd remembered, only more so.

Daniel rubbed her lips with his, the crinkly texture of his mustache pleasing in a very sensual way. Willow felt a flush sweep up from her heart to her cheeks. The heat of his mouth was contagious, and she sighed, wanting more.

He complied. Molding his mouth fully to hers, Daniel pressed her lips open, and Willow felt the tip of his tongue seeking entrance. A tremor shook her, and she opened her lips wider, thrilled at the intimacy of their kiss. He explored the secrets of her mouth, teaching Willow how to kiss him in turn. Which she did, wanting to return the pleasure he generously gave.

A moan tore from Daniel's throat, and he deepened their kiss. It turned wild, demanding, intoxicating, and hot. Willow was stunned by the rushing sensations it stirred within her. Her knees went weak, her hands clung to his shoulders, and her lips returned his passion in kind.

With a gasp, Daniel tore his mouth from hers. He pressed his forehead to hers, and Willow felt the strong *thump-thump* of his heart against her breast. She drew in a trembling breath and ran her tongue over her tingling lips. He groaned, and when she met his gaze, she realized he'd been looking at her mouth. She had no doubt he'd liked that kiss. It hadn't been given out of duty, nor had he been tricked into the caress. This kiss, like their other one, had come spontaneously, catching both of them up in its power, its heat.

"Why?" he asked.

"Wh-why what?"

"Why did you leave without me?"

"Oh!" Willow pulled away an inch or two, then just enough to see his need to know reflected in his beautiful blue eyes. "I felt out of place. There were a lot of other women there, and since I knew you'd been put on the spot earlier and had brought me to the dance most reluctantly, I felt it was best if I left you to find a partner of your choice."

"Nay, lassie, 'twasn't reluctance you saw. I had . . . something else on my mind. There was no other woman I wanted to be with. I thought I'd made that perfectly clear."

Willow pulled away and returned to her hay bale. She ran her fingers over Daniel's violin. "Thank you for the music."

"Which music? What I played at the barn or what I played here?"

"Both, I guess."

"You're very welcome, since 'twas for you I played both times."

"Oh!"

"Yes, oh! Then you ran out on me, you did."

Willow lifted one shoulder. "I'm sorry. But I'm glad you came."

"So you're glad I came. Is there a chance I could sit with you for a while? Or is that bale only for one?"

She finally gave in to the giddy feeling that had bubbled inside her since she'd noticed his presence. She laughed and stood. "Here, I can do better than that. The hay on the ground is fresh. I spread it right before Dr. Wirtz came and took Missy home with him." Gathering her two quilts from the corner where she'd folded them earlier, she spread one over the dried grasses. "We can sit in comfort. Of sorts."

"The most elegant of furnishings, indeed."

Cold as it had become, Willow opened the other quilt and spread it over her legs once she'd sat down. Daniel joined her, then asked, "Might I share the top one, too?"

"Of course."

Both got comfortable and sat silently for a moment. Then, "Tell me again, lass. What was it that made you run? I can't believe you still worried about my supposed reluctance. Not after we'd danced and talked and shared that cider. Not to mention the music I played for you."

Willow felt her cheeks heating again. "Why don't we just drop this?"

"Because I really want to know. I don't want to lose you again."

His words resonated in her heart, but she warned herself not to read more into them than their face value. But how was she to confess her jealousy? Especially of the very bold, beautiful, and polished-looking blond girl? As full of himself as Daniel Callaghan was, she didn't want to give him any more reason to strut.

"Ah . . . well, you looked . . . busy. There was a crowd around you. Seeing as I thought you'd brought me against your wishes . . . I figured I'd let you enjoy your musical success. Then, once I left, you'd be free to choose your companion for the rest of the time."

"That makes no damn sense, woman! Everyone was about to leave. Why would you think I'd be wantin' to choose a partner at that late date? Especially since I'd brought you in the first place."

He wasn't going to let her off gracefully. Fine! He wanted to know? She'd tell him. "If you must know, you blasted strutting lady-killer, it was that silly, corkscrew-headed twit hanging on your arm. And you, lapping up her attention as if you were a tomcat, and she a bowl of cream!"

For a moment Daniel looked stunned. Then he burst out laughing.

"You . . . horrid beast, you! How dare you laugh?"

As she went to stand, a warm paw clamped around her

forearm, preventing her escape. "Sit, lass. Neither of us is going anywhere until we settle this."

"There's nothing to settle. You're just the biggest, rudest brute—"

Daniel shut her up the only way he knew how. With his mouth, with his passion, and with his love. She'd been jealous! Thank the Saints and the Angels, she cared enough to feel jealous of the women who'd surrounded him, even though he'd hardly paid attention to any of them. His behavior had actually bordered on rude. All because he'd wanted to hold this hellcat in his arms, kiss her as deeply and as long as he was finally doing now.

At first she struggled, but when he parted her lips with his tongue, she trembled and allowed him in. Her arms soon curled around his neck and her fingers burrowed into the hair at the nape of his neck. She loved him. He knew she loved him. She knew it, too. But damned if the ornery creature wasn't going to make every step of their growing relationship as difficult as she possibly could!

Secretly Daniel hoped she never quit challenging him, tempting him, driving him wild with her quick wit, her passion, the desire he tasted on her sweet, soft lips.

A whimper rolled into his mouth, and his heartbeat kicked up again. Willow was warm and fluid in his arms, a living flame against his body. He felt her breasts against his chest, her thighs against his. Running his hands down her sides, he curved his hand over her hip, the fullness of her bottom leading him farther in his exploration. She was firm, and strong, and her honest passion burned its way straight to his heart.

On its trip back up, his hand paused at her ribs, and Daniel wondered if she'd break their kiss when he sought more secrets still. Then her tongue engaged his in a duel, and passion took over his thoughts. He cupped her breast, her nipple budding against his palm. She was so responsive . . . Daniel nearly lost what little control he retained. But he caught himself before tearing at her clothes, seeking those secrets she still held.

Needing air, Daniel tore his mouth away from hers. He glanced at his hand, filled with her bounty, and the attendant reaction in his trousers made him wince. It was getting uncomfortable inside his clothes.

Another glance showed her eyes, slumberous with passion, her lips, red and swollen from his, her breathing ragged, as labored as his. He also found a series of buttons running from the bottom of the lace V of her bodice to the tight waist of her dress. Seconds later, he'd unfastened the first pearl.

The others followed suit, and his lips traced the curve of Willow's jaw. He kissed his way down her neck, all the while opening the last button on her dress. Only when he'd parted the lace lapels did he look up. He beheld the treasures he'd uncovered.

Her breasts were full, round, and displayed her arousal in the tightened deep rose tips. They peaked against a sheer white chemise, more revealing than obscuring, a temptation of the most delicious sort. Daniel caught the end of a slender satin ribbon bow between his teeth and with a firm tug opened the dainty undergarment. Then, at his leisure, he gazed on her beauty as his need for her grew.

He came closer to her flesh and blew gently across a taut crest. Willow stretched sinuously, like a contented cat, raising her breasts closer to Daniel's mouth. He remembered that she'd called him a cat, one who'd lapped at cream. He felt fortunate, since this feast before him would satisfy more than the cream ever would have.

With a gentle stroke of his tongue, he tasted Willow's skin. She was sweet, an herbal scent rising from the cleft between her breasts. The flavors of her filled his mouth, intoxicating him more than any drink. It's no wonder he'd lost all common sense after meeting her. She was magic, a woodland sprite, a faery who'd cast a spell on him. A spell he wasn't ready to break.

His fingers shook, betraying his need. Despite the rare weakness, he found his way beneath her skirts. A froth of lace kept him from her silky skin, and he quickly found ties to pull, garments to remove.

Under the cover of her quilt, Daniel never paused to think she might want him to stop. He prayed she didn't, because he feared his willpower was lessening. He doubted he could retreat, since his body and his heart urged him to claim the woman he loved.

Then she was bare. Completely bare. Her golden-brown eyes showed her passion, her curiosity, and a slight hint of fear. But he was afraid as well. This was something new for him, too. He'd never made love to the woman he loved. Not before tonight. He'd had wonderful encounters with ladies he'd known and liked well enough, but Daniel had never been in love before. The strength and depth of his feelings awed him. "I love you, Willow."

She gasped, her eyes widening. Tears gathered on her lashes. "I . . . I love you, too, Daniel," she whispered.

"You what?" He wanted to make damn sure he'd heard what he thought she'd said. She was, after all, Willow Stimson. *His* stubborn, maddening, flummoxing Willow Stimson.

She smiled and cupped her hand around his bearded jaw. He felt her thumb test the hair on his face, and noticed how much wider her smile grew. "I love you," she repeated, this time in a clear, strong voice.

"I thought that's what you said . . ." He resumed his explorations, his hand running from a slender shoulder, over a full breast, past a narrow waist, a curved hip, and down to a silky smooth leg. Willow pressed her body closer to his and, to his surprise, began to work at the buttons on his shirt. He let her follow her bold impulse, thrilled to see her boldness equal his own. They were perfectly matched, and if these delicious caresses were anything to go by, they were about to soar higher than Paradise. He recognized this as a turning point in his life. Once he'd made love to Willow, there'd be no going back. He'd give his heart, his soul, his life to her with the intimacy they were about to share.

Her clever hands stripped him of his clothes, and he clasped her closer to him. A fragmented sigh escaped her lips and then a gasp when she felt his arousal against her skin. She flushed and refused to meet his eyes. "Oh, no, lass. Don't tell me you're going to kill me now."

That made her look up fast. "Kill you?"

"You're about to stop me, aren't you?"

"Stop you? Why would I do that? Especially since I finally got your clothes off."

Daniel chuckled in relief. "Well, when you wouldn't look at me anymore, I was afraid you'd changed your mind. . . ."

"I didn't want to appear unseemly eager—"

"Be as eager as you want, love," he whispered against her lips and resumed the kisses that had lit the fire in them. Their caresses heated up. Their kisses went on and on. Willow undulated against Daniel, stoking his ardor hotter and higher still.

She moaned. "Please . . ."

He wouldn't make her beg. He parted her thighs with his knees, found the welcoming cradle of her hips. With another deep kiss, he found his way to heaven, his very own heaven on earth. Her cry of surprise flew into his mouth as he went deep indeed, and Daniel knew this was right—this was the love, the woman, the very moment life had held in store for him, only for him.

With long, deep strokes he made love to Willow, relishing the soft sounds she made, her breathless wonder, her instinctive responses that nudged them both higher and higher, until she reached the crest.

She cried out, and the intimate clasp of her climax hurled Daniel over the edge to ecstasy. They were one.

16

*T*HE SOFT CORAL tones of dawn painted the eastern sky, and its fresh light swept the dregs of night away. That blushing light reached inside the Sheep Building and alerted Willow of morning's approach. All at once she remembered why she was here instead of at the Meisters' home, she remembered who she was with, and what she'd done with him.

She even remembered confessing her love for Daniel— after he'd confessed his for her. She couldn't even credit her memories to a dream or fantasy. Not even impending lunacy. Proof of her sanity abounded, since her lips felt puffy, her chin and cheeks still stung from the friction of Daniel's beard, her body was tired in places she'd never known could get that way, and there was no ignoring the mild soreness between her legs. Daniel had made love to her, and she'd participated fully, returning caress for caress, kiss for kiss.

Would he remember his avowal of love today? Or would he go back to being the swelled-headed tomcat, more certain than ever of his appeal to the opposite sex?

The cat emitted a muffled groan by her ear. Then the springy mat of his beard stroked her neck, and Willow arched instinctively, giving him greater access still. Although this was the worst possible position to be found in, a deep, spontaneously feminine part of her didn't want the loving to stop, didn't want the night to end. Even though it had.

When the dampness of Daniel's tongue reached her earlobe, sending frissons of feelings through her body, she relived the wonder of their passion. But this wasn't the time to resume where they'd left off. They were in a public place, a place that would soon be crawling with fair attendees, judges, exhibitors; any of a number of friends and strangers would be passing close to the open stall where they lay.

Willow rolled over and, inspired by her boldness of the night before, reached up and kissed Daniel gently on the lips. A deep rumble in his chest told her how well he liked her daring. She smiled and kissed him again.

As he deepened the kiss, Willow had to fight to retain control of her wits. Every part of her longed to melt into that caress, to wrap herself in his warm strength, to again seek the pleasure he'd shown her in the night. But common sense prevailed. This wasn't the time. Or the place.

Pulling back, she found it nearly impossible to break contact with the hungry lips that followed her, and she laughed from the joy of knowing herself desired. Loved.

What luxury! Daniel Callaghan loved her.

Planting a final smacking kiss on his lips, she shook her head. "No more, Daniel. Not now. It's morning already and the animals sound restless. Everyone's about to get here, and you and I aren't exactly dressed for it."

He groaned in protest, but soon his enormous shoulders were shaking with mirth. The blue eyes she so loved opened, a twinkle of mischief dancing in their depths. "Aye, lass. Can you imagine the scandal?"

"Only too well, Daniel Callaghan. And you once said you wouldn't lead me astray."

"I never said such a thing! I merely said I hadn't done so *yet*. See? Now that you gave me the chance, I have you exactly where I've been wantin' you."

He waggled his brows in mock threat, and Willow laughed so hard tears pooled in her eyes. He went on. "Well, I sort of have you where I want you, lass. I'd rather it be someplace less public, as you said. But I'm not proud. I'll take you as I can have you."

"Get off me, you . . . you cock of the walk, you! I knew you'd be trouble the moment I laid eyes on you that first morning of the fair."

"Goes both ways. You've turned me on my ear, you have."

"Good. At least we're both in the same boat."

"But you're right, you know—"

"Could I have that in writing?"

"What?"

"You admitted I was right, at least once, and under no duress."

He planted a smart tap on her bottom. "Get up with you, Willow Stimson, or you'll cause the greatest scandal on this planet, never mind the fair!"

Willow scrambled up, keeping her corner of the quilt clutched to her breasts. "Ooops!" she cried. "I guess I'd best stay down while I get dressed. I'm afraid I've reached the extremes of my daring." She felt self-conscious of her naked state before him, and knelt back down at his side. The cloak of darkness had provided some cover the night before, and she missed it in the raw light of day.

Which was ridiculous, as he'd mapped her entire body with those large, warm hands of his. There was little he could have missed seeing, even by the smoky lantern light. She knew she'd seen her fair share.

Her cheeks warmed at the distinct image that formed in

her mind. She hadn't found anything to dislike last night. And she'd made it quite clear to the man at her side. The huge man who suddenly stood, naked as the day he was born, and calmly shook out his denim trousers.

"For heaven's sake, Daniel! You're naked!"

Another chuckle set those shoulders shaking again. "Only way I know how to do what we were doin' last night—"

"Hush! You're as reprehensible as that ram of yours. And as randy, I might add."

"Any complaints?"

"Oh—you beast!" Willow grabbed his blue shirt, wadded it in her hands, then threw it at his face. "Go! Get away before I tell you a thing or two."

He caught the shirt in one hand, and with the other, he smoothed her tangled hair. "Seems to me you told me plenty last night."

"Too much, perhaps."

"Nay, lass. Those were important words, and we both said them."

She nodded, his hand cupping her jaw. "I meant them," she whispered, unable to meet his piercing gaze.

"As did I." Throwing the shirt over one shoulder, he slipped his other arm around her. With gentle pressure, he brought her to his side. "I love you, Willow. Don't know how or why, but, by God I love you, lass. Last night . . . last night was magic."

"Magic," she said in complete accord. "But today is here, and we should get ready for the ribbon presentation. I need to change, feed the animals . . ."

"Go," he whispered, then tenderly kissed her nose, her cheeks, her chin. Finally, with a softness that brought tears of joy to Willow's eyes, his lips captured hers and wrote his love for her on her flesh.

When he pulled away, she whispered, "I love you, too."

Then she covered her tingling lips with her fingers, as if to seal his kiss upon them.

As Daniel walked off, Willow speculated on what today might bring. Surely something wonderful was likely to happen. Miracles like last night's didn't happen in vain.

She wondered what would occur when she and Daniel met again.

At eight o'clock sharp Willow and her sheep, minus Missy of course, were at their places in the exhibition arena. The Fritzmeier twins were busy with her rams, and she had plenty to do with her two-year-old ewes. Casting a quick look around, she saw Daniel approaching, the leather lead he held pulled tight. Without even seeing the beast, Willow knew it was Lugh at the end of that leash.

Approaching the display blocks, he paused, searched through the gathered crowd, then smiled intimately when he caught her gaze. She smiled back, thrilled that the closeness established last night seemed likely to continue. Maybe there was hope for them. Maybe she could begin to dream of a future. Maybe love had finally found her.

Silence blanketed the crowd when Otis Hillenbaugh and his assistant judges stepped inside the exhibition circle. Tension gathered, and Willow's heart began to pound. Yesterday, when he came and decided to take Missy to his clinic, Dr. Wirtz had assured Willow that he'd already spoken to the head sheep judge about the ewe's sudden illness. Mr. Hillenbaugh hadn't disqualified Missy, so for all intents and purposes, Willow's ewe was still in the running for the Best of Show ribbon.

Her fingers, cold and clammy, clenched around the tethers attached to Daisy and Rosebud. An erratically bouncing ball had taken residence where her stomach had once lived, and its volleys were making her queasy. She didn't do well when her nerves were stretched to their limits.

In a ponderous voice Mr. Hillenbaugh welcomed all to the final event of the fair. At least, it was the last for the sheep. Although everyone knew that the decision had been made at a meeting between the judges last night, the four somber men took a silent but studious final look at the entrants. A violin string would have snapped had it been pulled as tight as the air in the arena.

Finally, nodding in satisfaction, Otis Hillenbaugh came back to the center of the ring and cleared his throat. Clamping reading spectacles on the bridge of his patrician nose, he unrolled a parchment with winners' names on it.

"In the category of two year-old-rams, the Best of Show ribbon and the five dollar cash award go to . . . Daniel Callaghan, of Callaghan's Dairy! Second place goes to . . . Miss Willow Stimson!"

Half of Willow felt pride in Daniel's accomplishment; her other side was knocked down a peg. Still, she hadn't hoped to win all the prizes, she'd only been certain of Missy's chances. So she smiled at Daniel as he collected his winnings.

The head sheep judge then took up another rolled parchment, cleared his throat, and ceremoniously unfurled the page. "In the category of four-year-old rams, the Best of Show ribbon and the five dollar cash award go to . . . Daniel Callaghan, of Callaghan's Dairy! Ladies and gentlemen, if you haven't had the opportunity to see this animal, allow me to encourage you to do so after the ceremony. Lugh is the finest example of adult male sheep I have ever seen."

Enthusiastic clapping rolled through the crowd, enhancing the excitement of the moment. Willow could easily smile at this win. She didn't even have a four-year-old ram entered in the competition. Besides, the moment she'd set eyes on the libidinous Lugh, she'd known she was seeing the ribbon winner in his category. Lugh was a master specimen indeed.

As he collected his ribbon and his money, Daniel turned to Willow and tipped his mustache in a wicked smile. Then he winked. At her! Before an enormous crowd, even. Although she tried her best to send him a glare, the best she managed was a widening smile and, she suspected, a besotted look. Lord, what that rogue could do to her with just one touch of those blazing blue eyes!

"Harrumph!"

At the sudden sound Willow glanced at Otis Hillenbaugh, and blushed to the roots of her hair. The head judge had missed none of the visual exchange between her and Daniel. He hadn't been impressed. In fact, he wore that same pruned look he'd worn when Lugh had lunged at Missy.

Was last night's intimacy that glaringly obvious? Did mere looks betray all their secrets? Oh, dear. Daniel Callaghan was far more dangerous than she'd ever suspected.

Another flapping of stiff paper caught her attention, bringing it back to the matter at hand. The two-year-old ewes were next. Her three ewes, Missy in particular, stood an excellent chance of winning.

"In the category of two-year-old ewes, a most difficult choice this year. The ribbon goes to . . . Daniel Callaghan, of Callaghan's Dairy, for Brigid, a nearly perfect natural black ewe. Second place goes to . . . Miss Willow Stimson, for her beautiful white Missy."

Mr. Hillenbaugh could as easily have slugged her in the gut. Willow's head spun. Her knees weakened. Her blood chilled, rushing from her head, her face, her limbs. She began to teeter and feared she was about to faint.

But she couldn't. Not yet. Not now, while so many people were watching. Especially that Irish devil himself.

With strength she'd never known she possessed, Willow gulped in air, once, twice, thrice—she did so until she felt reasonably sure she wasn't about to lose consciousness. Then she stepped forward into the arena and accepted her ribbon and the cash that came with the second place. She even managed a weak "Thank you" for the judge. It wasn't his fault he was nearly blind and abysmally biased in his surrogate nephew's favor. It was all that Irish devil's doing.

And she'd played right into his crafty hands.

With a sidewise glance she noticed him trying to capture her attention. Concern looked good when adopted with such practised ease. But she knew better. In fact, she began to wonder if he hadn't done something to make Missy fall ill in the first place.

He'd been so determined to win. So sure of his success.

Narrowing her eyes, she sent a venomous glower his way and knew pride when his jaw flapped open, leaving him looking like a hairy catfish dangling from a hook at the end of a fishing line.

Tears, unbidden and unwelcome, stung her eyelids, and since all her hopes had just been cut off at the knees, she tipped her chin upward, squared her shoulders, and with all the dignity she could call up, she led her animals away from the scene of her Waterloo.

It wasn't time to dissect what had happened. It wasn't time yet to reconsider her situation. It was merely time to recognize the ache in her heart, admit the sense of betrayal she felt, and determine never to look into dazzling blue eyes again.

Fighting back her tears, Willow entered the Sheep Building behind the Fritzmeier twins.

"So sorry choo didn't vin, Miss Stimson," said Lucas.

"But choo didn't all lose," offered Matthew. "Choo second place von."

"Second place. Where does that leave me, boys?"

Lucas scratched his head. Then he grinned. "Mit a ribbon-vinning flock of sheep!"

Willow squeezed out a sickly smile. It wasn't their fault she'd gone up against the maleficent musician. She'd been outclassed, outdone, out . . . out—everythinged!

She paid the twins from her winnings and laughed bitterly when she saw what she had left. Nothing. No hope at all.

She was going to have to sell her sheep for mutton.

And she felt as criminal as if she were the one who'd do the killing. There was nothing left to do. She had to pay the mortgage, and the taxes were more than overdue. She didn't think she'd be able to wangle any sort of extension. In fact, she didn't think the banker she'd dealt with was willing to even speak to her again, she owed so much. If she didn't sell the sheep, she'd lose the farm.

Her love for Aunt Lucie and her respect for her late parents made that option impossible to consider. As impossible as it was to lead her sheep to slaughter.

A scuffling of animal feet sounded at the entrance to the building. Willow glanced up and saw her nemesis leading his pack of winners to their stalls. A congratulatory train of admirers chugged along behind him, all their hot air nearly visible above his conceited red head.

Something where her heart used to be experienced a sharp stab, and the pain nearly felled her. But remembering Aunt Lucie's refusal to bow before adversity, Willow set her shoulders in a regal line and continued packing her belongings. There was nothing left at the York County Fair for her.

As if with blinders, she focused on the task before her. She wanted to leave this damnable place as soon as she could. She didn't know what she'd do if that rutting ram of a man tried to romance her out of her rage.

Looking up at the sound of approaching footsteps, Willow groaned. She'd never known her thoughts had such potent summoning qualities. On the other side of the stall gate stood the damnable Irish bard, contrived concern blaring from his expression.

"What do you want?" she asked rudely.

He blinked. Then frowned. "What in the name of all that's holy is wrong with you now, woman?"

"Ha! Playing innocent doesn't suit you, Daniel Callaghan! You know what's wrong with me."

"Fine. Missy didn't win. So what? She still placed second."

"Second won't command a high enough price, and you know it."

"I don't see why not."

"Because women around here have been seduced by glib merchants into buying their fabrics and yarns, that's why. All you men are the same. You don't consider anyone else's situation. You just barge ahead, blinded by greed and ambition. I should have known better. After all, you abandoned your entire family in exchange for the good life in Philadelphia."

Daniel recoiled as if wounded. His eyes grew stormy. His beard twitched. Willow saw that her words had pierced his self-assured exterior, and she was glad. If she couldn't hurt him as he'd hurt her, then at least she could engage his temper. He deserved some trouble for all he'd cost her.

He'd even taken her self-respect. She felt herself blanch again, and shook her head, reminding herself it wasn't time to think about last night. Perhaps it would never be time to ponder her loss of sanity. Perhaps all that was best left in oblivion.

As if she could forget.

The silence between them, heavy and charged right from the start, threatened to stifle her, so she returned to her chores. Then she heard him open the stall gate.

"What do you think you're doing?"

"Comin' to shake some sense into you."

"If you so much as touch me, I'll scream rape."

"You'd like to believe that was what happened last night, wouldn't you? It would be easier on your pride to stomach today if you persuaded yourself that I'd forced you. But I didn't, an' you know it damn well. You sighed and cried and kissed me back for all you're worth. An' I've no intention of lettin' you forget that."

He was right, but she'd be damned if she'd acknowledge it. "You need to puff yourself up in your eyes, don't you? That way you can pretend you aren't as shallow, selfish, and crude as you really are."

"Oh, Willow, enough o' this, lass! I'd rather not argue with you. Not today. Last night—"

"Leave last night out of this. It's bad enough to know I've been played as masterfully as your violin."

Daniel ran his hands through his hair. His jaw jutted out, squarer than ever, the set lines evident even under his springy beard. His eyes blazed blue-hot fire, and his cheeks grew redder by the minute. "Fine. You want to think me a devil, then go right ahead and do so. Just remember, lady, last night you swore you loved me and you took me in deep enough that I thought I'd reached your heart. Looks as if you don't have a heart for me to touch."

Willow swallowed, remembering their vows of love, their intimacy, the magic in their lovemaking. A giant hand squeezed the remnants of her heart, and she knew she couldn't take much more at his side.

"What did you come here for? Aside from reminding me of the greatest mistake I ever made."

"Mistake? You're daft, woman! Stark, ravin', blitherin' mad." Frustration was evident in his stance, his frown, his clenched fists, and Willow felt only marginally better. Before she could respond, he went on. "I came to offer for your sheep. I need to enlarge my herd, an' since your animals were second only to mine, I'd be a fool not to help you out of your financial bind and help myself at the same time."

"See? It's just as I said. You only think of yourself. You don't want to see that I have feelings about all this." But her feelings didn't count. Or they surely couldn't at a moment like this. She had to decide if she was going to save her animals or keep her family's dreams alive. Not a good position to be in, she admitted.

What would Aunt Lucie have done? Then she knew the depth of her defeat. The land. The land had always been uppermost in her aunt's thoughts. Despite her fierce love for her animals, Aunt Lucie knew that more would come in the spring, while the land you lost was impossible to regain.

Willow named her price. It was high, she knew, but that was what she needed to pay off the mortgage. She'd worry about the taxes once the property was cleared of the bank's lien. Then, gathering her courage, she added, "And you'll keep them for their wool."

"What?" Daniel's budding smile turned into a howl of ridicule. "I'm not insane, Willow. I can't afford to keep a flock of sheep when wool won't bring in a fraction of the money their meat will. Certainly not, when I've the hotels and restaurants in town willing to pay for good, fresh mutton."

The knife defeat had planted in her heart gave its final twist. She'd lost. Her animals faced imminent death, and there was nothing she could do about it. Bitterness left a hideous taste in her mouth.

"Then I hope their deaths land on your conscience. Doesn't seem as though anything ever could, though."

"Aye, Willow Stimson, 'tis easy for you to believe me a cold, callous bastard, but I'm not, and I suspect you know it, too. I doubt you'd have given yourself to that sort of man as freely and passionately as you did." He turned and left the stall. Latching the gate, he paused on the walkway. He sighed deeply, and although she knew better, Willow wondered if he was in pain.

"I'll leave you to your accusations and insults, then. See how they sit on your conscience. Perhaps yours will work better an' sooner than you think mine will." He began to walk away. Then he swung his head back, and Willow was stunned by the look he gave her. If she weren't sure of his shallow nature, she would have sworn she'd hurt him as much as he had her.

"I'll be right back with your money, lass." He walked away, his shoulders slumped.

Willow nibbled on her bottom lip. Had she made more of his winnings than there was to make?

She considered his close relationship with Otis Hillenbaugh and his friendship with Hiram Becker, another fair official. Daniel's wealth and social position in town could also be added to the equation.

Hans's voice came back to her. *He intends to win.*

Daniel had indeed won.

Willow had lost, more than she'd ever thought she stood to lose.

Then Daniel was back, a grim row of furrows marring his high brow, the crinkles at the corner of his eyes scoring grooves on his temples. His mustache sat straight over his tightly clamped lips.

Although he looked more forbidding than ever—a giant of a man, anger and stung pride evident in his rigid shoulders, his unequivocal steps, the brittle blue glaze over eyes that had looked at her with fire and desire only the night before—Willow wasn't ready to admit defeat.

She cared enough about her animals to resort to a plea. "Spare my flock, Daniel. I—I'll find a market for their wool. Don't kill them straight away. Give me a chance—"

"I can't," he bit off. "I also have demands on my funds. I can't afford to feed animals who won't pay for their keep. Here's your money. 'Tis all there. All you asked for."

For a moment Willow hesitated to take the bills. Her heart was broken, her dreams crushed. Once she took the money, it was all she'd have left. That, and a farm. Suddenly she wondered if this was what Mr. Meister had meant when he'd warned her that pride made a poor companion.

Willow couldn't think about that yet. The bank had given her until tomorrow, Friday, to pay. With trembling fingers, she took the money.

"Remember, lass. In spite of even this, I love you. I always will."

Willow turned her back to him. She didn't want him to see that her tears had begun to fall.

17

*F*ORCING HERSELF TO keep moving, Willow finished gathering her belongings and made sure the stall was ready to be cleared of the hay on the ground. It was hard to look down and not remember the passionate interlude shared upon those golden grasses. Each time her gaze returned to the corner by the hay bale, a vision of Daniel's face, taut with restrained passion, formed in her mind. Her heart wept.

She couldn't cry, though. This was too public a place, as she'd said in Daniel's arms just hours ago. Her grief had to wait until she was back at the farm.

It was grief she felt. She'd lost a number of friends; her sheep had been her closest contacts in those months since Aunt Lucie had died. Yes, the Meisters had tried to comfort her, but Willow hadn't been ready to accept it. She also hadn't wanted to rely on anyone else for her healing. She'd felt time and a lot of work would help blunt the sharp edges of her pain.

She'd thought herself over the worst of it, but now, after failing in her efforts to inspire an interest in spinning, she'd lost her sheep. Her conscience felt burdened; she'd failed her aunt. She was certain Aunt Lucie would have found a way to keep the animals alive.

If it hadn't been for that scurrilous Irish rogue, she wouldn't have lost sight of what was really important. Surely if he hadn't distracted her, she would have done a better job of demonstrating the positive elements of spinning. After all, that morning when she'd taught Maribeth the basics of the wheel, an appreciative group of women had come around to watch. They'd seemed interested, too. They were, that is, until that fulminating beast showed up, spewing dragonish flames from his bearded mouth.

A knot of pain formed in her throat, and Willow found herself gulping to keep it from unraveling into sobs. It was so difficult to stop thinking of Daniel. Everything about the York County Fair reminded her of his better qualities, few though they'd turned out to be. She had to wonder if she'd ever be able to come back and show her animals here. Perhaps she wouldn't have to, if the Agricultural Society went ahead with their plans to move the location of the fairgrounds.

The way she felt right now, she never wanted to remember the man. She certainly wanted to forget his rich voice, his merry laughter, the lilt of his brogue . . . his kisses, caresses, his lovemaking.

Would she ever forget? Something in her heart said no.

She couldn't believe she'd again fallen for a handsome face, a practiced collection of caresses, the seeming honesty of a voice that whispered "I love you."

Those miserable words. Willow hoped she never heard them again. For the second time in her life, she'd let her loneliness, her need for human love, blind her. No more. This time she'd learned her lesson. Never again would she let another male near her, much less let one kiss her senseless, caress her to a frenzy, then steal everything she had while she was too besotted to care.

Once the haze of passion cleared, reality arrived, piercing

and brutal. She'd been a fool. Twice over, yet. That was more than enough.

Squaring her shoulders, she set out to retrieve her wagon and Rufus, her ancient gelding. She'd left them at William Moore's livery nearby. She'd known, from years of Aunt Lucie's experience, that Mr. Moore, crotchety though he was, would take excellent care of her horse.

With brisk motions she loaded her bundles and parcels onto the rough wagon bed, then sat to wait until Mr. Wicked-Weasel Callaghan came for his newly purchased sheep. It was so hard to think of Daisy and Rosebud as someone's Sunday dinner. Her two-year-old rams, too.

Suddenly she realized they'd never discussed Missy. Fear squeezed her heart. The ewe was still at Dr. Wirtz's clinic. Would Daniel insist on taking Missy, too? Willow wasn't sure she could survive the loss of her favorite ewe, that dainty white lamb she'd held on her lap at a time when she'd thought she'd die from the pain of loss and betrayal. Missy was more to Willow than just an animal, more than just a producer of wool. Missy was a friend, and at this moment, a loyal friend was what Willow needed most.

"'Morning, Miss Stimson," Hans Brenneman called from the doorway of the Sheep Building. Sitting in her wagon near the entrance, Willow swallowed hard. The time had come to bid farewell to her flock. Since she'd kissed her latest dream of love good-bye, she might as well say good-bye to her last friends, too.

Despite that logic, however, Willow didn't think she could face them again without falling apart. "Hans," she said, her voice strained. "The sheep are in their pens. Feel free to take them when you're ready."

"Thank you. And I'm sorry you didn't win—"

"Let's not talk about that, shall we? As soon as you take

the sheep, I'll be on my way home. I have things to do at the farm."

Hans's lips turned downward, his brow lined with concern. "Are you sure you're all right?"

Willow's wry chuckle came out on a sob. "As I'll ever be."

The young man paused and studied Willow's face. His scrutiny made her uncomfortable. Although he looked as if he wanted to say something of import, he shrugged, then simply said, "I'll make sure they're well cared for."

"Until he kills them, that is."

Hans jerked as if butted by an angry ram, shock in his expression. "He's not a monster, you know. Just a farmer."

Willow waved dismissively. "I appreciate your concern but I'd rather not discuss your employer. In fact, I'd much rather go home. Can you handle the transfer of the animals?"

"Of course. Go ahead, I'll take care of everything."

"It's for the best."

Hans sought her gaze. Willow allowed the contact for a brief moment. "I wonder," he murmured, skepticism in his voice. "I really wonder."

Willow did, too, but she couldn't let anyone see her doubts. Certainly not Daniel's employee. "Godspeed, then, Hans."

"Good luck, Miss Stimson."

"Willow, remember?"

"Good luck, Willow."

Between them hung the part of the phrase he hadn't uttered. *"You'll need it."*

At the farm, after checking on the three sheep she'd had the youngest Fritzmeier boy watch during Fair Week, then seeing to Rufus's needs, Willow walked straight through the house to the kitchen. It had always been her favorite room. The large window with a southern exposure consistently provided cheer, and the red-and-white-checked curtains appealed to her sense of color.

Today, however, even being home didn't help. Neither did the film of dust that blanketed every surface. Amazing how even a few days could give a room a neglected, lonely look. It reflected the way she felt inside.

Pulling out a chair, she sat at the table and clasped her hands. She held them tightly, fearing that if she yielded to any sudden relaxation, everything would come crashing down around her, and she wasn't ready to face the pain. She did admit to hurting. Failure was never easy to deal with.

Then again, neither was a broken heart.

Despite her valiant effort, tears filled her eyes, and this time she couldn't summon the strength to keep them from flowing down her face.

How could Daniel have romanced her so callously? He'd lulled her into a sense of ease, diverting her attention from those all-important ribbons. Even poor Missy's cold had fallen like manna from heaven into his huge, masterful hands. Why couldn't the luck have been hers for once? Why couldn't she have won the ribbons? Why couldn't she have caught the interest of the women at the fair with her spinning wheel and lovable flock?

Why had Daniel said those damnable three words?

That was what hurt the worst, the fact that he'd vowed a love he surely hadn't felt. He'd simply been seducing the ignorant country bumpkin, all the while turning every advantage his way. After all, he'd won. He'd ended up with her animals.

And her heart.

Despite everything, she still remembered his kisses, his gazes, his loving caresses, the passion he uncovered in her.

She couldn't bear to think it had all been a carefully crafted plan to ensure his success. But Hans had said that Daniel always got what he wanted.

Had he ever gotten everything this time! The ribbons, the money, the sheep, and a willing woman, to boot.

Much good the brass ring had done her. She'd been a fool. She didn't seem to have learned a thing from the fiasco with Milford Philpott. No, sirree. This time she hadn't merely given her love. This time she'd given Daniel everything there was to her, and he'd only been after ensuring his success.

As the tears continued, anger joined her pain. How could she have let him do this to her?

The answer was clear. He'd made her love him, and loving Daniel Callaghan was an all-or-nothing proposition.

Willow had indeed given her all.

Expecting Elijah Stoltzfus at half past four, Willow was still caught by surprise when the knock came at the front door. She glanced at the clock on the parlor mantel on her way to answer and noticed it was precisely twenty-five minutes past four. She'd always remarked how punctilious the employees of the York National Bank seemed, but none could compare with Mr. Stoltzfus. He was always early.

"Come on in," she said, opening the door.

The tall, gaunt man entered, sparing only a nod in greeting. His lack of manners piqued Willow's temper, but this was a business meeting, not a tea party. Knowing she had the money she'd borrowed, she firmed up her spine and swept through the room to her favorite armchair.

"Ahem!" Donning silver-framed spectacles, Mr. Stoltzfus made a production of opening a substantial leather portfolio and withdrawing a number of papers. "You do understand, Miss Stimson, that unless you pay what you owe the bank, we will be forced to seize the property and put it up for public auction?"

"You made that abundantly clear the last time we spoke."

"Good. Where do we stand as of today?"

For the wildest moment Willow felt like retorting, *We're not standing, we're sitting,* but common sense prevailed. With a deep breath for courage, she took the document Mr. Stoltzfus held out to her. "I have the money I borrowed. I can pay back the mortgage."

"Oh. I see."

Willow could have sworn the banker looked disappointed at her news, but she wondered if it was just her horrible mood that distorted her perceptions.

"Very well, then," he said, gesturing for her to read.

Certain it was the note she'd signed when she'd borrowed the money, Willow only scanned the legal verbiage. "Yes, Mr. Stoltzfus, this is the note, and that's my signature at the bottom. If you'll excuse me, I have the money in the kitchen."

As she left, she caught sight of his raised eyebrow. He didn't believe her! Stodgy old penny-grubber. She'd show him. And she'd do it in cash.

Armed with the contents of Aunt Lucie's old cookie jar, one that hadn't seen a cookie in her lifetime, Willow returned to the parlor. Treading silently, she caught Mr. Stoltzfus eyeing the furniture, the lamps, even the fireplace.

So that was why he'd looked disappointed when she said she could pay! He'd been hoping to get his hands on the Stimson property. Scheming louse. He'd probably been rubbing his greedy hands together, all the while she worked like a horse to come up with the money she'd borrowed.

"Here," she said, wanting the ordeal over.

Still looking skeptical, the banker took the proffered bills. Tugging firmly on the currency, he studied the paper by the light of the parlor lamp. Willow's temper heated as he demonstrated his lack of trust. "That's it?" he asked when he'd performed the ritual with each bill.

"Of course. It's the exact amount I signed the note for."

"We have a problem, then." A smile spread across his pinched face.

"What sort of problem?"

"You're shy of the balance in the amount of the interest accrued."

"Interest?"

"Yes, the percentage the bank charges for letting you use our money."

"You mean . . . I have to pay you *more* than I borrowed?"

"You used our money for over a year, with no payment received."

"That's because I signed an eighteen-month note."

"So you had the bank's money for eighteen months."

"Are you saying I have to pay *rent* for that money?"

"You have a curious way of wording it, Miss Stimson, but I guess one could say you rented our money."

Willow stood, her mind reeling. She hadn't taken much time to read the infernally long and indecipherable mess of words in the bank note. At the time she'd gone to borrow the funds, she'd been so distraught by the damage the flood had caused, and it hadn't been long since Aunt Lucie's death and Milford's betrayal . . .

All she'd wanted was to repair her farm. To keep what was rightfully hers. And now, because she'd been so consumed with fears—feeling alone in the world and determined to make her own way—she'd neglected to pay the close attention a business matter demanded. Now what?

"Would you allow me an extension? I could come up with enough—"

"Miss Stimson," the vinegary man cut in, "you haven't listened to me."

Willow felt like screaming, but she checked her temper. Her fear . . . well, there was no controlling that emotion. It was galloping away with her remaining hope. "Then tell me again, and I'll try to understand."

With a fraudulent display of patience, Mr. Stoltzfus sighed, took off his spectacles, wiped them with a flowing bile-green handkerchief, then stuck them right back where they'd been all along. "Miss Stimson, the bank doesn't give out its money for the pleasure of it. We lend our money to people who need cash, and in return they pay us for the use of that money. If I borrowed your horse for eighteen months, you'd expect something in return. The bank does the same."

"How much . . . ?"

"A percentage of the amount you borrowed."

Gathering the papers strewn across his bony lap, the banker made a show of looking for the answer to Willow's question, but from the way he'd been appraising her home, she knew he had that sum engraved on his brain.

She fast grew tired of his pretense. "Mr. Stoltzfus, I've been away from the farm for Fair Week. There are countless things that need done. If you don't mind, please get to the point."

When he looked her way, she caught the gleam of victory in his marble-round black eyes. He named a sum that might as well have been in the millions. She probably couldn't come up with it even if she sold Rufus, her old wagon, her three remaining sheep, and the handful of chickens she kept for eggs. Besides, who'd buy them?

The only assets she'd had were the sheep and the farm.

As they sat in silence, Willow faced reality. This was defeat. There was nothing left to do. She'd taken a gamble.

She'd lost. Everything. She couldn't pay the bank, and she didn't have the money for the taxes. Lord knew those were late and due as well.

A gnawing emptiness in her middle hit her hard, so hard she nearly huddled into a ball, but she wouldn't show this man how she felt inside. If nothing else, she could keep her dignity. She stood, held herself as proudly as ever, and faced her uncertain future. "As you well know, I don't have that much. I was unaware of the matter of interest, and I guess I must pay for my oversight. What is the next step?"

"You must come in to town as there are a number of documents to be signed. I can't come back another time since your signature must be duly witnessed. After you sign over the title to the property, we'll take possession, then put it up for auction."

Each word he spoke killed another piece of Willow's heart. Tears again threatened, but she fought them valiantly. There'd be plenty of time to cry tonight, tomorrow, too. "How soon do I need to vacate the property?"

"Depending on the auctioneer's plans . . . perhaps three weeks."

"When must I sign the papers?"

"If you would come to the offices tomorrow morning, we could take care of that matter directly. No need to prolong the situation. The bank is anxious to recover its losses."

"Don't speak to *me* of loss, Mr. Stoltzfus. I doubt you even know the meaning of the word. Since you want me in the office tomorrow morning, I'll be there no later than nine o'clock."

The banker removed his spectacles, slipped them into a brown leather case, and placed them inside the matching portfolio. Then he returned the papers that had ruined Willow's future to the center compartment of the case. Finally he stood, gave the parlor another careful study, then smiled. "Let me give you some advice, Miss Stimson. If you mean to do business, learn the way business is done. You must read everything, even the complicated terms and the small print. They're there for a reason."

Willow bit the inside of her cheek to keep from saying something unacceptable. "It's getting late. As I said before, I have much to do. More than I'd expected."

With another jerky nod, the man picked up his plain brown hat and plopped it on his balding pate. "Tomorrow, then."

"Indeed."

As Mr. Stoltzfus stepped out onto the porch, a large shadow flitted past the parlor window. It wasn't late enough for darkness to have caused what Willow saw, but when she followed the acerbic banker, she found nothing unusual. Perhaps she was imagining things. She felt lightheaded enough that ghostly visions could explain what she'd seen.

Closing the door, she went upstairs and dropped on her bed. As if a dam had broken, the sobs tore out from her heart. Dear God, she had nothing left. Nothing at all.

What in the world was she going to do?

Hurrying off the porch before Willow spotted him, Daniel made his way to where a black buggy awaited the shifty-looking devil who'd just left her parlor. He didn't know what was going on, but he knew it entailed a sum of money Willow couldn't pay. Daniel was going to make good and sure he knew every last detail of her situation.

The day had been unmitigated hell. He'd been less than worthless, heartsick over the way matters had ended between him and Willow. Not one to sit and let trouble claim its toll, after he and Hans made sure the animals were settled, Daniel had taken his horse and headed for Willow's farm. After dismounting, he had approached her front door and caught the sounds of a conversation, a strained, unpleasant exchange. Discretion and curiosity led him to employ stealth, and he'd sidled up to an open window. He'd heard enough to give rise to misgivings.

The grin Elijah Stoltzfus wore on his cadaverous face when he walked away from Willow's front door reminded Daniel of a jack-o'-lantern. He'd never cared for the sour banker.

"Elijah!" Daniel called. He got no response, since the man was engrossed in a study of the farm buildings. Was Willow selling her home? Was that what the conversation had been about? No . . . that didn't make sense.

"Elijah Stoltzfus," he said, louder. Startled, the ghoul dropped his portfolio. As the man scurried to pick up the leather satchel, Daniel could have sworn he sported whiskers on his rodent's nose and a long skinny tail.

"Yes?"

"Doin' business with Miss Stimson, were you?"

"In a way."

"Hmmm . . . what way?"

With a self-righteous snort the banker proceeded toward his buggy. "I never discuss a bank client's business with curious strangers."

"An' if that stranger turns out not to be a stranger?"

"You're not saying you're related to her—"

"In a way." Daniel threw the sanctimonious prig's words back at him.

Tipping his pointy nose up, the banker climbed into his vehicle. "I suppose you'll explain your comment."

"What if I told you Miss Stimson and I are about to marry?"

"I'd say you were marrying a fair amount of trouble. Debt, too."

Daniel was momentarily taken aback. "What sort of debt?"

A frustrated sigh seeped from pale, pinched lips. "If you really must know, Miss Stimson borrowed a sum to effect repairs on her property after the Codorus Creek flooded a year and a half ago. She took out an eighteen-month note and never paid a cent on it. Until today. She covered the principal but was ignorant of the interest owed. The bank is seizing the property as provided by the note she signed. We'll auction the farm."

Daniel frowned. Willow hadn't said a word about this. She'd spoken of difficulties and needing to win ribbons for the money, but he'd never suspected she was about to lose her home.

Besides, although he'd told Stoltzfus that Willow was his intended just to learn what he wanted to know, the idea took root, and Daniel liked the way it sounded more and more. He especially liked the idea of protecting her, championing her cause. "Tell me, how much does my bride owe?"

"A percentage of the total loaned," said Mr. Stoltzfus while rummaging in his now dusty portfolio. "Here. It's a copy of the note she signed."

Daniel scanned the document, and when he reached the paragraph covering interest he was shocked. Willow was about to lose her farm for a paltry sum, and a woman as proud and strong as Willow wouldn't easily part with what was hers. This matter of the interest must have licked her but good, particularly after her loss at the fair. She had to be crushed.

He'd never known she was up against a giant of such enormous dimensions. She was hardly large enough to squabble, never mind do battle with a behemoth. He'd have to buttress her strength with his own in order to defeat her foe. After the results of the fair, he knew he had to prove himself to the woman he loved. Perhaps then she'd grant him her forgiveness, even though he'd done nothing that needed forgiving. Then again, Willow was Willow, and she believed he'd done her wrong.

Extending his hand to the miserable wretch who'd lobbed a crushing blow at his stubborn, independent shepherdess, Daniel said, "What d'you say we have a wee man-to-man talk? Mustn't tell my bride a word of this, though. I'd be likin' to surprise her at our weddin'."

18

$\mathcal{W}$ITH A SENSE of impending doom, Willow paced off the distance between Mr. Moore's livery, where she'd again left Rufus and her wagon, and the York National Bank. Every muscle in her body begged her to stop, turn around, run back to the farm, and barricade herself on her family's land.

But reality wouldn't let her do it. Reality made her place one foot before the other, each step further tightening her stomach muscles.

She'd spent a sleepless night, alternating between despondent sobbing and incensed raging. What was a woman to do once she'd lost everything that mattered to her? What good was life without meaning? What was she going to do with the life that extended before her like a barren desert?

Since those were the very thoughts that had plunged her into the depths of despair during the black hours of night, Willow shook herself and fought to keep her mind blank. She couldn't afford the luxury of misery just as she was about to enter the bank.

Before she knew it, she stood before the brass and glass doors of the York National Bank. Her heart implored her to flee, but reason led her to grasp the cool metal handle and let herself in. Familiar with the building's layout, Willow went directly to Mr. Stoltzfus's secretary. The bespectacled young man behind the desk looked like another member of the vulturine Stoltzfus family.

"I'm here to see him," Willow said, gesturing toward the banker's closed office door. She couldn't bring herself to speak his name; her stomach lurched each time she did.

The young man stood and, with disdain, asked, "Does he expect you?"

"With bated breath."

His only reaction to her response was a fast and furious blinking, followed by a reproving sniff. "Follow me."

"Good morning, Willow," she heard in a voice she hadn't heard for nearly two years. When she turned, she saw Milford Philpott rise from a chair near the secretary's desk. In the chair next to his sat a pudgy young woman of nondescript coloring.

Willow swallowed her surprise, remembering that Mrs. Meister had mentioned his return. "It's been a long time. Are you in town for the fair?"

Milford came closer, then ran his fingers through the thick, waving black hair at the nape of his neck. "You could say that. I came to buy livestock for my father-in-law's stockyard."

Distaste twisted Willow's lips. She allowed herself to meet his dark gaze, the gaze that once had thrilled her so well. She felt nothing, and that was something to celebrate. "I see," she said. "Since you have a mission, and I have business with Mr. Stoltzfus, I'll let you go on with your plans. So long." She followed the secretary who'd watched the exchange with curiosity.

So Milford had come to buy animals for his rich father-in-law to kill. Willow thought of the mousy girl who'd married her former fiancé. The couple brought to mind a peacock and his dowdy peahen. She smiled and shook her head. All she felt was relief that she hadn't married the handsome man. If nothing else could do it at this time, the thought of her narrow escape bolstered her sagging spirits.

With her every step the clicking of her heels against the granite floor ricocheted off the walls of the bank's large lobby, sounding like shots being fired through the fabric of her dreams.

"Come in," said Mr. Stoltzfus in response to his secretary's knock.

With a deep breath for courage and a firming of her spine, Willow stepped into the raptor's nest.

"Ah, Miss Stimson. Precisely on time."

Despite the positive words, his face displayed annoyance. He'd obviously wanted to start their meeting by placing her at an even greater disadvantage. Willow was glad she'd made sure to arrive at least five minutes early. "I prefer to be punctual."

Nodding, he picked up a sheaf of papers. "You'll be glad to know—"

"Let's not try to fool anyone. Nothing could make me glad at this moment. I'd prefer to avoid the pleasantries and finish our business."

"That's just it, Miss Stimson. We no longer have business together."

Willow couldn't credit her ears. What on earth was going on here? "Excuse me, but aren't you the one who came to the farm yesterday and told me I was to sign over the deed to my property?"

Mr. Stoltzfus took out an aubergine-colored handkerchief. As the old buzzard took his time wiping his shiny brow and upper lip, he appeared disinclined to answer her question. Finally, after folding the monstrous square of fabric, he tucked it back into his coat pocket and faced

Willow. "I indeed went to your place yesterday, and I requested your presence here this morning. Something came up, however, and there's been . . . a change."

"Change? What sort of change? And how does a change translate into no more business?"

The man's glowing scalp turned a mottled medley of puce and plum while his eyes shifted all over the room, anywhere but where Willow could meet his gaze. Something was going on here. Mr. Stoltzfus was clearly involved. Willow wasn't pleased.

"Look," she said, "I have a signed note. I owe more than I can pay. You said the bank was entitled to the farm as a result of my default. You asked me to meet you today, and here I am. I demand an explanation."

Then Willow noticed the banker's shaking fingers. He was nervous! He was also hiding something. "If you don't satisfy my questions, sir, I'll be forced to report this to the bank president and the Board of Trustees. It certainly wouldn't look good for you."

The ugly handkerchief came back out and mopped the banker's damp pate. "Fine!" he cried, waving the fabric. "Your fiancé paid the interest. He also provided the funds to pay your tax debt. The title to your farm is now free and clear."

Willow's jaw hung open. Her . . . *what* . . . had paid her debt? "My fiancé? You're mistaken. I don't have a fiancé. Where do I sign so I can leave?"

Finally Mr. Stoltzfus faced her. He was serious. Willow took in a sharp breath. "I—"

"Miss Stimson," said the banker, cutting her off, "listen to what I said. You owe nothing on your farm. We no longer have the deed. It's free and clear. You owe *nothing*."

"Who?"

"Who what?"

"Who paid my debt?"

"Look, miss, he told me he wanted to surprise you on your wedding day. I promised not to breathe a word of this, and you've already made me say too much. Go home. It's legally yours."

Willow crossed her arms over her chest, as if by doing so she could keep her heart from pounding in burgeoning hope. "You'd better say a lot more. I *don't* have a fiancé, nor am I aware of any wedding, much less its date. I'm not leaving until you clear up this mess."

Out came the eggplant-purple handkerchief one more time. The banker's knobby claws twisted the fabric mercilessly. He mopped his brow, dabbed under his beak of a nose. With an uncomfortable twitch, he stood and began pacing, clearly weighing his options. Willow took a seat, prepared to wait him out.

Finally he spun around. "I'll tell you everything, but you must make it clear to him that I revealed the details unwillingly."

"Who is this *him*?"

"Daniel Callaghan—"

"Daniel Callaghan?"

"Yes, he stopped me as I left your house and said you were about to marry. He paid off the interest and the taxes and said he wanted to give you the deed as a wedding gift. He has your deed, and if you want to know anything further, you'll have to ask him. I wash my hands of this matter."

Daniel. At the mention of his name, her stomach pitched and her heart beat faster, but her head restored her common sense. After all, according to Mr. Stoltzfus, the Irish louse now held the deed to the Stimson farm. It hadn't been enough for him to take those ribbons and the prize money; he'd had to swoop in for the kill. He'd been after her farm as well.

She should have held on to her initial suspicions about Daniel. They'd proved right. Like Milford, he'd been after something tangible, the easy gain of financial success. Like Milford, would Daniel have dropped his pursuit of her if he'd found a riper plum?

That thought ripped through the final layer of scarring over her heart. This fresh wound hurt worse than Milford's betrayal. This one tore her foolish heart in two.

Just what was she expected to do now? And what was all that talk of a wedding? Obviously Mr. Forked-Tongued-Fiend Callaghan had no concept of honesty. And Mrs. Meister had said his reputation was so sterling pure. Hah! The man had no scruples. He'd stolen her heart, bedded her, won her ribbons, bought her sheep, then swiped her farm right under her very eyes.

The banker was right. She had no further business with him. "I'll be on my way, then, but I can't say it's been a pleasure."

"Hmph!" was all the vulture said.

Closing the heavy wooden door behind her, Willow squared her shoulders and started toward the wall of glass at the bank's street exit. Milford stepped in her way.

Willow didn't like his smarmy smile. "What do you want?" she asked, impatient to leave.

"Seems I've gotten everything I wanted," he answered, pride puffing out his chest.

"Well, you *did* marry the money you were too lazy to earn."

Milford laughed. "Poor Willow. I broke your heart when I left, but it was the best thing for both of us. I'm not cut out for a life of sacrifice and struggle. Besides, now that I have all the money I could want at my disposal, I can buy what I couldn't afford years ago."

Willow again thanked her lucky stars she'd escaped a

lifetime of misery with him. She also marveled at his acting talent. For years he'd pretended to want her, when in reality he'd only wanted the Stimson property, a successful farm that must have looked prosperous indeed to the fatherless boy whose mother cleaned houses to put food on the table.

Still, understanding Milford's motives didn't make them any more palatable. Especially since he no longer bothered with his suitor's mask. "Ducky for you!"

He didn't seem to hear her. "Yes, sir! I'm even going to get the Stimson farm. After all those years of wanting your land and your sheep, I'll be buying it all for a song! As you can see, richer is far better than not."

He was buying her farm? "What are you talking about?"

Milford opened his well-tailored coat and slipped his thumbs under the red suspenders holding up his elegant navy trousers. He rocked back on the heels of gleaming black shoes. "I'm buying your farm from the bank for your delinquent interest and taxes. I'll hire a tenant farmer and raise mutton for the stockyard and to sell to local restaurants."

Willow didn't know whether to scream in frustration or laugh at the irony. She found herself in the same situation Aunt Lucie once had. Her two suitors had only donned the mask of lover in order to claim the Stimson farm. When Milford found a greener pasture, he dropped his mask and ran. Now, he'd returned for her farm, money in hand. Poor Milford. It looked like a more experienced conniving swine had caught the plum.

"I hate to dampen your enthusiasm," she lied, "but the debt has been paid. The title is free and clear."

"Paid?" Milford said with a frown. "Who paid for it? I was assured you hadn't the slightest chance of coming up with the money."

"You were well informed. I didn't pay for it, Daniel Callaghan did."

Milford's lips pressed tight, anger making an appearance in his long-lashed black eyes. "He couldn't have. I'd made arrangements with Stoltzfus. The fool wouldn't have dared act without speaking to me first."

"Looks like another weasel made Mr. Stoltzfus an offer he couldn't refuse." If only to see Milford so rattled, Willow was momentarily glad about Daniel's actions.

"We'll see about that," Milford said, a menacing tone to his smooth voice and an ugly cast to his handsome features. He spun around, hauled his wife out of her chair and propelled her into Mr. Stoltzfus's office.

For about a second Willow wished she were a fly on the office wall, but the errant wish flew away on the heels of another thought. Milford wanted to sell mutton to York eateries. She recalled an Irish-tinged baritone stating the same goal.

The baritone of the man who'd also admitted to having wanted a sheep farm as long ago as when he first returned to York.

Feeling sick to her stomach, Willow left the bank and arrived at the livery, almost without notice. Her thoughts and emotions were in a vicious tangle. Only one thing remained clear. Daniel had paid off the debt on her farm, and by doing so he'd eliminated Milford's chances to compete against him for the local hotel trade. She remembered Hans telling her of Daniel's determination and his talent for getting what he wanted.

So much for the wedding-day surprise.

Beneath a veneer of rage, Willow felt the anguish of betrayal. Her lonely heart had spun dreams of a future with Daniel. She'd fallen in love easier than she'd ever done anything else, and she had learned the difference between infatuation and love. She'd been infatuated with the slick Milford Philpott, and she was in love with the seemingly rough, but more accomplished scoundrel, Daniel Callaghan. It seemed that no matter what he did, no matter how hurt she was, her foolish heart continued to beat his name. She wished she could stop caring, kill her love for him, but by simply closing her eyes, she still saw his face, remembered the carousel ride, the shared lemonade, the passionate kisses, the dreamy waltz. How could it all have felt so real, when it had been no more than a plan to further Daniel's ambitions?

He'd left her nothing. Not even her self-respect. The money he'd paid for the farm made her feel dirty, used. Just as she'd felt after learning how Milford had tried to use her. Although at the time she'd never have believed it, she'd been lucky in her dealings with Milford, who'd left her as soon as he found a wealthier pigeon to pluck. She never gave Milford all she'd given Daniel. It hurt to recognize how gullible she'd been.

But it wasn't time to regret her mistakes. She had one last thing to do. She had to face Daniel one more time. If for no other reason, she had to speak her mind to tell him how despicable his actions were. She hoped she had the strength to do so without falling apart. She'd never be able to live with herself if she did. Then . . .

Willow didn't know what would come after their confrontation, but she knew she was strong enough to survive. All she had to do was figure out how to mend her broken heart, how to go on after her world and her dreams had come crashing down around her.

After taking care of Willow's financial problems, Daniel had slept like a babe. His dreams were filled with visions of the beautiful shepherdess turned princess and the questing

lord who defeated monsters and giants, and won riches
untold. When he woke up, he laughed at himself, abashed
by the blatantly romantic fantasies his subconscious had
concocted. The influence of a fey mother never seemed to
go away.

Daniel dressed and took care of matters at the dairy, time
passing in a flurry of activity. He had to separate a number
of animals he'd agreed to sell from those he intended to
keep, he had the farm's books to attend to, and on top of
everything else, he still had to come up with a solution to
Maribeth's problems.

He'd agreed to let her stay with the Meisters last night,
but Mrs. Meister was due to bring the girl home later this
morning. Daniel no longer had a housekeeper to watch over
the child, and he had more work than any single man could
manage. What was he going to do with his niece?

The imp on his shoulder whispered Willow's name, but
Daniel stifled it, for he still held doubts about Willow's
fanciful nature. Yes, he loved the woman, and now that he'd
come to feel comfortable with the idea, he intended to marry
her. But that didn't mean she was the right person to raise
his niece.

Of course that brought up the question of children that he
and Willow could have someday. He had no idea what he'd
do in that situation, either. He only knew one thing—he'd
never allow a child to be taught to base her actions on myths
and legends and the pantheon of the Pagan Celts. Fantasy
was fantasy. Insubstantial, fleeting, and, in the end, not to be
trusted. It made a person lose sight of what was truly
important, forget duty and love in exchange for impossible
dreams and heroic quests.

Reality, however, meant that life had rules for one to
follow, and as long as a person followed those rules, life
went on in its peaceful, sensible way. Trouble occurred

when one modeled one's actions after fantasies and fairy tales.

As always the image of his work-weary father formed in his mind. A vision of his mother, busy relating tales of wonder, appeared, too. There had been times Daniel had sought the mother for comfort, but found the dreamer instead. Times when Darby had needed a partner, but found a whimsical storyteller instead. And it had seemed to Daniel that Darby then redoubled his efforts, working himself to an early grave.

But . . . Mrs. Meister remembered Maeve's stories having a different impact on his father. Could she be right? Could he be wrong?

Regardless of what Darby had thought of Maeve's tales, Daniel would never forget how he'd broken his father's heart, and more than likely the man's will to live, as well. Darby had wanted his son to work at his side, the two of them giving life to his vision for the dairy. But Daniel had left the farm, and Darby had labored alone—until he'd found someone to carry on his dream. After Maggie and Will took up the reins to the dairy, Darby had died.

Always present in Daniel's thoughts was the pain he'd caused his family when he left for Philadelphia, full of the stuff of Maeve's myths. From childhood, she'd instilled in him the hunger for adventure, for the quest of an elusive, idealized goal. He'd set out to conquer the monsters of business and prejudice, determined to prove that an Irishman had the right and the capability to match any other man in America when it came to achieving his goals.

Instead, he'd found that prejudice seemed indelibly etched in the soul of many he met, and business . . . well, business kept a man busy, but success of that kind brought an empty sort of victory. If a man didn't have anyone to share his triumphs, little satisfaction came from his accomplishments.

He'd learned. 'Twas too late to right the wrongs he'd done his parents, but he had come back for Maribeth's sake. He'd found that the land he'd once disdained now called to him with his father's voice, and the dairy was his newfound goal. He willingly put everything he had into this new enterprise, and he was reaping prosperity.

That was why, when he realized Willow stood to lose her farm, Daniel couldn't stand by and let the inevitable happen. He'd lost so much and lived daily with the pain of those losses. He'd wanted to spare Willow the crushing loss of what she had left of her folks, especially since he had the means to give her that gift. Her farm. He'd understood how much it meant to her; it was evident in her determination, her devotion to her animals, her pride, and her dignity. All of which he found himself admiring and respecting. Well, maybe not that damned aversion to mutton and her almost unearthly ability to communicate with Missy.

Ah, she was something, she was, his shepherdess. The more he thought of her that way, the better it sounded. Aye, he'd have to do something about it later today. He wasn't willing to leave the future undecided. He wanted Willow, and by God he was going to marry her.

Every chore he tackled seemed like child's play, so optimistic was his mood. When he heard the crunching of gravel on the drive to the dairy, he grinned from ear to ear when he spied his lady-love. "Willow! Welcome to Callaghan's Dairy."

But as she flung the reins down, whirled, and debarked the wagon, his smile melted into a frown. "What in hell is wrong with you now, lass?"

He heard her swallow hard and saw the shine of tears in her eyes. "You know perfectly well what's wrong with me," she spit out. "How dare you seduce me to steal my ribbons and my farm?"

"What? Have you gone mad now? I did no such thing! Where did you get that damnfool notion?"

Her eyes darkened to black, and their glare was so piercing, Daniel felt the skin of his neck prickle. She was staring in that general direction, obviously to avoid his questioning gaze. Still, the damp evidence of her vulnerability shone in her eyes.

"It's not a damnfool notion," she said, her voice uneven. "You won the ribbons, right?"

"Aye, can't deny fact."

"You paid my debts and have the deed to my farm."

"'Tis true, as well."

"Do you deny kissing and . . . and . . ."

Daniel smiled as she faltered. At least she remembered the magic in the hay. "Can't say it, lass? Can't you say 'tis love we made?"

Her chin flew skyward, wobbling on its way up. "I see no *we* in your scenario. You were busy distracting me to win those ribbons, and you can't deny you'd been making inquiries about buying an established sheep operation. Then, when you realized that I couldn't pay off my debt, you found a way to get what you wanted at a bargain price. Especially after hearing that Milford Philpott was back in York looking to supply the hotels with mutton. You didn't want the competition."

At Daniel's bewildered expression, Willow paused, then went on, remembering how she'd been fooled by Milford. But Daniel had outdone her former fiancé, so she refused to be fooled by his accomplished performance. "That is what you said you invested in sheep for, isn't it? Are you denying it now?"

"Of course, an' I'm not! 'Tis a legitimate interest I have,

but I've never heard of this . . . this Milpott fellow, nor did I know anyone wanted to do the same as I do."

Willow snorted. "Do you deny romancing me in order to get the property if I managed to cover my debts? Why else would you have said you loved me?"

Daniel rammed his hands through his hair. He cursed the air blue around them and stormed into the house. He yelled back at her to wait for him. "An' don't be plantin' that fanny on that wagon seat till I come back outside!"

Willow watched an enraged Daniel storm off into his house. He was angry, angrier than she'd seen him yet. A tiny question made a brief appearance in her thoughts, but she dismissed it. Daniel was adept at putting up a front. She'd found out what he'd been after all along, and he didn't like having his ulterior motives revealed. He probably didn't want that sterling reputation of his besmirched.

But what about her? Lord knew she felt besmirched. Swindled, to boot. Used and discarded. Like Milford, Daniel had found he didn't need her to get what he wanted in the end. She'd been a puppet in his play. He'd won, and he no longer needed to romance a backward sheep farmer.

No, she wouldn't wait until he came back outside to justify his actions again. She'd go home, pack her belongings, and prepare to turn over her family's farm to its new owner, Mr. Callaghan's Dairy, himself.

Hurrying, she reached her wagon and climbed in. She bent down to pick up the reins and suddenly found herself flying through the air, a steely forearm clamped around her waist.

With a furious twist, she fought to escape his grip, even though her traitorous body urged her to relax into his strength, his enervating warmth. "Put me down, you monster, you! I won't stay another minute in the presence of a dishonest louse like you. Let me go, I said! I want to go home."

Daniel did nothing of the sort. Instead, he kept her feet off the ground and his arm around her middle. Taking giant, swallowing steps to his front stoop, he carried her to his home. He threw open the door, then kicked it shut behind him. A moment later he dumped her onto a navy velvet sofa in the ample parlor.

Immediately she missed the heat of his touch, and that made her hurt even more. He really had stolen a lot from her. Her hopes, her dreams, her future, her love. But she wouldn't let him see how deeply he'd wounded her. She had to retain at least her dignity. So she firmed up her spine, stood, and hid behind her anger. "You have some nerve, Mr. Callaghan! I said I was leaving and I mean to do just that. Good day."

He was there in a flash, flapping a piece of paper before her nose, his paw shackling her arm. "Read this, before you go, Willow Stimson. The farm is yours, free and clear. I have plenty with the dairy and the sheep. 'Tis not your farm I'm wantin'. I don't need it. I realized a while back that I only needed a larger flock, not another whole business to run. I bought your sheep for more than they're worth. I knew you needed the money, so I didn't argue the price. I know you love that farm. I didn't want you to lose it for a sum I was happy to give you."

Trying her best to shut out his words, Willow glanced at the deed and the canceled bank note. According to the papers, the property was free and clear of debt, and owned by one Willow M. Stimson, sole proprietor. Still, she couldn't believe. "You're so full of blarney, you even make your actions sound noble. You paid the money, though, didn't you?" she asked, keeping the tears out of her voice.

"I just said so, didn't I?"

"Did I ask you to do that?"

He snorted. "Nay. You'd never ask anyone for help, no matter how bad things got. You're too damn stubborn to see what's best for you."

"And what is best for me, Mr. All-Knowing Callaghan?" The mean little insult registered, and his brows crashed together in a frown. At least she mattered enough to upset him with her words.

"You know damn well what's best for you. Take the deed and rebuild your flock."

"That's it? Just like that, you give me a farm?"

"I'm not givin' you anything. The damn farm is yours. Always was."

"In exchange for what? A night in the hay?"

She'd once compared him to a fire-breathing dragon, but she'd never seen anything like the salvo of flames that now flared in his gaze, that made him breathe roughly, that made him take a step closer to her.

She held her ground.

He came closer still. She caught her breath. If she wasn't so sure he hadn't a heart, she would have thought she saw pain behind his rage.

Through clenched jaws, he said, "I don't like what you're insinuatin', Willow. I told you I loved you, and I meant it. I have never—will never—pay a woman for what should be freely given. An' you know, as well as I do, that we both gave. You said you loved me, but I guess you can't stand not gettin' your way, since now that you lost the ribbons, you no longer love me."

Her heart fluttered when he said he loved her. It urged her to cry out her love in turn, but Willow couldn't trust Daniel. Too many of his actions resembled those of Milford.

Besides, he hadn't said a word about her sheep.

"It wasn't the ribbons I wanted," she said. "I wanted to

win so I could sell my sheep for their wool. I don't want them slaughtered. I wanted to teach women the joy in creating something useful from a puff of froth. My plans failed when I couldn't concentrate on what I was doing. You chased me, caught me, and bedded me. I feel as if you've paid for and bought me, and people can't be bought and sold like sheep. Since you say you want me to keep what I love, have you decided to spare my flock?"

He gave a dismissive wave with his large hand. "I told you from the start, lass, I can't afford to keep animals on sentiment alone. 'Tis a business I run."

Swallowing her misery, she met his fiery blue gaze. "I see. As with Milford, business comes first. Should I expect you to continue your seduction until you take the farm from me?"

Daniel's jaw twitched, and she saw his lips press shut. Then he reached across the space between them and clasped her shoulders in his hands. "You're makin' no sense. I don't know any Milford, I never paid for you, nor have I bought you, lass. I love you and I want you for my bride."

"And you thought that by paying my debt I'd be so grateful I wouldn't question your motives? That I'd conveniently fall into your hands?"

"There's nothing convenient about you," he muttered. "I saw a problem I could fix. That's all. I thought you might forgive my winning those damn ribbons if I helped you keep your farm. Not that I did anything wrong, mind you, but you seemed so fixed on blamin' me for that."

"You thought you'd be earning my undying gratitude by flying in and taking care of everything?" At his nod, Willow rolled her eyes ceiling-ward. "You don't know me at all. In fact, I don't know you, either. We only just met five days ago. How could you presume on such short acquaintance that I'd want a knight on a white charger to rescue me from my troubles? I'm Lucie Stimson's niece. She turned down a few proposals in her time, especially since her suitors, although they liked her well enough, wanted her property more than they did her."

Daniel opened his mouth to respond, but Willow couldn't afford to fall under the spell of his rich, musical voice again. There was no telling what new tales he'd tell.

"Don't say a word," she ordered, counting on a final burst of anger to hold her tears at bay. "I still have things to say to you, so listen. You didn't compete for those ribbons out of need. You simply followed your drive for success. You turned your back on your family—"

Willow pulled up short when she saw him flinch. That had hit him but good. When he went to respond to her hurtful words, she clapped her hand over his lips. "I told you to listen," she said. "You left York because you wanted money and fancy city living. When you came back you brought with you that same hunger for more. It didn't matter that you'd returned to one of the most successful farms in the area. You *still* wanted more. And you were willing to do anything to get it. Including buying yourself a wife to further your plans."

He shook his head fiercely. His eyes gleamed dangerously.

Willow held on. She was almost done. "I'm not for sale and I don't need a knight to save me or my farm. I never wanted grand gestures or great riches. I wanted your love. I wanted you."

Taking her hand from his mouth, she spun around.

"Willow," he said, a warning in his voice.

She ignored him and picked up the deed she'd dropped. "Here's your sheep farm, Mr. Callaghan. Be sure to treat it well." Her fury propelling her, Willow reached the front door. Turning the knob, she paused. "I pity Maribeth. She has no one left but you, and you seem to feel that by buying her a keeper you've done right by her. She needs parents, a family, and I doubt you have the heart to understand what that is. Let her know she's always welcome to visit me, no matter how unsuitable you think I am, no matter where I end up going."

When she opened the door, the first thing she saw was Maribeth's horrified face. Dear God, how much had she heard? Willow whispered the child's name, but the girl shook her head and ran off.

19

$\mathcal{A}$S WILLOW TOOK off after Maribeth, Daniel ran to the door. "Maribeth!" he cried. "Willow!"

Neither one bothered to answer. Neither one returned.

"What on earth was that all about?" asked Reba Meister from the porch steps. Daniel, who hadn't seen her arrive, looked at her in surprise, then remembered she'd been due to bring Maribeth home.

Willow rounded the corner of the barn, and he gestured toward her. "She's gone mad," Daniel answered. "She wasn't makin' much sense before Maribeth appeared, and the child must have overheard some of Willow's irrational comments."

Mrs. Meister came off the steps, trying to see where the other two had gone. "Irrational does not sound like Willow."

Daniel raised a skeptical eyebrow.

Willow's friend gave him a reproving glare. "Willow may be unconventional, but when it really matters, she has more common sense than most."

He snorted. "Saints preserve us, then, if the rest of us have less than she!"

"What makes you say that?"

Daniel ran a hand through his tousled hair. "She stormed in here a while ago, accusin' me of actin' like some Philford somebody who tried to swindle her out of her farm. She threw the deed to the property in my face when she learned I'd paid the debt for her, then went on about killin' sheep, romancin' the farm away from her, and that Milpott fellow competin' with me for the hotel mutton trade. Who is he, anyway?"

As the two of them watched, it became evident that Willow hadn't found Maribeth. She spared Daniel a look full of misery, climbed into her wagon, and left without another word.

Mrs. Meister faced Daniel, subjecting him to a minute study. "How much time do you have?"

"Right now?"

Mrs. Meister nodded.

"All the time in the world. I have no idea where Maribeth went, an' chasin' her only seems to encourage her efforts to vanish, so I'd best let her be for a while. Judgin' from her last words to me, Willow wouldn't welcome my comin' after her, either."

He opened the door and gestured Mrs. Meister to follow him inside. When they'd both taken a seat in the parlor, Daniel waited for her to speak.

With a sigh, Mrs. Meister began. "Paying that money was your first mistake, son. Willow could only have seen your efforts on her behalf as a blow to her self-respect. Keeping that farm is something she thinks she has to do herself. She feels she must measure up to Lucie Stimson's unrealistic standards. I don't believe she should even try, since I know Lucie missed much while she invested her entire life in the farm. But Willow feels she must follow in her aunt's footsteps, she sees it as a matter of family pride, of proving her mettle as a Stimson."

"I didn't know. Even if I had, how can my help do her self-respect any harm? How could the way she solves the

problem matter more than just solving it? I don't understand. I only want to help her keep somethin' that's
important to her. Especially since my Brigid took the ribbon
Willow had hoped Missy would win, and she holds that
against me. I've lost so much, I couldn't stand to watch her
lose everythin' when I had the means to prevent it."

Mrs. Meister nodded, understanding in her expression.
"It's not me you have to persuade, Daniel. I know why you
did what you did. I also know why she feels the way she
does."

Mrs. Meister fell silent. He again waited. "Well?" he
prodded.

An unusually vague shrug lifted Mrs. Meister's shoulders. "I don't know. . . . I'm not sure I should be the one
to tell you the rest."

"Will she?"

"Not right now."

Daniel threw his hands up in frustration. "Then what in
hell am I to do? Keep blunderin' around in the dark? At that
rate we'll both be too old to bother with marriage!"

Mrs. Meister smiled. "So you've come far enough to
think that way."

"Think nothing! I proposed, an' she threw my proposal
back in my face. Together with the deed to the farm."

Shaking her head and chuckling softly, Mrs. Meister took
off her gloves. She settled back into the gray-and-blue
striped armchair, and proceeded to illuminate Daniel about
the romantic blunder in Willow's past.

"I'll never understand women," he muttered as he watched
Mrs. Meister drive her open-fronted buggy to the road, then
head toward York. It seemed inconceivable that his formidable shepherdess had painted him with the same murky
brush as her former fiancé. And if Daniel ever came across

that fool, he'd make sure to thank the idiot for walking away from Willow.

Since Willow was sure to need more time to get over her disappointments, hurt pride, and unnecessary heartache, Daniel decided to try and find Maribeth. He hadn't asked Mrs. Meister for any pointers on how to deal with his niece, but the girl surely would be more tractable than Willow was at present.

As had happened so often of late, however, Daniel found no trace of his niece. Like Willow, he figured Maribeth needed privacy to deal with what she'd heard, to cope with her feelings, before he tried to talk with her. So he returned to the house.

It was obvious that Willow was hurting; her pain had caused her to hurl those insults at him. Although Daniel didn't wish her pain, he hoped her pain stemmed from her feelings for him. A person had to care a lot for perceived wrongs to wound them. Besides, he was sure that had Willow not loved him as much as he loved her, last night's lovemaking would never have happened.

He'd give her the time to cool off, as he was letting Maribeth calm down. He'd let her think through her irrational accusations and her absurd arguments. Then he'd return to her side. It would take a lot of patience and probably some effort to wait her out, but Daniel wasn't willing to give up on their love.

Not without one hell of a fight.

And this better be the last time she compared him to that idiot from her past.

Utterly drained, even though it was scant mid-day, Daniel retreated to his office. He'd do some paperwork instead of the more physical chores that needed to be done around the farm. Hans could handle those.

But sitting behind his great oak desk, Daniel found he

couldn't concentrate on dairy business. He kept replaying
Willow's words in his mind. He now knew who Milford
was, and he agreed with Willow that the man was despicable, but Daniel couldn't accept the comparison she'd
drawn between the two of them. He hadn't done a thing to
hurt her, whereas Milford had done nothing but.

He now agreed that paying off her debts without inform-
ing her had not been the wisest thing to do. Even though
he'd given her the deed to her farm showing that she still
owned the land, it was easy to see how someone who'd been
betrayed as Willow had would connect the two sets of
circumstances.

But, dammit, she'd never told him about Philpott. She'd
only accused Daniel of using her. That hurt. He'd only tried
to help her, to please her; he'd only wished to make things
better for her.

"Damn!" Patience had never been one of Daniel's strong
suits.

Then the office door crashed open. A flurry of red pigtails
and filthy blue calico flew at Daniel, clawing and pummeling and kicking wildly.

"Maribeth! Control yourself! What are you doin', lass?"

Between massive, rending sobs, fractured phrases assailed
Daniel, and the girl's tears drenched them both. "I hate
you. . . . You're mean. . . . You only care about business. . . . I hate you. . . . You sent Willow away. . . .
Mrs. Reba and Willow are my only friends. . . . I hate
you. . . . You want to kill our sheep. . . . I hate you. . . .
I want Willow . . . my mo-mother . . . my father . . . not
you!"

Although he knew it was her anger, grief, and frustration
speaking, Daniel couldn't dodge the impact of his niece's
words. Nobody but Maribeth had ever said they hated him.
Her ravaged features and heartrending cries lent credence to

her words. He hoped it was only heartache making her say such things. He loved her, wanted the best for her, but didn't know how to show her.

Where was Willow when they needed her most?

He doubted she'd be receptive right now. She'd probably snatch Maribeth from his arms and, like a protective mother bear, tear him limb from limb. What's worse, he was sure Maribeth would be only too happy to help her.

In a measured voice, he sought to calm the girl down, to ask and learn what made her so miserable, beyond her obvious anger. "Maribeth, lass, we must talk about this. You can't just say you hate me. Tell me what's wrong this time?"

At first Maribeth continued crying and hitting. Daniel managed to deflect most of her blows while holding her in his arms. Then the punching began to lessen. The mean words died out. Still, the sobs continued; the tears did, too.

Finally, with a loud sniffle, Maribeth withdrew her head from where she'd used it to batter Daniel's middle. "You don't like me—"

"Of course I do! I love you—"

"No, you don't. You only yell and punish me and leave me with nasty old Mrs. Hulbert—"

"Can't anymore," he interjected with a hopeful smile.

Maribeth wasn't buying. "Fine, but you never listen to me, and you always send me away when I want to see what you're doing. You make fun of me, and now you did something horrible to Willow. It must have been really bad, since she was . . . was *pitying* me. And she said you were going to kill the sheep! You didn't say no. How could you, Uncle Danny? What have the sheep done to you? Don't kill them. They're all I have left."

After that extraordinary speech, she wrenched out of his arms and ran to the door.

"Maribeth, listen to me—"

She shook her head. "Did you fight with Willow?"

Daniel frowned but was forced to nod. "Sort of."

"Sort of?" she scoffed. "Hah! You chased her away."

"I did not!"

"Did, too." Blue eyes blazed at him. "Did you take her sheep?"

He tried to keep the fire out of his. "I bought her sheep."

A shoulder bobbed up. "Same thing. Are you going to kill them?"

"Maribeth, listen to me, lassie. I'm sellin' them to the hotel—"

"Are you going to kill the sheep?" she insisted, sounding just like Willow Stimson.

"I'm not. 'Tis the butcher who'll do that."

"But you're sending them to the butcher, right?"

"Well, yes. How else could the chef cook the mutton?" He was fast growing tired of the inquisition, and he wished the girl was still five years old so he could send her to a corner. But Maribeth was too old for that sort of treatment, and she deserved straight answers. "Maribeth, 'tis a farm I run. I raise animals for their food value—the cows for milk and the sheep for meat. I don't raise pets. If 'tis what you want, next spring you can choose a lamb all your own. One we won't sell—"

"But how can I choose one to live when the rest are going to be killed? And do we *really* have to eat them? Can't we eat corn and potatoes and bread and apples and cheese and . . . and other stuff?"

Good God, Willow had gotten to the child, after all. 'Twas a fine mess for a farmer to be in! "Ah . . . you can eat what you want, but I can't be keepin' those sheep for you. I can't afford to raise them with no hope of return."

Maribeth's pinched lips grew a white edge. Her blue eyes narrowed. She'd never looked more like her mother than she did right then. Daniel remembered Maggie arguing with him. He'd never won a single bout with his fiery sister. This one with her daughter was one he *couldn't* lose. His vow to his late father was one he couldn't afford to break.

With a shuddering breath, Maribeth swiped tears from her cheek. "Willow was right. You don't have a heart. I don't want to be with you anymore. I'm going to my room, so don't come after me. I'll let you know when I decide to leave."

With a violent slam to the door, she was gone. Daniel closed his gaping jaw. How had his life gotten so terribly confused?

Women. That was how.

Later that night Daniel stood at his bedroom window, staring out into the dark. He'd spent the last two hours thrashing on the bed, seeking elusive sleep. What was he going to do about Willow? Maribeth?

It had all seemed so simple when he'd spoken to Elijah Stoltzfus. He would pay Willow's debts, give her the deed to the farm, marry her, and between the two of them—with great caution on his part—raise Maribeth.

But now Willow had stomped off in a dither, Maribeth didn't even want to be near him, and although he still wanted to marry her, he had no way of knowing whether Willow would be amenable any time in the near future. Maribeth needed parents right away. Daniel felt more helpless than ever.

He was also scared to death. Maribeth's final words had carried a warning. *"I'll let you know when I decide to leave."* He had to do something, anything to keep her from running away again. He had to do it fast.

Still, a niggling corner of his mind reminded him that Maribeth's antics had been influenced by her contact with

Willow, who was more than conversant with the same old tales and legends his mother had favored. The last thing he needed was to walk outside one day and find the two of them communing with trees and faeries and leprechauns.

He certainly couldn't see Willow's supposed common sense, no matter how much Mrs. Meister assured him it was there in its proper place. He couldn't let Willow fill Maribeth's imagination with dreams of quests and adventures and princes and magic. The girl needed to grow up equipped to handle the realities of life.

He pounded the windowsill. "Damn!"

It was getting late, and he was as awake as ever. What was he going to do?

Another hour went by before Daniel found peace from his thoughts, before he finally slept.

A slender shadow crossed the distance between the farmhouse and the large barn nearby. Its enormous crossbuck door opened silently, and the wraith slipped inside. A horse nickered in greeting. A sheep baahed, too.

Moments later a more substantial shadow traced the same path. The horse welcomed this newcomer. The sheep joined in.

Then the larger shadow took something from a pocket, the *scritch* of a match hung in the air, and a kerosene lamp flared to life.

"Oh!" cried Maribeth, turning her back to the mare she was saddling.

Bearing the lantern, Hans approached. "What are you doing?"

"What do you *think* I'm doing, stupid?"

Hans came closer, anger on his features. "Let's try it again. *Why* are you saddling Grianne?"

With a defiant toss of red pigtails, Maribeth returned to what she'd been doing. "Because I'm going to ride her."

"Where to?"

"None of your business."

Hans grew impatient. "Grianne is my business. I work for your uncle—"

Maribeth snorted. "My uncle, the butcher."

"The *butcher*! Are you crazy, little girl?" he egged her on, unable to stop himself. Maribeth was acting like a brat.

Blue eyes shot daggers of rage at him, but she didn't answer. "Where are you going?" he asked again. "It's the middle of the night. Everyone's asleep."

Childish lips formed a sneer. "Aren't you the bright one!"

"Brighter than you. No one in their right mind would go out now." He then jabbed at her pride. "Much less a child."

Mutiny showed in her pout. "I'm not a child, Hans. I'm a *young lady*."

"Then act like one! Where do you think you're going this late?"

"I don't think, I *know* where I'm going. It's none of your business."

For a pittance Hans would have throttled her. "We already discussed that. Grianne is my business as long as I work for your uncle. Where are you taking that horse?"

With an impatient gesture she tossed a braid off her shoulder. "You're not working for him right now, are you? He's sleeping, and if you were doing what you say everyone else is doing, you'd be sleeping, too. So, why are *you* following *me* around?"

Red circles appeared on Hans's fair cheeks. "Never mind about me. I'm a man. You're just a child. Take that saddle off that horse and go back to the house."

But Maribeth's eyes suddenly gleamed. "Aha! So . . . you're up to something, too. What would Uncle Danny say if I told him I found you in the barn in the middle of the night?"

With a furtive glance toward the barn doors, Hans laughed nervously, trying for nonchalance. "Nothing. I . . . just . . . came to check on the sheep."

"In the middle of the night? When you're supposed to be home?"

Hans switched the lantern from his right hand to his left. "Ah . . . well, I heard noises, a sheep crying. I came to see what was wrong."

"You heard them from all the way at your house? I don't hear any crying, do you?"

"Mustn't have been important."

Then the barn door squeaked as it opened further. "Pssst, Hans!" hissed a feminine voice.

Maribeth swung her head its way.

Hans mirrored her actions.

In the doorway they saw a disheveled young woman. "What's taking you so long?" she asked in a whiny voice. "I should have been home hours ago. If Papa finds my bed empty, I won't be able to meet you any more."

Hans groaned.

Maribeth chuckled.

Hans's friend frowned, then pointed at Maribeth. "Who's she?"

"Daniel's niece. Get back in the wagon. I'll take you home."

"I'll be waiting," said the young lady in an inviting way.

Hans's eyes widened.

Maribeth snickered. "*I'll be waiting. . . . Oooh, Hansie, boy, I'll be waiting. . . .*" she mimicked, hiding her jealousy behind the mocking words. "Goodness, Hans, what would Uncle Danny think about *her*? And that you brought her *here*?"

The young man gulped. "No-nothing. He's not going to know."

"Oh, really?" Maribeth asked, getting some of her own back as he squirmed.

Then Hans's eyes narrowed. "Yes, Maribeth, really. Because you're not going to tell him."

Donning bravado, Maribeth went back to saddling her horse. "Oh, really? Why shouldn't I tell him you've been smooching a girl here at the farm at night?"

"Because if you do, I'll have to go tell your uncle Danny right away that you're saddling Grianne. You wouldn't get far."

Maribeth paused, then laughed and loosened the cinch she'd just tightened. "He's not going to know, because *you're* not going to tell him. If you tell, I'll have to tell your *employer* that you've been smooching girls at the farm."

Hans sighed in relief. "It's a deal. Neither one of us tells. Now go back to bed so I can take Amanda home."

Maribeth felt the stab of jealousy again, but hid behind her mocking words. "Oooh, Hansie, boy! Amanda's waiting. Mustn't make her wait!" she chanted, waggling her index finger in front of Hans's nose.

Hans swatted her hand away and laughed. "Brat! Go back to bed and forget you came out here tonight. Forget you saw me."

Maribeth studied Hans for a moment. All humor left her. "Sure, Hans. Go take Amanda home. I'll go back to bed. I won't tell Uncle Danny."

Hans relaxed his stance. "I won't tell your uncle that you were out here, either. We're friends, right? Friends don't tell on friends."

"Sure, Hans, we're . . . *friends.*"

With a quick smile Hans replaced the lantern on the hook where it normally hung. "Thanks, Maribeth!"

As he ran out of the barn, he heard the girl mutter something about her only friend. Good. Maybe now that she'd seen him with a *woman* Maribeth would get over her silly crush on him. He began to whistle, climbed into the wagon, stole another kiss from Amanda, and headed for York.

Standing in the doorway of the barn, Maribeth watched it all. The kiss stabbed her lonely heart. She wasn't a child anymore, and she didn't want to be Hans's friend. She wanted more, even though he saw her as a child. Even though he was seven years older. Nineteen wasn't *that* old.

Someday, she thought. The present was for friends. She only had two of those.

Mrs. Reba Meister and Willow.

20

$\mathcal{W}$ILLOW BLEW HER raw, red nose for the millionth time that night. The only other time she'd felt this wretched was right after Aunt Lucie died and Milford ditched her. Although she hadn't suffered another death in her family, she was mourning the sheep she'd sold Daniel, and she was trying to cope with the heartache she'd suffered as a result of his self-seeking courtship.

Rough pounding sounded at the door. Slowly approaching, Willow wiped her swollen eyes. Her heart was truly broken this time. The pain of Daniel's betrayal went far deeper than Milford's defection.

She opened the door and found Maribeth Miller on her front porch. "What's wrong? Why are you here so late? Is—is Daniel hurt?"

With a "Hmmph!" Maribeth swept into Willow's parlor, dragging a lumpy feed sack behind her. "You said it yourself. Uncle Danny doesn't have a heart. He doesn't like me, and I'm not going to live with him anymore. I've decided to live with you and your sheep."

Willow's eyes widened. She looked from the girl to the sack, which probably contained Maribeth's every possession, and back to the girl again. "I don't think you want to do that. Your uncle paid for my farm earlier today. It belongs to him now and"—Willow tipped up her chin—"I must leave it to him."

Maribeth crossed her arms across her flat chest, nodding sagely. "I told you he was horrid. It's simple, then. I'll go with you, since I won't go back to Uncle Danny."

Willow bit her bottom lip, wondering what to do next. If she knew anything about Daniel, she knew he was sure to become frantic the moment he learned his niece was gone this late. She knew how much he loved the child, even though he had no notion how to cope with her. And no matter how much Willow wanted to comfort Maribeth, she couldn't encourage that penchant for running away.

She approached Daniel's niece and wrapped an arm around thin shoulders. "I'm afraid you can't stay with me. Your uncle loves you very much—"

"Hah!" Maribeth stomped her foot. "Shows how much you know. He doesn't like me at all!"

But Willow realized she *did* know a lot about Daniel, enough to reassure the girl. "Listen to me, Maribeth. Your uncle does love you, he just doesn't know how to raise a girl. He's never been a girl and he's never been a father. He needs your patience and help so he can learn what to do."

"Too bad he's *not* a girl," Maribeth muttered, sounding very much like her uncle.

Willow chuckled. No, it wasn't too bad Daniel was a man. There was much to be said for many of his masculine attributes. Only not to his niece. "Well, he's not, and what matters now is that you tell me what's wrong."

"*You* know," Maribeth said, staring at Willow as if Willow had suddenly kissed her common sense good-bye. "He started yelling at you and ran you off the farm. And he still wants to kill our sheep."

For a moment Willow frowned, weighing Maribeth's words. Then with a clear recollection of what had happened, she was forced to shake her head. "No, Maribeth, if I'm to be perfectly honest, I have to tell you that he didn't start yelling at me. I was already upset when I went to the farm. While I was there, I hardly let him say a word. I'm afraid I'm more at fault for that argument than he is."

Maribeth jutted out her jaw. She hadn't liked Willow's response. "But he's going to kill the sheep! I can't believe he wants to *eat* them. He's like those people who eat people. You know, in other places."

Willow groaned, remembering when she'd accused Daniel of cannibalism. Had she sounded as childish as Maribeth now did? Oh, dear. "I don't think we can say those two things are the same. Most people—civilized people— eat animals. Your uncle is just like everyone else."

"*You* don't eat animals, do you? Well, I've decided I won't either."

"Oh, I've been known to eat a chicken leg before. Mind you, the older I get the less I enjoy eating meat, but I won't mislead you." As she watched, Willow saw that this response didn't go over any better than her earlier one.

"Oh."

Maribeth fell silent, apparently still searching for more to hold against her uncle. Willow wondered if she hadn't responded to her disappointment with the fair results in precisely the same fashion. Could she have made more of the situation than it warranted? Had Daniel indeed done nothing more than show his sheep—which he was entitled to do—and try to help her out of a financial bind? Could she really have not known about Milford's plans?

A forgotten fact suddenly appeared in her thoughts. Daniel had been in Philadelphia when Milford jilted her just days before their announced wedding. It was quite possible that Maggie Miller hadn't bothered to relate the latest county gossip to her Philadelphia-businessman brother.

Willow also had to consider that while Milford had scouted property in the area during Fair Week, Daniel had been either at the fairgrounds or at her side. She hadn't seen Milford until she went to the bank earlier this morning. It was entirely possible that Daniel might not have heard of the potential competition until she told him about it today.

Could he possibly have been telling the truth? Had she been too stubborn, angry—unreasonable—to listen to him?

There was only one way to find out. "Come on, Maribeth. We both need to go back to Callaghan's Dairy. We have a lot of talking to do with Mr. Daniel Callaghan himself."

Daniel bolted upright in bed. The room was pitch black, the sky outside the window reflecting the orange of approaching dawn. His heart pounded wildly. His breathing became shallow pants. What had woken him up in this condition?

Then he heard it. The bone-chilling sound of panicked animals. The infernal hiss and crackle of fire.

Leaping to the window, Daniel realized that what he'd thought was dawn was actually the glow of a raging fire. In the barn.

Without wasting a second, he dragged on his trousers, stamped into his boots, and grabbed a flannel shirt as he ran out of the room.

Seconds later he stood close enough to feel the fury of the flames, the fear of the animals. Cows bellowed, sheep bleated, horses neighed. All around him mountains of smoke rose skyward, making the situation more hellish still.

The cacophony of threatened animals and devouring flames gripped Daniel's heart. Good God, he had to save those poor beasts. They didn't deserve to die. He'd worry about dousing the flames once he'd saved his stock.

He ran to the house and grabbed a thick woolen blanket. Back outside, he dunked it into a watering trough and threw it over his head. He ran into the barn, noting that the flames were somewhat contained in the rear and to one side of the structure.

As he opened the first stall, he heard Hans call his name outside. "Let them into the pasture," he responded. "They'll be fine there."

Hurrying, he dragged the frightened sheep to the barn doors. Without waiting, he thrust them at Hans and returned for more. Over and over they repeated their motions, trying to beat the greedy hunger of the fire. Sheep, cows, horses, one by one Daniel dragged them from certain death. Finally the flames spread too far. Two sheep remained in the last stall, but Daniel feared that if he went back for them, they'd all three die.

The animals in question were Willow's ewes.

"Damn!" he spat, kicking the door frame. He felt sick at heart for those two animals. They'd merely had the misfortune of being housed at the back of the barn. Daniel had placed them there, and now it didn't look good for them.

Still, they were Willow's sheep. He knew how she felt about them.

He vacillated another moment, then took a step toward the barn. Hans grabbed his arm, holding him back.

"Stop, Daniel! You can't go in there again. The fire's spread too far. It's too dangerous."

Daniel pulled on his sleeve. Hans held firm.

"Let me go, boy-o! I must get those sheep. They're Willow's ewes."

"I know they are, Daniel, but you can't go. You could die!"

Daniel didn't want to hear what Hans had to say. In his mind two voices kept arguing on behalf of the sheep, two feminine voices that pled with him to spare them. In a sudden burst of awareness Daniel understood Willow's bond with her animals.

It was the same feeling he'd experienced when he realized that unless he did something about it, his cows and sheep and horses would die. He'd willingly risked his life for the animals he'd come to love. Willow would have done no less.

He couldn't let Daisy and Rosebud die. He couldn't fail Willow.

Tearing his arm from Hans's grip, Daniel threw the wet blanket over his head and dove floorward into the barn.

Hans watched his employer throw himself into the thick of the smoke, and he knew a helplessness he'd never known before. As he watched, his heart in his throat, from just behind him he heard an anguished woman's wail.

"Daniel, noooo . . ."

Hans spun around and saw Willow hurtle past him. He looked. Blinked. Looked again. Where had she come from? Why was she standing at the door to the barn, so close to the fire, twisting her hands and crying?

"Willow!" he called. "Get away from there. You'll be hurt."

"No, Hans, I-I have to help him. He's in there!"

"Yes, he's in there, but there's nothing you can do. Move back!"

She took a step toward Hans, then one toward the barn. "Why did he go in?"

Hans hesitated. "Daisy and Rosebud are still inside."

Willow's eyes widened. "What? Is he crazy? He went after my two sheep? But what about *him*? He could get hurt, or—or worse."

"He said he couldn't let your sheep die."

"So instead he's going to get himself killed? How's that going to help? What about Maribeth? What about me? I can't let him die!" With that she followed Daniel into the blazing furnace that had once been a barn.

As Hans's spirits plummeted, flames crawled out the hayloft window, licking upward, scorching the wood. He was forced to watch in helpless impotence. He heard Daisy and Rosebud crying. The sizzle of the fire surrounded him.

Desperation stung him. He had to do something. Anything. He couldn't stand there and watch the fire destroy the barn, kill those sheep, take two lives. He had to do whatever he could to help. Grabbing a pail, he filled it at the pump not more than ten feet away, then dumped it on the nearest patch of flames. When he turned around with the empty bucket, he noticed Hiram Becker and his two sons approaching.

"We came to help!" cried the older man.

"We brought buckets, too," added Ned, a taller, heftier version of his father. His brother, Arthur, waved another pail in the air.

Hans felt a surge of hope strengthen his waning spirits. "Thank you. We need more water. Willow and Daniel are in there, trying to get the last two sheep. Why don't you three start a bucket line on that side, while I stay here. We can work inward."

The three newcomers arranged themselves between the water pump and the open-doored barn, and began to hurl water at the fire.

When Hans turned around to refill his bucket, he felt a tug on his shirtsleeve. With a sidewise glance, he saw Maribeth's horrified face, her slender body shaking visibly. "What are you doing here?" he asked, shocked to see her.

"Th-that doesn't m-matter. Uncle Danny and Willow are . . . are in there. Can't you . . . can't you help them?"

Hans pulled his arm away from her and pumped vigorously. "I'm doing what I can. We have to control the fire, put it out."

"But you're wasting time. Don't you understand? They're *in* there!"

"Don't *you* understand? I can't help them if I go in after them." After dumping more water on the ever-present flames, he ran back to the pump and glared at Maribeth. "Go back to bed. I can't talk to you now. I *am* trying to help them."

He heard her snort, then to his horror, saw her slip into the billows of smoke pouring out the barn door. "Maribeth!" he hollered, more scared than he'd ever been in his life. Throwing the bucket down, Hans flew after her, using his larger bulk to tackle her to the ground before she'd crossed the threshold. "What are you, stupid? It won't do you or them any good if you get yourself killed. Daniel never fails. He always succeeds. He-he'll get them out."

When he faltered, she gasped. Damn! He shouldn't have said anything. At least, not about Willow's and Daniel's chances of getting out. Anyone with eyes could see those chances were virtually nonexistent.

Maribeth tried to wrestle out of his arms. Hans held on tight.

"Let me go!" screamed his boss's niece. "I don't have anyone else. Everyone's dead. Now Daisy, Rosebud, Willow, and even Uncle Danny are going to die, too!"

"How's it going to make things better if you get yourself killed?"

"I won't have to hurt all alone."

Maribeth's words hit Hans in the deepest part of his heart. She *was* all alone, all alone save her uncle, Willow, and himself. "Hey," he said with sympathy, "you're not all alone. What about me?"

Maribeth pummeled Hans's shoulders. He rolled off to

her side. She bounced up, aiming her venomous blue stare at him. "You? Hah! All you want is Amanda."

Hans stood, too, wiped his hands against his trousers, then grabbed Maribeth's hand and dragged her away from the doorway of the burning barn. "Nah, brat, I'm all for keeping you around." With gentle care, he walked her to the water pump.

When he looked around, he realized more neighbors had come out to help. Three separate bucket brigades were running, and unless his eyes betrayed him, it looked as if the fire was coming under control.

Just then a sheep cried piteously from inside the barn. Maribeth screamed and took a step toward the sound, but Hans pulled her close to his chest. As she cried, he patted her back, not knowing what he was going to do with the weeping girl once it became obvious her uncle and Willow were no longer alive. Tears stung his eyelids, but he fought to keep himself strong. Maribeth needed him.

Then a miracle occurred. A sooty sheep bounded out the door. Shouts of relief rivaled the loud sucking sound of the devouring fire. Moments later the other ewe, just as disheveled and ash-covered, followed the first. This time total silence gripped the crowd.

Were Daniel and Willow still alive?

Silent seconds ticked by.

All one could hear was the hiss of the water when it hit the flames and the sharp popping of wood when it surrendered to the heat. No one stopped in their efforts to douse the fire, but no one dared speak. They were too afraid of what they'd have to say.

Finally a blanket-shrouded ball rolled out of the barn. It came to a stop at Hans's feet. Cheers went up, then suddenly died, since no one knew if both Daniel and Willow had made it out. The blanket covered the ball.

Then, "Get off me, you mountain of mule—"

"Don't you ever call me that again, lass—"

"Then get your enormous body off me! I can't breathe."

The fire-fighters gave in to nervous snickering, then burst into relieved laughter as Willow and Daniel continued to bicker under the blanket. Maribeth tore out of Hans's arms and flung herself on the sparring pair, slugging them indiscriminately as hard as she could.

"Don't you ever scare me that bad again, Uncle Danny!"

The wriggling bundle under the girl grew absolutely still. An ominous silence again fell over those gathered in the Callaghan barnyard. Maribeth hastily—wisely—backed off. The blanket flew up, and Daniel stood. His eyebrows crashed together over the bridge of his nose. His jaw was even more squared than usual. "What in he—"

"Daniel . . ." warned Willow, also standing.

Daniel cleared his throat. "What in the world are you doing outside, lassie? Shouldn't you be in bed?"

Maribeth's brows mirrored her uncle Danny's. "I'm not a baby anymore! I want to help."

Daniel grabbed the bucket someone stuck in his hands, then passed it on to Hans, who'd gone to stand at his side. "Fine, Maribeth. You aren't a baby, but you're also not an adult yet. As long as you're a child you're my responsibility. I can't let you stay out here just because you want to. This is dangerous, not child's play. Go on inside, and we'll talk about it tomorrow."

Then he turned back to the barn and noticed that the blaze was dying down. He saw Willow grasp an empty bucket and send it back to the water pump. He was glad she was there. He was glad they'd saved her sheep. But what was she doing at his farm? When had she gotten here? How could she have put herself in so much danger as to rush into the burning barn?

He passed the dripping pail Hans gave him to Arthur Becker, then rushed to Willow's side. As she swung an empty pail to the woman at her left, Daniel slipped in at her right. When she noticed him, her eyes widened.

"Why?" he asked.

A frown crinkled her forehead. "Why what?"

"Why did you come here? Last time I saw you, you thought I sported horns, tail, and smoking pitchfork."

Eyelids came down over those brown eyes. She shoved the sloshing bucket of water at his middle, then turned to study the barnyard pump. "I decided I owed you the opportunity to explain yourself. I never let you answer my accusations."

Willow Stimson backing down! Miracles did still happen. "What made you come to that conclusion?"

Slamming her fists on her slim hips, Willow turned to face him. Daggers of energy shot out from her eyes. "This time, after your last to-do with Maribeth, she decided to move in with me. When I listened to her complaints about you and her accusations, well . . . ah . . . they sounded . . ." One hand waved away the importance of her words, the other slid over her lips, muffling her words. *"Cserjersh."*

"Excuse me?" Any minute now, Daniel expected her to stomp a foot, she was so defiant. The woman had no notion what repentance meant.

"Childish, dammit!"

A smile widened his lips. A chuckle threatened to escape, but Daniel suspected if it did, they'd be back to where they'd been before she came to give him a chance. "Your apology is duly accepted *a'sto'ri'n,* and I'll tell you again that I'm innocent of all your charges." She shoved another bucket at his middle, reminding him of the mutton stew incident. He sent it on to the front of the line. "I never wanted your farm, Willow. I don't want it now. All I want is you."

Her head swiveled, and their eyes met. Silent communication flowed between them, broken only when the empty pail came back to Daniel. As he passed it on to her, their fingers touched. A shot of fire flew up his arm, and he watched her eyes widen in surprise. "Why did you go into the barn?"

Willow mouthed a word, too softly for Daniel to hear. "What was that?"

She faced him, and he met her haunted gaze. "You were in there. I couldn't just let you die for the sake of two sheep."

"Even if they were your own?"

"Even then."

At that moment Daniel noticed the woman to her left listening intently. He ran a finger over Willow's sooty cheek. "We'll talk later, lass."

"Later," she repeated. Then she nodded slowly, her eyes veiled.

Lord, the woman was still a mystery to him. But one thing was now absolutely clear. He'd never let anything come between them again. He would never survive another separation, another worry about the woman he loved.

For the rest of their lives he intended to care for her, protect her, provide for her. Daniel Callaghan now knew that Willow Stimson was the only woman for him.

As Hiram Becker, the last of his neighbors to leave, drove his wagon out of the Callaghan's Dairy drive, Daniel allowed himself a moment to relax. To his amazement, his knees sagged, and he drooped to the ground near the farmyard pump. The ground was damp and cold, but he relished that coolness after the hours of fighting the killing heat of the blaze.

He'd been lucky, unbelievably lucky. None of his animals had died; no one was injured. Well, he couldn't count the blisters on his hands and the scrape across his cheek. After all, when one went about saving lives, minor wounds didn't matter much.

Glancing around, he wondered where Willow had gone to. It had been a while since he last saw her. The need to see her, hold her safe in his arms, propelled him upright again. Slapping his hands free of damp dirt, he started toward the house.

"Daniel!" called Hans from behind him, apprehension in his voice.

Daniel spun around, responding to that note of concern. "What is it? Is anyone . . . ?"

At the look of misery on his farmhand's youthful features, a knot formed in Daniel's gut. "Tell me, boy-o, what's wrong?"

"Seems boy-o is right, after all," the youth answered, keeping his gaze in the vicinity of Daniel's charred, filthy work boots. Then, squaring his shoulders, Hans lifted his head and met Daniel's gaze.

Guilt, Daniel read in that clear stare. "What have you done?" he asked.

Hans clenched his fists, as if bracing for a blow. "I hardly know how to say it, and I know I deserve whatever you decide to do with me, but . . . earlier last night . . . I-I went to the barn. I heard one of the sheep crying, and . . . and, well, I thought I should check on it."

"When was this?"

"About ten o'clock."

Daniel frowned. "What were you doing here so late? Didn't you go home as usual?"

"Yes, b-but I came back."

"Why?"

Hans rubbed his face with a shaking hand, and Daniel felt sympathy join his apprehension. "Well, get on with it, son."

"I-I was meeting someone out here."

"Someone?" Daniel asked, his patience fading. "Who?"

Hans blushed to the roots of his blond hair, his ears glowing red. "Ah . . . er, Amanda . . . Amanda Neuhaus."

Daniel frowned again. He didn't understand why in heaven's name Hans was telling him about his romantic escapade. "Is there a reason you're telling me this?"

Hans nodded and swiped his damp upper lip. "Yes . . . umm . . . when I was going to take her home, I heard the sheep, so I lit the lantern when I went in, and—"

"An' you left it burnin' when you left. Damn!" Daniel's anger raged hotly, as hot as the fire had burned just a short time ago. Hans's youthful negligence had cost him a barn and a night of fear. It also nearly cost him the lives of his animals, his own, and worse yet, Willow's.

Still, there was little he could say that would make Hans any more miserable or regret his mistake any more than he already did. They'd have to deal with the matter of the fire sooner or later, but for Daniel, later would be soon enough. He had more important matters to attend to. He had a proposal to make, a future wife to persuade. He had to make Willow see that marriage was the only thing for the two of them.

And he wasn't going to wait a second longer than he had to. Life was too fragile, too precious to waste.

With a sharp nod and a sigh, he said, "I understand, lad. We'll talk about it later. You did yourself proud organizin' the bucket brigades, though. I'll take that into consideration."

"I don't deserve any consideration—"

"Let me decide that, will you? Get on home, son. You've earned a rest, regardless."

Hans's heartfelt "Thank you" rang out as he trudged to where he'd tied his gelding. With an easy swing, he mounted, and rode out to the road. As Daniel watched his farmhand leave, he again thought they'd have to come to some form of understanding. After all, Hans's mistake had threatened Daniel's stock, and Willow's and his own lives. He'd also caused Daniel's barn to burn down to cinders.

Suddenly Hans led his horse back onto the drive, and Daniel looked up at the young man, a question in his gaze.

Hans looked ready to pop, and Daniel wondered how many more confessions he could expect at this time. "What is it now?"

Squirming in his saddle, Hans shrugged. "Ah . . . well, you see, Maribeth was really angry when you sent her back to bed. I saw her running to the pasture . . . and I think you'd better see if Grianne is still there. She might have run—"

"Away again," Daniel finished with a long-suffering sigh. "Tell me, how was it you came along at just the right time to help fight the fire?"

Hans flushed again. "I was coming home from taking Amanda home."

Daniel smiled wryly. "Of course. Anything else?"

With an ambiguous hand gesture, Hans then fiddled with the reins. "I don't know if it has anything to do with Maribeth, but I saw Willow drive her wagon down the road right after I saw Maribeth in the pasture."

Daniel chuckled without humor and wondered if this excruciating night would ever end. "Great! Now I have the two of them to find. Is that it? Have you any more sins to share?"

Hans shook his head. "I don't think so. I mean, I hope not,

sir. Except . . . I'm pretty sure Willow didn't go home. I don't know why, but she was heading toward town."

Daniel thought for a moment.

Hans fell silent, too. Then he said, "Maybe . . . maybe Maribeth went to that friend of Willow's. You know, the big lady Maribeth stayed with toward the end of the fair. Right before I left with Amanda, I heard her mumble something about her only friend . . . maybe friends. At first I thought she meant I was her only friend, but the more I think about it, the more I believe she meant Willow and that lady."

Daniel slapped his forehead. "'Course, an' that's where the wee lass went. Willow was here, fighting the fire. If Maribeth was going to run away, she'd go to someone she trusted. She certainly took to Reba Meister and wasn't ready to come back to the farm after the time she spent at the Meisters' home."

Slapping Hans's horse on the flank, he gestured the youth away. "Go on now, lad. I'll get the two of them back. 'Tis home I'm bringin' them, right where they belong. I'll be havin' to find ways to make them want to stay with me forever."

21

THE RIDE INTO York took very little time. Scarcely enough for a man to have a monumental revelation, but somewhere on the road between Callaghan's Dairy and the town of York, Daniel experienced his own epiphany. The shock of the fire and his driving need to act had shed light on any number of conflicts he'd been carrying around for years. It was too bad it took him this long to understand his parents as well as he now did.

For the first time in his life, Daniel knew exactly why his father had been so single-minded about the dairy. It had been Darby's dream, one he was willing to work himself to death for. In that split second of decision, as Daniel realized all the Callaghan's Dairy animals would die in the fire if he didn't rescue them, he recognized that his father's dream had become his own over the last year. He couldn't let even one of his animals die in the blaze.

He now could also accept that Darby had shared some of Maeve's more whimsical tendencies. His father had followed a quest, his own brand of adventure, and it had led him from Ireland to Pennsylvania, and ultimately to Callaghan's Dairy. At the same time, thanks to what Mrs. Meister had said, he understood that Maeve hadn't been nearly the flighty, otherworldly idealist he'd thought her for

so long. She'd given her family love, happiness, fed their
imaginations, and fueled their spiritual growth. She was the
one who had given Daniel the secure sense of family that
allowed him to test his wings. It wasn't her fault that Daniel
left the farm, and when viewed this way, Daniel had to
wonder how damaging his departure had really been.

Yes, he'd seen Philadelphia as a kingdom to conquer, but
he'd learned much about business during those years. He'd
gathered knowledge and experience that had shown him
how to maximize the success of his father's farm—his own
farm now. Besides, had he stayed home, he and Darby
might have found themselves in a tug-o'-war over the dairy,
as opinionated as both were. Darby might have continued
his hardworking ways regardless of who was there to help.

Daniel also learned that when it really mattered, family
meant much more to him than success. It was the memory
of the happy family life Maeve had nurtured during all those
years that he found himself missing after Darby, Maeve, and
Maggie had died. It was that same family feeling he wanted
to provide for Maribeth.

He could no longer think of Willow as an ineffective
dreamer. Her farm was scrupulously maintained, her sheep
were outstanding, healthy representatives of their breed, and
she'd even taken up the defense and care of his own niece!
Her flight after Maribeth showed a strong sense of duty, of
maturity, and a profound desire to nurture.

That she liked Celtic myths and Irish folk tales was
merely a bonus. And her faith in luck? Well, she was
entitled to her own touch of whimsy. After all, he played the
violin, and that had never detracted from his strength, either
in business or his personal life. As he'd recently learned,
thanks to Miss Willow Stimson herself.

Remembering the barn dance where she forced him to
publicly acknowledge that private part of himself, Daniel

was grateful for the relief her actions had brought him. He could take the best of both worlds, he could succeed in the dairy business, and he could also indulge his more spiritual side. That God-given part of him was what gave him the wings to soar to heights of wonder, the voice with which to express the deep love he was capable of feeling.

He loved her. Just as she was. Yes, his shepherdess was indeed a prize. And he was going to win her.

In the end all he'd lost were some foolish misconceptions, and a perfectly good barn, a small price to pay for his sudden peace of mind.

Still, something didn't feel right, but for the life of him Daniel couldn't place his finger on what it was. It had bothered him since he'd left Hans and headed for York. Even now, as he approached the Meisters' home, the nagging twinge of unease refused to let up.

Turning into the drive, Daniel guided his horse around to the back by the stone carriage house. There he found an old horse and wagon, patiently waiting. They looked like the ones Willow had driven to Callaghan's Dairy yesterday morning.

Looping the reins through the ring on a post, Daniel hurried to the main house. Lights were on in what he was sure was the library where he'd caught Willow reading Irish folk tales to Maribeth. Either his two ladies were here, or the Meisters kept strange hours indeed.

At his knock, the door swung open, and Mrs. Meister pulled him inside. "Finally! We were wondering how long it would be before you got here. The fire is out, right?"

Startled, Daniel nodded. "You were waitin' for me?"

"Well, of course, son," she said, marching him down the hallway in the direction of the library. "Maribeth got here first, crying her heart out, unable — or unwilling — to tell me why she was in such a state. Then Willow rushed in, all dirty, sooty, wet, and smelly. She mumbled something about your barn burning, then ran to Maribeth, trying to comfort her. But the child just keeps crying."

Meek as a lamb, Daniel allowed himself to be led. He'd thought most of his problems had been solved when the fire was put out, especially since he'd untangled those personal conflicts he'd been toting around for years. Now it seemed Maribeth hadn't run off in a lather, as had been the case before. This much crying was extreme, even for his recently moody niece.

Mrs. Meister gestured him into the library, then closed the door behind him. He found Maribeth sitting on the bloodred Persian rug, her head buried in her arms on the cushion of a coffee-brown settee, while Willow sat as close to the girl as she could get. Pain-filled sobs wracked Maribeth, giving evidence to her misery. Willow, dirty and damp, continued rubbing the girl's back and smoothing her disheveled red hair.

As he approached, Willow glanced up. Her eyes widened, and a tentative smile curved her lips. Despite the swath of soot darkening one cheek and the tip of her nose, she was the most welcome sight Daniel had ever seen. Her smile meant the world. He smiled back.

He sat on the settee, at his niece's other side. Laying his hand on her shoulder, he pressed gently. "Maribeth, lass, please tell me what's wrong."

At the sound of his voice, the sobbing came to an abrupt halt. Her shoulders quit shaking, and she gulped down huge lungfuls of air. Then she lifted her head, squared her shoulders, and stood. Red-rimmed eyes met his gaze.

She clasped her hands at her waist. "I-I'm so very so-sorry, Uncle Danny. I really di-didn't mean to do it. Honest, I didn't. And I'm sure you're going to get . . . get rid of me, and I understand."

Daniel was speechless, clueless, and even breathless. "What are you sayin'?"

White-knuckled fingers began to twist a fold of dirty green-and-gold plaid skirt. "That I understand, Uncle Danny. You don't need to-to put up with me anymore. Especially since you never wanted me in the first place, and now that all this happened, I know you'll finally send me away."

Pressing the heels of his palms into his tired eyes, Daniel sought to make sense of what the girl said. But no matter how many ways he considered her mistaken notion, he came up with many missing pieces to Maribeth's puzzling statements.

Unable to sit, he stood and began pacing. "Maribeth, lass, is this the first time you've run away?"

She met his gaze momentarily, then glanced down toward the rich-hued rug. "No," she said, her voice small and scared.

He wanted to run to her, hold her, try to ease her fear away, but Daniel didn't even know where to start, so he again tried to reason with the girl. "Haven't I chased after you, brought you home each time?"

"Yes."

"Then why would you think I don't want you? If I didn't, I wouldn't go to the trouble of fetchin' you back, now would I?"

A shoulder jerked up, but blue eyes widened.

"So what is it you've done this time to persuade yourself that I'll send you away for good?"

A huge sob ripped through her, and tears again welled in her eyes. "I-I burned down your barn."

Daniel froze. *"You did what?"*

In a gesture very like Willow's, Maribeth tipped her chin up. "I burned down your barn."

By God, and he now knew what had bothered him on the

ride into town! Hans had said he'd heard Maribeth talking about friends as he drove away from the barn with the Neuhaus girl, but he'd never mentioned that Maribeth had been in the barn at the same time he was there. "Well, an' I'll be damned . . . I have two culprits and one charred barn."

Maribeth stole a peek at him, then looked away again. "Two culprits?"

Daniel rocked back on his heels. This was getting interesting. "Amazin' things, coincidences. Just before I came to town, Hans confessed to torchin' down my barn. Now you're doin' the same. How did you and Hans get together to burn down that barn?"

Maribeth stared past Daniel to a point behind him. "We didn't. I went out to saddle Grianne because I was leaving the farm. I was going to Willow. But Hans . . . he came in the barn and sent me back to bed. I pretended to do that, then came back and rode Grianne to Willow's."

Fighting to stifle a chuckle, Daniel asked, "What was Hans doin' in the barn at night? Hadn't he gone home?"

Maribeth turned her back to Daniel. "Ah . . . er . . . he-he was checking on the sheep."

"Didn't that strike you as odd? Shouldn't he have been at home?"

A shoulder jerked up again.

Daniel suspected her shrug concealed more pain than it revealed. Maribeth, infatuated with Hans, was likely hurting after seeing him with a girl. Poor wee lass. "Very well, Maribeth, I can see we'll have to talk this out between the three of us. You, Hans, and me. But I'm not sendin' you away. Understood?"

Maribeth nodded. Then she startled Daniel by running at him, throwing her arms around his neck, and hugging him. "I don't want to go away. I don't really hate you."

Awkwardly Daniel held the girl close, surprised at the prickling behind his eyelids. Lord, what these females put a man through! "And I love you, Maribeth," he murmured, patting her shoulder. "Right now, though, I want a moment alone with Willow. Go along and tell Mrs. Meister we'll be out directly."

"With Willow?" his niece asked, an odd expression on her face.

Gesturing toward Willow, he said, "Yes, of course—" He cut off his words when he turned and realized Willow no longer occupied the settee. "Where the hell—er, excuse me! Where in the world did that woman go?"

Maribeth's lips twitched with a poorly concealed smile. "I don't know where she went, Uncle Danny, but she left the library while you were pacing back and forth."

Daniel threw his hands up in helplessness. "So much for the chance to explain myself," he muttered, thinking of what Willow had said to him in the bucket line. She'd offered him a chance, and he was going to take it. No matter what.

Miss Willow Stimson and Daniel Callaghan had some fence-mending to do, and nothing was going to stand in his way.

She'd finally gotten home when dawn painted the eastern sky a delicate shade of rose. After tending to Rufus and checking on her three remaining sheep, Willow went to her room, undressed, washed off the worst of the grime from her fire-fighting efforts, and collapsed on her bed. Sleep claimed her immediately.

For the first time in her entire adult life—most of her childhood, too—she allowed herself the luxury of sleeping late in the morning. It was already past ten o'clock.

Hairbrush in hand, Willow approached the window. She began to work through the knots in her hair as she took in the essence of the day. It was a beautiful autumn morning, clear, crisp, comforting. The Pennsylvania countryside wore a vibrant palette of reds, golds, greens, browns. Across the road, cornfields were covered with the drying stubble that remained after the harvest, and the pastures beyond still shone green and bright. The sky, a brilliant blue, sported random, gossamer wisps of cloud. It was all so beautiful that she was reluctant to move.

Her thoughts refused to pause, though, and they inevitably led straight to a stubborn, irritating, fascinating Irish rogue. Willow hadn't been surprised to see Daniel arrive at the Meisters' last night. He had, after all, made a habit of chasing Maribeth back every time she ran away. Still, she hadn't known what she would do when he finished speaking with his niece. So Willow slipped away. He'd promised— maybe threatened was more the case—they would have another chance to talk things out. But Willow hadn't been ready to do so when her nerves were still so rattled by the events in the night.

She still didn't know what she would do about Daniel. She did, however, realize she should get dressed soon. Since she'd been the one to leave, she was probably the one who ought to make the next move. And she didn't want to postpone that conversation indefinitely. She wanted to know how Daniel really felt.

Turning away from the window, she walked to her large oak dresser and took out undergarments, a crisp white shirtwaist, and a fresh pair of black stockings. From the wardrobe closet she chose a serviceable navy serge skirt. But before she had time to change, a strange conglomeration of sounds wafted up from the road.

What on earth was going on out there? She'd just been at the window, and the road had looked deserted. She threw her clothes on the bed and ran back to her earlier post, only to see a large group of sheep advancing down the road. A dog kept them moving, circling continuously, barking vigorously. Baas and bleats argued back.

Occasional squeaks could be heard from the rear of the flock, but Willow couldn't identify their source, since the animals were so loud. Curiosity propelling her, and despite her cotton flannel nightgown, she flew down the stairs and out to the front porch.

That's when she saw him. Bringing up the rear of the odd procession was Daniel Callaghan, animatedly playing the violin. Willow's eyes widened in surprise. Her heart began pounding. She found it impossible to tear her gaze away from his face.

Slowly, as he approached, Willow caught snippets of music. Every step he took made the tune clearer, teasing her with its familiarity, although she couldn't yet hear it distinctly enough to identify the piece.

Then Daniel smiled. That devilish, tilted, mustachioed grin of his that stole her heart on opening day at the York County Fair. Despite seeing it a number of times since then, she'd grown no more used to the wild rush it sent through her, the excitement it awoke.

The dog rounded up the last of the sheep, directing the herd into Willow's yard. Daniel followed, then whistled sharply, calling the dog to his side. Through it all, the crazy man never stopped fiddling. Which allowed Willow to recognize the tune he played. It was, of course, "Danny Boy."

Like Moses parting the Red Sea, Daniel made his way through the milling balls of fleece, then took her front steps in two leaps. The last notes of Danny Boy faded, and he dove right into a sprightly Irish jig. Willow could no longer stifle her mirth. She burst out laughing, feeling lighter than she had in a very long time.

"What *are* you doing?" she asked between chuckles.

He winked. "Fiddling. And dancing." Sure enough, he danced a few steps around her and kept right on playing.

She turned in place, trying to keep him in sight. "I can see that, but what are all these sheep doing here? And why are you here, fiddling and dancing, in the middle of the day?"

He jerked his head toward the sheep, bow still sailing over tight strings. "They're yours."

Willow blinked, startled. "What do you mean, they're mine?"

"Just what I said," he answered, continuing his serenade. "They're yours. You can do whatever you want with them. Every last one of them can be a wool-making machine, for all I care."

Willow's breath caught. Was he saying what he seemed to be saying? "I can do whatever I want with them?"

He nodded, launching his bow into yet another grand flourish of sound.

Willow was still having trouble giving credence to her ears and her eyes. "I see Daisy and Rosebud . . . oh! and Jethro and Zebulon, too. But where did you get the rest?"

"They were mine. And look carefully, *a'sto'ri'n*, you have another friend among them."

Willow swept the flock with a careful eye, then smiled, exclaiming, "Missy! I thought she was with Dr. Wirtz."

Daniel nodded, approaching on the notes of the waltz they once danced to. "She was. I went to see the good doctor and told him it was time for that lass to come home. So I brought her with the rest of your flock."

Suddenly he tucked his bow under his arm and began patting his chest. Taking folded papers out of a pocket, he offered them to her. "Here, love, I don't want to forget this. It's your deed. With your name right on it. The other paper is a note drawn up in the amount of money you owe me.

Since you were so opposed to letting me pay off your debts, you can now make good on your debt to me. If you'll notice, the terms are most liberal."

Willow turned serious, but she never bothered to look at the documents. She sought the answer she needed in his eyes. "Then you *really* weren't interested in the farm?"

"Not in the least. I can barely handle what I have on my plate right now. When I considered expanding, I was pushing myself beyond reasonable boundaries, thinking I still had to prove myself to my father. But last night I realized that's not what he would have wanted me to do. He would only have expected me to do my best, for Callaghan's Dairy and for Maribeth, not to live up to an unreasonable standard he would never have held me to."

"But why give away the sheep? Why not sell them? Won't you be taking a loss?"

He shrugged, then set the violin down on a chair behind him and crammed his hands in his pockets. "Because you and Maribeth made a very good point. There are losses . . . and then there are losses. I couldn't bring myself to let even one of them die in a fire, never mind send the bunch of them to be turned into Sunday dinner leg-o'mutton roasts."

Willow raised her eyebrows. "This from the man who called me barmy when I expressed that very sentiment?"

Daniel's cheeks turned red. "Yes, well . . . but don't go tellin' everyone! I'd never live it down."

Willow laughed long and hard, so long that tears filled her eyes, so hard they spilled onto her cheeks. "And why the serenade?"

"Well, I'd always thought of my fiddlin' as a weakness I didn't want to admit to. But you showed me it was a strength. No one saw me as any less the successful businessman after the barn dance. And I owe you my gratitude. 'Twas a gift my mother first gave me, and I was able to make peace with my talent when you gave it to me again."

Willow's heart took flight. Maybe there was hope for them after all. "Oh, Daniel, I'm glad! So glad your mother taught you to play."

Daniel let out a breath that resonated with relief. "Well, then," he went on, "let's get the sheep into the barn and go tell Maribeth the news. We have a lot of details to see to before the weddin'."

Willow frowned. There he went again with that wedding business. He'd never consulted her in the first place. Hmmph! "So . . . who's getting married?"

Daniel snorted. "Don't joke about it, lass. It's been hard enough as it 'tis."

"I'm missing something here. I don't know who is marrying whom."

"Saints preserve us, we are! You, me." Daniel's cheeks ruddied again. "We go to church, have a ceremony." He rubbed the palms of his hands down his face. "What the hell do you mean, you don't know who's marryin' whom? Why else would I be here, givin' you a mess of sheep and makin' a fool of myself?"

Willow planted her fists on her hips, growing more disgusted by the second with the recalcitrant brute. "Aside from Milford Philpott two and a half years ago, I don't remember anyone asking me to marry him. Especially not you."

His eyebrows slid together, and his jaw jutted out. "Remind me to thank Mr. Philpott for jiltin' you, if I ever come across the fool." He came closer, so close Willow felt the warmth of his body, the fresh scent of his soap. Then he stabbed his chest with his thumb. "Aye, lass, you're marryin' me. Maribeth and I need you, and you know it, too."

At his mention of his niece, Willow crossed her arms over

her chest and tipped her chin up. "Maribeth needs a neglectful person who uses poor judgment? A woman who's daft, barmy, and who knows what else?"

The bright red blush spread from above Daniel's beard to the roots of his hair. "Ah . . . well, you see, lass . . ."

"Yes?" she pushed.

"Er . . . I've always had a wee problem with . . . oh, I'd say, idealistic folk. Those who like my mother could be considered . . . eccentric." His hands came out from his pockets and dug furrows through his hair. A clear sign of discomfort.

Willow smiled wickedly.

With random gestures, he went on. "Well, an' you're an idealist, and you're superstitious, and you even tell the same tales my mother told me when I was a lad!"

"And *that's* why you decided I wasn't good enough to take care of Maribeth?"

"Well, you can't blame me for not wantin' the lass to end up chattin' with leprechauns and communin' with trees!"

"You think *I* talk with trees and little men?"

"Well . . . not exactly."

Willow threw her hands up in frustration. She narrowly avoided throttling the man. "You're so dense! I bet you considered my optimism about Missy's chances of winning as some deep and dark and damning superstition or oddly mystical belief, didn't you?"

He shuffled in place, refusing to meet her gaze. "I did have a mother like that."

He was back to muttering! The man was going to drive her as batty as he'd initially thought her. The crazy one between them was really him. Willow had had it with his half-witted assumptions.

"It seems she must have dropped you on your head a time or two!" she said. "Go take your small-minded objections and your presumptuous notion that I'd marry a stubborn, blind fool like you and . . . and . . . Oh, I don't know what you can do with them, but do it far away from here."

She whirled around, stomped into the house, and tried to slam the door shut behind her with all her strength. Daniel blocked it with one enormous shoulder.

"Oh, no, you don't, lass," he countered in a warning tone. "It's taken me damn long to get us where we are. You're not gettin' away now."

He was coming straight at her, his big hands reaching for her. But Willow knew she couldn't let him touch her; his warmth and that indefinable something about him would melt her on the spot. She backed away but came up against a small table.

Dodging to the left, she asked, "How can you be so thick as to think I'll marry any crazy who just up and assumes I'm willing to do so? You never even asked if I was interested in marrying you!"

Daniel followed and came closer still. "Hell and damnation, Willow, will you stop your foolishness? You'd never have let me lay a finger on you if you hadn't loved me, never mind givin' yourself to me—"

"That's enough! And you're close enough, too." Willow felt embarrassment glow from the tip of her toes to the top of her head. "You don't need to rehash every private detail."

"Why? Who else is here?" He cast glances all around. "From what I can see, it's just the two of us. You were there. So was I. What's the difference?"

"The difference, you muttonhead, is that a woman wants to be *asked*! I may be a farmer, but I'm a woman first."

"Ah, Willow, let's not argue, love," he murmured, approaching yet again.

"Oh, no!" Willow put her hand up, palm outward. "Stop right where you are. Don't you dare smack those lips of yours anywhere on me! Not until you at least get this part right."

Daniel chuckled and slipped his fingers between the ones she held up. "I love you, you know? As ornery and contrary as you are."

"Ornery!" She tried to reclaim her hand. It was a hopeless cause. "Contrary!" She darted to her right. He held her tethered by her fingers. "How dare you? You're the ornery—"

Daniel was again forced to resort to the only way he knew to shut her up. He kissed her. It was a homecoming, the warmth of her lips against his. "I love you," he murmured against her mouth.

A dozen kisses led him to her ear. "I love you," he whispered.

Another smattering of caresses brought his mouth to the pulse point in her slender neck. "I love you, and you love me, too."

That made her chuckle. He pulled away.

Meeting her dark gaze, Daniel felt a tremor cross his body that left him breathless with the strength of his feelings for the beautiful young woman in his arms. Stepping away, he gave her what she wanted.

He knelt at her feet. "Marry me, Willow. Marry me and be mine."

"Oh, Daniel!" Tears again filled her eyes, but this time there was no laughter. Instead a dazzling smile curved her lips. "Yes! Yes! Yes! Of course, I'll marry you."

"Say it," he demanded, standing again.

"What?"

His cheeks heated up, but he no longer cared. He wrapped his arms around her and hung on for dear life. "You know."

She gave him a wry smile. "I love you, Daniel Callaghan. And I always will."

His responding smile came with a sigh of relief. Until she began to wriggle in his grasp. "Where do you think you're goin' now?"

"Just wait. I'll only be a moment."

She ran up the stairs, her heavy white nightgown flapping just enough to give Daniel a glimpse of shapely calves. He'd have to do something about her nightwear; surely she wouldn't always wear that thick white armor? Especially since nothing suited her so very well.

He remembered the loving in the hay. He'd have to make sure they repeated that on a fairly regular basis. But he'd control the matter of privacy in their future romps in the hay. After all, they'd soon be man and wife.

True to her words, she was back in a flash, a radiant glow in her features. Holding something out on the palm of her hand, she came to him. "I was right," she said, smiling smugly. "I told you it meant good luck. I paid off the mortgage, I still have my flock—even though I *will* pay you back—and now I even have you."

Daniel glanced at her hand and saw the carousel's brass ring. Good luck, providence, fate . . . who cared? She loved him, and he loved her.

Suddenly he remembered he still had another surprise for her. So he walked to the table where she'd dropped the deed and the note. "Make sure you're satisfied with these terms," he said. "I intend to hold you to them. *Especially* now that you've promised to marry me."

Willow gave him a skeptical look, then took the paper gingerly, holding it away from her. She began to read. Then she started laughing. "You wretch! This can't possibly be legal!"

"Well, of course, an' it 'tis. Those are my conditions."

"'The debt shall be paid in full upon the voicing of wedding vows by the parties hereof.'" She cocked an eyebrow, still looking at him. "And when shall this wedding take place?"

In a prayerful voice he answered. "As soon as possible!"

"Saints preserve us," she cried, mimicking his brogue, "an' we finally agree on somethin'."

Daniel's arms came around her, lifted her up high, and spun them in circles. Then, ever so slowly, allowing himself the pleasure of feeling every inch of her slender body against his, he let her back down. "I love you, lass."

As his lips claimed hers, Willow closed her hand, taking full grasp of the brass ring.

Our Town
...where love is always right around the corner!

__Harbor Lights by Linda Kreisel__ 0-515-11899-0/$5.99
On Maryland's Silchester Island...the perfect summer holiday sparks a perfect summer fling.

__Humble Pie by Deborah Lawrence__ 0-515-11900-8/$5.99
In Moose Gulch, Montana...a waitress with a secret meets a stranger with a heart.

__Candy Kiss by Ginny Aiken__ 0-515-11941-5/$5.99
In Everleigh, Pennsylvania...a sweet country girl finds the love of a city lawyer with kisses sweeter than candy.

__Cedar Creek by Willa Hix__ 0-515-11958-X/$5.99
In Cedarburg, Wisconsin...a young widow falls in love with the local saloon owner, but she has promised her hand to a family friend — and she has to keep her word.

__Sugar and Spice by DeWanna Pace__ 0-515-11970-9/$5.99
In Valiant, Texas...an eligible bachelor pines for his first love.

__Cross Roads by Carol Card Otten__ 0-515-11985-7/$5.99
In Pensacola, Florida...Viola Mae Smith meets her match in the infuriating Yankee crew boss, Seth Rowe. Once her heart takes a fancy to a man, there's no turning back...

__Blue Ribbon by Jessie Gray__ 0-515-12003-0/$5.99
In Louisville, Kentucky...a young woman chases her dreams in the world of horseracing, only to end up in the most wonderful chase of all — love...

__The Lighthouse by Linda Eberhardt__ 0-515-12020-0/$5.99
In New Clare, Indiana Fiona witnesses one of the worst shipwrecks ever — and finds herself drawn to the ship's lone survivor, Travis Paine.